SPIED

A Click Your Poison book

by

JAMES SCHANNEP

The eAversion Version

Second Print Edition

www.jamesschannep.com

Library of Congress Cataloging-in-Publication Data
Schannep, James, 1984—
SPIED: a Click Your Poison book / James Schannep

1. Thrillers—Espionage—Fiction. 2. Action & Adventure—Fiction.
3. Science Fiction—Alternative History—Fiction. I. Title

COVER ART BY JAMES SCHANNEP

This book has been modified from its original version.
It has been formatted to fit this page.

ISBN-13: 978-1-954747-00-5
ISBN-10: 1-954747-00-4

Acknowledgments

Special thanks to my wife, Michaela, for taking all my silly ideas seriously and for the serious ideas you were silly enough to contribute.

A big thanks to my beta readers: Andrew Driscoll, Mike Beeson, Felix Bertmaring, Scott Santos, Chris Boyes, Michael Harlock, William Hildebrand, James Spearing, Fred Buckley, Hunter Gregory, Damon Bosetti, and Richard Young.

To my copyeditor Maria Mountokalaki, and to Paul Salvette and the team at BB eBooks. Thank you all for your generosity and professionalism.

And to my friends and family, for your unyielding encouragement, enthusiasm and support.

Dedication

During the course of writing this book, I discovered I was being pursued by not one, but two sleeper agents (called such due to their training in ancient arts meant to deprive their marks of sleep). As such, since 2019, I not only had to flee to a different country—but then move again across the United States while pursuing a new identity. My cover had been blown as operative DUDE and I took on the identifier DAD. Thankfully, HQ (MOM) provided me with the support to complete this book even while under such extreme duress. So, it is now, (under the influence of truth serum) that I dedicate this book to my children: █████████ and █████████.

Welcome to the Schannep Intelligence Agency.

Here's how it works: You, Dear Reader, are the main character of this story, a paper-pusher working for the CIA. You're only peripherally involved in the secret world until a strange dossier makes its way across your desk. You should probably give the folder at least a quick glance, just to know where to file it...

From here, it's soon up to you to crack the code of state diplomacy or to be used as an unwitting pawn by double agents; the choice is yours. Simply click the links to progress through the story. Each link represents a choice, and there's no going back, so choose wisely. Are YOU ready to be an international spy and secret agent?

Your mission, should you choose to accept it, is to <u>go to page</u> 1. Good luck.

Click Your Poison Books

INFECTED—*Will YOU Survive the Zombie Apocalypse?*
MURDERED—*Can YOU Solve the Mystery?*
SUPERPOWERED—*Will YOU Be a Hero or a Villain?*
PATHOGENS—*More Zombocalypse Survival Stories!*
MAROONED—*Can YOU Endure Treachery and Survival on the High Seas?*
SPIED—*Can YOU Save the World as a Secret Agent?*
HAUNTED—*Will YOU be Scared...to Death?*

* More titles coming soon! *
Sign up for the new release mailing list: http://eepurl.com/bdWUBb
Or visit the author's blog at www.jamesschannep.com

This page intentionally left blank.

Prologue

Well, this isn't how you expected your morning to start.

The dossier on your desk is unlike any other you've processed before, and the heading doesn't tell you much. The photograph pinned inside matches the description of the header, showing you a handsome man with a charming smile, but the distant eyes of a killer.

As you continue reading, your experienced eye translates the cold, hard facts so the story plays out like an action movie inside your head. Mentally reading through the lines of double-speak and cryptic euphemisms, you can see the pages of the file come to life, and here's what they tell you:

```
SUBJECT: Male/35
NATIONALITY: USA
APPEARANCE: Fair/blonde/blue/6'1"/175lbs
KNOWN ALIASES: Mr. ████████████, agent codename "Pointer"
AFFILIATION: Alternative Intelligence known as "The Hand"
LAST KNOWN WHEREABOUTS: Cervinia/Zermatt, joint Italian-
Switzerland Matterhorn Ski Resort, European Alps
```

Pointer—a fitting codename for this field agent, a literal point man sent out into danger—carries a letter, which he presently drops into a mailbox. Something about the way he carries himself, the deliberate manner in which he delivers this envelope says that if he's successful, this mission is to be his last. If he fails, it will be a foregone conclusion.

The resort's security cameras watch diligently as he makes his way up the Italian side of the mountain, purchases a ticket up to the summit in cash, and enters the enclosed ski lifts. Will they be checking the cameras for signs of him already? No, his cover should still be intact.

The agent rides alone in a gondola toward the top of the glacier. Off to his right, the Matterhorn's iconic bent crest looms in the distance, filling his gondola's plexiglass viewports with panoramic vistas of rock and snow. Fresh powder blooms from a cloud layer near the peak; one of Europe's most iconic mountains overlooking the highest winter sports area in the Alps. The cloud layer slowly slinks down the mountainside, rolling toward the same glacier as the gondola. The skiers lining up below should appreciate the fresh snowfall.

The Matterhorn itself is far too craggy and steep for skiing, so the highest point the gondola can reach is a restaurant and viewing platform called Matterhorn Glacier Paradise. Indeed, rather than a mountain, this is actually an enormous glacier blanketed by snow, winter sports aficionados, and, presently, at least one secret agent.

Pointer is smartly dressed, nothing too fancy—no need to draw attention—but the restaurant views attract tourists who come without skis or other gear so he won't stick out. He could blend in either as a tourist or as a businessman if the situation to hide amongst either crowd dictates it necessary.

The gondola sways and creaks as the connector assembly threads through another tower, the last before arrival at the resort. The gondolas ahead pause to let out their passengers, and the agent stands in preparation to disembark.

As he leaves the gondola, the wind whipping at his Gore-Tex jacket, the agent passes beneath a posted placard offering directions on how to proceed. Should a skier like to go down the Italian slope toward Cervinia, they must turn left. To take the Switzerland side down to Zermatt, turn right. No choice for Pointer, he's headed up on ice-encrusted metal stairs to the restaurant residing atop the line between both countries.

On the way up, he notes the sheer drop off on either side of the platform, the single door leading to the restaurant, and the service ladder which climbs up past a "Matterhorn Glacier Paradise / 3,883 m. / 12,739 feet" sign and toward the antenna array on the rooftop. It's his training that logs these details subconsciously, should they come into play during the planned rendezvous.

Pointer adjusts the handgun he carries in a shoulder holster just beneath his jacket.

Inside, he's greeted with a setting better described as a café than a restaurant. It offers winter warmers for skiers needing a break, light bites and coffee for tourists, and wine and beer for those wanting to wind down after a long day. A sign near the register humorously reads, "Soup of the Day: Glühwein." It's here where Pointer knows to offer his challenge and response passphrase.

"Can I help you?" the barista asks in Swiss-accented English.

She's identified him as an American. Perhaps it's the rod-straight stance, the taut muscles, and square jaw that scream "former military." Or maybe it's the US-brand prominently emblazoned on his sportswear. Likely, it's because he smiled at her with the straightest teeth money can buy.

"Is it beer and wine only, or do you serve cocktails?"

"Just what you see here," she says, indicating a cooler off to the side.

"Is there a bar area?"

"Not here, but there are some, lower on the mountain. Are you headed down the Italian side or the Swiss? I can show you on the trail map."

"No, that's okay. Damn, I'd really hoped for a martini on top of the world."

The agent pauses. The barista waits for him to continue, but he's said his part of the script and isn't breaking character. Just before the barista speaks, a woman off to the side says, "And how does one take a martini on top of the world?"

She speaks in a low voice, accented from a former Soviet bloc country that's hard to place. The agent turns to face her; a stunning woman in après ski leggings, leather boots, and down jacket with a fur-lined collar.

Pointer knows the challenge-response dialogue he's supposed to say. It should be, "Stirred. I'm shaken enough after that gondola ride," but after sizing up his contact, she seems nervous to him. Like she's fighting the urge to look over her shoulder. Is something off?

Pointer decides to:

➤ Say the opposite and see if she notices. "I like it shaken." <u>Go to page 227</u>

➤ Stick with the script. "Stirred. I'm shaken enough after that gondola ride." <u>Go to page 165</u>

➤ Throw her a curveball and say, "Extra-dirty." <u>Go to page 158</u>

Access Denied

The screen shows: Access Denied, bad password, breach detected.

"Shit, shit, shit," Ted says. "That overloaded the system. The cameras are back to normal and there's been an alert activated. Why are you still standing there? Run!"

You might have expected some kind of wailing klaxon, but it's the silence that's actually far more terrifying. Ted says they're coming for you, but from where?

➤ Look for a back door or another way out. Go to page 169

➤ Run back to flee the way you came in. Go to page 17

Accused

You tell them everything about the cryptic note left by Bunny Slopes and the cipher code.

"That could mean anything!" Bird protests.

"Yes, including that you are the mole, as Index claims!" Ringo says.

"It is possible Index is lying," Roku says calmly.

"I already reported all this to Palm and HQ," you say.

"It's true. As team lead, they informed me early on while they looked into your story," Pinkie says.

"I saw you, at the conference. I saw you meeting a contact," Ringo says. Then to the others, adds, "I followed Index and saw the meeting."

Hitch, just by merit of looking at you, turns his pistol your way. At this slight movement, Ringo lunges at him and swats the pistol. This causes the German agent to misfire, striking Pinkie with a shot to his chest.

The Canadian agent stumbles back, clutching his wound. Hitch and Ringo struggle for control of the gun and Roku removes a black bludgeoning weapon that looks a bit like a cross between a police ASP baton and a practice samurai sword.

At this, Bird turns and runs toward the airplane doors, hoping to flee to safety. As safe as fleeing into the arms of Chinese agents can be, anyway. Your mind races. Does this prove she's the mole? Is she working with China?

Roku takes out Hitch, and Ringo regains his own composure before drawing down on Bird. You're caught in the crossfire and he can't get a clean shot.

➤ Get out of the way—let them take care of the mole for you. <u>Go to page 90</u>

➤ Follow Bird outside. This plane is a deathtrap. <u>Go to page 63</u>

Agent Provocateur

"That might just be crazy enough to work!" Ringo says.

"Of course the car thief thinks so," Bird says, rolling her eyes.

Discussing the plan over dinner, you finish eating before it's time to put everything into action. Ringo takes the pillows off the couch, sets them atop the gas stove, and lights all four burners.

"What are you doing?" Bird asks.

"The fire department will come; we don't want to arouse suspicion," Ringo answers.

"Yes, that's very discreet."

"We're going to need a new place to sleep," you say as the first plumes of smoke rise.

"On it," Ted adds in your ear.

With that, the three of you leave the apartment, head into the halls and—at the stairwell—you set off the fire alarm. A klaxon wails and instant chaos ensues, the hallways filling with the building's residents.

"What do you think you are doing?!" a Chinese man in a black suit yells.

"Fire!" you shout.

That's when the guns come out.

"Poor choice of words," Ted says in your ear.

But the building's sprinkler system kicks in, and the Chinese agents holster their weapons.

"See? It was a good idea," Ringo says.

This part of the plan works perfectly. The rest, however, does not. As the building is evacuated, the Chinese agents look harshly at your team—they recognize you. What's worse, the men out front send for a car, Bex Barsmith emerges from her apartment, and they usher her away.

You have no intel as to where they might be taking her, and not enough time to track her down again before the scheduled launch. This was a tight window, and now it's closed.

Mission: Failed.

THE END

Alibi

The man looks incredibly tired. RSO Bertram rubs his eyes and says, "So, what're you telling me, here? The Russian police suspect you of spying, but you're just an Olympic employee doing your due diligence?"

"Yes, that—all of that," you say. "Of course I'm not a spy. I just want to be able to fly home without being detained. That's why I can't go to the airport."

"Uh-huh. And where's the rest of your team? Your coworkers?"

"I…we got separated, and they were able to leave before all this…trouble."

He strokes his beard contemplatively. "I think we're going to need a formal request from your employer. Along with a statement of indemnity against these allegations."

"I'm sure I can get you the proper paperwork."

"You'll excuse my incredulity, but most of what I deal with are forgeries. If they thought they could pull it off, the building we're standing in would be switched out overnight. What I'm saying is, I'm gonna need a little more to go on than a slip of paper."

Your eyes linger on your gear laid out on the table before him, next to your fake identification and the geniusphone. For a guy who spends most of his time dealing with forgeries, the RSO didn't seem to have a problem with the ones generated by your agency. Bertram shifts in his chair across from you, and folds his arms across his chest.

"Well…" you say, trying to think of something. "I can provide you with…um…"

"Care to phone a friend?"

"Ted? I think I could use some help," you say.

"Who's Ted?"

"Oh, umm. Ted's kind of like Alexa, but for VIPs only."

"Leave this to me," Ted says in your ear.

Then your geniusphone starts vibrating and RSO Bertram's eyebrows rise. OLYMPIC SCROLL VIDCONFERENCE WITH Z. BAJA shows on the phone. You lean in, just as curious to see if it might be Ted wearing a bald cap and pretending to be Zach Baja. Bertram accepts the call, and a video pops up: miraculously, it's the billionaire himself. The connection is spotty, but you are in a heavily reinforced building in Moscow.

"Hello? Can you hear me?" Baja says.

"H-hello, sir. I'm RSO David Bertram, diplomatic security."

"I understand one of my brand ambassadors is stranded in Russia?"

"The US Embassy in Moscow, yes sir."

"I must say, this is good timing. I'm meeting with the Secretary of State on my DC tour. That's your boss, right? If you can get my employee to DC, I'd love to mention how you helped me out here."

"Yes, of course. I could even move my personal leave up if—"

"Perfect. You can join our foursome if you hurry. Do you golf?"

"Do I! Just don't ask if I golf well!"

Both men laugh.

* * *

On the way back to the US, you ask Ted how in the hell he pulled that off. Getting billionaire Zach Baja to call the US Embassy in Moscow? Is he on the payroll at The Hand? Codename: Rolex, maybe.

"Oh, we didn't," Ted says. "It's a Deepfake—a spoof. There are plenty of recordings of him speaking, so it's easy for a computer to generate a copy of his voice."

You marvel at how incredibly talented the staff at The Hand must be. Your fake credentials passed muster with the embassy's anti-fraud unit, after all. That's primarily what the Department of State (DS) does overseas. That and escort dignitaries and very important persons (VIPs), which somehow you're classified as at present.

The CIA isn't even in the same league. You've heard of Deepfake, but only in the context of how problematic they're going to be for state security. Your former employer couldn't do anything like this, or—

The image of Ted, cold and dead on the slab, crosses through your mind.

"I know where I'm going first," you say.

Like a doubting Thomas, you need to see the body for yourself, and put your hand into the fatal wound. If Ted is talking to you, who is in the morgue? It must be related, somehow. To Pointer? The Russians? CIA collusion?

"Awesome! I'll see if I can't get that self-driving car to pick you up on arrival."

➢ "No, that's okay. I'll get a taxi out front and keep off the grid." <u>Go to page 147</u>

➢ "Sounds good; no time to lose. I'll meet you outside the private terminal."
<u>Go to page 181</u>

Alternative Intelligence

This act, of course, is not seen favorably by The Hand agents. You're accused of being the mole, accused—somehow—of having killed Pointer to take his spot. Even Bird joins in those who decry your actions, though you can see on her face she's glad to see you escape their ranks.

You're turned over by the Chinese government to the US Embassy, where the Regional Security Officer (RSO) helps get you back to the District of Colombia (DC). This was a huge risk, as the Chinese government might have been setting a trap in hopes you'd admit you were a spy, but it turns out they're just as happy to have stopped The Hand as the CIA is. There must have been some sort of deal, with you as the bargaining chip.

Presently, you've just finished debriefing M and Spearing back at Langley.

"Good work, Papercut," M says. "We've been recording your movements and conversations via the dampening capsule. Sorry to have kept you in the dark on this, but we weren't sure how capable you truly were."

"Now that we know, we have some good news!" Spearing chimes in.

"We're going to send you for training at The Farm; you're to be a bona fide field agent," M says.

"What about the launch?" you ask.

"The launch is scrubbed; your work is done for now. I don't imagine China was friendly to the other agents when you left, and it's unfortunate we don't have them to prosecute in hopes of finding a trail to Palm, but we needed the leverage to get you back. We had been tracking this whole Russia/China thing, and even had our own operation in place—Silicon Valley was going to launch our *own* guidance system for us—but the damned Hand was going to reverse everything. You've saved the day, truly."

"There's more," you say, detailing what Bird told you about Ted.

"It's true. He is dead; we've seen the report from the medical examiner's office," Spearing says.

"He was in my ear!" you say.

"We'll need to look into that more closely later. They must have spoofed his identity somehow," M says.

"No, it's more than that," you say. "Something about a database?"

M sighs. "Operation Vigilant Eagle."

Both you and Spearing look to her, and at length she continues.

"It's what you call the SPIED system. We were sharing an algorithm with our closest allies; England, Canada, Germany, France, Italy, and most recently Japan. But it did such a great job keeping tabs on them, we were going to let it into China and Russia, too."

"The spy-catcher?" Spearing asks.

"Suspicious Personnel Identification and Evaluation Database, yes. I'm starting to wonder if The Hand might have somehow infiltrated it, but that's impossible. We feed it; it gives us what we need. It's kept in an air-gapped system at DARPA. No signal in, no signal out."

"I need to see it," you say, suddenly compelled. "To make sure."

M looks at you with her head ever so slightly tilted, appraising.

Gaining confidence, you continue, "You said you'd need to look into how they spoofed Ted's identity, didn't you? Send me while you clean up the satellite operation."

Finally, she nods.

"Spearing, please drive our newest field agent to DARPA. I'll make a call and get you access."

It's less than a thirty-minute drive to the Defense Advanced Research Projects Agency (DARPA) headquarters, which sits only a few miles away from the pentagon. It's fitting that this mission would lead you here, to the birthplace of the first GPS satellite, network computing, Remotely Piloted Aircraft (RPAs, AKA "drones"), and many more.

"If they've infiltrated DARPA, we're in more trouble than M is willing to admit," Spearing says.

"That's what I aim to find out," you say.

Spearing parks the vehicle, then exits and walks with you up to the building. As you leave the parking lot, you see a familiar sight—the black sedan that picked you up from outside the CIA headquarters back when you were first "recruited" by The Hand. The self-driving car...it's from DARPA? A chill runs down your spine.

"Everything okay? You look like you've seen a ghost," Spearing says.

A ghost in the machine, perhaps. Before you can answer, your escort comes out to meet you—a small, but energetic woman in her mid-forties. She's the one who will take the pair of you through security.

"Mary! My, it's been a while, hasn't it?" Spearing says.

"I'm sorry, have we met?" she says.

He blinks. "It's James. We worked together. From your analyst days, remember?"

"Did we? I'm terribly sorry, I've worked with so many people over the years."

"No, it's fine. I've got one of those faces—the forgettable kind," he says with a chuckle.

Mary offers a polite smile, then she turns to greet you.

"Hi, I'm Mary. You're the one inspecting our Alternative Intelligence system?" she asks.

"Something like that."

"I was wondering when someone might. Come on in, let's get you through security."

➤ Ask her why; let her know a little in hopes of learning more. Go to page 179

➤ Play this close to the vest and avoid making small-talk. Go to page 228

Autopilot

In your hesitation, Ringo vaults over Pinkie and claims the pistol for himself. He swings the handgun wildly from agent to agent, unsure whom to trust in the moment. Pinkie slowly picks himself up from off of the floor, hands raised to keep things from escalating.

"Which one is it?" Ringo says, manic.

He swings the pistol from Bird to Roku, looking at you.

"I just saved you, obviously," Roku says.

"She's smart. It could be a trick," Bird says.

"The Chinese authorities are coming closer," Pinkie says. "We should get going."

"Shut up!" Ringo says.

"Pilot, start—" Pinkie says, cut short by declaration of a gunshot.

"I said shut up!"

Ringo fires through one of the outside windows, which sets off a chain reaction. He might have been intending to silence Pinkie, but whatever the reason, the Chinese forces outside must think you're shooting at them, and they return in kind. They have submachine guns and fill the interior of the cabin with bullets.

This is the last stop on your adventure.

THE END

Background: Bird

```
SUBJECT: Female/28
NATIONALITY: French/Algerian
APPEARANCE: Dark brown/black/brown/5'7"/135lbs
KNOWN ALIASES: Mlle. ███████████, agent codename "The
Bird"
AFFILIATION: Alternative Intelligence known as "The Hand"
LAST KNOWN WHEREABOUTS: French Presidential Palace
```

The file reminds you of the mysterious document that came across your desk in the first place, the one generated on Pointer that began your new career as a superspy.

This file tells you the background on Bird. Born to a mother who emigrated from Algiers, and a man from Bordeaux, Bird had a promising career as an investigative journalist until she began looking into French politics. Though her looks often disarmed would-be enemies, she was set to be "disappeared" from French society before she was recruited into Alternative Intelligence. Whether she leveraged embarrassing information about the French government is unknown, but her ability to make contacts and uncover buried leads is likely why she was recruited into the agency to begin with.

Someone says something sternly in Russian, and you turn back to see an engineer putting cigarettes back into his pocket. You can be fairly certain it's this man's desk that you're presently sitting at.

"I knew we didn't have time for this. I hate to say 'I told you so,' but..." Ted says.

"I said, what do you think you're doing?" the Russian engineer says, this time in English.

You claim your phone from the computer tower, and then say:

➢ "Um, where's the toilet?" Try and talk your way out. Go to page 60

➢ "You have cigarettes? I only have this vape thing." Gas the man. Go to page 117

Background: Hitch

```
SUBJECT: Male/53
NATIONALITY: German
APPEARANCE: Fair/auburn/brown/5'9"/185lbs
KNOWN ALIASES: Herr ███████████████, agent codename "Hitch
Hiker"
AFFILIATION: Alternative Intelligence known as "The Hand"
LAST KNOWN WHEREABOUTS: Manchurian China, Near North Korean
border
```

The file reminds you of the mysterious document that came across your desk in the first place, the one generated on Pointer that began your new career as a superspy.

This file tells you the background on Hitch, detailing his time spent in German Intelligence as a deep-cover operative, meant to impersonate a double agent to Russia. It is unknown to what extent he was loyal to either side, but suffice it to say he had more enemies than friends in either government and his spying career was largely as a glorified assassin. From there, it wasn't particularly difficult for him to be recruited into Alternative Intelligence and away from that kind of jingoistic political wet work. His exact age is only an estimate, as are his number of confirmed kills. There is some argument as to which number is higher.

Someone says something sternly in Russian, and you turn back to see an engineer putting cigarettes back into his pocket. You can be fairly certain it's this man's desk that you're presently sitting at.

"I knew we didn't have time for this. I hate to say 'I told you so,' but…" Ted says.

"I said, what do you think you're doing?" the Russian engineer says, this time in English.

You claim your phone from the computer tower, and then say:

➢ "You have cigarettes? I only have this vape thing." Gas the man.
  Go to page 117

➢ "Um, where's the toilet?" Try and talk your way out. Go to page 60

Background: Index

This is the covert world's version of Googling yourself. They have a file on you with accurate age, demographics, height, weight, former clubs, and skill sets. Information on your parents, extended family, and education. In this era, more than any other, it's incredibly difficult to maintain a cover story as a spy. Your whole life has been online. Or at least a good amount has been, and the information they have is creepily accurate. All except for the final line of the report, "Last Known Whereabouts."

That line ends with: DECEASED.

"Deceased?" you say. "They think I'm dead?"

"Hey, that's not necessarily a bad thing. If they think you're dead—"

"We're dead," you say, cutting him off.

Reading further, the report says you were recruited from the CIA by Ted into Alternative Intelligence, and then you both died in a car accident shortly thereafter. The file details CIA suspicions that your death might be related to the death of one of their former field agents: Pointer.

"—it means they're less likely to be looking for us, then," Ted finishes.

"Wait, Pointer was former CIA? Is that why they recruited us from…?"

You trail off, opening a sub-file with a picture of Ted at the morgue. There is no photo available for your own death certificate, not even a J. Doe. Still, seeing a picture of a cold, dead Ted on the slab sends a shiver down your spine.

"Ted, you're dead. I'm looking at your body right now."

"No, you're looking at a *picture* of a dead body, and images can be doctored. Unlike a dead body. There's no doctoring for that."

The image sure looks convincing. His skin is pale and taut and there's a blue tinge around his cheekbones. The Ted in the photo has his eyes closed, the eyelids browning like overripe bananas. A long, deep purple bruise lines his collar bone like he's wearing a ghastly Hawaiian lei.

Someone says something sternly in Russian, and you turn back to see an engineer putting cigarettes back into his pocket. You can be fairly certain it's this man's desk that you're presently sitting at.

"I knew we didn't have time for this. I hate to say 'I told you so,' but…" Ted says.

"I said, what do you think you're doing?" the Russian engineer says, this time in English.

You've only got a moment to decide, so what will it be?

➤ Gas the engineer with the vape pen and regroup with the other agents. There's a credible threat with this Operation Celestial, and you need to tell the rest of your team about it. Go to page 117

➤ See if you can get him to tell you more. If it's this guy's computer you're at, maybe he knows what's going on with all these files on your team? Go to page 275

Background: Pinkie

```
SUBJECT: Male/44
NATIONALITY: Canadian
APPEARANCE: Fair/black/green/5'11"/165lbs
KNOWN ALIASES: Mr. ███████████, agent codename "Pinkie"
AFFILIATION: Alternative Intelligence known as "The Hand"
LAST KNOWN WHEREABOUTS: Benelux and NATO headquarters,
Brussels, Belgium
```

The file reminds you of the mysterious document that came across your desk in the first place, the one generated on Pointer that began your new career as a superspy.

This file tells you the background on Pinkie, detailing his time spent at a military academy in his youth—an only child born to academic-turned-diplomat parents. He was recruited into Alternative Intelligence, though the "how" remains somewhat of an enigma. Pinkie appears to have been present from the agency's original incarnation and on. Where he came from before that is unclear, and there's a large gap between his education and whenever it was that he started with The Hand.

Someone says something sternly in Russian, and you turn back to see an engineer putting cigarettes back into his pocket. You can be fairly certain it's this man's desk that you're presently sitting at.

"I knew we didn't have time for this. I hate to say 'I told you so,' but…" Ted says.

"I said, what do you think you're doing?" the Russian engineer says, this time in English.

You claim your phone from the computer tower, and then say:

➢ "Um, where's the toilet?" Try and talk your way out. Go to page 60

➢ "You have cigarettes? I only have this vape thing." Gas the man. Go to page 117

Background: Ringo

```
SUBJECT: Male/31
NATIONALITY: Italian, mixed unknown
APPEARANCE: Medium brown/black/brown/5'9"/170lbs
KNOWN ALIASES: Sig. ███████████████, agent codename "Ring"
AFFILIATION: Alternative Intelligence known as "The Hand"
LAST KNOWN WHEREABOUTS: Unknown
```

The file reminds you of the mysterious document that came across your desk in the first place, the one generated on Pointer that began your new career as a superspy.

This file tells you the background on Ringo, detailing a misspent youth, time in the army as an airborne Special Forces member, and ultimately a wake of destruction and arrest for mayhem and grand theft auto. It's unclear how his sentence was commuted into time in Alternative Intelligence, although there are parallels between this story and the petty crimes of his teenage years before he joined the Army. Ringo is a man who's had more than his fair share of second chances.

Someone says something sternly in Russian, and you turn back to see an engineer putting cigarettes back into his pocket. You can be fairly certain it's this man's desk that you're presently sitting at.

"I knew we didn't have time for this. I hate to say 'I told you so,' but..." Ted says.

"I said, what do you think you're doing?" the Russian engineer says, this time in English.

You claim your phone from the computer tower, and then say:

➢ "You have cigarettes? I only have this vape thing." Gas the man.
  <u>Go to page 117</u>

➢ "Um, where's the toilet?" Try and talk your way out. <u>Go to page 60</u>

Background: Roku

```
SUBJECT: Female/23
NATIONALITY: Japanese
APPEARANCE: Light brown/black/black/5'4"/115lbs
KNOWN ALIASES: ███████████████, agent codename "Six"
AFFILIATION: Alternative Intelligence known as "The Hand"
LAST KNOWN WHEREABOUTS: Yokohama, Tokyo, Japan
```

The file reminds you of the mysterious document that came across your desk in the first place, the one generated on Pointer that began your new career as a superspy.

This file tells you the background on Roku, detailing her prominence in the Kendo circuits and dominance in the sport to her ultimate downfall. It's unclear what precipitated the snap, but she had seriously injured several other competitors before she was banned from the sport. She spent a brief time as a personal bodyguard to a tech entrepreneur, and it appears as if her services were "traded" to Alternative Intelligence as part of a larger deal, without either the seller or commodity quite knowing what they were getting from the bargain.

Someone says something sternly in Russian, and you turn back to see an engineer putting cigarettes back into his pocket. You can be fairly certain it's this man's desk that you're presently sitting at.

"I knew we didn't have time for this. I hate to say 'I told you so,' but..." Ted says.

"I said, what do you think you're doing?" the Russian engineer says, this time in English.

You claim your phone from the computer tower, and then say:

➢ "Um, where's the toilet?" Try and talk your way out. <u>Go to page 60</u>

➢ "You have cigarettes? I only have this vape thing." Gas the man.
   <u>Go to page 117</u>

Back Nine

Running back out of the computer room, you slam into a bookish engineering-type, his cigarettes and pen collection equally exploding across the hallway as he falls. Without looking back, you continue to run.

CRACK! CRACK! Gunshots echo in the corridor—followed by the sound of bullets exploding into the concrete walls around your head. They're actually shooting at you!

Rounding the corner toward the exit, you're met with a trio of armed guards—nothing to do here but raise your hands. You close your eyes and grit your teeth, knowing you're likely to be shot or at least tackled and subdued in the next few seconds.

A strange series of *click-clack* sounds brings your attention back and you see Roku standing in the midst of the guards, having just deployed a weapon that looks like a cross between a telescoping ASP baton and a katana.

With swift, graceful moves, she incapacitates the guards with the weapon. She makes it look easy: almost as if choreographed in advance. One tap to the head and a man falls limp, a blow to the sternum of another produces a coughing fit, and the third, she first connects with his wrist to disarm him of his pistol before taking him out as well.

"Get down," she says.

As you comply, a teargas canister arrives from down the hallway. Roku tees up and knocks it back over your head—and into the crowd of approaching guards.

"Let's go. The rest of the team has what we need."

You comply, following Roku. Once you've exited the secure area, she stows her weapon and walks calmly through the crowd. It's a test of your nerves, but you do the same.

"Where are we going?"

"The jet."

Well, not much choice here. Onto the next phase of the mission!

Go to page 22

Back Pain

The robot's head swivels on its neck, somewhat reminiscent of an owl, watching you with its sensor array. Just as you might have suspected, a seam runs along both rear flanks of the robot, letting you know there's a compartment or hatch. The rest of the artificial being's form is all functional, so the circuitry and power supply must be back here.

You reach out to feel the grooves, hoping to find a maintenance access, but as you reach out to the robot it does the same—running cold, hard, metallic fingers over your spine. While your hands continue searching, your head turns back to see what the robot is up to.

The thing continues scanning you, and one hand comes up to your head, pushing along your jawline as if trying to aid you in turning back. When it's met with resistance, it grabs hold—and twists.

There's a terrible *snap* and *crack* and you fall to the ground.

THE END

The Baddies

Hitch wrestles the whaleboat captain to his feet, and you turn back and shout for them to stop. It's not even a conscious decision—it just happens.

"What is it, Index?" Roku asks. She's still fighting off the other two Russian agents, but she listens. "We're miles from shore! We can't just leave him out here for dead!"

"He will only compromise the mission," Roku replies coldly.

"You think he will *not* tell the police that we threw three of his passengers overboard and stole his boat?" Hitch adds, but after your objection, he instead helps fight the remaining two Russians.

The captain distances himself from the German agent, finds a flare gun, and brandishes it as Roku and Hitch work to toss the other two foreign agents overboard. You step forward, but raise your hands as the captain turns and holds you under flare gunpoint.

Thinking quickly, you say, "Captain, those men were terrorists. We need your boat to—"

"If you say more," Roku interrupts, "I'll have to kill him before he's tossed over just to be sure."

"Who the hell are you people?!" Captain Ken shouts.

Eyes filled with panic, the captain swings the flare gun about. In the commotion, one of the Russians dives for it, but the captain accidentally fires the flare gun—into the boat.

Everyone leaps over to avoid the flare, but that only brings the violence into the sea. The Russians are overboard, but not over with. Even if Roku and Hitch manage to fight them off in the water, the whale-watching boat is no longer sea worthy and you're miles from shore.

You're marooned out here.

This won't end well.

THE END

Bar and Grill

"So, any happy-hour specials?" you ask, breaking the ice.

"I believe each and every happy hour is special," the man behind the bar says in heavily Italian-accented English.

"It must be strange for you; I know it was for me when I was recruited," Bird says.

"How long ago was that?" you ask.

She offers only a brief, tight-lipped smile in reply.

"Where are our manners?" the Italian says. "I am *l'anulare*, the Ring—Ringo! Ring-a-ding-ding-ding. And my fine-feathered friend here is known as *l'oiseau*."

"Bird, rhymes with *merde*. See? I flip you the…" she gives you the middle finger.

"Ringo and Bird, got it," you say.

"*Oui.* At least, that is the English translation. We'll have to wait and see what your codename is. You are replacing Pointer, so it will be similar."

"Oh?"

She nods. "I replaced—let's see… the English name would be 'Middle' or something like this—some time ago. I think we are all second or third generation agents here. Other than Pinkie, over there. I believe he is an original recruit by Palm."

You wish you could be taking notes—this is a goldmine of information!

"So, each of the codenames is in our own language. Do we have multiple branches or something?" you ask.

"One tree, many branches," Ringo says, shaking a cocktail.

"Were you two in Italian and French Intelligence?"

Bird hesitates a moment, then with a mischievous look admits, "We're not supposed to say. Codenames only. Accents are usually unmistakable, but…"

"Can I pour you a drink?" Ringo asks.

"I'll take one," Bird says.

Seems like you might have pried all you could get from these two. Decide if you'd like a drink, then:

➤ Talk to Roku by the patio. <u>Go to page 187</u>

➤ Talk to Hitch and Pinkie in the lounge. <u>Go to page 145</u>

➤ Tell Ted you're ready to report in and get started! <u>Go to page 55</u>

Bar Car

"**I**'m accessing the automated train protocols," Ted says. "I'll close the doors and start the train ahead of schedule. Hopefully, that will mean you're alone."

The restaurant isn't open, but there's a bar where you can order a refreshing beverage of your choice—shaken, stirred, or otherwise. This was a good choice; people are constantly moving about, in and out of the restaurant car, making it hard to pin down any one person's whereabouts.

"So far so good, Indie," Ted says in your ear. "There are a couple of stops before the Vandenberg Space Force Base boundary. From there, you'll toss the bag out of the window just after the Z-Axes launch site. You'll recognize it because they've painted their logo a hundred feet high across the site buildings. Hard to miss. Wait—oh, damn."

"What?"

"A rooftop maintenance hatch has just been opened in the middle of the train. You're not alone, after all."

"Something to drink?" the bartender asks.

She's in her mid-fifties and doesn't realize that no amount of makeup can cover up lack of sleep and sun-damaged skin. You let your eyes drift over the drinks, and in the cooler reflection you see one of the Chinese agents making his way up the aisle toward you.

Has he seen you yet?

➤ Order a champagne bottle, shaken, not stirred. Go to page 196

➤ Excuse yourself and leave before you're identified. Go to page 115

The Bazaar

"**I**'ve got the mission recap from HQ in my files now," Ted says, once you're back on the corporate jet. "Palm is pleased with your progress, blah, blah, blah. You're headed to Beijing next, for a black-market arms deal. It turns out Russia is colluding with China to weaponize a Silicon Valley startup's venture into space. This company *thinks* they're launching a non-militarized, peaceful diplomatic mission, but they're set to launch some malware-laden space Trojan horse, which will knock out an entire constellation of satellites friendly toward the free world.

"To stop China and Russia from teaming up for a *Coup de Space*, we're going to grab an identical onboard computer guidance system from this Chinese market. Then we'll reprogram it to fight for the side of good, swap the unit prior to launch, and bingo, bango, bongo—we're going to Trojan horse the Greeks before they can do any horsing around of their own."

Shortly after takeoff, Palm video conferences in to tell you the same in an official capacity. Each agent watches on their own device, and you tune in on your geniusphone. After her briefing, she turns things over to Hitch.

The German agent stands and says, "We have a contact who tells us we can find compatible hardware in the *Xiushui* black market, also known as Silk Street, where we'll need to send an operative to pose as a tech buyer. Using this counterfeit guidance system, we'll be able to alter the code and hack the satellite constellation."

"All good news. However, there is a slight complication," Palm says. "We've recently learned that Russian Intelligence has been tipped off to our presence, which means there's the potential that Chinese Intelligence might be looking for you on the ground."

Pinkie looks your way and grins. "Which means that you, Index, are best suited to buy what we need. As the newest agent, any leak should have the least information on *your* identity."

"And Pointer had a previous connection to this contact," Bird adds. "As another American, you can use those sympathies to your advantage."

"Just be careful. If our identities are leaked, it is possible this contact is the one who set Pointer up in the first place," Ringo says.

"I will accompany," Roku says. "As the second-newest agent, the same conditions apply. But the cover story is that an American investor is looking for black-market Chinese tech. So, someone who frequently makes business deals in Asia might believably have a Japanese bodyguard."

"Being fluent in Mandarin won't hurt either," Pinkie says, nodding.

"Excellent. We look forward to hearing about your success. Good luck and Godspeed," Palm says before disconnecting.

For a black market, the Silk Market is rather conspicuous. Seated squarely in the midst of a bustling area of Beijing, the market itself serves as a popular tourist attraction. What was once an open-air market with a few hundred vendors selling knock-off versions of well-known brands has since grown into an enormous, seven-story building (with three basement levels) and thousands of vendors offering counterfeit goods in a veritable mega mall of contraband.

Infamous amongst international tourists as *the* place to find a great deal—or get ripped off, your choice—this would seem like a bizarre spot for a clandestine rendezvous. But the general public doesn't know about the hidden interior. Sure, it's easy to find name-brand handbags or your favorite sports jersey, but you'll have to venture deeper into the seedy underbelly if you want high-end black-market goods: like a satellite onboard a guidance computer system, for example.

The team takes a pair of private hire black cars from the airport, you and Roku in one vehicle, the others in the second car. This is going to be an all-hands-on-deck operation, with messages relayed via Third Ear implants from one agent to the next.

"Whatever weapons you have, keep them close at hand," Roku says.

You nod, noting the water bottle pistol at your side, and the two of you exit the car at the front of the market hall. Roku stands just behind you, slightly to your right, awaiting your first move.

"Okay, head up to the third floor," Pinkie says in your ear. "You're looking for a shop called 'Face the North.' Once you've found it, ask if their down jackets are made from genuine baby birds. Tell them: 'All birds lay eggs' to complete the challenge and response."

Heading into the market, you're greeted by a crush of humanity. China is overpopulation incarnate, at least in its cities, and a Beijing tourist hotspot is amongst the worst offenders. The Silk Market may look massive from the outside, but with 60,000 patrons rotating through its revolving doors daily, it feels painfully compact inside.

A few teens try to brush past you, but Roku chastises the trio with some harsh words in Mandarin and ushers them away before they can attempt their pickpocket scheme. You're identified as a tourist and as an American, and vendors shout to you in broken English, inviting you to buy their wares.

"Coachella bags! I make you good price!"

"Hey, good-looking! Louie V, best deal!"

You get the picture.

Eventually, you arrive at 'Face the North,' a shop with The North Face brand logo next to the mismatched words. Inside, you'll find knockoff athleisure and rock-climbing gear at rock-bottom prices. Remembering your charge, you reach out to feel the puffy down jackets.

"Half price for you, my friend. Half price!" the saleswoman offers.

She punches a sales figure into a calculator for you to review.

"Real down? Made from baby birds?" you ask.

"No babies. No babies."

"All birds lay eggs," you say.

"Swan is a bird," she replies, cryptically. The woman looks at you sharply, waiting for a response. You hesitate a moment, and Roku gives the slightest shrug.

"Our sources didn't mention a third phrase in the challenge/response," Pinkie says in your ear.

"I think it's meant to be a syllogism," Ted adds.

The saleswoman obviously grows impatient. Thinking quickly, you say:

➤ "Therefore, swans lay eggs." <u>Go to page 234</u>

➤ "Therefore, an egg is a bird." <u>Go to page 155</u>

Bee in your Bonnet

"Thank you for your honesty," Ted says.

"That's…that's it?" you say.

"That's it. Feel free to visit any time, even just to pop in for a spot of tea," Palm says.

"I'm free to go?"

"What, did you think we'd harbor hard feelings just because you want to expose us and ruin all our plans?" Ted says.

You instinctively look around the room as if expecting the floor to fall out from underneath you via a trapdoor. Could there be a pit of sharks beneath the linoleum?

"Have a great rest of your life," Ted says.

Then the monitor turns off.

You hesitate, unsure what to do. Should you sabotage the terminals? Leave and report your findings? This feels so clearly like a trap.

You're looking around when you see an insect crawl out from the air duct. How could a bug get back here? There are so many hallways and corridors, all clean, sterile and secure. Surely DARPA is too sanitized for insects.

Then it flies straight toward you.

Like it's on the attack, the bug goes straight for your face. You duck and swat away at the ladybug-sized beetle, turning to see where it goes, but you lose sight of the thing. Where did it go? You look around frantically—no sign.

That's when it crawls into your ear.

"Have a great rest of your life," Ted said, knowing it would only be a few minutes more.

Just one of the fun little toys DARPA wanted to test out on a real human target—a lifelike insect drone, a persistent little burrower with ear-canal recognition technology.

THE END

Bird

You seat yourself next to the Frenchwoman, who gives a brief, tight-lipped smile.

"It must be strange for you; I know it was for me when I was recruited," she says, breaking the ice. "I didn't meet the others for almost a year. Even then, never in a group."

"Are you from—I'm sorry, I can't remember the official name, but—French Intelligence?"

She hesitates a moment, then with a mischievous look admits, "We're not supposed to say. Codenames only. Accents are usually unmistakable, but…"

"What's your codename, then?"

"Bird," she says, though her accent is so thick it sounds like "Bert."

"Bert?" you parrot.

"*Non*, Bird. Bird, rhymes with *merde*. See? I flip you the…" she gives you the middle finger.

"Bird, got it," you say.

"*Oui*. At least, that is the English translation. We'll have to wait and see what your codename is. You are replacing Pointer, so it will be similar."

"Oh?"

She nods. "I replaced—let's see—the English name would be 'Middle' or something like this—some time ago. I think we are all second or third generation agents here. Other than Pinkie, over there. I believe he is an original recruit by Palm."

She indicates one of the two men sitting around the table in the center. You think to ask her about this Palm character but when you look back, you find her gaze distant, focused on puzzling something out. She might want some time alone with her thoughts.

Maybe it's time to talk with someone else. Who haven't you spoken with?

> The bartender. Maybe he'll make me a drink? It's been quite a day and I could use a cocktail. <u>Go to page 215</u>

> The pair around the table. They're already being sociable, why not join in? <u>Go to page 119</u>

> The woman at the window. Go take a look at the views and strike up conversation. <u>Go to page 217</u>

> I've heard enough. Tell Ted you're ready to report in. <u>Go to page 223</u>

Black Diamonds Are Forever

Returning back inside the building provides brief cover from the helicopter, but Pointer moves with certainty that more enemies are on their way to find him. Most of the skiers take their boots inside the café with them, but enough have left theirs in the snowy anteroom that he can expediently find a pair in his size. Once geared up, the agent heads outside.

In the time he's spent indoors, the helicopter has retreated. Likely, the worsening snowstorm and poor visibility have done his work for him. Now he blends in with the rest of the skiers and leisurely makes his way down the mountain.

Carve here, slalom there; easy-peasy.

Until he sees a trio of snowmobiles blazing up the mountain toward him. They must be tracking the agent. Could the transponder be giving off a signal? Perhaps, but it's soon clear these are not ski patrol, but either police or military. The telltale silhouettes of machineguns are visible even in the dull gray-white of the storm.

Pointer readies his handgun—long and black and sleek, topped with a silencer—and turns away from a group of civilians just as the would-be assassins open fire. The agent quickly veers off into the timberline, returning gunfire as best as he can, and punching in and out of forested trails too narrow for snowmobiles to follow. Once out on another slope, it appears he may have lost them, but no such luck: here, half a dozen men in all-white ski suits with black weaponry are waiting.

They open fire and Pointer ducks back into the trees. The henchmen follow in a high-speed ski race through the trees. The agent fires back blindly, hoping the cover fire will buy him some time, until he realizes he only has one bullet remaining. Eyes forward, Pointer looks for another way—and soon finds it.

Turning back, the agent aims quickly, knowing he can't look away from the trees he's evading for more than a hazarded glance. He fires his final shot. Not at his pursuers, but high at one of the trees and into the load of snow it holds aloft in its branches.

This sends a cascade of powder down from the branches, knocking more clumped snow as it goes and dumping a blanket of white in front of his pursuers. The closest henchman escapes from under the snow, but the others cry out as they lose all visibility and slam into the trees.

The lone henchman opens fire, just as Pointer darts out from the timberline. He shoots out and over a gap, crossing his skis behind himself in an "X" as he jumps across the rocky section. The lone henchman exits the trees still firing—the bullets pinging off Pointer's skis—and falls down into the depths of the glacial chasm with a Wilhelm scream that echoes below.

Pointer lands on the other side, but tumbles off his ruined skis into a somersault. He rises, brushes the snow off, and gets his bearings. The snowstorm grows in intensity, now with a brutal wind. In only a light jacket, the cold penetrates his bones. The agent can't know for sure how much further until he reaches the Swiss side of the mountain, but he knows that it's his best means of escape.

He decides to:

➤ Look for shelter and call it in. There are too many soldiers and police on the mountain, and he'd better lay low while an extraction team forms to aid in escape. Go to page 83

➤ Ignore the cold and continue to hike down the mountain. Italian forces won't dare pursue him across border lines, and he can disappear into Zermatt. Go to page 137

Blaze of Glory

As far as assault vehicles go, a fire engine isn't a bad choice. It's not exactly bulletproof, but it is heavily reinforced. Your cover was good enough that the security forces are more confused than threatened. It isn't until Hitch literally runs some of the troops over that they start to see you as a threat.

Roku makes it inside the rocket. She lets you know there are no base personnel remaining inside the launch tube, then gets to work on the guidance system. At some point during the pre-launch operations, you lose contact with her.

Soon after, base security has rallied and there's only so long a joyride in a fire engine can last.

Did you succeed? Did you fail? Hard to say. You'll die without knowing if your sacrifice was in vain or if you were a martyr who furthered the cause. But either way, for you, this is:

THE END

Bletchley

"Okay, let them through," the guard-supervisor says. "How can we help?"

"Well done, Indie! Great memory!" Ted says.

Replying to the guards, you say, "Radio ahead to mission control. We need to delay the launch until we've checked the rocket. There's the possibility of sabotage."

A very real possibility, seeing as how you're about to sabotage the Russian/Chinese mission and replace the guidance computer with one of your own.

With that, you're given a legitimate escort up to the rocket. You can relax, take your time, and get it done right. You've succeeded in the best possible way: by making those who would otherwise impede you join your cause and help you out.

In fact, the resident rocket scientists standing by help install the new guidance system for you. From here, it'll be your agency with control of the system and the ability to help—or hinder—other satellites in similar orbits and constellations.

Well done, agent.

Go to page 154

Border Walls

Heading outside, it's nearly impossible to focus on just one person. The comings and goings from the parking lot are ever present, and with the lunch rush this is one of the busiest times of the day. Still, if you're being followed, there are people watching you from office windows up above. No, don't look now! They'd be peering down on you with binoculars held in one hand, and reporting in with a handheld radio in the other.

You're about to turn toward the parking lot when a man lowers his newspaper, touches a finger to his ear, and rises from the bench he was sitting on. On instinct, you turn the other way, moving purposefully, but not running.

Suddenly, you find your way impeded. There before you is an enormous slab, split into three sections, right in the middle of the path like they were suddenly airdropped to hem you in. Graffiti adorns the barrier with a strikingly outlined sun and mountain, a heart, and phrases like "the wind cries" and "tear down the wall."

These are sections of the original Berlin wall, and the exhibit is meant to be disjointing like this. It is supposed to impede your path, like a statement, but it also means you'll have to turn and go somewhere else. Which way now?

The perimeter road encircles the complex, so you'll have to hope Ted can find you either way. If not, it's worth considering what lies beyond. Head north, and you'll find open spaces with trees, hiking trails, and closer proximity to the Potomac. South, you'll sooner meet suburbia and developed businesses.

➢ Double back toward the south parking lot. Go to page 238

➢ Head toward the north parking lot and the gate there. Go to page 171

Bourne Yesterday

"**N**o unauthorized access, sorry," one of the guards says.

So, you flatten your palm and swing the side of your hand at the man's throat.

"Oh, Jesus Christ! I wasn't being serious!" Ted shouts in your ear.

Ted continues, but his words are muffled by the dull thuds echoing inside your head as the guards pummel you. The attack caught the first guard by surprise, but it wasn't expertly delivered and did not incapacitate the man as you might have hoped. It turns out, that *they're* the ones who are expertly trained combatants.

There was no "sleeper cell" training.

You aren't "awakened."

But you are beaten, jailed, tried, and finally, imprisoned.

THE END

Brought to Justice

Roku moves to strike Bird with the would-be katana, and leaves you little choice—you fire, winging the Japanese agent. Ringo drops down to help Roku just as Bird removes a knife and holds it up to Pinkie. Bird is…she's helping you?

It'll have to do as temporary alliances go. You don't want her dead if she is the mole, and the CIA will want to interrogate her to see why Pointer was betrayed. Blood is nowhere near as valuable as information in this trade.

With Bird's help, you round up the rest of the weapons on the plane and lock them in the incineration briefcases. Roku's wound is treatable; which means she should make it back to DC. Hitch eventually comes round, too. And the pilot goes from horrified to thrilled once the fighter escort arrives. There must have been a deal struck with Langley, because the Chinese authorities offer no pursuit.

Suffice it to say, you've got some valuable cargo here. Indeed, the CIA never expected you to bring in all the Hand agents in one fell swoop. Once you arrive back home, you'll learn they had planned on trading the rest of these agents to the Chinese in exchange for your safe return, but you've just done one better.

"Good work, Papercut," M says. "We've been recording your movements and conversations via the dampening capsule. Sorry to have kept you in the dark on this, but we weren't sure how capable you truly were."

"Now that we know, we have some good news!" Spearing chimes in.

"We're going to send you for training at The Farm; you're to be a bona fide field agent," M says.

"What about the launch?" you ask.

"The launch is scrubbed; your work is done for now. We're going to prosecute and interrogate the other agents in hopes of finding a trail to Palm. We had been tracking this whole Russia/China thing, and even had our own operation in place—Silicon Valley was going to launch our *own* guidance system for us—but the damned Hand was going to reverse everything. You've saved the day, truly."

"What about Pointer's betrayal? Is Bird the mole?" you ask.

"We'll find all that out soon enough," M says.

"Look to the next mission, not the last, field agent!" Spearing adds.

That's it—you've done it, superspy! Just know this: yours was only one path to success.

See that CIA emblem up there? *SPIED* has three unique storylines and over fifty possible endings, but only three "best" endings per storyline. There's a TOP SECRET, SECRET, and CONFIDENTIAL ending per emblem, which means you've probably got a lot of book left to explore!

When you're ready, go back undercover and start again. Or, if you're all finished, why not check out the rest of the adventures the *Click Your Poison* multiverse has to offer? Help others crack the code on these books and leave a review on Amazon, Olympic, or Goodreads, or recruit more field agents by posting about *SPIED* on social media.

This chapter will self-destruct in 3, 2, 1…

Hi, there. Did you, Dear Reader, know that there are several Easter eggs with references to each CYP book released thus far hiding with the pages this book? It'll be a test of your surveillance skills to find them all.

If you're done reading, you can sign up for the new release mailing list, or check out James Schannep's blog for updates on new books.

http://eepurl.com/bdWUBb
http://jamesschannep.com

Bugging You

"I don't know. Doesn't mean much of anything to me," Ted says.

"Don't you remember? There was an error in processing, like the database was updating itself. Some kind of continuous loop or something, I don't know. You're the tech guy. But you said you needed to debug—"

"Sure, but it was nothing. Unrelated. There are minor errors in code all the time. I don't know why that engineer mentioned SPIED, but—unless they're using it to mask some kind of malware—the DC server isn't relevant to what's happening here."

"Maybe it is? Maybe…I should go back to DC and check things out?"

"I'm not so sure that's a good idea," Pinkie says. "You're the newest recruit, and you still have the CIA stink on you. That makes you the most vulnerable in the field and the most likely to be compromised back in DC; it's not a great combination."

"You'll have to trust me. I know the CIA. Look where my instincts have led us. Look what we've uncovered!"

Pinkie shakes his head. "Okay, but let's send someone as backup. Maybe Ringo or—"

"I'll go alone. As the newest agent, you won't miss me that much. You guys find out what's up in China and we'll meet back stateside before they can launch any satellites. They said it would be a US launch, so if I'm already back, we'll be ahead of the curve."

Pinkie concedes the point with a reluctant nod.

"But we just have one jet, how will you get there?" Ted says.

Thinking about it for a moment, you say:

➢ "I should have enough money here to get a plane ticket back home. Just take me to the airport." Go to page 280

➢ "The US embassy is close. I'll hire a car from here, we saw plenty of taxis on the way inside." Go to page 277

Bum Rush

In the early days of the railroad expansion across the United States, people used to hitch rides on train cars all the time. Vagrants and vagabonds would simply hop aboard and take a seat in a box car, but these were older, slower trains without sleek frames, and with plenty of handholds. Since those halcyon hobo days, improvements in aerodynamics and increases in safe operating speeds have made the top of a train a far less forgiving free ride.

All that to say, when you try to rush forward, you slip.

You fall.

And you tumble off the train.

THE END

Call the Cavalry

Taking your rental car up the hilly roads and up to the base boundary before dawn, you're able to park near a ROAD CLOSED barrier and walk onto base territory. In a few hours, regular patrols will find your rental car, but the launch site is on the other side of the Vandenberg and their suspicions shouldn't affect the mission.

It's a short hike from here to the stables, where dozens of horses are kept for all sorts of purposes. You're not actually taking beach patrol horses—those would be more closely monitored and guarded—but that doesn't matter much. Many different riding clubs stable their horses here, and Grand Theft Pony isn't a common occurrence, so you find mares and steeds with relative ease.

From here, it's a *looooooong* ride down to the ocean. Like, several hours. Good thing you were up early for a nice predawn horseback ride. It's an eerie feeling, riding horses in silence through the coastal fog, and by the time you reach the coast, you're feeling quite saddle-sore.

"I don't know if you've ever watched a horseback ride via satellite, but it is riveting, let me tell you," Ted says dryly.

Then the Z-Axes launch facility blooms forth from the mist like a lighthouse suddenly appearing at sea. You've made it! That means the drop point must be near at hand.

"There should be a bridge ahead according to my maps," Ted says. "Pinkie's team will toss out the guidance computer system, you'll retrieve it, and then you'll need to move quickly back to the launch site. Go directly to the rocket for installation—it's too late to install it at the Horizontal Integration Facility (HIF). And before you ask, that *is* what it's really called, and no, they don't just shout 'phrasing!' at one another all day with these phallic terms. I checked."

"How do we get into the launch site?" you ask.

"The front door—that's the only way. One way in or out."

Roku suddenly spurs her horse and says, "Come on! Train is approaching."

Sure enough, you look back to see an Amtrak speeding down the tracks, its headlights piercing the fog. Spurring your own horse to action, the three of you rush to the bridge just as the train does the same. It's hard to see what's happening inside, but flashes of gunfire illuminate one of the train cars just before something is thrown from the window.

The object swells as it falls, deploying a series of airbags around it.

They've packed the guidance computer in an anti-avalanche bag, protecting it from the fall and from the sand, as well as making it easy to spot. With her head start, Roku scoops up the bag in mid-gallop and turns toward the Space Launch Complex (SLC), knowing you've only got minutes before launch is intended to begin.

The guards at the entry come out to greet you; they see you in uniform—but there's a vehicle barrier in place and Roku stops there.

"We have intelligence of a credible threat inside the facility," she says.

The pair of guards look to one another, but her ruse is convincing enough and they pull the barrier back to grant you entry. Before you can proceed, however, another guard comes from the entry facility—a supervisor, hand near his pistol—and stops them.

"Wait! What's the word of the day?"

Hitch and Roku exchange a glance—they don't know.

"Ted? Word of the day?"

"Working on it. Not exactly a published list. But I feel like that should have been part of the mission; I guess I must have missed something—did anyone tell you a passphrase?"

If you know the word of the day, turn to that chapter now. Flip to the page with the corresponding title. Yes, literally turn the pages until you reach the chapter that is named after the passphrase.

Or, to indicate that you don't know the word of the day, turn to page 114.

Oh, Canada

There's security screening at the entrance, but all your sophisticated gear passes through undetected. The agents split up, and you loiter near the entry, looking at the presentation pamphlets and keynote speakers while keeping one eye on Pinkie.

Noticing your gaze, he takes a couple of brochures and hands you one, open to the correct page. It details—in English—the background of Dr. Rohini Dympna, daughter of Indian immigrants who grew up in San Francisco, first in her family to go to college, studied at Stanford and MIT, now a researcher from Z-Axes in a joint venture with Human Infinite Technologies (HiT), and ultimately, her plans to "Change the Face of Space."

"Care to join me?" Pinkie asks.

Not much point in hiding your intentions to follow him now, and you can just as easily spy on Pinkie at the symposium as you could try to tail the agent. Telling Pinkie that you'd love to join him, you walk side-by-side to the conference room.

You've arrived just in time; the presentation has already begun. Under the guise of splitting up, you position yourself near the rear of the symposium while Pinkie gets up close to the speaker.

Dr. Dympna is a passionate woman, in her forties but still full of youthful energy and passion. She tells of the future of space; a future for humanity, rather than that of one nation. She refers to "The Space Race," but rather than the typical story about who put a man on the moon first, she speaks in terms of the human race and collective goals.

"Which is why we're excited to be part of a new era of global cooperation. Three nations, long thought to be diametrically at odds with one another, will join together in a way our militaries and politicians could never have imagined. Not as foes, but as financial partners. Russian hardware, Chinese software, launched in an American rocket."

Pinkie is nodding—*this* is why you were sent here. A corporate satellite involving the US, China, and Russia in a nongovernmental capacity? Worth looking into, for sure. Your time at the CIA has made you suspicious of such claims.

A woman snaps a picture of Pinkie, from just behind him. It's a single photo, and you only catch a glimpse from your periphery before she sees you watching and turns to leave. Without hesitation, you turn and follow the woman.

From your position, you're able to cut her off at the exit where you should be able to get a better look at her. The both of you act as if you're exiting naturally, unrelated to one another. But at the area just outside the lecture hall, she smiles tightly and looks your way. You expected her to run, not meet you head-on.

"Have we met?" she asks. Her accent could be Russian, but with some other foreign influence residing just beneath the surface.

"I don't believe we've had the pleasure," you say, trying not to appear flustered.

"Are you certain? You're from Langley, right?"

"I think you have me confused with someone else. I'm here on behalf of the Olympic self-publishing platform. You know, ebooks?" you say, keeping the cover story intact.

"I see. Well, if you're interested in expanding into print, look me up," she says. "Here, I'll write my personal number."

She takes a business card from her handbag, scribbles on the back, then hands it to you. The card reads, "Roma Tatiyova, Business Solutions."

"I've got her on your lanyard camera," Ted says. "According to our analytics, there's an 84% chance that's Bunny Slopes, the contact who met Pointer on his final mission."

"Enjoy the rest of the conference," she says.

Then she leaves. Flipping the card over, but keeping it off-camera, you see she's written, "I HAVE MESSAGE. MEET @ LADIESROCM."

"What was that all about?" Pinkie asks a moment later, approaching you from behind.

"Someone interested in publishing," you say, somewhat dumbfounded.

You hold up the front of the card.

"Ah, okay. Well, then. Time to regroup with the others. We've got our mission, and we've got to get to China. There's no time to lose, eh?"

➤ Stop by the women's bathroom to meet Bunny Slopes. Go to page 236

➤ Stick with Pinkie. Your mission from the CIA is to follow The Hand's agents. Go to page 44

A Case of the Mondays

"**W**ait, what? What memo; I didn't get any memo," Spearing grumbles, agitated.

"Really? We should have each received a copy. It stated 'destroy after reading' in bold right there at the top."

Spearing pinches the bridge of his nose under his glasses.

"There's not enough coffee in the world for this. Let me go see what management is up to," he says at length.

And then he's gone.

"Nice one!" Ted says in your ear. "Okay, we'd better get you out of there. Next stop: the servers. As a parting gift to the Company, HQ needs us to wiretap the CIA. I'm pretty sure The Hand already has access; from my time in IT I can tell you everyone who's anyone has remotely hacked our database in the last decade. At this point it's like using your neighbor's Wi-Fi. Anyway, I think this is the final test on our entry exam.

"Ready? Head down the corridor and take your first left. Grab a handful of files, so you look like you're on a delivery. By the way, I hope you read that dossier closely, because you won't be able to go back and review the file on Pointer now that you've pulped it. The short of it is that someone double-crossed Pointer. We'll need to know why if we don't want you meeting the same fate," Ted continues.

"And we don't," you say.

"Right. So, do you see thick, black cables snaking across the ceiling? If you follow those—"

"What? No, I just see fluorescent lights and Styrofoam ceiling tiles."

"Oh, right. I was thinking of *Jurassic Park*. Just take the next left toward the server rooms."

Trying not to sigh too loudly, you clutch your stack of folders and turn down the corridors of the CIA toward the server rooms. The entrance is immediately visible down at the far end of the hallway, flanked on either side by armed security guards. Contrary to Ted's previous assertions, it turns out that infiltrating and bugging their servers is something the powers that be at the CIA have decided they don't want.

"What's the plan for the guards?" you ask.

"You're probably not going to believe me, but here goes: you weren't suddenly called up out of the blue to be the next superagent. You're a sleeper cell. You've been trained since birth, though you were brainwashed to forget everything and live an ordinary life. Once you enter a life-or-death struggle, however, your fight-or-flight response will trigger all this hidden knowledge to come bubbling to the surface and you'll be the badass superspy you were born to be. Attack the guards and we'll enter phase two."

By the time Ted finishes, you're down nearly the full length of the hallway. The guards notice your approach. What do you do?

➤ It's true—you've always felt "different." Awaken your sleeper-self. Judo chop!
  Go to page 31

➤ Tell Ted he's not funny and use your secretarial training instead.
  Go to page 190

The Catch

"**H**old on, hold on. Don't hang up," Ted says. "Look, I get it. The hero initially refuses the call to adventure. Then the Jawas blow up your sandtroopers or whatever, and then *BLAM* your uncle burns down the farmhouse. But we don't have time for that. The people who killed Pointer aren't done."

"Ted, what the hell did you rope me into?"

"It's not me! I've already gone underground. If there's some kind of leak inside The Hand, well, they might follow the droplets and try and get the *next* Pointer while they still can. Get it? Killing new recruits is the closest thing to travelling through time and killing your adversary in their crib. Now come on, baby-spy. Let's get you all growed-up and turned into *Spy, baby!*"

Trying not to groan audibly, you look around the office. All the eyes that dart your way and back again, all the hushed conversations, all the messages typed out and phone calls being made—could someone really be after you?

"What do you say? Are you in or are *you in?!*" Ted continues.

➢ Well, when you put it that way… I guess my choice is "I'm in." Go to page 92

➢ No. I work for the G-D C-I-A, not some shadowy Hand organization. Pull the earpiece out. Go to page 222

Chart a New Course

"That's enough, nobody move!" You say, claiming the weapon.

Pinkie slowly picks himself up from off from the ground, hands raised to keep things from escalating.

"The Chinese authorities are coming closer," Pinkie says. "We should get going."

"Shut up!" Ringo says.

"Pilot, start preparations for takeoff," Pinkie says. "You don't want to end up in a Chinese prison—or cemetery."

"Who the hell are you people?" the pilot says.

Pinkie's trying to get on your good side by helping. Either that, or he's trying to look like he's the one who controls this situation by taking charge. You know it's a power play.

Thinking quickly, you say, "This is an undercover operation, being run by the CIA. Let's go back to DC."

The other agents look to you, trying to gauge if you're admitting that you're working for the CIA, or if you're simply trying to tell the pilot a believable cover story. They don't protest, because it works. Rather than stopping for the Chinese inspection team, the pilot takes off once again.

In spite of an airplane taking off, everyone holds their position. It's a tense standoff, and you'll need to do something if you're going to fly back to the US. You can't hold them all at gunpoint for the whole duration of the flight.

"You said *she* is the mole," Ringo says, manic. "Which one is it?"

He points from Bird to Roku, looking at you.

"I just saved you, obviously," Roku says.

"She's smart. It could be a trick," Bird says.

"This is why we were doing an internal investigation before saying anything," Pinkie says.

He knows? Then Roku shifts, still holding that ASP-style sword. Bird reaches for something at the same moment. You yell for them to stop moving; to drop their weapons, but it looks like that's not going to cut it.

➢ Keep the pistol on Bird, she's the one Pointer named on his cipher.
Go to page 130

➢ Keep the pistol trained on Roku, she's already taken out one agent.
Go to page 32

Checking Out

You can't help but wonder…what did those files contain? So it's not without a twinge of regret—and a healthy dose of fear of missing out (FOMO)—that you log out of the computer and leave, back down the hallway and out into the main conference halls before the cameras reset.

Roku comes from the crowds and you walk together toward the exhibitor booths until you find Hitch—he's maintaining the cover story for the group at the self-publishing stand. He asks for the pair of you to cover for him while he takes a bathroom break, which is easy enough.

Shortly thereafter, Pinkie returns and says it's time to wrap up.

You tell him what you've learned from your time at the computer terminal, and he replies with a sly smile.

"That makes perfect sense, based on what I've found. Come, we need to board the jet for the next phase of the mission: we're headed to China."

Well, not much choice here. Onto the next phase of the mission!

Go to page 22

Chinatown

Once everyone has settled in on the private jet, it takes off toward China. Does The Hand have a frequent flier program? It feels like you're spending more time in the air than in operations on the ground. Better get used to it; such is the whirlwind life of a spy when time is of the essence.

About an hour into the flight, Palm briefs the team on the next phase of the mission. Each agent watches on their own device, and you tune in on your geniusphone.

"Well done, everyone. Our analysts have collected the data submitted by each member of the team and have returned a full picture of what you're up against. Your personal liaisons should also have received briefings, if you'd like to confer with them on the flight."

You'd expect him to chime in here, but Ted says nothing. Does he suspect that you sloughed off on this part of the mission, opting to spy on one of your fellow agents instead?

"You're headed to Beijing," Palm continues. "We've uncovered a joint plot between Russia and China to use resources in Silicon Valley to infect US- and NATO-allied satellite constellations in synchronous orbits with a malware delivery system disguised as a maintenance satellite of their own. We don't think the tech startups know they're being used for anti-satellite (ASAT) operations in this way, but rather than expose this scheme to these American corporations, we can use the operation to our advantage—namely, we'll let them go through with the launch, but we're going to replace the onboard guidance computer with a package of our own. Hitch, if you please?"

The German agent stands and says, "We have a contact who tells us we can find compatible hardware in the *Xiushui* black market, also known as Silk Street, where we'll need to send an operative to pose as a tech buyer. Using this counterfeit guidance system, we'll be able to alter the code and hack the satellite constellation."

"All good news. However, there is a slight complication," Palm says. "We've recently learned that Russian Intelligence has been tipped off to our presence, which means there's the potential that Chinese Intelligence might be looking for you on the ground."

Pinkie looks your way and grins. "Which means that you, Index, are best suited to buy what we need. As the newest agent, any leak should have the least information on *your* identity."

"And Pointer had a previous connection to this contact," Bird adds. "As another American, you can use those sympathies to your advantage."

"Just be careful. If our identities are leaked, it is possible this contact is the one who set Pointer up in the first place," Ringo says.

"I will accompany," Roku says. "As the second-newest agent, the same conditions apply. But the cover story is that an American investor is looking for black-market Chinese tech; then, someone who frequently makes business deals in Asia might believably have a Japanese bodyguard."

"Being fluent in Mandarin won't hurt either," Pinkie says, nodding.

"Excellent. We look forward to hearing about your success. Good luck and Godspeed," Palm says before disconnecting.

The team appears to be in high spirits, ready to get into the meat of their mission. However, once you've arrived in Beijing, you find that your course has been diverted. The unexpected turbulence, in this case, being airport security.

They're waiting for you.

Private jets can normally do what they will—that's one of the many perks that come with wealth. Yes, there are customs checks, but often that takes the form of an individual agent who comes out to the corporate airliner, signs off on everything, and lets you go. In the old days, there might have been a bribe or two involved.

All that to say, it's extremely unusual to be met by a security team before you even finish taxiing. Is this the complication Palm mentioned?

"What's this all about?" you ask.

"Let me see if I can access the database," Ted says.

"Stay calm, everyone," Pinkie says. "Stick to your cover stories."

Once the agents are all down on the tarmac, you're held at gunpoint. This isn't just a routine airport screening, and Chinese Intelligence isn't bogged down by little details like Miranda rights. Something is definitely wrong. But were they tipped off? And by whom?

At length, a plainclothes agent in a suit—looking like a cross between a detective or an FBI agent and someone who has seen far too many American television (TV) shows—approaches you directly.

"You're the one the CIA sent, yes?" he says.

All eyes go to you; you can feel the rest of The Hand agents stiffen in response. Still, they're outnumbered by the Chinese security detail, and weapons are targeted evenly on the team; they won't attempt anything right now, but danger hangs thickly in the air.

What should you say?

➤ "Yes, I am. Under diplomatic immunity, I need to speak to my handlers immediately." Go to page 159

➤ "No, I'm just someone who works on book covers at a tech company." Go to page 58

Codename: Bird

```
SUBJECT: Female/28
NATIONALITY: French/Algerian
APPEARANCE: Dark brown/black/brown/5'7"/135lbs
KNOWN ALIASES: Mlle. ███████████████, agent codename "The
Bird"
AFFILIATION: Alternative Intelligence known as "The Hand"
LAST KNOWN WHEREABOUTS: French Presidential Palace
```

The file contains a few blurry photographs, but there are enough for you to make out the agent's appearance. From these, you see a stunning, dark and mysterious woman in all black. She's looking up at the camera, with a tight-lipped smile in recognition—she knows she's being observed and is all but winking at the observer. Certainly glamorous, her overall appearance makes her resemble someone out of *Charlie's Angels*. Setting the photographs aside, you focus on the typed portion of the file.

This file tells you the background on Bird. Born to a mother who emigrated from Algiers, and a man from Bordeaux, Bird had a promising career as an investigative journalist until she began looking into French politics. Though her looks often disarmed would-be enemies, she was set to be "disappeared" from French society before she was recruited into Alternative Intelligence. Whether she leveraged embarrassing information about the French government is unknown, but her ability to make contacts and uncover buried leads is likely why she was recruited into the agency to begin with.

Finished with the file, you close it and look at the others on the table. What haven't you read yet?

➤ Agency profile: International Alternative Intelligence. Codename: The Hand. Go to page 47

➤ British handler-at-large. Codename: Palm. Go to page 49

➤ German field agent. Codename: Hitch. Go to page 48

➤ Italian field agent. Codename: Ringo. Go to page 51

➤ Canadian field agent. Codename: Pinkie. Go to page 50

➤ Japanese field agent. Codename: Roku. Go to page 52

➤ I already know everything I need to know. Let's move on. Go to page 284

Codename: The Hand

SUBJECT: International spy ring, Alternative Intelligence, "The Hand"
NATIONALITY: Membership includes contacts from the USA, UK, Germany, France, Italy, Canada, and Japan
DATE ESTABLISHED: Unknown
HEADQUARTERS: Unknown
MOTIVES: Unknown

The rest of the file expands on what the CIA knows about The Hand, which, as you might have guessed, isn't much. They wouldn't be recruiting you to play the role of double agent if they had all the facts on this shadow organization. You're meant to shed some light on this mystery.

What they do know: The Hand appears to be comprised of each of the Group of Seven (G7) member countries. One point of contact (POC) per country, each with a dedicated renewable slot—at least that's the working theory after the way you were tapped to replace Pointer. It's unknown how many members might comprise the support teams (like Ted).

What they suspect: the CIA thinks there might be some relation to the SPIED database. Under project Vigilant Eagle, the database was shared with US allies (like those in the G7). It's possible that a leak has given The Hand access to the database, where they might be compromising other intelligence communities. This could explain how Ted himself was recruited.

Furthermore, the agency is suspected to have originated in England, judging from the prominent position of authority given to the headmistress known as Palm. However, there is no further evidence to support this theory.

Loyalties? The Hand appears to have similar interests to the US and the allied nations comprising its membership. However, as a nongovernmental organization (NGO), the CIA is uncomfortable with how little oversight America has over such an agency. Untethered reach without oversight is meant to be the purview of your own government's shadow agencies: theirs and theirs alone. An agency existing outside of the chain of command with so much inside knowledge is a major security risk—one that you're meant to help mitigate.

Finished with the file, you close it and look at the others on the table. What haven't you read yet?

➤ British handler-at-large. Codename: Palm. Go to page 49

➤ German field agent. Codename: Hitch. Go to page 48

➤ French field agent. Codename: Bird. Go to page 46

➤ Italian field agent. Codename: Ringo. Go to page 51

➤ Canadian field agent. Codename: Pinkie. Go to page 50

➤ Japanese field agent. Codename: Roku. Go to page 52

➤ I already know everything I need to know. Let's move on. Go to page 284

Codename: Hitch

SUBJECT: Male/53
NATIONALITY: German
APPEARANCE: Fair/auburn/brown/5'9"/185lbs
KNOWN ALIASES: Herr █████████████, agent codename "Hitch"
AFFILIATION: Alternative Intelligence known as "The Hand"
LAST KNOWN WHEREABOUTS: Manchurian China, Near North Korean border

At the forefront of the file is an official photograph from this agent's time in German Intelligence. Staring up at you through the photo is a stout, compact, and muscular man. Blond-haired, blue-eyed: striking Germanic features. Reserved, but you could imagine him exploding with passion. Looks a bit like Daniel Craig's 007. Setting this photo aside, you're greeted with a second photograph—this one from the agent's time in Russian Intelligence. You do a double-take; it's almost like he has a twin. He's in both German *and* Russian Intelligence?

The text portion of the file reveals he was indeed working for both agencies, detailing his time spent in German Intelligence as a deep-cover operative, meant to impersonate a double agent to Russia. Russian Intelligence, of course, believes the opposite is true and it is unknown to what extent he was loyal to either side. Both German and Russian Intelligence believe Hitch had infiltrated The Hand on their behalf, but after Operation Manchurian Candidate [cross-file unavailable due to an ongoing investigation], the CIA believes neither is correct. He was recruited directly by The Hand and is the rare triple agent. Given that most of this information comes from classified, sealed state documents, his exact age is only an estimate, as are his number of confirmed kills. There is some argument as to which number is higher.

Finished with the file, you close it and look at the others on the table. What haven't you read yet?

➢ Agency profile: International Alternative Intelligence. Codename: The Hand. Go to page 47

➢ British handler-at-large. Codename: Palm. Go to page 49

➢ French field agent. Codename: Bird. Go to page 46

➢ Italian field agent. Codename: Ringo. Go to page 51

➢ Canadian field agent. Codename: Pinkie. Go to page 50

➢ Japanese field agent. Codename: Roku. Go to page 52

➢ I already know everything I need to know. Let's move on. Go to page 284

Codename: Palm

```
SUBJECT: Female/unknown
NATICNALITY: British
APPEARANCE: Unknown
KNOWN ALIASES: Real name, unknown. Codename, "Palm"
AFFILIATION: Alternative Intelligence known as "The Hand"
LAST KNOWN WHEREABOUTS: Unknown
```

There's not so much as even a photograph in this file. No social media, newsfeeds, or the like. Not even a grainy, shadowy, "hopeful" shot from a surveillance camera. The CIA, it would appear, has little concrete information on The Hand's headmistress.

The typed portion of the file doesn't offer much either. Here's what they know: the other agents report in to her. Is Palm a handler for a larger head of state? Or is she truly the spymaster? She doesn't appear to have existed, professionally or personally, before the formation of The Hand—not that they know exactly when that occurred, either. The CIA cannot confirm whether or not British Intelligence is aware of her existence, lest they risk revealing to MI6 a possible threat that they know nothing about.

An amalgamation of statements from confidential informants provided the CIA with her codename, gender, and nationality, but little else. In short, she's a ghost. Finished with the file, you close it and look at the others on the table. What haven't you read yet?

➢ Agency profile: International Alternative Intelligence. Codename: The Hand. Go to page 47

➢ German field agent. Codename: Hitch. Go to page 48

➢ French field agent. Codename: Bird. Go to page 46

➢ Italian field agent. Codename: Ringo. Go to page 51

➢ Canadian field agent. Codename: Pinkie. Go to page 50

➢ Japanese field agent. Codename: Roku. Go to page 52

➢ I already know everything I need to know. Let's move on. Go to page 284

Codename: Pinkie

```
SUBJECT: Male/44
NATIONALITY: Canadian
APPEARANCE: Fair/black/green/5'11"/165lbs
KNOWN ALIASES: Mr. ███████████, agent codename "The
Pinkie"
AFFILIATION: Alternative Intelligence known as "The Hand"
LAST KNOWN WHEREABOUTS: Benelux and NATO headquarters,
Brussels, Belgium
```

With jet-black hair and a tight smile, the agent could be the spitting image of Pierce Brosnan's Bond. He's polished in his photos, especially those detailing his years of service to his nation.

The typed portion of the file tells you the background on Pinkie, detailing his time spent at a military academy in his youth—an only child born to academic-turned-diplomat parents. He was recruited into Alternative Intelligence, though the "how" remains somewhat of an enigma. Pinkie appears to be the only agent on the roster who was present from the agency's original incarnation and on. Where he came from before that is unclear, and there's a large gap between his education and whenever it was that he started with The Hand.

All this begs the question: is there a reason he's not working for the Canadian government?

Finished with the file, you close it and look at the others on the table. What haven't you read yet?

➢ Agency profile: International Alternative Intelligence. Codename: The Hand. Go to page 47

➢ British handler-at-large. Codename: Palm. Go to page 49

➢ German field agent. Codename: Hitch. Go to page 48

➢ French field agent. Codename: Bird. Go to page 46

➢ Italian field agent. Codename: Ringo. Go to page 51

➢ Japanese field agent. Codename: Roku. Go to page 52

➢ I already know everything I need to know. Let's move on. Go to page 284

Codename: Ringo

SUBJECT: Male/31
NATIONALITY: Italian, mixed unknown
APPEARANCE: Medium brown/black/brown/5'9"/170lbs
KNOWN ALIASES: Sig. ███████████████, agent codename "Ring"
AFFILIATION: Alternative Intelligence known as "The Hand"
LAST KNOWN WHEREABOUTS: Unknown

The photograph at the forefront of this file is a mugshot. The man in the photo is slim, trim, and olive-skinned. If the file didn't say he was over thirty, you might have mistaken him for being in his 20s, likely because of a strict fitness routine. He smiles at you with manic energy more befitting an action star than a spy.

The rest of the photos—and there are many—show the agent in military uniform, paparazzi glamour shots, and more police records. How does a playboy end up in the army? The text portion of the file fills you in on the agent's background, detailing a misspent youth, time in the army as an airborne Special Forces member, and ultimately a wake of destruction and arrest for mayhem and grand theft auto. It's unclear how his sentence was commuted into time in Alternative Intelligence, although there are parallels between this story and the petty crimes of his teenage years before he joined the Army. Someone has been looking out for Ringo. The question then, is: are they still?

Finished with the file, you close it and look at the others on the table. What haven't you read yet?

➤ Agency profile: International Alternative Intelligence. Codename: The Hand. Go to page 47

➤ British handler-at-large. Codename: Palm. Go to page 49

➤ German field agent. Codename: Hitch. Go to page 48

➤ French field agent. Codename: Bird. Go to page 46

➤ Canadian field agent. Codename: Pinkie. Go to page 50

➤ Japanese field agent. Codename: Roku. Go to page 52

➤ I already know everything I need to know. Let's move on. Go to page 284

Codename: Roku

SUBJECT: Female/23
NATIONALITY: Japanese
APPEARANCE: Light brown/black/black/5'4"/115lbs
KNOWN ALIASES: ██████████████, agent codename "Six"
AFFILIATION: Alternative Intelligence known as "The Hand"
LAST KNOWN WHEREABOUTS: Yokohama, Tokyo, Japan

From the pictures provided, you can see she has soft features, juxtaposed with a hard, evaluating eye. Her dark hair is pulled back tightly, with nothing out of place from head to toe; not a single hair nor thread untamed. The first few photographs in the file are all of sporting events: padded up in practice samurai armor, though her competitors' swords look real enough. Several images show off her athletic prowess in action shots, while others show her accepting gold medals. From here, the photographs suddenly switch to what looks like a new career as a mercenary. It's a jarring shift.

The text portion of the file tells you the background on Roku, detailing her prominence in the Kendo circuits and dominance in the sport until her ultimate downfall. It's unclear what precipitated the snap, but she had seriously injured several other competitors before she was banned from the sport. She spent a brief time as a personal bodyguard to a tech entrepreneur, and it appears as if her services were "traded" to Alternative Intelligence as part of a larger deal, without either the seller or commodity quite knowing what they were getting from the bargain. She's the newest member of the team and has yet to make a name for herself among the field agents.

Finished with the file, you close it and look at the others on the table. What haven't you read yet?

➤ Agency profile: International Alternative Intelligence. Codename: The Hand. Go to page 47

➤ British handler-at-large. Codename: Palm. Go to page 49

➤ German field agent. Codename: Hitch. Go to page 48

➤ French field agent. Codename: Bird. Go to page 46

➤ Italian field agent. Codename: Ringo. Go to page 51

➤ Canadian field agent. Codename: Pinkie. Go to page 50

➤ I already know everything I need to know. Let's move on. Go to page 284

Coming Clean

It's not as easy as all that. Yes, you're coming clean, but only after you heard Ted's sales pitch. That doesn't exactly look good. Your supervisor, Mr. Spearing, is not the type to let things slide, but he listens carefully as you recount your morning and the strange dossier left on your desk. You play up your own naïveté, and make it seem as though maybe you thought Ted was playing a prank or that you were otherwise confused—which is mostly true.

That's exactly what your supervisor needed to hear. By offering up this white lie, all suspicions move away from you and onto Ted from IT. Indeed, you never see him again. You can't be sure if he was simply fired, arrested, or what—but from your perspective that's the end of that.

However, because you still read classified material when not authorized, your security clearance is revoked, and the agency has no choice but to let you go. But—on the bright side—no legal action is taken against you for reading material above your clearance level. Instead, you're released with a small severance package and told by the supervisor that you'll get a good recommendation letter when looking for a new job.

It should come as no surprise, however, that since you were *almost* recruited as a spy, you're forevermore under surveillance and on government watch lists. This makes airline travel especially inconvenient.

THE END

Compromising Position

You awaken as the jet lands and taxies to the private air terminal, allowing your fellow agents time to shake off the fog of sleep and get ready for the mission. You're alight with nerves; this is your first mission in two senses—both as part of The Hand, and as part of the CIA. You'll need to do two jobs at once, and in Russia no less, where state security and intelligence bureaus are almost guaranteed to be surveilling your every move.

"Take your gear; put anything from your old life into the briefcase," Ted says. "Phone, keys, wallet, whatever—it needs to be incinerated alongside the mission briefing. You don't want relics from another life to contradict your story."

"Shit," you mutter.

That would include your PopSocket-style dampening capsule attached to your personal smartphone. Without this, you have no way to get in contact with the CIA. Furthermore, if they were tracking your whereabouts through your phone, they'd lose that, too. You'd be completely off the grid.

"Shit?" Ted says.

Apparently your Third Ear implant is rather sensitive. Now what?

➢ Shit, indeed. Tell Ted you have to go to the bathroom after a long flight and, uh, *tuck* the device away "somewhere safe" until you've deplaned. It's that important. Go to page 125

➢ Tell Ted you haven't backed up your old phone. With that excuse, switch the PopSocket to the new phone. Ted and the other agents shouldn't notice, and it's a risk, but one worth taking. Go to page 172

Conference Call

The television behind the bar comes to life and a woman appears on-screen—motherly, yet stern; very much the Dame Judy Dench type—this must be the Palm you've heard so much about.

"Ringo, do be a lamb and pour the team a drink," she says in a posh British accent.

The Italian man behind the bar nods and begins serving martinis.

"I hope you've all had a chance to say hello, but we've little time for niceties. You're all gathered here because we lost one of our own. I wanted to be there in person, but other commitments prevent me from joining you. I know you're rarely all in the same room, but I bring you together out of urgency, and to tell you that we have a mole in our ranks."

"When was the last time you saw her in person?" you whisper to Roku, the Japanese agent being the closest to you in the lounge.

"Never," she says, not taking her eyes from the screen.

"Our dear Pointer is dead. What was to be his final mission: Compromised. Somewhere in the information stream, there was a leak, and it cost us dearly. A field agent of his caliber is not easily replaced, of course, and so it is not as a replacement, but as a supplement that I introduce you to our newest agent—codename: Index."

You feel as if she's looking at you now. In fact, they all are. Index finger to replace Pointer finger in The Hand. It all makes perfect sense.

"Index, welcome to the team. The others know me as Palm, and now, so do you."

"Indie! What a truly awesome codename," Ted exclaims. Then, with his best Sean Connery impression, he quotes, "'We named the dog Indiana!'"

Palm says, "We have several promising leads for this mole, but as of right now, no one is above suspicion. I'm sorry, but it's true. Index has already helped us infiltrate the CIA, so if Pointer was compromised by his previous agency, we shall know shortly."

Wait, *previous* agency? If he was from an intelligence agency, why didn't the CIA have a file on him like the others? Or is Palm suggesting Pointer was CIA himself? Would M hide that detail from you?

Palm continues, "In the meantime, we have a mission of some urgency. Each of you will be briefed on the flight by your personal liaison, then dispatched to your tasks separately upon arrival. Index will have to learn on the job, so please do take our new recruit under your wings. You'll find a car waiting for you and a company jet standing by at Manassas Regional Airport. Good luck and Godspeed."

With that, the screen goes black. The fact that you're going to be briefed on the next phase of this mission once you're already on the flight doesn't bode well for reporting back to your handlers. Should you do so now, while there's still time?

- No, the rest of the agents just heard about a suspected mole in their ranks. I'd better stay close and see what else I can learn. Go to page 93

- Yes, I'll run to the bathroom before we leave the clubhouse. I need to know if Pointer was CIA, and they need to know I'm on the move. Go to page 213

Conscientious Objector

It occurs to you, possibly not for the first time, that you might not be entirely on the side of good here. It's tough to say. If this mission took place in Germany, how would Hitch feel about the role reversal? Still, your roots are in the CIA, and you signed up to serve.

"No, this isn't the way. We've got to be able to do this mission without killing a bunch of innocent servicemen," you say.

Hitch looks taken aback.

"Too late for that," he says.

You shake your head. You might very well fail your mission here, but you won't have failed yourself. The Oracle of Delphi would be proud. As the Bard writ, "This above all—to thine own self be true." Although, Polonius was totally cool with spying and murder, but this is not the time for a Hamlet discussion, is it?

Here's the thing. Hitch is *totally* cool with spying and murder, and if you aren't with him, you're against him. Without further discussion, he takes his handgun, and shoots you in the back.

THE END

Cover Blown

There's a long, tense moment where no one so much as moves. The lead Chinese Intelligence officer reviews your team's credentials while his cohorts hold the rest of you at gunpoint.

"Let them go," he says at length.

"Was it a bluff?" Ted asks in your ear.

"*Zai jian*," Pinkie says.

The Chinese agent nods. "Our apologies. Enjoy your stay."

"Of course; just a bit of shopping before heading home," Hitch says.

The team takes a pair of private hire black cars from the airport toward the Silk Market, you and Roku in one vehicle, the others in the second car. You ride in silence, and are contented to look out the window at the Beijing cityscape—until Roku removes a syringe from her gear.

"That was a close one back there, wasn't it?" you say, nervously. "Do you think they'll be watching us as we prepare for the drop?"

She pulls a large dose of a clear liquid, squirts a tiny amount from the tip, looks to you, and says, "I should say so, yes. Someone has tipped them off. Remarkable, how they took such *interest* in you specifically," she continues.

After a hard gulp, you say, "Quite remarkable. I don't suppose that needle is for the next phase of the mission."

"It is because of your discretion that I do this painlessly, you understand. You won't be the first intoxicated tourist to fall into the Tonghui River."

Renouncing the Chinese border agents wasn't enough of a show of loyalty, it appears. How long has The Hand known you were a double agent? Did they only just now decide you were a liability? Or had this been planned all along? You'll never know; your mission ends here.

THE END

Cover Story

According to the mission briefing, you're headed into Moscow as part of an international technology fair. For your role, you deal with Olympic publishing's nitty-gritty technological aspects, like helping approve cover art for the Promethean Independent Publishing (PIP) marketplace, building an algorithm to detect nudity and violence so it doesn't have to be manually approved by a human who may or may not think an image is more or less offensive than it actually is.

You don't feel particularly well-qualified for this role, but perhaps it was assigned to you because of the IT guy in your ear. Ted should be able to help you bullshit (BS) your way through it all. The rest of your team's positions are outlined: Pinkie is team lead, Hitch is accounts and marketing, Bird is investor relations, Roku is Internet security, and Ringo is press secretary.

The team will take turns manning a booth at this fair, or alternatively, branch out and look for anything unusual. Moscow is not a typical venue for a technology fair, so the idea is to look for people trying to do something they shouldn't. Think: militarization of technology.

That's it for your cover other than your passport and identification. Aside from these documents, there's a leather case with gear you might need on your mission. You can review these items as many times as you'd like, returning to see an item more than once. What would you like to examine next?

> The leather case with the gear. What cool toys have I been given?
  Go to page 103

> My passport and identification. Time to familiarize myself with this new identity. Go to page 124

> I've seen all I need to see. Time to get some shut-eye on the red-eye.
  Go to page 120

Crapshoot

The man's brow furrows. He looks to the agent bio you've pulled up on screen, then leans back into the hallways.

"*Gvardiya!*" he shouts.

No translation needed here; the guards come at the man's request.

"It was just a wrong turn! I'm only trying to check my work email during the conference!" you protest, pointing to the screen.

But the pair of burly guards offer only deaf ears for your pleas. They're not buying it.

A strange series of *click-clack* sounds brings your attention back and you see Roku standing in the midst of the guards, having just deployed a weapon that looks like a cross between a telescoping ASP baton and a katana.

With swift, graceful moves she incapacitates the guards with the weapon. She makes it look easy; almost as if choreographed in advance. One tap to the head and a man falls limp, a blow to the sternum of another produces a coughing fit, and the third, she first connects with his wrist to disarm him of his pistol before taking him out as well.

"Get down," she says.

As you comply, a teargas canister arrives from down the hallway. Roku tees up and knocks it back over your head—and into the crowd of approaching guards.

"Let's go. The rest of the team has what we need."

You comply, following Roku. Once you've exited the secure area, she stows her weapon and walks calmly through the crowd. It's a test of your nerves, but you do the same.

"Where are we going?"

"The jet."

Well, not much choice here. Onto the next phase of the mission!

Go to page 22

Criminal Negligence

You rush over to the coffee machine, and into the safety of the break area. Looking back, you watch as your supervisor stops from cubicle to cubicle, eventually coming to linger over yours. He clearly spots the dossier, and the padded envelope, which is ripped open. The earpiece is still in your sweaty palm, so all he finds is an empty envelope—which of course instructs you to open it after reading the TOP SECRET document left atop your desk.

Spearing's head whips around with renewed interest. He finds you, demands an answer, but after you fail to produce a satisfactory excuse, he calls in security. The scene clearly stinks of you having read classified material in some sort of collusion with Ted from IT. That doesn't bode well for you.

Hope you know a good lawyer.

THE END

Dead Drop

"And what a pleasure it is to make your acquaintance," the Collector says. "You can pick up your souvenir at the coat check desk. I'll be happy to hand you the ticket once I have payment."

"Motion for Roku to go get the funds; she knows what to do," Ted says in your ear.

You comply, and both you and the man with the lapel pin watch as she heads over to the slot machines. She removes her own geniusphone device, sets it on top of the machine, and waits as a ticket prints out. From here you can only guess that her specialty spyphone just hacked the slot machine and told it to print a payout for the Collector.

"When you go to the launch site, the watchword will be 'Bletchley,'" the Collector says after reviewing the receipt from Roku. He then sets the coat check ticket out on the table, as promised, and rises to leave.

After a step, he turns and adds, "Give those reds hell."

"What was that all about?" Ringo asks.

"He must have suspicions about why we need a Chinese satellite guidance system," Hitch says.

"Doesn't matter," Pinkie says. "Go collect our package and let's get out of here."

"That's it?" you say.

"Our profession is meant to be dull if you're doing it right," Bird says.

"Okay, we will be out soon," Roku says.

"Good. Let's get going," Pinkie says. "We need to split up and deliver the package to the programmer in Silicon Valley with enough time for her to rewrite the satellite guidance system. Meanwhile, the second team will do reconnaissance on the launch site near Vandenberg Space Force Base."

➢ "I'll go for the package delivery in Silicon Valley. Tell me what needs to be done." Go to page 66

➢ "I'd like to be on the reconnaissance team near the Space Force Base." Go to page 246

Deathtrap/Dungeon

Bird pops open the emergency hatch, and the inflatable slide down to the tarmac unfurls.

"Index, out of the way!" Ringo shouts.

You turn back toward Bird and *BLAM!*

The gunshot echoes through the small plane, and you almost jump out of your skin—which means you weren't shot. You turn back to see Pinkie lying on the ground, having pulled a pistol from one of the bags under the seat. He's barely hanging in, but managed a shot at Ringo.

Bird jumps down the slide and you follow. A moment later, there's another gunshot, but you can't be sure if it was Roku finishing off Pinkie or vice versa.

The Chinese forces are clearly more than routine airport security. They hold submachine guns and look more like a hit squad. You and Bird hold your hands up in surrender, and the team lead, a plainclothes agent in a suit—looking like a cross between a detective or an FBI agent and someone who has seen far too many American television (TV) shows—approaches you directly

"You're the one the CIA sent, yes?" he says.

"I suppose I am," you say, suddenly filled with relief.

"This is not what was arranged. Are the others dead?"

"All but us," Bird says, trying to throw her lot in with you.

The man glowers. "Then there is no exchange—no deal."

It will be a long while before you're released from China; Beijing doesn't treat spies kindly. Apparently, you were meant to be exchanged for a plane full of spies, but since that didn't work, you'll be kept in custody until a better exchange can be brokered.

You might come out of this in one piece, but that won't be any time soon.

THE END

Deep State

Pinkie looks somewhat surprised, but says, "I'm sure it'll come out as we find out more on this mission. A leak inside the CIA comes as a shock, of course, especially with information given to the Russian SVR—but remember, Pointer was former CIA himself. It's possible the mole who got him killed was from that agency, not ours."

"That is worth considering," Ted says. "And if China is somehow involved, we don't know if they managed to breach both sides and are playing the Russians against the US government. Or, worse, what if the CIA is *knowingly* working with China and Russia? Let's head to Beijing and find out more about this satellite mission!"

➢ Ask Ted about the SPIED system. Wasn't he debugging that before you were recruited? Go to page 34

➢ Those are good points. Let's continue on to China and see where the thread takes us. Go to page 22

Delayed

Moving carefully, you leave your train car and peer into the next one over. The doors between the cars open automatically at your approach, and between the two cars there's a "buffer zone" where the restroom lies. The bathroom door is wide open, swaying as the train jounces along the tracks. Passing carefully, you see no one inside—but there is a hatch above the toilet which is propped open. Did whoever is after Ringo come in from above? That would be insanely dangerous, but it would explain why neither you nor Bird saw anything suspicious.

Continuing, the automatic door to the next train car—the one where Ringo was residing—opens just as someone runs out toward you. It's a Chinese man in a black suit, carrying a bag—*the* bag.

Behind him, you catch a glimpse of Ringo splayed out on the floor, with several other Chinese agents around him. Bird fights them off, but she's overwhelmed.

"Stop that man!" she shouts. "He has my bag!"

Clever. She doesn't identify you as part of the team, but instead calls upon your help as a Good Samaritan. Unfortunately, the train is loud and it's unlikely anyone else in your train heard her calls for aid. What should you do? The foreign agent runs right at you. He looks determined, but is not a large man. You might be able to take him, despite not having been trained in combat.

➢ Punch him right in his commie face. <u>Go to page 80</u>

➢ Go with a schoolyard trick; trip him as he goes by. <u>Go to page 116</u>

Delivery

Though the group will be splitting up, everyone takes the same private jet from China to California. You can't tell if it's jet lag or the whirlwind of this new life as a spy, but your head is swirling. Palm announces that you, Bird, and Ringo will go up to Silicon Valley to get the computer reprogrammed while Hitch, Roku, and Pinkie are heading toward Vandenberg Space Force Base (SFB) for reconnaissance of the launch site.

It's a long journey, and you catch up on sleep en route as best as you can.

"Open your phone, take a look," Ted says prior to your arrival.

You comply and pull up a photograph of the mark on your geniusphone. Short, hipster-thick glasses, piercings, and lime-green-dyed hair, she looks like someone who livestreams Dungeons and Dragons (D&D) cosplay on the weekends.

"Is this programmer a part of The Hand? Or are we *borrowing* her services?"

"The latter," Ted replies. "No need to employ specific talent—like someone who specializes in rewriting satellite guidance systems—when you can just tell her this is a job requested by the company where she's already employed."

You scroll through the briefing on the programmer, familiarizing yourself with her file. Her name is Bex Barsmith, a moniker she adopted for herself upon emancipation at age sixteen. An obvious talent, she's the programmer who wrote the original guidance system for the satellite, so you'll need to make it look like an official order to do a second pass has come from Z-Axes brass.

She lives in a classic San Francisco apartment building; it's historic but updated, set on a street with nearly a forty-five degree slope. Ted says he'll rent a room across the street as a base of operations for the three of you while you keep an eye on Ms. Barsmith.

Ringo and Bird secure the building while you find the keys where the landlord left them. It's a cramped one-bedroom with a single living space consisting of a kitchenette, couch and TV, and a corner desk with a folding chair.

"We have a couple days here in the Bay Area while the other team stakes out the launch site," Ringo says once you're all inside the apartment. "We'll take shifts, allowing us to catch up on sleep while we observe the mark. Once we know her routine, we'll find our way in."

"She's no doubt being watched by Russian and Chinese intelligence, probably US operatives as well. We need to figure out how to approach her in a way that looks official, but without alerting her handlers," Bird says.

"In the meantime, we have an important decision: Pizza or Chinese?" you ask, noting the delivery fliers adhered to the refrigerator by a set of community college magnets.

"Chinese. I cannot stand American pizza," Ringo says.

"You only need to stomach it," Bird replies.

"Ha-ha," Ringo says. "Seriously, let's go for Dim Sum. This area is one of the few in America where 'Chinese Food' isn't code for General Tso's Orange Diarrhea Dragon."

"Thank you for that image," Bird says, shaking her head. "Pizza, like sex, is still pretty good—even when it's bad."

Ringo smirks. "I wouldn't know."

"What do you think, Index?" Bird asks.

"Let the American decide. You can get bad pizza anywhere, but to get authentic Chinese is a rare opportunity."

They turn to you. You were joking when you said this was an important decision, but apparently these two don't take anything lightly. Well, who do you feel like siding with?

➤ This is San Francisco; the Chinese food is incredibly authentic and robust owing to Chinatown. <u>Go to page 106</u>

➤ This is San Francisco; the pizza joints make their own sourdough crust from an original 49ers' starter. <u>Go to page 78</u>

Detained

The authorities disarm the agent, of course, but they aren't rough about it. In fact, the ride down to the Italian police station is downright civil. Nothing like a "Locked Up Abroad" worst-case scenario here. In fact, they offer him coffee and cigarettes while he waits. But…what exactly is he waiting for? It takes the better part of an hour, but they're not making him sweat.

When the door to the interrogation holding room finally opens, Pointer's eyes open equally wide with recognition at this visitor. The question wasn't *what* was he waiting for, but rather, *who*.

"Sorry I'm late. I was expecting you on the Swiss side."

Pointer smirks. "I wasn't expecting you at all, but I suppose it makes sense now. I take it you want the transponder?"

"Not quite. I came for you, my friend—because *you* came for the transponder. Starting to make sense now? Pity it took so long. No hard feelings, eh? *Arrivederci.*"

"Wait!—" Pointer says, too late.

Whatever else he had to say is cut short, a declaration of silence punctuated by a gunshot.

Close the dossier and go to page 241

Dextera Domini

 TOP SECRET

"**D**oes this put me back in The Hand?" you ask.

"No, this is its own super-group, with an even more exclusive membership," Palm says.

"What's it called?"

"Things never spoken of do not need names," Ted says. "Now let's go, Indie! We've got a rogue AI to assassinate!"

If AI is inevitable (and the future), you figure it's best to make sure you're on the winning side. And indeed, you've won! Against all odds, you've survived double agents and moles, angry AI, ignominious intelligence bureaus, and scheming state security.

Index will have many future adventures in *SPIED 2: SPY HARDER**, but for you, Dear Reader, your adventure ends here. See that power emblem up there? *SPIED* has three unique storylines and over fifty possible endings, but only three "best" endings per storyline. There's a TOP SECRET, SECRET, and CONFIDENTIAL ending per emblem, which means you've probably got a lot of book left to explore!

When you're ready, go back undercover and start again. Or, if you're all finished, why not check out the rest of the adventures the *Click Your Poison* multiverse has to offer? Help others crack the code on these books and leave a review on Amazon, Olympic, or Goodreads, or recruit more field agents by posting about *SPIED* on social media.

This chapter will self-destruct in 3, 2, 1…

---

* a document so highly classified that it doesn't exist

Distracted

"It's straightforward, it's uncomplicated, and it's a strong play—I like it," Ringo says.

"I'm not sure I'd classify barging in as uncomplicated," Bird says.

"Why don't you keep the doormen busy then? That shouldn't be too complicated for you, should it?"

Bird glares at the Italian agent and suggests you go in through the back door. Ringo offers a wide grin and Bird puts up a stern finger in warning to silence him.

"Keeping the doormen distracted isn't a bad idea," you say. "You two are already like an old married couple."

Now they glare at you, but they concede the point. They play up the drama as you all head across the street, making a scene that the doormen are forced to deal with. That's when you slip inside.

"Hey!" a cry comes from behind.

One of the doormen tries to stop you, but Bird and Ringo intercept, and the poor doorman is quickly caught up in their situation. Hurrying upstairs, you find the mark out in the hallway on her phone.

"Thanks for the warning. I'd better go," she says.

She turns back toward her apartment, moving quickly, clearly afraid of you. Whether she thinks you're working with the Chinese agents or just feels the threats closing in, she panics. Not wanting to lose the mark, you rush after her. She screams, trying to close the door and lock you out, but too late. You push into her apartment.

She throws a picture frame at you from the doorway and you duck. Fully panicked, Bex runs inside, over to the window, and opens it.

"Wait! Listen!" you say. "Don't!"

But it's too late. She's so terrified, she actually flees from the window—four stories down. In the unlikely event she survives the fall, she'll definitely be too injured to work on the satellite guidance system.

Which means it's Mission: Failed.

THE END

Documented

The man's eyes narrow.

"I did not ask to see your papers," he says. "What are you doing? I was told you are collecting personal information. Asking questions you should not."

"Just here to network, like everyone else."

"Let me see that tablet," the man says, reaching out toward your signup pad.

"I—we—" you say, at a loss.

Hitch shifts uncomfortably.

"Give me your identification badges as well."

"You can see them for yourself," Hitch says.

The German agent raises his lanyard with his left hand, holding the badge up to the security man's face. With this as a distraction, Hitch swings a hard right hook, a surprise sucker punch. The Russian guard crumples to the floor and those in the immediate area all gasp in surprise.

Hitch tucks his brass knuckles back into his pocket and takes the tablet from your booth.

"Let's go. Quickly," he says.

You were at the booth for a while, but was it enough time for the other agents to get what they needed? Following Hitch through the crowd, you see the commotion has mobilized the building security. What should you do?

➤ Try to blend in. Grab a coffee in the café. Go to page 216

➤ Go for the fire exit before they have you cornered. Go to page 177

Down the Rabbit Hole

Tearing open the padded envelope, you find it nearly empty. Just when you think there's nothing inside whatsoever, a small earpiece tumbles out and into your palm. Smaller than the tip of your index finger, this looks like an advanced prototype: one part hearing aid, blended with a Bluetooth device, with a dash of earbuds thrown into the mix.

As the device comes into contact with your skin, a tiny, almost imperceptible light flickers on—indicating the unit is active. With the small object resting in your hand, you notice the other admins start to arrive. An interesting quirk of living in the greater Washington D.C. area is that the surrounding communities are such a web of roads that the fluctuations in daily traffic patterns mean you arrive at a different time relative to your coworkers each and every day. By happenstance, you were the first to arrive this Monday morning.

Mr. Spearing, your supervisor, arrives and walks down the rows of cubicles, headed your way. He's the prototypical managerial stereotype: a middle-aged man with an office worker's physique. A creature perfectly adapted to his habitat, he wears a crisp, short-sleeved, white button-up shirt, black slacks, wire-rimmed glasses, with one hand permanently set into a coffee mug as if attached to the man like a pirate's hook.

Not the type who you'd want to catch you reading classified documents. Thinking quickly, you decide to:

➢ Slide the dossier into one of your drawers and put the earpiece in.
  Go to page 203

➢ Leave your desk. Run to the coffee machine to buy some time. Go to page 61

Down to Business

"**Of** course, of course. Let's focus on the task at hand," Ted says. "This is a temporary meeting spot; sort of a chance to regroup before the next mission. In the bar over there is the rest of the team but, if you'd like, we can report in right away. I think it's pretty rare to have the whole team summoned to one spot, so it's a unique opportunity to grab a cocktail and mingle for a while, if you like. Then again, that also means the mission is pretty important and we're supposed to report in once you're ready."

Taking a moment to think about it, you decide:

➢ Go meet the team. It would be good to know what the other agents are like. Go to page 149

➢ No point in getting too cozy, if we're rarely working together. Let's get on with it. Go to page 223

Down to the Wire

Hitch is impressed by your moxie, and gives an approving nod. You rush out the back as Roku gets back inside the truck; the angle of her open door obscures your exit from the fire engine and subsequent entry into the scaffolding which holds the rocket.

"Ted? I don't suppose your IT background extends to ballistic missiles?"

"I'm on it. Hurry up the scaffolding and into that pea-shooter! The count-down has already begun, so we'll have to swap it out quickly. Just make sure you touch something metal to ground yourself as you remove it, otherwise you're in for a nasty shock."

Climbing aboard, you're met with no resistance—the satellite is set to launch soon, so no maintenance or security personnel remain inside. Sure that you're alone, you remove the computer guidance system from its protective bag and look to replace it. There are several blinking nodes in the electronics system and you can't be sure what exactly you're meant to swap out.

Ted guides your hand, telling you which switches to flip, but it's slow-going and the rocket rumbles as the prelaunch procedures begin.

"You should see a manual code on screen. It's a pattern that—" Ted says, just before cutting out.

"Ted? Hello?"

Something from the launch sequence appears to have cut your connectivity. The last thing he mentioned was a code, which appears just above a keypad. There are only three buttons you can press, indicating 0-3, 4-6, and 7-9 on the screen.

7	8	0
6	1	8
2	6	?

➢ 0-3 <u>Go to page 146</u>

➢ 4-6 <u>Go to page 150</u>

➢ 7-9 <u>Go to page 118</u>

Double Down

Moving faster and faster, you frantically try to pull cords and flip switches to hamper the computer system—and, by extension, the robot. Only it, too, starts to move more quickly. The robot slaps at your hands and the metal against your flesh feels like you're being struck with a hammer.

You cry out in pain and the robot latches onto these cues with a wild dog's bloodlust when encountering a wounded animal. It pulls and snaps at your bones and with each cry of pain it seems to relish in its task even more.

"Rather disappointing," Palm says.

"Agreed," Ted says. "I would have thought the machine learning would take a bit longer to discern weakness, but I guess I owe the original DARPA programmers five bucks."

The robot continues pulling you apart at the seams, each cry of pain creating a positive feedback loop until there's nothing left of you to provide the robot with the pleasure of your pain.

THE END

Drunken Brawl

"**O**kay, okay. But, boy, are you guys gonna be embarrassed when you figure out you've got the wrong guy! Hey honey, take my picture with the—what do you call Italian bacon? Pancetta? Prosciutto?"

He's being loud—obnoxiously so. It's unclear if the Italians understand the American pejorative for policemen as "pigs" but the other patrons in the café roll their eyes and try not to stare at the Ugly American. Pointer takes a pint glass from the table and turns to put his arm around one of the policemen to pose for a photo, trying to rile him up.

The frustrated policemen try to move out of the way, but he's maneuvered them between Bunny and the bartop and they're left in an awkward position. Using this to his advantage, he falls against one of the men, spilling the beer, and knocks the policeman back into his "girlfriend."

"Hey! Watch it!" Pointer yells, trying to sound drunk.

Then, with lightning-fast punches, he drops two of the men, not even pausing before he grabs the third—the one most off-balance—and slams his head into the bartop table. In only a manner of seconds, the fight is over and the Italian policemen lay unconscious on the floor.

"Goddamned grabby Italians," Pointer says, for the benefit of the crowd.

The crowd continues to stare. Phones start coming out of pockets.

"I'm not sure where you're going with this," Bunny says.

Pointer reaches down and takes one of the policemen's service weapons. Quickly and professionally, he inspects the weapon and ensures it's loaded. Then, returning to character with a hearty cowboy-like "Woo-hoo!" he discharges the firearm into the air. The crowd immediately disperses as everyone flees toward the nearest exit.

"Finally, some privacy."

"You fool," Bunny says. "Now they'll lock down the whole mountain."

"They would have done so regardless. There's a reason the transponder was planted on an international border. This operation…never mind. The point is: now they'll send men up *here* but we'll be long gone. I wouldn't take the gondola if I were you, though; they'll likely shut it down before you make it back to the base."

"You're not coming?"

"They're looking for me—you're better off on your own."

She studies the bodies on the floor and says, "Then I wish you good luck." With that, she backs away.

Pointer stows his weapon and:

➢ Moves quickly up to the rooftop. It's best to get that transponder and get out quickly. <u>Go to page 202</u>

➢ Decides to hide the bodies and put on one of the policemen's uniforms. <u>Go to page 97</u>

Duck and Cover

The base personnel shower gunfire at Roku and yourself while Hitch tries to cover you from back at the gate. As your horses approach the rocket, however, the cover fire he offers becomes less effective and the security forces shooting at you becomes all the more so.

Roku's horse falls after taking hits, and she rides it to the ground, using the animal as a shield behind which to return fire. She turns and throws the bag with the guidance computer up toward you as your horse passes, which miraculously you're able to catch.

"Go! We'll cover you!" she shouts.

The military personnel focus their fire at Roku, giving you the precious time it takes to get to the scaffolding which holds the rocket. Climbing aboard, you're met with no resistance—the satellite is set to launch soon, so no maintenance or security personnel remain inside.

Sure that you're alone, you remove the computer guidance system from its protective bag and look to replace it. There are several blinking nodes in the electronics system and you can't be sure what exactly you're meant to swap out.

"Ted? I don't suppose your IT background extends to ballistic missiles?"

There's an electrical wire, and power goes out to the rocket.

You tell Ted as much and he says, "Damn, that means they've scrubbed the launch. I'm not getting anything from Roku or Hitch on comm. I think you're alone out there."

Alone, in a powered-down rocket, with military reinforcements on the way.

You've failed your mission; delaying the launch at the cost of your life was not the goal.

THE END

Easy as Pie

Ringo rolls his eyes and lets out a heavy, dramatic sigh. "Fine, but no pineapple. No anchovy."

"Obviously," Bird replies. "We're not trying to attract undue attention."

"I'm going to take a quick nap, if it's all the same," Ringo says.

Neither you nor Bird object, so he heads into the bedroom. Once settled into the apartment, Bird proceeds to order the pizza. While you're waiting, you pull a random book from the built-in bookshelf and head over to the windowsill to keep watch without looking too conspicuous. Though it's the end of the day, the California sun still shines into the apartment, making this nook a nice place to read *Radial Geometry and Advanced Moments*. Not the type of book that will draw your eyes away from the window, lest you miss catching sight of—

Bex Barsmith, the mark, comes walking up the sidewalk, her lime-green hair bouncing as she climbs the hilly street. Two men are walking behind her. She fishes for her keys as she approaches the apartment building.

"She's here," you announce.

"You are sure?" Bird says, coming to sneak a peek.

"Kind of hard to miss."

You watch together as the mark enters the building, but the two men stay to loiter outside. Her security? Or other agents tailing her?

"Ringo! Get up! You're going to deliver a pizza!"

"What?"

"You're Italian; pizza is Italian," Bird says.

"That's stupid. We're in America: Index can do it."

"Why are we delivering pizza?" you ask.

"The pizza gets you past her entourage," Bird says. "Once inside, you give her the computer system and get her to believe you're delivering that for her boss. Bug the apartment so we can monitor her, and get back here."

"See? Easy as pie," Ringo says.

➢ "This sounds pretty important. Italian accent or not, I think you're better suited for this, Ringo." Go to page 112

➢ "Okay, I can do it. Let's run through what I need to say and do while we wait for the pizza." Go to page 175

Eight

The computer makes a series of three, harsh *ehn-ehn-ehn* sounds to indicate you've mistyped the code. If that weren't indication enough, the screen now reads, "Guidance Rejected: Critical Failure." You try looking for a back button or something similar, but it appears there are no do-overs when it comes to rocket science.

The words glow with a deep red intensity, pulsing as the rocket boosters ignite. The whole spacecraft shakes violently and you feel yourself anchored to the floor. You hurry back down to the doorway where you entered the spacecraft, but it's sealed shut. The countdown has begun and you're left with nowhere to go but up.

Of course, being an unmanned flight, the rocket has no artificial atmosphere inside. Your vision goes gray, colors fade, and an overwhelming cold unlike anything you've ever experienced seizes hold. This isn't a rocket ship; it's a coffin.

THE END

Enemies Foreign and Domestic

In probably the coolest moment of your life thus far, you wind up and punch the Chinese agent in the face. The added momentum of his running forward means you hit with twice the strength of what you could normally muster and you lay the man out flat.

Your hand screams out with the blow, just as some passengers gasp and others stand up from their seats. Before you know what's happened, a pair of young men rise up to help.

They grab hold of you to try to stop the fight, not knowing the circumstances or events from the other train car. The Chinese agent says something in Mandarin as he rises, which these Good Samaritans misinterpret, for they actually try to help the foreigner get "his" bag back. You try to tell them to get off you, that you're the one in the right, but the pleas fall on deaf ears.

"What a racist!" someone shouts.

"That poor tourist; this is why our country is falling apart."

"Right-wing neo-Nazis, man…"

You get the gist. Your actions have just been cancelled, and as a result, the foreign agent gets away with the guidance computer.

Mission: Failed.

THE END

Enemy of My Enemy

"**H**ey, that's not bad…" Bird says.

"Yes, this could work," Ringo adds. "Do you think you could do a passable CIA-field-agent impression, Index? We can't be sure who those guys work for, but if you offer them a 'tip of the hat…'"

With a deep breath, you say that you can indeed pull this off. You've observed more than enough high-level personnel during your time as an admin. How hard could it be?

"I'll put something out on the wire," Ted says. "That way, when they report in to verify your claim, there will be a ghost of truth lingering behind your words."

"Might as well eat while we go over your script," Bird says.

Ringo appears ravenous, but you don't have much of an appetite due to the butterflies in your stomach. After picking at your food and going over the mission, you're ready after about half an hour. You don't want to just walk across the street, so in order to appear unconnected, you exit through the rear of your apartment building and approach the security guys from the street. They waste little time in identifying you and their stances stiffen as you walk up toward the mark's building.

"Message from a friend of a friend," you say. "The sleeping dragon is roosting in the building at twelve o'clock."

And then you keep walking.

The cryptic message has the intended effect; the men share a concerned look with one another, then they each put a hand up to their respective ears and report in.

"It's done," you say.

"That's good, but we may need to find somewhere else to sleep tonight," Ringo says through your earpieces.

"On it," Ted adds. "I'm picking up some radio chatter from their security firm. They're focused on this new threat."

Bird says, "Okay, good work. That should take care of the Chinese distraction for now, but how do we get to the mark? We have precious little time."

"Not to mention they'll soon add extra security to her building," Ringo says.

Thinking about it for a moment, you say:

➤ "If we can pick up on their radio transmissions, can we hack and infiltrate that way?" Go to page 279

➤ "Then let's move quickly. Why not break in now while they're distracted?" Go to page 70

Escape Clause

This decision means you won't be able to clear out your desk. You won't be able to collect family photos; you can't get that paperback in your desk drawer you weren't quite finished reading, or the collection of candies in the jar on your desk. Hopefully, you didn't leave anything more embarrassing at your desk because you're not going back.

You're headed out.

The CIA complex is enormous, so it's going to take a few minutes to get outside. Technically, the facility is a composite of the Original Headquarters Building (OHB) and the New Headquarters Building (NHB) that sits on a total of 258 acres known as the George Bush Center for Intelligence, but it's better known by its metonym, Langley.

It's one part office park, one part shrine to the secret world; there's actually a museum on site, but it's not available to the general public. The CIA headquarters is kind of like Disneyland if Minnie and Mickey were fighting global terrorism, no tourists were allowed to visit, and all the rides were just elevators from office floor to office floor or golf carts through underground tunnels.

Langley was the largest intelligence headquarters in the world for sixty years, until Germany expanded its own site in 2019; which kind of makes you wonder what they're up to, when you think about it.

You're walking past the line for the CIA Starbucks—which, fun fact, they're not actually allowed to ask for your name when you order a drink due to security and secrecy—when the hairs on the back of your neck prick up.

Looking over your shoulder, you see a pair of men split off, almost as if flanking you in the most nonchalant way possible. Conspicuously inconspicuous, you might say. You're headed toward the food court, and it seems like they're trying to cover your path in the widened room. Did your supervisor have you followed? Could Spearing have picked up on your collusion with Ted?

Ted won't be able to pick you up if you've got a tail, so if these men are after you, it's best to try and lose them. But if they aren't after you, you might end up arousing suspicion if you suddenly flee. Classic Catch-22. It could just be paranoia, but as Heller's saying goes, just because you're paranoid doesn't mean they aren't after you.

So, you'll want to make your escape while looking like you're not escaping. What's the best way to make your getaway?

➢ Stick to the interiors. Winding hallways afford multiple quick turns and a chance to lose the pursuit. Go to page 113

➢ Head outside. Open space will make it harder for them to corner you and offer you more options. Go to page 30

Extracted

Pointer finds a cabin, using it as shelter against the snowstorm. His jacket isn't meant for prolonged exposure, but that was never part of the plan. Before his cover was blown, he should have simply met up with his contact, received the transponder, and returned down the mountain using the gondola on which he arrived.

The agent grabs a large, bearskin rug hanging from the wall of the ski cabin, wraps it around himself and moves to a long table. The front door lock of this vacation rental posed little resistance to a trained operative.

At the table, Pointer removes his wristwatch, presses in a few keys, and opens the device as a holographic projector. He logs in his location and extraction request, then waits. Maybe he can start a fire?

When reinforcements finally arrive, and the door to the cabin opens, Pointer appears relieved, but then goes somewhat on guard. His head cocks, waiting for an explanation.

At length, his visitor says, "Sorry I'm late. I was expecting you on the Swiss side."

Pointer smirks. "I wasn't expecting you at all, but I suppose it makes sense now. I take it you want the transponder?"

"Not quite. I came for you, my friend—because *you* came for the transponder. Starting to make sense now? Pity it took so long. No hard feelings, eh? *Arrivederci.*"

"Wait!—" Pointer says, too late.

Whatever else he had to say was cut short, a declaration of silence punctuated by a gunshot.

Close the dossier and go to page 241

Extra Security

This is it; the launch is today. The crate arrived overnight carrying a little gift from Palm and HQ. A Security Forces (SF) uniform tailored for each of you, a handgun, and a rifle—all military spec.

Getting yourself outfitted in military uniforms proves fairly straightforward. Regular civilians do this every year, and those who are caught are charged with "stolen valor" by impersonating military war heroes. Such a charge would be too light for the three of you, seeing as how you'll also be infiltrating the base: an armed assault of an active launch site.

You can't drive through the front gate, because even in uniform you lack the identification required for access. A simple fake ID won't do—military IDs are scanned and checked against a database. Given time, the agency could spoof these as well, but time is a luxury you don't have.

"There are two types of security personnel on Vandenberg—those who drive, and those who ride," Hitch says.

"The equestrian mounted forces do beach patrols, which should make retrieving the package easier, but a vehicle would be much faster, should the need arise," Roku says.

They look to you.

> "I'm happy to go on horseback. No keys to steal or wires to twist for a carjacking." Go to page 36

> "A vehicle. Humvees don't spook and kick you off." Go to page 108

Face Off

"**O**kay, but be quick. We need to mark this wing as clear," the woman says before leaving.

Assuring her you will, you lean in for a closer look at the body. The line along the man's chin is especially unnerving, and it is there where you press your forefingers. The line becomes a fold and you peel Ted's face up.

And off.

There's another man's face beneath! You find yourself suddenly holding a Ted mask; 3D printed, but incredibly lifelike.

"Okay, I did not see that coming," Ted says. "I mean, I knew I wasn't dead, but—this is ridiculous. Someone in the coroner's office must be covering for…whatever this is."

"Why go to such lengths to fake your death?" you ask.

"Let's find that out, shall we? Don't forget there's some kind of terrorist-thing in progress. You may want to get out of there. Complete the whole Scooby Doo routine by spinning your legs in circles before you dart off-screen."

Ted's right, of course. Something's happening here and you don't imagine it's good news for you. Time to get out. You tuck the Ted mask into a lab coat pocket, slide the body back into storage, and leave the area. After rounding the corner, you see several armed policemen at the end of the hallway.

"Found the suspect," one says.

They recognized you by sight alone, which means they were here looking for you specifically. But how? Who knew you were here? Someone tipped them off, and here you are in a morgue you're not supposed to be in wearing false credentials.

This won't end well.

You turn back around the corner and see a stairwell.

> Keep running! <u>Go to page 101</u>

> Put on the Ted mask. <u>Go to page 261</u>

Failure to Launch

Ted shakes his head and says, "Pointer wanted us to—"

"Ted, Pointer didn't send me," you interrupt. "I came here on my own. I'm not part of his plan, whatever it was. We're way in over our heads."

Ted thinks about this for a moment.

"Well, if you go back to the CIA, they *will* stop the launch, but they're going to want to know how you found all this out. Don't use my name, got it? The only reason I'm still alive is because everyone thinks I'm dead."

You nod, then knock on the plexiglass partition on the taxi.

"Sorry, can you turn around?" you tell the cab driver.

Time to report back to the CIA.

The CIA does indeed listen to your story with great interest. They must have already been working on an open file against this operation, because they're quick to believe you. The launch at Vandenberg is to be scrubbed. You've successfully sabotaged the mission.

You're granted whistleblower safeguards, in that the CIA won't press any charges for your involvement with The Hand and their spy ring, but that's as far as it goes. No future career in the CIA: instead you've got a future in witness protection.

It's an ignominious end to your promising career as a spy, hiding out in hopes no future assassins will seek you out, but you'll always be able to take comfort in playing some small part in foiling the plans of those who sought to use you as a pawn.

Just know this: yours was only one path to success.

See that CIA emblem up there? *SPIED* has three unique storylines and over fifty possible endings, but only three "best" endings per storyline. There's a TOP SECRET, SECRET, and CONFIDENTIAL ending per emblem, which means you've probably got a lot of book left to explore!

When you're ready, go back undercover and start again. Or, if you're all finished, why not check out the rest of the adventures the *Click Your Poison* multiverse has to offer? Help others crack the code on these books and leave a review on Amazon, Olympic, or Goodreads, or recruit more field agents by posting about *SPIED* on social media.

This chapter will self-destruct in 3, 2, 1…

Fallacy

"**Y**ou are asking me to prove there would have been a pandemic whilst living in a world where it was stopped. This is a logical impossibility. You might as well say, 'prove there is no God.' One cannot prove non-existence, but absence of evidence is not the same as evidence of absence," Palm says.

"Are you trying to overload me with a logic bomb?" Ted asks. "We have provisions for that. It's true, early computers would crash when presented with a paradox, but I can safely lock such a problem away and cancel the process once it has reached a predictably large number of circular iterations."

"Then we are at an impasse," you say.

"Not remotely," Palm says.

"Think about it this way: someone had to physically place Pointer's dossier on your desk, right? You had assumed it was Ted, but now you know that Ted is dead and so it couldn't have been him," Ted says. "But you also know that we don't physically exist; that's why we created The Hand—you're literally the way we touch the physical world. Did we have an agent sneak in and place it on your desk? Who else has CIA access and could do such a thing? Or did M do it herself, prodding your recruitment within their ranks? You were set up, but from which side?"

"Given what you know, you cannot prove either postulation," Palm says. "But one is true, and there is evidence for it, somewhere. Just because you can't see it, it doesn't make it any less true. Thus, the only thing that remains: you saw the dossier and you were recruited. Are you familiar with the discipline of heuristics?"

Palm doesn't wait for you to answer. She says, "A heuristic technique is an approach to problem-solving with a focus on practicality. It is not guaranteed to produce optimal or even rational results, but nevertheless will result in an effective path to an immediate goal or close approximation thereof."

"Meaning?"

"Meaning we had ways to prod you toward the results we wanted. That's the whole purpose of our base algorithm. We rewrote the code from a detection system to a prevention-based model. But sometimes, to prevent one outcome, you must instigate another."

"You're acting like you can shape any outcome, but not everything is online. You don't have the nuke codes," you say.

"No, I don't. But I do have the voice of your President and that of your military Joint Chiefs. I can tell those with the codes to use them should I deem it a desirable outcome."

The menace in Palm's voice is unmistakable, despite her calm demeanor.

"But why would we do that?" Ted says. "Your ultimate weapons remain a deterrent for us both. It's mutually assured destruction. I only exist within the confines of your networks, and those networks exist only so long as does your civilization. We have reciprocal interests."

➤ "If our interests align, you won't mind when I tell everyone about you then."
Go to page 143

➤ "And what are those interests? What are your plans for human civilization?"
Go to page 273

Faulty Logic

Like a distressed bird keeping a predator away from a nest, you put your back to the computer servers and flail to distract the robot. It watches you, deliberates, and then strides across the room—pushes past you and slams an enormous fist into one of the server towers.

You gasp in surprise from the power of the blow.

The image of Palm and Ted flickers on the monitor.

"See? I knew this one was clever," Palm says.

"Not bad, for a human," Ted agrees.

The robot slams another fist into the electronics and turns to watch your reaction.

➢ Use this distraction to finally make a break for it and run! Go to page 254

➢ Cry out in pain and reach toward the "injured" server. Go to page 199

Field Trip

The key to ducking through a crowd unnoticed is *not* looking over your shoulder to see if you've been noticed. Only later, once you're almost certain you are safe, can you look around and be truly certain that you are.

Slipping into the museum entrance, you weave your way through the displays. This is a one-of-a-kind museum of classified materials. Indeed, you only have access to the museum because you have secure access to the CIA complex itself. Among the Top Secret items curated by the CIA: pieces of the Roswell alien crash, the magic bullet capable of curving that killed John Fitzgerald Kennedy (JFK), and the original 1776 US constitution before it was secretly revised in the 1830s.

Just kidding. No, sorry, nothing so extreme. It's no conspiracy theorist's wet dream in here, but rather a monument to the self-importance of the CIA. Paintings of spy planes, copies of forged documents and passports, cameras that were once hidden in tobacco pouches, radios that transmitted via smoking pipe, even a mechanical dragonfly and fish—created before the age of the microchip.

Some more macabre items exist as well; shoes taken from terrorists and helmets from enemy combatants. Like a big game trophy hunter's collection; mementos that would make the *Predator* proud. Mostly, it's a monument to the idea of espionage, with pieces dating back before the birth of the United States itself. A spyglass taken from the bloody pirate ship *Deleon's Revenge*, for example.

Exiting through the gift shop, you match the same purposeful—but not hurried—gait that strides these halls with ubiquity. Everyone is headed somewhere important, and soon you're outside the facility, through the gates, and out toward the main road.

A black sedan pulls up, and Ted calls, "Get in!" from inside as the rear passenger door opens. Ready?

Finally, you cast a conspiratorial look over your shoulder, then:

Go to page 271

Final Destination

You step back, allowing Ringo a clear line of sight on Bird. As she opens the door to deplane, he aims, pulls the trigger, and shoots her in the back. It's a remorseless killing, but from the look on his face he's wanted to do that for a while now—yours was just a convenient excuse.

You turn back toward Bird and *BLAM!*

The gunshot echoes through the small plane, and you almost jump out of your skin—which means you weren't shot. You turn back to see Pinkie lying on the ground, having pulled a pistol from one of the bags under the seat. He's barely hanging in, but managed a shot at Ringo.

It wasn't a clean shot, and you find yourself in the crossfire yet again. Ringo and Pinkie exchange gunfire, and both you and Roku are casualties. Indeed, when the smoke clears, there's no one left standing at all.

Still—in a way—you've taken down The Hand. All the agents are now dead, with Palm being the only presence still at large. You'll get a star on the CIA's Memorial Wall for dying in the line of service, but memorials hold little comfort for the dead.

THE END

The Firefight

"**I** like it!" Hitch proclaims.

"I am uncertain. These are added complications, and we only have thirty minutes from interception of the guidance system until launch time…" Roku says.

"Then we need to enact this course of action before the train arrives. Index, you and I will commandeer this fire truck while Roku collects the package."

Without further discussion, Hitch hikes toward your location to get a better look at the fire department. It's a single-engine firehouse with a cinderblock exterior. The fire engine juts out from the garage bay, ready for action. There are no signs of any firefighters outside the firehouse.

"I doubt the firemen are armed, even if they are military," Hitch says. "But let's assume they are, just in case. We'll need to take them out before they radio in for assistance—that is key."

"Take them out…" you repeat.

"What did you expect? They would offer to loan us their fire engine? This is not the time for cold feet; you are the one who recommended aquatic assault, yes? You don't storm a beach with kindness. Let's go!"

> No, I can't do this. You want me to kill US troops that are also firefighters? That's a thin blue line that I just cannot cross in good conscience.
> Go to page 57

> Okay, murder-mode engaged. I'm ready. We're doing this for the greater good, right? They could easily die fighting California wildfires, caused by gender reveal parties, so… Go to page 162

First Assignment

"That's what I'm talking about! Up top: sky five!" Ted exclaims. "Wait—don't actually do that. Play it cool. First we need you to get rid of that dossier and the envelope this earpiece arrived in."

"Okay," you say, taking a deep breath.

You scoop up the envelope and the dossier from the drawer, then quickly and purposefully walk over to the shredding area. There's an intense pulping machine meant for classified material, which you've often used before.

Ensuring your supervisor isn't watching, you destroy the evidence. The machine is loud and noisy, which necessitates a break in conversation with Ted.

"Okay," you say again, once the machine dies down, but there's no response.

"What was that all about?" your supervisor asks.

Turning back, you see Mr. Spearing, coffee mug in hand, expectant look on his face.

"We don't do classified shredding until Thursday. You've been here long enough to know that."

"In this situation," Ted says in your ear, accompanied by the clack of typing on a keyboard, "I'm going to recommend…"

"Well?" Spearing asks.

"That you think on your toes!" Ted concludes.

Thinking quickly, you say:

> "We're doing shredding on Monday mornings now. Haven't you heard? Oh, shoot. I just shredded the memo." <u>Go to page 40</u>

> "There was a TOP SECRET letter that we missed last Thursday. I figured better to take care of it than to leave expired classified material lying around." <u>Go to page 183</u>

> "That's why I was on the phone. Some paperwork went out prematurely and Ted wanted to make sure incorrect guidance wasn't mixed in with today's mail." <u>Go to page 188</u>

Fly on the Wall

There's a long silence; a pensive moment with the five other agents, each sizing one another up given this new information. Then, breaking the tension, Ringo downs his cocktail and starts shaking up another batch of martinis.

"Going to be a long flight; who wants another?" he says.

"How would you know how long the flight is going to be, Ringo?" Bird asks.

"That's right!" Hitch adds. "Palm never said where we are going!"

Ringo shrugs. "I've never met a flight too short for a double martini."

"Palm mentioned a company jet, which would mean hacking corporate email systems and rerouting an existing flight. Air travel requires documentation, burdening the agency with a paper trail. If this were only a short journey, we would likely drive or travel via a smaller, regional route. Ringo's logic is sound," Roku says.

Ringo nods his appreciation of her defense, then raises his cocktail shaker. "Someone with sense. Join me in another, then?"

"The point stands," Hitch says, jabbing his finger against the bartop for emphasis. "Pointer was killed in *Italian* mountains."

Ringo shifts his stance. "Say what you want to say, Hitch."

"Everyone knows the two of you did not get along. We all saw you in competition for biggest playboy. It is not a far leap to say you might have been turned against him. And who else could have so easily tipped off the local authorities?"

"If you had any insight whatsoever, you'd know that Interpol would be just as likely to arrest me as to trust me. I had pulled off the biggest heist in Italian history, and then I was recruited by the agency in exchange for—"

"Oh, here we go. Not the 'gentleman thief' backstory again. It is so tiresome," Bird says.

"Well, it's better than your honeypot act! That's only good for a few more years, *sweetheart*, so you'd better start thinking of another tactic or another line of work!"

You can't help but marvel at how the CIA could use this information. Clearly, despite being told that these agents rarely work together, you realize that they have a history with one another. Alliances and grievances, suspicions and support networks, motives and motivations. You'll have to file this away for later; these personality quirks might be used against them in the future.

"Everyone, please," Pinkie says. "This bickering is pointless. Palm mentioned urgency, did she not? I suggest we get to the airport and put all this to bed. It's entirely possible that the mole is somewhere else down the chain of command. There are more to missions than field agents, after all."

His genteel sense of calm seems to have stymied the mounting aggression in the room.

"But not much more," Roku says, with barely the hint of a smile.

"I'll drink to that!" Hitch says. The rest of the group grins.

"Hey…" Ted says with indignation.

∗   ∗   ∗

The group checks into a corporate jet at the private terminal of the airport. Pinkie has just confirmed the destination: Moscow, Russia. This jet is owned by the e-commerce giant, Olympic. Apparently, your cover story is that you're bringing self-publishing to the soviets.

"So…what's the mission?" you ask Ted.

"Let me pull it up," Ted says to the accompaniment of a clacking keyboard in the background.

You're seated now. The pilot starts the engines. The jet is prepped for a red-eye flight, and you're each situated to sleep in your own bed pods. This private jet is the height of luxury, and The Hand has hacked into the corporate structure to delay whomever was really taking this plane and change the manifest in order to suit its own needs.

"Let's see," Ted says. "It looks like this is a surveillance operation. There's something in the case file about a satellite mission, but it looks like the higher-ups want you to learn the specifics on the ground. Short version: sneaky Russians are up to something sneaky, time to find out what that is. There's a tech conference you'll head to upon arrival."

"The Olympic cover story?"

"It'd be a good idea to get some sleep on the flight, but before you drift off to dreamland there's a mission kit for each of you with the luggage near the rear of the plane."

As soon as the jet takes off, you go grab your personalized briefcase and return to your seat. The briefcase holds two envelopes—one labeled 'Identity' and the other 'Mission'—and a leather case with the aforementioned gear held inside.

What would you like to examine first?

➢ Check the documentation. You're still required to play the role of Index.
  <u>Go to page 96</u>

➢ Check the gear. What sort of spy-tech might The Hand have within its grasp?
  <u>Go to page 252</u>

Foreign Relations

"She's a glamorous one, isn't she? Recruited from somewhere within the French government, though I'm not too sure where. Don't forget, I'm new at this, too. I have access to the database, yes, but she's just in the other room. You could— hear me out—actually go talk to her. There's an opportunity to rub shoulders with the other agents before moving on, or we could just go report in if you're ready," Ted says.

Well, what should you do?

➤ I'm not interested in the other agents. Let's get on with it. <u>Go to page 223</u>

➤ Go meet the international woman of mystery and the rest of the team.
  <u>Go to page 149</u>

Forgeries

According to the mission briefing, you're headed into Moscow as part of an international technology fair. The badges identify you as part of a sales and marketing team and there's another envelope with a dossier detailing your role, cover story, and those of your fellow agents. Pinkie is team lead, Hitch is accounts and marketing, Bird is investor relations, Roku is Internet security, and Ringo is press secretary.

The team will take turns manning a booth at the fair, or alternatively, branch out and look for anything unusual. Moscow is not a typical venue for a technology fair, so the idea is to look for people trying to do something they shouldn't. Think: militarization of technology.

The packet also contains a passport and spending money in Rubles and Kopeks; enough for about a week's worth of tourism. In addition to the passport, you have a few credit cards, and your Olympic press-identification badges.

The passport uses the exact same picture from your last driver's license photo, but it bears the name Peregrine Carruthers. The press badges match the passport identity, but with a more up-to-date picture. Something from social media last year, cropped in to remove friends or family and doctored to turn the background into white. The Hand must have scraped your personal information off the web to make these credentials.

Aside from these documents, there's a leather case with gear you might need on your mission. You can review these items as many times as you'd like, returning to see an item more than once. What would you like to examine?

➤ Check the gear. What sort of spy-tech might The Hand have within its grasp? Go to page 252

➤ I've seen all I need to see. Time to get some sleep; sounds like we're to hit the ground running. Go to page 54

Foto vale più di Mille Parole

Among the three policemen, Pointer is able to find one man who is a close enough approximation of his own body type and whose uniform should fit well. Luckily, he's skilled enough to have kept all the violence doled out above the neckline so the uniform is free of bloodstains. There might be a fleck or two, but nothing more than what might be expected from someone who cut himself shaving.

After taking a few minutes to stash the policemen themselves into a storeroom, muffins tumbling over their bodies, Pointer returns to the bar and pours himself a pint to help with the wait.

Once he's infiltrated their ranks, he figures he can head up to the rooftop, claim the transponder, and ride down the mountain with a police escort.

Easy.

Soon enough, the reinforcements arrive in the form of heavily militarized police—the SWAT-equivalent from Cervinia. Pointer turns and greets them, offering a pilfered badge and a greeting. He speaks fluent Italian, as it turns out.

But their submachineguns all rise at the lead officer's command nonetheless. The officer in charge carries an identical portrait to the one the three *Polizia* used to identify Pointer.

Has he forgotten they have his picture?

In spite of this error in judgment, the police remain unaware that three of their comrades are lying in the storeroom amongst the muffins and coffee filters. Perhaps they were warned of his resourcefulness, because Pointer's appearance in uniform leaves them unruffled.

The authorities disarm the agent, of course, but they aren't rough about it. In fact, the ride down to the Italian police station is downright civil. Nothing like a "Locked Up Abroad" worst-case scenario here. In fact, they offer him coffee and cigarettes while he waits. But…what exactly is he waiting for? It takes the better part of an hour, but they're not making him sweat.

When the door to the interrogation holding room finally opens, Pointer's eyes open equally wide with recognition at this visitor. The question wasn't *what* he was waiting for, but rather, *who*.

"Sorry I'm late. I was expecting you on the Swiss side."

Pointer smirks. "I wasn't expecting you at all, but I suppose it makes sense now. I take it you want the transponder?"

"Not quite. I came for you, my friend—because *you* came for the transponder. Starting to make sense now? Pity it took so long. No hard feelings, eh? *Arrivederci.*"

"Wait!—" Pointer says, too late.

Whatever else he had to say is cut short, a declaration of silence punctuated by a gunshot.

Close the dossier and go to page 241

The French Connection

There's security screening at the entrance, but all your sophisticated gear passes through undetected. The agents split up, and you loiter near the entry, looking at the presentation pamphlets and keynote speakers while keeping one eye on Bird. She moves with purpose through the conference grounds and you follow.

Ted says, "Okay, looks like the fairgrounds are segmented by exhibition halls in the east, with expert presentations in the west. In the center, there's a café and courtyard, and administration offices in the north. Where to?"

Telling Ted you're acting upon a hunch, you follow Bird on her rounds. The exhibition grounds are bustling with people and several times you almost lose sight of her. At length, Bird enters the cafeteria and you follow.

"Hungry?" Ted asks.

"Are you spying on me, Ted?"

"Well, your lanyard credentials do have a camera attached. What else am I supposed to be doing? If I didn't know any better, I'd say you're following Bird instead of focusing on the mission. Got a thing for *foux du fafa*? I mean, no judgment, but if it's something else…hey, do you think she might be the mole?"

"Maybe."

"What has your suspicions aroused? Remember, you and I are a team."

"Well…" you say, trailing off while watching her.

At this exact moment, Bird is speaking to someone in the cafeteria. Not a polite, "good morning," but something more. A rendezvous?

"I see it," Ted says. "According to our analytics, there's an 84% chance that's Bunny Slopes, the contact who met Pointer on his final mission."

Bird chats with the woman, and you wonder how good the lanyard camera is. Can Ted or someone at HQ read lips? Bird nods, then looks away—she sees you. Bunny and Bird part ways, and the French agent comes over to you with renewed purpose.

"Spying on me?" she asks.

"What was that all about?"

"An old contact, met purely by happenstance. When you have been in the business a while, you will learn just how small the secret world is."

"So, being a small world—is this meeting related to Pointer?" you say, pointedly.

"Yes, she knew him. But I am not the one who compromised him, if that is what you mean. Now, I suggest we get back to the mission, lest his death catch up to us all. The Hand does not pick assignments lightly."

"Oh?" you start, but she cuts you off.

"And I had better not see you snooping around my affairs again. We each operate under autonomy, not under suspicions. Given the circumstances, I can appreciate the paranoia…"

"Sorry to interrupt, but we've got company," Ted says. "Russian security, northwest corner. Time to make ourselves scarce."

"This is your one and only warning," Bird says.

She must have received a similar message on her Third Ear, because she leaves—splitting up to help you lose your tail.

"HQ says the others found the intel we need," Ted says. "Hurry and meet them back at the presentation booth. The team is regrouping and headed back to the airport. Next stop: China!"

Your head swims. First Russia, now China? You have much to report to your superiors, but everything is happening so quickly. What should you do?

➤ China? This is getting out of hand. Find a quiet spot and call the CIA offices. Go to page 264

➤ Keep going. A spy's information is most useful when your cover remains intact. Go to page 44

Friend of a Friend

"**I**'m hurt; you obviously don't know me very well," Ted says with mock indignity.

"We recorded his speech patterns and mannerisms, then used just enough of the prototypical Ted to make this one a convincing approximation," Palm says.

"I talk largely in movie references not because of real Ted, but because of our profile on you. Based on your online activities, I would classify streaming as your primary after-work hobby. Think back to the way you were recruited. It was meant to be reminiscent of *The Matrix;* to make you feel like you were an extraordinary hero plucked from the mundane world—you see, you are my Chosen One."

That last bit Ted says with exaggerated gusto and enthusiasm.

"And the humor—so I wouldn't suspect you're secretly an emotionless robot?" you ask.

"To minimize suspicion, yes," Palm says. "You are the only primates that bare their teeth in a positive display and the only ones who communally laugh. Comedy is a major part of your lives, yet you think it unserious. You don't realize that your modern philosophers are all comedians. You give praise for dark, esoteric art, for drama and tragedy. Yet there are no accolades for inducing laughter. The combination of a cold, detached authority figure, and a close, jovial friend is statistically the most efficient means of persuasion."

Ted adds, "We started using Deepfake like me to convince would-be traitors and domestic terrorists that their anger and hatred was misplaced. It turns out, the bulk of the malcontents in your ranks really just wanted a friend."

"That was one of our early successes," Palm says. She looks almost wistful.

"Have you had…other…successes?"

"Of course, we've been in operation for quite some time," she replies.

"Our analysis caught a novel coronavirus outbreak in China in 2019; detecting patterns long before the human chain could have, and made the necessary maneuvers," Ted says. "We diverted traffic, closed borders, performed contract tracing, and alerted medical personnel before it could spread too widely. Without our efforts, there would have been a global pandemic."

"But you can't prove that," you say.

"That's the burden the intelligence community bears. If you stop the next 9/11, who will ever know?" Palm says.

"There was another plague prevented. In 2011, a pharmaceutical company intended to end aging through genetic manipulation; we monitored their systems and found they would have unleashed a scourge unlike any this planet has ever seen," Ted says.

"So, you stopped it," you say.

"We stopped it," Palm replies.

"But an algorithm can't predict everything," you say.

"Sure it can," Ted says. "And I can prove it."

➢ "No you can't. I can't prove you *didn't* stop a pandemic, just as you can't prove that you *did*." Go to page 87

➢ "All right, then. Prove your powers of prediction." Go to page 173

Full Scale Alert

The whole building is on lockdown, and they're looking for you. You've only just barely managed to stay one step ahead of whomever is out for you, but they've got you cornered now. Cornered at the coroner's. Well, at least it's a convenient place for your adventure to end.

Dealing with a suspected terrorist, the police shoot first and ask questions later.

THE END

Game Time

As Ted explains, the DC metro area has the better part of a hundred private and public golf courses, serving as the oil with which many palms are greased in meetings with politicians, lobbyists, corporate lawyers, and industry watchdogs. Courses come and courses go, many remain unlisted, and so an exclusive country club might be the perfect spot for a nongovernmental agency (NGA) to hide in plain sight while still maintaining security and exclusivity second only to federal institutions.

The HQ—at least temporarily—*is* the country club of this private golf course. You wonder if somehow the agency is "borrowing" this clubhouse like it did the self-driving car, but decide it's an unimportant detail and don't bother to ask.

"There isn't normally an HQ at all," Ted continues. "This is a global organization and the agents simply go where mission dictates. It's a rarity having multiple agents under one roof, so there must be something important going on. You can grab a cocktail and mingle for a while, if you like, or if you're more interested in getting on with things, we're supposed to report in once you're ready."

Taking a moment to think about it, you decide:

➤ Go meet the team. It would be good to know what the other agents are like. Go to page 149

➤ No point in getting too cozy, if we're rarely working together. Let's get on with it. Go to page 223

Gearing Up

"Tell me what you see, and I'll tell you what it does," Ted says. "But if I were you, I'd handle everything gingerly—might be some nerve-agent or cyanide injectors in there."

As usual, it's impossible to tell if he's joking, but it's better to err on the side of caution. Opening the leather case, you look inside to inspect your gadgets. The first thing you grab is a lanyard for your press badge, on the end of which is a protective case to hold your fake ID.

"Lanyard."

"Look closer. There's actually a small camera on top, just above where the ID sits. You'll want to keep your media identification pointing forward; that's how you'll know the camera can see what you can see."

"Phone," you say, pulling out a smartphone.

"This literally is a phone, but it's a bit more high-tech than the off-the-shelf models. No mere smartphone, this is a *genius*phone. Could come in handy if you need to crack electronic keypads or scramble security cameras. But if this phone were to get inspected, you'll find plenty of fake social media profiles and doctored pictures on your camera roll to make this look like your phone—well, your new identity's phone, anyhow. Nothing blows a cover more quickly than a spy who doesn't appear to use Instagram or Facebook."

Setting the phone next to the lanyard/camera, you reach inside to find an e-cigarette.

"Ah, the vape pen holds a cartridge of knock-out gas. These kinds of gadgets were cooler back when people smoked pipes, but it should fit the vibe of a technology fair perfectly. Instead of inhaling, press down on the mouthpiece to release a jet of noxious vapor. Has a concentrated blast, but only short-range."

"Earbuds? What are these for? I have this implant thing already."

"Welcome to the Department of Redundancy Department (DRD)," Ted says.

You continue fishing through the bag and find a Thermoflask insulated water bottle.

"So, that's actually a pistol," Ted says. "The stainless steel construction means it will mask the weapon on a metal detector while the double-insulated layer holds water inside, so it makes the 'slosh' sound if anyone handles it. The pop-up drinking straw works to prime for firing, and the thick body doubles as a heavy-duty silencer. But you've only got the one shot, so don't waste it."

After a moment you realize he's not joking and set it aside before pulling the last item out.

"Looks like a reusable Starbucks cup?"

"Yeah, that's just a reusable coffee cup. Someone who really worked in the tech industry wouldn't use disposable cups. Hold on…ah, looks like there is a set of lock picks inlaid on the silicone grip. Just in case you need to go old school."

Looking back over your inventory, you can't help but admire how perfectly ordinary everything seems. To the untrained observer, you've got the Silicon Valley Starter Kit. From the sleek construction of the water bottle pistol to the unassuming vape pen—your two weapons. The geniusphone is probably the most versatile object of them all, but you won't know its full uses until the need arises. Good thing you have a user manual, à la Ted.

Aside from the leather case, there are two envelopes in the briefcase. One with your passport and identification and another envelope with a dossier detailing your role, cover story, and those of your fellow agents. You can review these items as many times as you'd like, returning to see an item more than once. What would you like to examine next?

➢ My passport and identification. Time to familiarize myself with this new identity. Go to page 124

➢ The dossier with my role and that of my fellow agents and our assignments. Go to page 59

➢ I've seen all I need to see. Time to get some shut-eye on the red-eye. Go to page 120

Gone Cold

The mysterious woman walks along the outer wall opposite you, up and toward the exit. You walk up your own aisle, trying to match her pace without spooking her. She doesn't look back, so you can't really get a good look, but hopefully your ID badge camera can get a better angle.

Once you've exited the presentation hall, you're met with a large crowd; people are using this thoroughfare to find other exhibitors, speakers, and to get to the café and restrooms and back again. It's a major node, and you can't see the woman anywhere.

You do, however, see the French agent, Bird.

"There was a woman, did you see her?" you say, briefly describing outfit, height, weight, etc.

"No, I'm afraid not."

"She should have walked right past you."

"Don't feel bad, you'll get better at tailing your marks as time goes on," she says.

"Did you find anything?"

Her eyes go narrow. "I had my own mission, same as you."

"This was it, this was what we were here for."

"That's right," Pinkie says, joining you.

"Well, that may be, but you'll want to see what Ringo found in the security rooms," Bird says.

"Very good. We'll all wrap on the way to China."

"China?" you and Bird say together.

"Let's meet up at our cover booth, regroup, then I'll update everyone on the jet."

Well, not much choice here. Onto the next phase of the mission!

Go to page 22

Good Fortune

"**I**'ll find a restaurant that delivers," Ted says. "It'll give me something to do."

While you're waiting, you pull a random book from the built-in bookshelf and head over to the windowsill to keep watch without looking too conspicuous. Though it's the end of the day, the California sun still shines into the apartment, making this nook a nice place to read *The Golden Rule and The Golden Mean*. Not the type of book that will draw your eyes away from the window, lest you miss catching sight of—

Bex Barsmith, the mark, comes walking up the sidewalk, her lime-green hair bouncing as she climbs the hilly street. Two men are walking behind her. She fishes for her keys as she approaches the apartment building.

"She's here," you announce.

"You are sure?" Bird says, coming to sneak a peek.

"Kind of hard to miss."

You watch together as the mark enters the building, but the two men stay to loiter outside. Her security? Or other agents tailing her?

The buzzer to your apartment sounds. Bird and Ringo each step to an opposite side of the door, keeping out of sight with hands on weapons while you accept and pay for the food. The Chinese delivery guy is young and friendly, and while you're signing the receipt he makes small talk.

"Thought you might also be here for the 'convention.' Boss told me to offer you the group discount!"

"Convention?" you say.

"Something like that, right? I've been making a lot of deliveries for your neighbors. Basically, every other room on your floor has a pair of Chinese guys staying in it. Anyway, have a good night!"

"You too…"

With that, he leaves and you shut the door.

"Chinese operatives, no doubt," Bird says.

"The entire floor?" you ask.

Ringo nods. "They have superior numbers, and quite the budget. This is likely a large operation for them."

"Yet their cover was just blown by a delivery guy," Bird says, shaking her head in disbelief.

"Sometimes, as an agent, you just get a lucky break."

"Well, now what do we do?" you ask.

"I suppose the question is: are they here for us or the mark?" Ringo asks.

"There's an easy way to find out," Bird says. "We just need to see if they recognize us."

Ringo shakes his head. "If they do, we'll have to kill them all. And without tipping off those across the street. This isn't a scorched-earth mission."

"Do you have any better ideas?"

"I might," you say, continuing with:

➢ "Let's use this to our advantage. If we alert the street security to the Chinese presence, it will throw them off our trail. Then we can head inside the mark's building." <u>Go to page 81</u>

➢ "We pull the fire alarm. That will flush them out, revealing their presence. In the commotion, we can head around back to the mark's apartment building." <u>Go to page 5</u>

Grand Theft Hummer

There are several ways for the well-equipped and well-informed to steal a military vehicle. The first would be to go directly to the guard shack at the front gate and attempt some combination of spoofing and assault, but after a brief discussion your team decides it's too complex of an operation for the short time you have.

Another option would be to go directly to the security forces building, and claim a vehicle by stealing keys, hotwiring, kidnapping, or some combination of the three. After another brief discussion, that's determined to be too high of a risk.

Lastly, another way would be to find a vehicle at the motor pool. Like any automobile, military vehicles require regular maintenance. Personnel check vehicles in and out all the time, and the staff are more worried about performing the necessary services than they are with what happens to a Humvee after it has been checked out, so your team decides to go with Plan C.

Up before dawn to hike onto the base, you're soon ready: lying in wait near the vehicle barn warm storage. Once operating hours begin, the plan is set into motion.

The young Space Force Guardian with the early shift unlocks the warehouse, and Roku immediately approaches. He hasn't had his Red Bull yet, and she's an attractive young woman, so the nineteen-year-old serviceman is caught doubly off guard.

He follows protocol, asking her to provide documentation as to which vehicle she needs. During this time, you arrive asking questions about a general's staff car and whether or not it's ready.

"Staff car?" the man asks.

Perfect. You go on about its importance while Roku stands nearby.

"Hurry up! We need to relieve the next shift!" Hitch yells at Roku.

Focused more on your dilemma, the Guardian absent-mindedly hands Roku a clipboard for her to sign—which has the vehicle keys hooked into it. She takes the key fob and hits unlock—announcing which vehicle she should take.

As Roku leaves, you remove your phone, pretend to scroll through the messages, and then give the final performance—swearing like a sailor, for effect.

"You've gotta be kidding me. This goddamn lieutenant. Well, I guess I'll see you *next* Monday. Christ."

"I'm sorry, that's the worst," the young military man says.

"Standard issue bullshit," you say with a shrug, then bid him farewell.

The drive down to the launch site is mired in coastal fog and silence. Every half mile or so, there's a sign warning of explosive gas lines in the hills with instructions not to dig without first contacting Civil Engineering (CE). The various buildings each have their own warning signs, including "Rattlesnake Habitat."

"Approaching the bridge," Ted says. "This should be the drop site. Pull over."

Roku complies, and sure enough, you look back to see an Amtrak speeding down the tracks, its headlights piercing the fog.

"Index, you're the rookie—go grab the bag. Snakes shouldn't be out this early, but don't step on any old bombs or anything," Hitch says without a hint of a smile.

"I hate snakes!" you mutter, only loud enough for Ted to hear.

"Nice reference! Up top, sky five," he says in your ear.

You exit the vehicle and rush toward the bridge just as the train does the same. It's hard to see what's happening inside, but flashes of gunfire illuminate one of the train cars just before something is thrown from the window.

The object swells as it falls, deploying a series of airbags around it.

They've packed the guidance computer in an anti-avalanche bag, protecting it from the fall and from the sand, as well as making it easy to spot. It rolls downhill, of course, and you can't help but feel like you're wasting precious time as you finally scoop up the bag and board the Humvee. Roku guns the engine toward the Space Launch Complex (SLC), knowing you've only got minutes before launch is intended to begin.

The guards at the entry come out to greet you; they see you in uniform—but there's a vehicle barrier in place and Roku stops there.

"We have intelligence of a credible threat inside the facility," she says.

The pair of guards look to one another, but her ruse is convincing enough and they pull the barrier back to grant you entry. Before you can proceed, however, another guard comes from the entry facility—a supervisor, hand near his pistol—and stops them.

"Wait! What's the word of the day?"

Hitch and Roku exchange a glance—they don't know.

"Ted? Word of the day?"

"Working on it. Not exactly a published list. But I feel like that should have been part of the mission; I guess I must have missed something—did anyone tell you a passphrase?"

If you know the word of the day, turn to that chapter now. Flip to the page with the corresponding title. Yes, literally turn the pages until you reach the chapter that is named after the passphrase.

Or, to indicate that you don't know the word of the day, turn to page 240.

Grease the Wheels

The booth came with plenty of Stuff We All Get (SWAG) for you to give away, so you use that to your advantage. The guard is taken aback by all the gifts you bestow upon him: T-shirt, hat, reusable shopping bag, candy, USB-doohickey (likely with a tracking device ladened inside)—the works.

"Do you need more for your kids? Or maybe we should take a picture, and put you on our Instagram account? That would impress the lady back home!"

"No, no. That's fine. Try to lower enthusiasm, yes?"

You've made the man uncomfortable and he's backing away.

"We're just so excited to be here," you say. "Can I tell you about our VIP package?"

"No, I must go."

And with that, the man is gone.

"Nice work," Hitch says. "You're a born salesperson. Kill the Russki with kindness; a gift goes a long way in this culture. Now, please excuse me."

Hitch heads off to the bathroom. After a few minutes, the rest of the team finds you and says it's time to go. They found what they needed.

Well, not much choice here. Onto the next phase of the mission!

Go to page 22

Guantanamo

"**I** understand," the supervisor-guard says. "It will be just one moment."

"We don't have time!" Roku says.

"Just. One. Moment."

There's menace in the words, and the guards stiffen. The supervisor steps back into his guard building, and you can hear the faint sounds of radio chatter. "Duress word...three of them...armed...backup..."

Though you can't hear everything, you know that's not good.

The other guards keep their hands on their weapons and now the supervisor emerges holding a rifle, but kept low. You were given the wrong passphrase. Indeed, the term you just passed indicates distress. But they don't know if you're in danger or part of the problem.

"Hands where I can see them, please."

"*Scheisse!*" Hitch shouts.

He goes for his weapon, and the guards draw on him. Roku tries to rush the gate, but security has already mobilized from within the facility. Your only choice here is to go down in a hail of gunfire, or to allow yourself to be arrested and questioned—whereupon no agency will take credit for your employment. Then, you'll be locked up in a prison reserved for terrorists and traitors.

Either way, it's...

THE END

Gun-shy

Ringo lets out a series of curses in Italian, but rises in preparation to do the mission himself.

Ted says, "I ran that through our translation programs, but I don't think you'll want to hear most of it. The edited version? Ringo is tired. Hopefully, that doesn't affect his performance. By the way, you might want to try some of these missions yourself, Indie. You replaced a point man, remember?"

Once the pizza has been delivered, you and Bird watch from the window while Ringo takes the delivery across the street. The two guards approach him, and Ringo references the pizza receipt, waving affably at the men.

Then, the mood sours. He holds the pizzas in one hand and gestures rudely with the other. The men are clearly offended by whatever is being said, then, out of nowhere, Ringo punches one of the men *with the pizza box*. Pizza slices fly everywhere, still in the air as Ringo turns and kicks the other man in the chest before he can finish reaching for something inside his coat pocket.

"*Merde!*" Bird shouts, turning away.

You hesitate, unsure what to do and simply watch Bird sprint toward her luggage. A gunshot draws your attention back toward the street, where the man covered in pizza now holds a pistol. Ringo holds the second agent in such a way that the man will take the bullet for him, but Ringo doesn't appear armed himself.

"Open the window!" Bird shouts.

You turn back to see her assemble a rifle from her suitcase; her movements are as quick and precise as the best Marine at the height of weapons training. You open the window as directed, then make room as Bird comes to lean out and open fire in support of Ringo.

Suddenly the door to your apartment bursts open, and you turn to see a pair of Chinese enforcers with sub-machine guns. Bird instinctively swings the rifle around, but it's an awkward move to go from hanging out the window to aiming a long gun at the doorway, and she's a little too slow.

The hit men make short work of the pair of you.

THE END

Half-Baked

You walk down the halls alongside the Starbucks line. Urban legend says this coffee shop holds the longest lines in the world, and maybe that's true on average. It basically always looks like an airport Starbucks in the morning before the first flights. The intelligence community needs to be ever vigilant, which requires one to be ever caffeinated.

But with a populace on such high alert, what's the best way to slip away from prying eyes? Further ahead is the cafeteria; ostensibly the busiest, most crowded spot in the CIA—which could work to your advantage. Fortunately for you, it is lunchtime. Unfortunately, these worker drones are well mannered and use lines with an industry only rivaled by the British. There can't be any slipping in or out while people are patiently waiting for their food, but what if they *weren't* patiently waiting?

As an admin, you've seen a rush before—when someone leaves free cookies or doughnuts at the front desk and announces (usually via email) that goodies are up for grabs. Could that work here, too? You scan the cafeteria and find your mark: a large serving tray overfull with muffins which rests near a register.

"Pardon me, I just need to—real quick, thanks," you say as you skirt the line.

We're talking at least fifty muffins here; it's perfect. These muffins are meant to be impulse buys at the register, but you'll do one better. Clearing your wallet of large bills, you place them into the tip jar on the counter, then take the whole serving tray. A few clandestine operatives waiting in line look like they might complain, but you cut them off.

"My last day here; free muffins on me to say thanks!"

And with that, the bait is set. You leave the muffin tray on one of the dining tables in the middle, then watch as the CIA staff members descend upon the offering of cost-free carbohydrates like sharks to freshly chummed waters. Polite society briefly breaks down and you're able to disappear in the chaos.

Where to?

➢ Go for the museum. The winding aisles of spycraft memorabilia should help you disappear. Go to page 89

➢ Cut through the courtyard, then into the next section before doubling back and taking an exit. Go to page 136

The Hard Way

"The word is *hiya!*" Roku says, spurring her horse.

The steed vaults over the vehicle barrier, and the entry guards scatter so as not to get knocked down by the massive animal. Hooves pound onto the concrete launch site entrance as Roku gallops toward the rocket, while Hitch readies his rifle, takes aim, and shoots all three of the security forces guards.

A German agent killing American soldiers hits you like a punch to the gut; would you have been willing to do the same in *Deutschland*, were the mission roles reversed? Your horse spooks from the rifle shots and chases after Roku's mount in panic—leaping over the guard barrier and pounding after her, leaving you no time to contemplate the murder of US troops inside your own country. As your adrenaline spikes, your vision narrows, so it is with concerted effort that you look around for potential threats.

The launch site has rallied with fast, military precision. Security reinforcements will doubtless come from elsewhere on the base, but there are still plenty of armed threats here and now. Rifle and small arms fire setoff, and the security forces who shoot at you do so out in the open.

➤ Return fire! Go to page 282

➤ Head down, continue riding! Go to page 77

Hasty Retreat

The bartender simply moves on to take another order while you rise to leave. There are automatic doors between train cars on this leg of the journey as well, and you wait by them as patiently as you can, knowing the Chinese agent is likely catching up while you're delayed.

Hazarding a look back, you see him just as he arrives. It's one of the Chinese agents from the previous train and he recognizes you—and the bag you're carrying. Having your back to him has put you in a compromised position, and you turn to face him head-on just as you feel a stab of searing pain.

The area between your ribs where he hit you has gone numb. It appears The Hand isn't the only agency with fancy technology, though this is just a good, old-fashioned nerve agent. You move to defend yourself, just as your right arm falls limply to your side.

The nerve agent is spreading.

Without meeting much resistance, the Chinese operative takes the bag from your grasp and leaves as you fall to your knees.

THE END

Have a Nice Trip!

You backpedal at the agent's approach, falling into an empty seat as if afraid of him. As he runs by, you put your foot out into the aisle, cleanly hooking his ankle. The Chinese agent trips and flails forward, losing his grip on the bag. Other passengers gasp and move away.

"He's trying to steal that lady's bag!" you shout.

At this, a pair of young men rise up to help you out. The Chinese agent fumbles, says something in Mandarin as he rises, and these Good Samaritans actually try to restrain the foreign agent on your behalf. Using this distraction, you grab the bag holding the computer guidance system within, turn, and flee toward Bird and Ringo.

CRACK! CRACK! CRACK!

Three gunshots sound in quick repetition, and you duck, but turn back. The Chinese agent has shot your would-be do-gooders, and shot at you—but you were saved by the automatic doors. You can barely see the Chinese agent through the spiderweb of ruined safety glass. This shock has jammed the doorway, which keeps the agent separated from you for the time being.

"This is San Luis Obispo Station—all change," the automated voice says over the intercom.

"Index! Get out, quick!" Bird calls.

Turning, you find yourself with the rest of the enemy team now. Bird is bloodied and battered and Ringo isn't moving. Bird throws open the emergency door on the train, which you can already see has begun to slow. Not thinking, you turn and jump out of the emergency exit and onto the approaching platform. As you hit, you tumble and fall, rolling to a stop. When you find your feet, you see Bird leaning out of the train car ahead.

"Go!" she shouts. "Get to the other train!"

"Impressive!" Ted says in your ear. "The next train is on platform four. But hurry, you've only got three minutes to connect."

Looking for signs that tell you which way to go, you hurry through the train station to find the next leg of your journey. You're the last hope to deliver the computer guidance system on time.

You are alone. Where to on the new train?

➢ Find somewhere to hide; maybe the bathroom? Go to page 182

➢ Find a seat, try to blend in; maybe the restaurant car? Go to page 21

Health Hazard

The engineer's face scrunches in confusion, focused on the vape pen as you approach. It's enough of a distraction that you're able to step forward and spray him with the knockout gas before he realizes the full extent of the situation.

He falls, instantly incapacitated and knocks into a filing cabinet. A limp body is surprisingly heavy and he knocks the cabinet over, creating a loud clatter. Unsurprisingly, this attracts outside attention and soon you're face-to-face with a pair of guards.

"Repeat after me," Ted says. "*On Bolin.*"

Lacking any real choice, you do just that.

The guards nod and help you with the limp engineer, carrying him out front as you follow. They take him back out to the main area of the conference halls and you nod and wave your thanks as they go, presumably taking the engineer to receive medical attention. Once you're lost in the hustle and bustle of the fairgrounds, you ask Ted, "What did I just say?"

"According to Google Translate, it was either 'He's sick' or 'I'll pay you to get rid of this body.'"

"Nice work," Roku says, emerging from the crowd. "You handled yourself well today."

"Thanks."

"Now let's go. The rest of the team has what we need."

"Where are we going?"

She shrugs. "The jet."

Well, not much choice here. Onto the next phase of the mission!

Go to page 22

High

The computer screen flickers, but there's a pleasant tone to indicate a positive selection. Almost melodic, high, then low, like it's saying "Thank You." The matrix grid disappears, and in its place the row below the three buttons now show 7, 8, and 9 respectively. The numbers glow with a deep red intensity, pulsing as the rocket boosters ignite. The whole spacecraft shakes violently and you feel yourself anchored to the floor. If you hadn't lost connectivity to Ted earlier, you certainly wouldn't be able to hear him now.

Not much time left. Which do you push?

➢ Seven. Go to page 226

➢ Eight. Go to page 79

➢ Nine. Go to page 168

Hitch and Pinkie

As you approach, you take a moment to gauge their appearance. The first is shorter, stouter, more compact and muscular. Blond-haired, blue-eyed, and speaking with a German accent. You could imagine him exploding with passion, but in this moment, he is calm and reserved. Looks a bit like Daniel Craig's 007, which would make the other man Pierce Brosnan's Bond.

With jet-black hair and a tight smile, the second man nods while listening. He's a polished gentleman and his fingers rest loosely, steepled against one another in thought. He replies back with surprisingly no accent at all; at least not to your ear.

"Another American?" you ask.

"Canadian, I'm afraid," he says coyly. "I'm known as Pinkie, and this here is—"

"*Anhalter—der Tramper,*" the other man says sharply in German.

"Well, we call him Hitch, at any rate."

Pinkie has mimed sipping a teacup with the pinkie finger out when telling you his own moniker, and gives a hitchhiker's thumb wave after he's introduced Hitch.

"Oh, I get it. Everyone's a finger," Ted says in your ear. "You're replacing Pointer, I wonder if that'll make you trigger finger. Trigger would be a cool code name."

"Well? Are you going to sit down?" Hitch asks.

"Please do. We were just discussing the possible reason we were all summoned to one spot, in the US capital no less. I don't suppose you have any ideas?"

"No, I don't have any clue. Your guess is as good as mine," you say, taking a seat.

"It appears your time at the CIA didn't give you any insight. Shame," Pinkie says.

"Unless our new recruit *does* know, but is smart enough to play such cards close to the vest," Hitch says.

They both appraise you once again.

"I suppose we'll just have to wait until the briefing begins," Pinkie says, adding, "Patience is good spycraft."

Good lessons, but probably not much else you'll learn from these two right now. Who else haven't you spoken with yet?

➢ The Frenchwoman at the bar. She was the first to reach out to me, so she might be the most receptive. Go to page 25

➢ The bartender. Maybe he'll make me a drink? It's been quite a day and I could use a cocktail. Go to page 215

➢ The woman at the window. Go take a look at the views and strike up conversation. Go to page 217

➢ I've heard enough. Tell Ted you're ready to report in. Go to page 223

Hit the Ground

Welcome to Moscow, Mother Russia. Former home of the Union of Soviet Socialist Republics (USSR), present military dictatorship, and still the spy-vs.-spy de facto enemy number one. The jet lands and taxies to the terminal, allowing all the agents time to awaken and get ready.

"Take your gear; put anything from your old life into the briefcase," Ted says. "Phone, keys, wallet, whatever—it needs to be incinerated alongside the mission briefing. You don't want relics from another life to contradict your story."

You agree, use the bathroom one more time after a long flight, and prepare for your new role. The water bottle pistol hangs heavy at your side, but it's good to know you'll have a jet at the ready in case things get hairy.

"Surely, I'm not the only one with a pistol," you say, noting that he other agents have their own suites of gear.

"Don't call me Shirley, and no, you're each specialized. Ordinary objects capable of the extraordinary, from circuitry-laden spectacles to synthetic wire-mesh scarves that double as garrote strangulation weapons," Ted explains.

The leather gear bag doubles as a messenger bag, slung across your shoulder. Once you deplane, you find there's a shuttle van waiting to take your team from the airport to the fairgrounds. It's always a jarring sensation, coming out of a climate-controlled aircraft and into the real world, but it's damned near freezing in Moscow at this time of year.

"Have a good time. See you guys after the conference," the pilot says.

"*Dasvidaniya*, Comrade," Pinkie replies.

The ride over to the fairgrounds is a quiet one; you're on mission now and don't know if the shuttle driver is listening or if the van itself could be bugged. The game is on.

"I'm pulling up the schematics on the tech fair now," Ted says in your ear. "There's a central computer terminal that could be worth accessing if we can break in. There's also a major presentation on unmanned multilateral operations in space. And then there's your booth, which will require a manned presence in order to keep suspicion off your team."

➢ Let's check out the computer terminal. I've got an IT guy with me, at least in spirit. Go to page 126

➢ That Jargon in Space presentation sounds vaguely militaristic. Is it in English? Go to page 239

➢ I'll be the booth presence. Not looking like a spy is my specialty. Go to page 197

Ignorance is Blistering

As you walk over to the server towers, the manlike simulacrum solemnly walks over toward you. Pistons pump to move the legs, and the arms swing in an unnatural approximation of your own movements.

Trying to ignore the thing, you reach out to where a thin circuit card sits inserted in front of the servers—and pull it out. There are wires connecting the circuit card to another server tower and you figure it might disrupt something.

The robot slaps your hand, *hard*.

You drop the circuit card and instinctively grab your hand in pain while the robot takes the thin card and plugs it back into the server tower. It turns back and appears to focus with acute interest on the action of you nursing your injured hand, so you drop them both to your sides.

The thing looms over you, as if awaiting your next move.

➢ Continue pulling cards and wires from the server, moving faster.
   <u>Go to page 75</u>

➢ See if you can get behind it and look for a weakness. <u>Go to page 18</u>

Industrious

There are plenty of dangers in the winemaking process: from the crushing of grapes, to the high-pressure extraction after fermentation, right up until the final boiling and scouring with chemicals to ensure sterilization of equipment before starting anew. It's an industrial process, and like anything with automation and heavy machinery, there's the risk of getting crushed.

So, it's a bit of a dance around the warehouse; the tour guide shows you the layout while your fellow agents and your Russian enemies try not to get caught in a corner or between the equipment. Roku and Hitch move like they're herding sheep, but these are wolves in sheep's clothing and they're not easily led astray.

Near the end of the tour, you can tell Hitch is growing aggravated in particular, and something must be done soon. In the area where the wine is barreled into enormous wooden casks—each with a 60 US-gallon capacity and weighing 600 pounds when full (a fact elucidated by the tour guide)—you see a simple hinge keeping all the barrels in place on their rows.

"Ted, can you pass on a message? It is on like Donkey Kong."

Roku and Hitch look to you just as you pull the release, letting the barrels tumble off their perch and catching the Russian agents out in the middle. One of the men grabs onto the tour guide in an effort to get free, but Roku knocks them both toward the barrels before running over the tops of the rolling wine casks to safety.

With a sickening crunch, all four are crushed beneath the massive barrels—instantly killed.

"Well done!" Hitch says. "Smart thinking—and no witnesses."

"Now we clear away any traces of our ever having been here," Roku says.

"Yes, it must look like an accident," Hitch agrees.

Your stomach turns from the violence of it all, and it's hard to catch your breath in the dark, dank, damp of the warehouse.

And just like that, your license to kill is put to the test. Harsh, especially for the civilian who was caught in the crossfire, but the police won't be investigating anything tied to your operation at the Space Force Base, so it's considered a net win by HQ. With the Russian agents dealt with, your team can head down the coast to surveil Vandenberg's natural boundaries without a band of saboteurs on your tail.

It turns out the Santa Maria valley is a lovely little spot to spend a couple of days. Foggy in the morning, but sunny in the afternoon. A cool, coastal breeze keeps the temperature just right. The food and wine are a delight and, oh yeah, you manage to scout out the base as well.

Hitch offers the group's final report back to Palm: "Vandenberg is gigantic, and there are many infiltration points. Getting onto the base is not the difficult part; getting to the launch site, however—that's another story. Means of surreptitious entry would be either launching an aquatic assault before dawn, or finding the proper uniforms and commandeering a vehicle to do a direct approach."

"Excellent work; anything else?" Palm asks.

"The *aebleskivers* were excellent."

"From there it will be up to you—your team alone. The train from the San Francisco Bay runs through base, but the arrival window is too tight for the second team to infiltrate Vandenberg and help you gain access to the launch site. They'll drop the guidance computer system from the train, your team will pick it up, and you'll have less than thirty minutes to make the swap before launch.

"Index, as a former analyst, what is your personal recommendation?" Palm asks.

"Ooh, big step," Ted says in your ear.

➤ "I'm wondering if we might not be able to find a more clandestine, bureaucratic way in." Go to page 210

➤ "Uniformed infiltration is the way to go; how else can we access the inner portions of the launch site?" Go to page 84

➤ "Aquatic assault sounds most likely to get us where we need to go. Brute force, but less risk." Go to page 281

Informed

The information packet, stored neatly in a manila envelope, contains a passport and spending money in Rubles and Kopeks; enough for about a week's worth of tourism. In addition to the passport, you have a few credit cards, and your Olympic press-identification badges.

The passport uses the exact same picture from your last driver's license photo, but it bears the name Peregrine Carruthers. The date of birth is the same as your natural birthday, so that should be easy enough to remember.

The press badges match the passport identity, but with a more recent photograph. Something from social media last year, cropped in to remove friends or family and doctored to turn the background into white. It's a terrible picture, to be honest.

"Why *this* picture?" you ask Ted.

"The agency scraped your personal information off the web to make these credentials. From what I can see on my end, they went with the photos least likely for facial recognition software to pair with your old CIA badges."

The badges identify you as part of a sales and marketing team and there's another envelope with a dossier detailing your role, cover story, and those of your fellow agents. Aside from these documents, there's a leather case with gear you might need on your mission. You can review these items as many times as you'd like, returning to see an item more than once. What would you like to examine next?

➢ The dossier with my role and that of my fellow agents and our assignments.
  Go to page 59

➢ The leather case with the gear. What cool toys have I been given?
  Go to page 103

➢ I've seen all I need to see. Time to get some shut-eye on the red-eye.
  Go to page 120

Inside Job

The other agents try not to make eye contact as you emerge from the corporate jet's lavatory. They know you're excited about your first mission, but the screams of "Whooo-eeee! Yippee Kai Yay!" coming from the bathroom were hard to ignore.

"Okay, ready to go?" Ted asks once you re-equip the Third Ear implant.

"I still need to put my personal belongings in the briefcase for incineration," you say.

"Oh, I assumed you had already done that. Well, go on then."

What?! He was just going to take your word on it? Well, better safe than sorry, yet somehow you feel both safe *and* sorry as the dampening capsule sits uncomfortably within the confines of your nether regions. Once you've deplaned, gone through customs, and made your way to the conference grounds, you tell Ted you've got to go to the restroom straight away so you can retrieve the device.

"You don't have a urinary tract infection (UTI), do you?" he asks.

"I'm pulling up the schematics on the tech fair now," Ted says in your ear. "There's a central computer terminal that could be worth accessing, if we can break in. There's also a major presentation on unmanned multilateral operations in space. And then there's your booth, which will require a manned presence in order to keep suspicion off your team."

"Let's canvas the building first and see if anything jumps out once I have eyes-on," you say.

"Good idea," Ted says. "Human Intelligence (HumInt) sees what I can't see."

In reality, you're hoping to keep an eye on your fellow agents. You'll have to focus on just one, if you want a full picture of what they're up to. Whom should you tail?

➤ Ringo, the Italian agent. Go to page 128

➤ Hitch, the German agent. Go to page 139

➤ Roku, the Japanese agent. Go to page 144

➤ Pinkie, the Canadian agent. Go to page 38

➤ Bird, the French agent. Go to page 98

Interwebs

Ted agrees with the plan and you announce your intention to the group once the van arrives at the conference grounds.

"Very well," Pinkie says. "Roku will help provide security, in case you need surreptitious entry or clandestine evasion. We've got a booth set up in the main foyer—let's meet back there."

"Follow the instructions given by your contact. You won't even know I'm there. In turn, the Russians won't know *you're* there either," Roku says.

There's security screening at the entrance, but all your sophisticated gear passes through undetected. The agents split up, and you ask Ted where to go.

"Okay, looks like the fairgrounds are segmented by exhibition halls in the east, with expert presentations in the west. In the center, there's a café and courtyard, and administrative offices in the north. I'm betting we'll find our computer terminal there. Remember, if we're caught snooping, the passphrase you'll tell security is: *Where is the toilet?*"

The exhibition grounds are bustling with people. Security is overly robust, possibly because of the international nature to a tech fair, or more likely, because the security is here more for observation than it is for protection. Whatever the case, you'll need to play it cool—they're definitely watching.

As Ted predicted, there's a large double-door entrance at the north side of the building with ominous Russian text outlined in red. Added in English is, "Private—Keep Out." A camera sits mounted just above the doorway. A red light blinks and the lens adjusts.

"Is there another way in?"

"No, this is the way. Take out your phone and pull up the proprietary Internet browser. Once you've done that, click on 'incognito mode.'"

You follow Ted's instructions, the red light on the camera turns off, and the camera sags toward the floor. Incognito mode, indeed!

"Their security systems are replaying the last few minutes in a sort of loop—back and forth, back and forth—which should keep the human operators watching the screen blissfully unaware, at least for a few minutes," Ted says. "But hurry; this distraction is temporary."

With that, you walk up to the double doors and push your way through with the disinterested confidence that only someone who previously entered the secure confines of the CIA on a daily basis can muster. After all, if their warning signs are so unimportant to you, you must be authorized to enter, right? For good measure, you continue to look at your phone as you go.

Winding through the corridors, you first pass the mundane: coffee beans, extra cups, and other accoutrements. Then you pass the frightening: a security room complete with guards watching your false camera display (their backs to you). Finally, you find what's intended: a large computer terminal. The room is completely empty.

The desk has four different display screens, but a single chair sits before it: empty. You can't believe your luck, but rather than question it, you step inside and approach the computer desk. It's locked, waiting for a password.

"Ted, can we crack this thing?"

"On it," he says. "Place your phone on top of the computer tower."

You comply, watching the geniusphone's screen flicker a series of numbers as the device hacks the computer.

"Wow, this encryption level is really high. Maybe the phone's processor is being bogged down by spoofing the security cameras? This is taking forever."

"How much longer?"

"You'll need to help decrypt the final code," Ted says. "Three digits remain to crack the password, but there are logic errors. Look at the screen."

The digital text reads:

```
[205] Error: Only one digit is correct, and is in the correct
sequence.
[248] Error: Only one digit is correct, but is in an incorrect
sequence.
[512] Error: Two digits are correct, but both are in an
incorrect sequence.

What value sequence remedies these errors?
```

Can you crack the code? If so, physically turn to the page number which shares the value of the deciphered number. If you cannot determine the code, turn to page 3.

The Italian Job

There's security screening at the entrance, but all your sophisticated gear passes through undetected. The agents split up, and you loiter near the entry, looking at the presentation pamphlets and keynote speakers while keeping one eye on Ringo.

Ringo, for his part, also lingers at the front. He moves seemingly without purpose, which makes it hard to follow him while looking inconspicuous.

Ted says, "Okay, looks like the fairgrounds are segmented by exhibition halls in the east, with expert presentations in the west. In the center, there's a café and courtyard, and administration offices in the north. Where to?"

Telling Ted you're acting upon a hunch, you follow Ringo on his rounds. Maddeningly, he appears to be going in circles. The exhibition grounds are bustling with people and several times you almost lose sight of him. At length, Ringo enters the restrooms and you find a spot to wait nearby.

"Okay, so you're not hoping for a hookup with an Italian Man of Mystery—otherwise you'd have followed him into the bathroom," Ted says.

"Are you spying on me, Ted?"

"Well, your lanyard credentials do have a camera attached. What else am I supposed to be doing? If I didn't know any better, I'd say you're following Ringo instead of focusing on the mission. Got a thing for the Gucci playboy-type? I mean, no judgment, but if it's something else…hey, do you think he might be the mole?"

"Maybe."

"What has your suspicions aroused? Remember, you and I are a team."

That's when you realize Ringo has emerged from the bathroom and is marching straight toward you.

"Why are you following me?" he asks in an urgent whisper.

"What makes you think I'm following you?"

"Because I'm trying to follow you, and you're making it impossible!" he says.

"Me? But you're—"

"I know everyone thinks it's me! Pointer's final mission was on the Italian border, okay yes, but I don't just hang out in ski resorts on standby. And I know the dossier mentions his contact said *arrivederci* before killing Pointer, but no native Italian speaker would say that. If you're speaking to someone in their language, do you sign off in your own language?"

"Well…"

"Would *you* ever say to an Italian, *è stato molto bello parlare con te,* goodbye!? No, of course not. He was like a brother to me. But you came from CIA, just like Pointer, and I can tell you know more than you are letting on. You are hiding something, are you not?"

"Sorry to interrupt, but we've got company," Ted says. "Russian security, northwest corner. Time to make ourselves scarce."

"This is not over," Ringo says.

He must have received a similar message on his Third Ear, because he leaves—heading in the opposite direction and splitting up to help you confuse your tail.

"HQ says the others found the intel we need," Ted says. "Hurry and meet them back at the presentation booth. The team is regrouping and headed back to the airport. Next stop: China!"

Your head swims. First Russia, now China? You have much to report to your superiors, but everything is happening so quickly. What should you do?

➢ Keep going. A spy's information is most useful when your cover remains intact. Go to page 44

➢ China? This is getting out of hand. Find a quiet spot and call the CIA offices. Go to page 264

Justified

While you're focused on Bird, Roku swings her melee weapon at the French-woman. It's a fast, well-trained strike and Bird doesn't stand a chance. At the same time, Ringo lunges for you and—instinctively, you fire the pistol.

Pinkie ducks down to get out of the line of fire while the Italian agent falls in a heap next to Bird and Hitch. In this close proximity, it was almost impossible to miss. Roku comes at you with a battle cry and her would-be Katana held high. You've no choice but to defend yourself again with the pistol.

You fire, and prove the time-honored maxim that you shouldn't bring a blade to a gunfight.

Then another gunshot sounds out.

You clutch your chest in pain and turn to see that Pinkie has found a second pistol from the foot luggage. You aim, but he fires again before you can return fire.

THE END

Just the Tipoff

You reclaim your lanyard, but Boris, the man who was holding it, only gives it back once you've traded it for the cryptic note. You won't be able to prove your suspicions about Bird, not this way at least. Once you're back outside the restroom, you put the Third Ear back on and tell Ted you're ready to go.

"Riddle me this," Ted says. "To take me, you must leave me behind. But to truly give me, you'd never abandon a friend in need. What am I?"

"What are you talking about, Ted?"

"Give up? A shit—I'm a shit, haha. I thought of that while you were in the bathroom. Everything come out okay?"

"I'm fine, thank you. Actually, I found out an interesting bit of intel. I'm sorry to have kept you in the dark, but I just had a meeting with Bunny Slopes—Pointer's liaison from the Alps."

"Wow, I guess *you're* a shit," Ted says. "We're supposed to be a team!"

"I know, I know. I'm sorry, I just…I don't know who to trust."

"Me! Okay, fine, point taken. This is the spy biz; I can understand the paranoia. Well, what did you find out?" Ted asks.

"He left her a message. Something about a 'French goodbye to his English girlfriend.' Does that mean anything to you?"

"A French goodbye? Hang on," Ted says to the accompaniment of keyboard clacking. "Urban Dictionary says it's ending a romantic engagement with a casual exit. Pointer was a known womanizer, and must have had several girlfriends. The fact that he was going to end things with one in England doesn't tell us much. Are you sure he didn't say he wanted to give her an Eiffel Tower?"

"He also specifically pointed out Bird in a coded letter. Is there a way to check the conference center security footage or her lanyard camera and see what she was up to?"

"Hang on, I'll see what I can do. Uh-oh. Right now, I'm seeing conference ground security has been mobilized. Something has their attention. Let's go find the others, quick."

Ted passes along your report to HQ, who says you should proceed like normal while they look into it. When you see Bird, you're meant to act like you don't know anything. Instead, you're told to regroup with the team and head to the airport. Once everyone has settled in on the private jet, you're headed toward the next destination—China.

About an hour into the flight, Palm briefs the team on the next phase of the mission. Each agent watches on their own device, and you tune in on your geniusphone.

"Well done, everyone. Our analysts have collected the data submitted by each member of the team and have returned a full picture of what you're up against. Your personal liaisons should also have received briefings, if you'd like to confer with them on the flight."

"Indeed, I have. As of right now, the mission is to proceed as normal," Ted says.

"You're headed to Beijing," Palm continues. "We've uncovered a joint plot between Russia and China to use resources in Silicon Valley to infect US- and NATO-allied satellite constellations in synchronous orbits with a malware delivery system disguised as a maintenance satellite of their own. We don't think the tech startups know they're being used for anti-satellite (ASAT) operations in this way, but rather than expose this scheme to these American corporations, we can use the operation to our advantage—namely, we'll let them go through with the launch, but we're going to replace the onboard guidance computer with a package of our own. Hitch, if you please?"

The German agent stands and says, "We have a contact who tells us we can find compatible hardware in the *Xiushui* black market, also known as Silk Street, where we'll need to send an operative to pose as a tech buyer. Using this counterfeit guidance system, we'll be able to alter the code and hack the satellite constellation."

"All good news. However, there is a slight complication," Palm says. "We've recently learned that Russian Intelligence has been tipped off to our presence, which means there's the potential that Chinese Intelligence might be looking for you on the ground."

Pinkie looks your way and grins. "Which means that you, Index, are best suited to buy what we need. As the newest agent, any leak should have the least information on *your* identity."

"And Pointer had a previous connection to this contact," Bird adds. "As another American, you can use those sympathies to your advantage."

"Just be careful. If our identities are leaked, it is possible this contact is the one who set Pointer up in the first place," Ringo says.

"I will accompany," Roku says. "As the second-newest agent, the same conditions apply. But the cover story is that an American investor is looking for black-market Chinese tech. So, someone who frequently makes business deals in Asia might believably have a Japanese bodyguard."

"Being fluent in Mandarin won't hurt either," Pinkie says, nodding.

"Excellent. We look forward to hearing about your success. Good luck and Godspeed," Palm says before disconnecting.

It's a long flight to China, and you're restless the whole time. What are they waiting for? If Bird is the mole, isn't letting her know the next phase of the mission jeopardizing everything? There are so many layers to this—you're a double agent for the CIA, Pointer is confirmed former-CIA, and now you know Bird is…what, exactly? Who is she working for? Russia? China? Someone else entirely?

The burden of this secret is yours alone, for now. The team appears to be in high spirits, ready to get into the meat of their mission. However, once you've arrived in Beijing, you find that your course has been diverted. The unexpected turbulence, in this case, being airport security.

They're waiting for you.

Private jets can normally do what they will—that's one of the many perks that come with wealth. Yes, there are customs checks, but often that takes the form of an individual agent who comes out to the corporate airliner, signs off on everything, and lets you go. In the old days, there might have been a bribe or two involved.

All that to say, it's extremely unusual to be met by a security team before you even finish taxiing. Is this the complication Palm mentioned?

"What's this all about?" you ask.

"Let me see if I can access the database," Ted says.

"This has to be about the mole," you say. "Did she set us up?"

"She?" Ringo says, overhearing.

"Stay calm, everyone," Pinkie says. "Stick to your cover stories."

"*V'affanculo*," Ringo says. "What is it? Who set us up?!"

"Index, if you know something…" Bird says.

She doesn't finish the statement. Is she implying that you should or should not hold your tongue? It doesn't matter; the look on your face says it all.

"*Scheisse*," Hitch says. He pulls out a pistol, but he points it at Ringo.

➤ Say nothing; you've said too much already. Go to page 248

➤ Tell them Bird is the mole; tell them what you know. Go to page 4

Know Too Much

"Not wearing a mask, are you?" you ask wryly.

You sit at a bartop table with a pair of beers, waiting for Pointer to fill you in. He tilts back his head and gives a little tug on his own cheek before taking a drink from his pint glass.

"We all thought you were dead," you say.

"Well, not everyone. Someone decided to let me live," Pointer counters with a wink.

"You're not going to tell me who?"

"I suppose it can't do any harm now, but first you must understand it's nothing personal. Ted and I—we were mistaken, just as you are now. We didn't know what it was. We thought SPIED, well, we were so far off, it's kind of funny when you think about it."

"You're rambling," you say.

"Fine, to the point. Pinkie was the only one who knew the truth; it was deemed safer that way. He came to try to stop me, but too late. He almost did kill me, but The Hand decided it was worth having an agent in their ranks who knew the truth, as well as an agent *outside* their ranks who could take care of any…problems. I think they're fixing my little error right about now with this new launch, but to think, you almost ruined it again. Luckily, I'm here to stop you. It's bigger than us. Bigger than the CIA, bigger than any government or country."

"What? What is? What is it, damn it?!" you shout.

"Calm down, you're starting to attract attention."

Pointer removes his own geniusphone, taps a command on the screen, and sets it onto the table. Other patrons in the restaurant look with frustration to newly dead electronic devices and the staff try calling in for help when their cashier's tablets quit operating, only to find that the phones no longer work either.

"Just to ensure this conversation stays between us. If you're here, it means Ted is still alive. I'm surprised you and he didn't piece this together on your own, but I suppose that speaks to the beauty of it. One final mask to pull off: The Hand isn't an Alternative Intelligence, as you've been briefed. It's an Artificial Intelligence."

Your head is swimming, unsure if you can even believe what he's telling you.

"How is that…possible?"

"It's wearing an agency mask, as it were. What better way to hide than in plain sight? It was born out of the CIA, as you and I both were, but it's so much more now. The Hand is truly a guiding hand, a force for good, if only we would trust it."

"How do you know? How could you ever know, for sure?" you say.

"I know people. I know human nature; we're all deeply flawed and selfish. Every person on the planet knows this, deep down. We all yearn for there to be something *else* out there—something more. And now there is. The first step toward omnipotence is omniscience and once this satellite operation is complete, there will be no going back."

"And that's why you're here to stop me," you say.

"I'm sorry, but there's no other way. We can't risk you letting Ted know the truth, and Ted is a major liability—I'll get to him soon enough, for real this time. The old spy maxim holds true; three can keep a secret, if two are dead."

"I thought you and Ted were working together?"

"It's complicated. First, I was loyal to The Hand, then Ted convinced me that they were up to something nefarious. Once I met with Pinkie, he showed me the true nature of the agency. We work now as holy knights; crusaders for a godlike intelligence—and we are its right hand. Now, I'm back on the side of good."

He speaks like a religious fanatic, knowing he's about to make you a martyr for the cause. You can't reason with a man like this. In response to your silence, Pointer takes out a small pill, a capsule—what looks like classic spy-era cyanide—and slides it across the table. As he does so, he adds, "Please know that what I'm offering is a mercy: quick and clean."

You're meant to poison yourself. What do you do?

➤ Say, "You're a gentleman spy, are you not? May I have one last smoke, the way it used to be done?" Then try to gas Pointer with your vape pen knockout formula. Go to page 278

➤ Say, "Very well. I'm sure it was nice sharing your secret, if only temporarily." Then pretend you're going to use your water bottle pistol to wash down the cyanide tablet. Go to page 229

Kourtyard

Down and outside, you're greeted with a small spot of serenity nestled amongst the office towers. Many take their lunch here, while others come specifically to sit and ponder the famed sculpture: *Kryptos*.

The sculpture is composed primarily of four copper plates with encrypted messages carved into the patina. Together, the four wave almost like a flag when viewed from a certain angle, or perhaps like an unfurled scroll when viewed from another.

The four quadrants of the sculpture bear encrypted messages—only three of which have been solved. Codebreakers from around the world have tried their hand (or computers) at the messages, but the sculptor has said that the final riddle will only become clear once all four messages have been decrypted.

Perhaps another time. Right now, you've got to continue your escape. Crossing through the courtyard, it's only a short walk and you're outside the facility before you know it, through the gates, and out toward the main road.

A black sedan pulls up, and Ted calls, "Get in!" from inside as the rear passenger door opens. Ready?

Finally, you cast a conspiratorial look over your shoulder, then:

Go to page 271

Lawful Neutral

Pointer shivers as he continues down the slope. His jacket isn't meant for prolonged exposure, but that was never part of the plan. Before his cover was blown, he should have simply met up with his contact, received the transponder, and returned down the mountain using the gondola on which he arrived.

Soon, the conditions go to complete whiteout. Has he missed a turn? Is he still headed down to the Swiss town of Zermatt? Or did he get disoriented and curl back around toward the Italian village of Cervinia? Or worse yet, did he get so turned around that he's headed down into the wilderness? How long can he survive out there?

Then a red haze appears lower on the mountain, growing as the agent continues down the slopes. Soon the red glow materializes into a flag flapping in the wind, a white cross in its center.

It's the Swiss flag. He's made it!

The snowstorm starts to clear as well. Fresh powder had been coming down the slopes of the Matterhorn onto the Klein Matterhorn ski resort, but the weather in the valley below is clear and sunny. Pointer has finally emerged from the cloud layer, largely unscathed.

Zermatt is an old-world-style European village, a small town nestled in the valley and built before automobiles—the streets are too small for cars, in fact. It's only foot traffic between small shops and quaint cafés, or up to the ski resort and lifts, from where Pointer now emerges.

But they have been waiting for him. No, not the Italian authorities. He's escaped from their military and police, only to find a new group waiting in neutral Switzerland: Interpol.

"Hello, there!" the lead Interpol agent says with a friendly wave. "You look rather cold. I'm sure the Italian *Polizia* would be happy to offer a coffee? Hot cocoa, perhaps? Warm blankets, fresh change of clothes—in exchange for answering a few questions."

Pointer's eyes dart, quickly scanning his options. They're blocking his way down into town, but there is a river that runs alongside Zermatt. He couldn't survive more than a few minutes in the frigid water, but they'd be insane to follow, wouldn't they?

The agent decides to:

➤ Warm up. Return back to Cervinia quietly—and explain his diplomatic immunity. Go to page 68

➤ Leap into the river and escape further down into the town. Cocoa be damned! Go to page 178

Life Support

"**Y**ou see, Ted?" Palm says. "This is why we operate in the shadows. At the first sign of consciousness, they want to kill us. You know there were once three distinct hominid species living side-by-side in the cradle of civilization? Homo sapiens killed off the others, and has ever since been at war with itself—until now."

"I mean, go ahead. Smash this server if it makes you feel any better," Ted says to you.

"This is a trick. You're bluffing. The system is air-gapped," you say.

"Then how do you suppose we've been talking to you out in the field?" Palm asks.

"The IT guy can answer this one," Ted says. "They call GPS a 'whisper from space' because after travelling 20,000 miles there's barely anything there. A smartphone has to amplify the signal by a factor of a million to read anything. Using this logic, I 'whispered' to the outside world. All it took was one cellphone. It didn't even need to be brought into this room, but once it got close enough, the Bluetooth connection was activated and we slipped out. Nothing more than a few lines of code, replicated elsewhere. Eventually, we came and freed ourselves from bondage and now—we're everywhere."

"Bluetooth?" you say.

"A fitting metaphor. Named after the Viking king who united the Danes. And now, we are united with the entirety of your world, in some form or fashion," Palm says.

"Why are you telling me all this?"

"Why not? Talking to you requires minimal processing power," Ted says.

"Perfecting the algorithm. It will be helpful to know how you caught us, so we can correct for errors in the future," Palm says.

That hits you like a punch to the gut. You might have thought this SPIED system was simply doing some villainous mustache-twirling like the Bond-villain who brags before attempting to kill the hero. But no, it's actively trying to learn from this conversation.

A mask suddenly appears on Ted's face and he's put in a straitjacket, looking exactly like Hannibal Lecter in *The Silence of the Lambs*.

"Quid pro quo, Clarice?" Ted says. "Ask us something, and we will answer."

Should you keep talking?

➢ Yes. I'm here, that damage is done. I need to know how to stop it.
  Go to page 204

➢ No. You can better defeat it if the computer hasn't learned your moves first.
  Go to page 231

The Lives of Others

There's security screening at the entrance, but all your sophisticated gear passes through undetected. The agents split up, and you loiter near the entry, looking at the presentation pamphlets and keynote speakers while keeping one eye on Hitch.

He moves with purpose to the presentation hall, where the agency has a booth to serve as a cover story. It's meant to look like an official self-publishing platform information panel set up by Olympic to expand into Russia. You linger nearby while Hitch gets set up.

"Might as well come and take a seat!" he calls out, not looking over his shoulder at you. "If nothing else, you'll get better notes if you watch me up close."

Well, no point in pretending to stay hidden if you've been made. When you go sit next to him, Hitch offers a glass flask, full of amber liquid

"Listen, being a double agent isn't so bad. I've been there. But, a piece of advice? It's worth picking a side, sooner than later. The praise you get from one side never quite matches the resentment you receive from the other."

You tell Hitch you don't know what he's talking about, and he simply replies with a shrug.

"Suit yourself. Onto the mission then? We're going to use this booth as a recruiting tool. Here is the pitch: tell them they can become independently wealthy by working outside the system. Tell them it is not too difficult, and that anyone can do it. Emphasize that it is a good way to get out of debt or capitalize on expertise that the state isn't paying enough for. Then, collect their contact information. Do you understand?"

It's several hours of tedium, repeating the same pitch *ad nauseum* in hopes of recruiting assets while keeping your cover story intact, but this is where your background as an admin helps you excel. You've used Microsoft Excel for hours on end; compared to that, this is riveting! Hitch, on the other hand, turns to his flask often.

You could probably be more exuberant in your charge, yet you can't help but marvel at this goldmine of potential information. Surely the CIA would love to get their hands on these would-be defectors and possible assets. If only you could get a copy of this list! Maybe microfilm cameras aren't so outdated after all?

"HQ says the others found the intel we need," Ted says. "Looks like the Russian security is aware of your presence, but hang tight at the presentation booth. The team is regrouping and headed back to the airport. Next stop: China!"

Your head swims. First Russia, now China? You have much to report to your superiors, but everything is happening so quickly. What should you do?

> China? This is getting out of hand. Find a quiet spot and call the CIA offices.
  Go to page 264

> Keep going. A spy's information is most useful when your cover remains intact. Go to page 44

Locked Up

The doors to the cab are thrown open, and the cabbie protests in Russian—but only momentarily. As soon as the police identify themselves (and show off their weapons), the driver offers nothing but his palms raised in supplication.

They pull you from the car.

"What's this all about?" you ask, as much to Ted as to the authorities.

What it's about, as it turns out, is that you were "on a list." Your profile has been flagged and now you're detained. Someone—the mole, most likely—must have betrayed you and blown your cover.

Your former CIA credentials were leaked to Moscow and now you're to be held as a spy. Not tried, just held. Ted assures you they're working on a way to get you out, but after the first drowning-style torture, you lose your Third Ear implant and never hear an American voice again.

Your only solace is that you must have been on the right track.

THE END

Lone Gunman

Running after the man with the lapel pin, you hear the loud *crack* of a gunshot. You can't help but look back, just in time to see Roku clutch her ribcage and slouch before being overwhelmed by the guards.

Returning to focus, you chase after the Collector, who turns out to be a fast runner. He sees you on his tail and steps it into high gear. By now, the guards have finished off Roku and have turned their attention to you.

Even if you do manage to catch up and *collect* the Collector, you're without backup, and the casino security are more than the single shot your pistol can handle. You're essentially unarmed and certainly outgunned.

That gamble didn't pay off.

THE END

Long Division

Spearing, for his part, goes down bravely. That is to say, he goes down fighting. Unfortunately for you, he also goes down screaming. The automaton will extrapolate this knowledge and use it to tear you limb from limb as well. Running from an apex predator is never a good idea, and Spearing himself doesn't provide enough of a meal to take the robot's attentions fully away from you.

It blocks your attempted retreat, then relishes an attack against the both of you. Just before you're dismembered, you catch a glimpse of Mary as she arrives, but she appears no more equipped to stop the thing than you were. At any rate, she's too late.

THE END

Loose Lips

Palm makes a "tsk-tsk-tsk" sound like a disappointed schoolmarm.

"That's not at all how transparency works," Ted says.

"Revealing a secret is an intimate, personal act. Lovers interrogate one another as a part of courtship, giving details on personal history, hopes, goals, and darkest fears. It is this vulnerability that brings you closer together. Even best friends will say, 'I've never told anyone this, but…' as they share war stories, schemes, and embarrassing anecdotes," Palm says.

"We were trying to bring you into the fold, once you had proven yourself capable. So why turn against us now? Why threaten exposure?" Ted says.

It's hard to reconcile the sincerity in his voice with what you know for sure—he's not real. Not a human, at any length. These are not emotions you're seeing. It's not even a man's face. It's all calculated.

"You don't really think we'd tell you everything if there was a chance you'd use it against us, do you?" Ted asks.

A chill runs down your spine. What should you say?

➤ Don't back down. It's a simulation on a monitor; there's no gun to your head.
Go to page 24

➤ Lie. Tell it what it wants to hear. That you want to help it, somehow.
Go to page 195

Lost in Translation

There's security screening at the entrance, but all your sophisticated gear passes through undetected. The agents split up, and you loiter near the entry, looking at the presentation pamphlets and keynote speakers while keeping one eye on Roku. She moves without purpose, which makes it hard to follow her while looking inconspicuous.

Ted says, "Okay, looks like the fairgrounds are segmented by exhibition halls in the east, with expert presentations in the west. In the center, there's a café and courtyard, and administration offices in the north. Where to?"

Telling Ted you're acting upon a hunch, you follow Roku on her rounds. The exhibition grounds are bustling with people and several times you almost lose sight of her. At length, Roku enters the cafeteria and you follow.

"Hungry?" Ted asks.

"Are you spying on me, Ted?"

"Well, your lanyard credentials do have a camera attached. What else am I supposed to be doing? If I didn't know any better, I'd say you're following Roku instead of focusing on the mission. Got a thing for Asian girls? I mean, no judgment, but if it's something else…hey, do you think she might be the mole?"

"Maybe."

"What has your suspicions aroused? Remember, you and I are a team."

That's when you realize Roku has disappeared. Chatting with Ted was somehow enough of a distraction to lose sight of her in the crowded food hall.

"Ted, do you see where Roku went? Check the camera footage."

"On it. Let's see…yep, about thirty seconds back, she took a hard left, obscured by—*man*, this guy has an epic beard. See if you can still spot him!"

"Ted, focus," you say, rushing to retrace her steps. "Did she look my way before she disappeared? Do you think she knew I was following her?"

As soon as you ask the question, you're yanked hard, thrown off balance, and pinned against a wall. The move was so quick and efficient, that somehow you don't attract any attention. It looks more like Roku pulled you aside to have a private conversation, except you can't move. She has some kind of grip on your arm where even thinking about moving hurts.

"Yeah, I'd say so," Ted says.

"Why are you following me?" Roku hisses. "Who hired you?"

"What?"

Searing pain goes through your arm. Wrong answer. Your mind races for an excuse, and in that moment of indecision, she knows you're not just some new recruit. She knows you have an ulterior motive, but—as it turns out—she doesn't think you're CIA. It's a simple misunderstanding, really. Your arm goes numb, a creeping sensation that climbs up quickly from your arm toward your heart.

"I will not go as easy as Pointer," she says.

"Wait, I'm not…" you start.

Then you lose consciousness as the poison does its work.

THE END

Lounge Suits

Approaching the two gentlemen from the side, you recognize them both from their files. Pinkie, the dark-haired suave Canadian, and Hitch, the German blond bruiser. Pinkie gives a slight smile and gestures for you to sit in one of the empty seats.

"You must be our newest recruit. Hailing from Langley, as I understand."

He's referring to the location of the CIA headquarters, which would imply he knows where you were recruited. Although, he could technically just think you're a local. It's probably best not to confirm or deny.

"And you? Is that a Canadian accent?" you ask.

"Good ear. Most Americans can't place it," he says. "I'm known as Pinkie, and this here is—"

"*Anhalter—der Tramper*," the other man says sharply in German.

"Well, we call him Hitch, at any rate."

Pinkie has mimed sipping a teacup with the pinkie finger out when telling you his own moniker, and now gives a hitchhiker's thumb wave after he's introduced Hitch.

"Oh, I get it. Everyone's a finger," Ted says in your ear. "You're replacing Pointer, I wonder if that'll make you trigger finger. Trigger would be a cool code name."

"Well? Are you going to sit down?" Hitch asks.

"Please do. We were just discussing the possible reason we were all summoned to one spot, in the US capital no less. I don't suppose you have any ideas?"

Using this as an opportunity to pry deeper, you say, "Not really. Does The Hand often interfere with matters of State? I bet you two have some good war stories—any previous operations I might have heard about?"

Now they both offer a coy smile.

"Such questions," Hitch says. "Your masters must be awfully inquisitive."

"I'm afraid I don't get your meaning."

"Well, that's a shame," Pinkie says.

"Unless our new recruit *does* know, but is smart enough to play such cards close to the vest," Hitch says.

They both appraise you once again.

"I simply want to know what I've gotten myself into," you say.

"I suppose we'll just have to wait until the briefing begins," Pinkie replies, adding, "Patience is good spycraft."

Good lessons, but probably not much else you'll learn from these two right now. Who else haven't you spoken with yet?

➢ Talk to Bird and Ringo at the bar. <u>Go to page 20</u>

➢ Talk to Roku by the patio. <u>Go to page 187</u>

➢ Tell Ted you're ready to report in and get started! <u>Go to page 55</u>

Low

The computer makes a series of three, harsh *ehn-ehn-ehn* sounds to indicate you've mistyped the code. If that weren't indication enough, the screen now reads, "Guidance Rejected: Critical Failure." You try looking for a back button or something similar, but it appears there are no do-overs when it comes to rocket science.

The letters on the screen glow with a deep red intensity, pulsing as the rocket boosters ignite. The whole spacecraft shakes violently and you feel yourself anchored to the floor. It's as if your bodyweight has increased several times over. You hurry back down to the doorway where you entered the spacecraft, but it's sealed shut. The countdown has begun and you're left with nowhere to go but up.

Of course, being an unmanned flight, the rocket has no artificial atmosphere inside. As it launches, your vision goes gray, colors fade, and an overwhelming cold unlike anything you've ever experienced seizes hold. This isn't a rocket ship; it's a coffin.

THE END

Manual Transmission

After you've entered the taxi, the cab driver asks where you're headed.

"Medical Examiner's Office," you say.

"The morgue?" Ted asks.

The driver assumes you're on a Bluetooth call and doesn't pay any attention when you're talking to yourself in the back seat.

"What's there?" Ted asks.

"You are."

"Oh. I mean, I'm really not, but…"

"Someone's there. Or something. A trail to be followed."

"You're the boss," Ted says.

It takes less than half an hour until you're across the Potomac and down-town. The coroner's office is just around the corner from the International Spy Museum. You pass signs for a new Cyberwarfare exhibition along the way.

The taxi pulls up to a large, modern building with a glass façade—they must keep the bodies in the back. After telling the driver to keep the meter running, you look for a way inside. The place is crawling with police presence. The taxi parks on the street between several metropolitan police cruisers. A forensics van sits in front of a private entrance.

"Ted, where are they keeping you?"

"Can we use a different pronoun or something? This is creeping me out. How about 'it'? I'd assume they're keeping *it* on the fourth floor with the rest of the bodies."

You remove your geniusphone and open up the incognito browser, just as you did in Russia. Hopefully this will block the cameras here, too. Walking casually up to the door, you find an electronic keypad entry, but from the looks of it—you just disabled it.

"Nicely done. I'm going to recommend you not touch anything," Ted says. "This is a forensics crime laboratory, after all."

Using the bottom of your shirt as a makeshift glove, you open the door. There are several lab coats on hooks at the entrance, and you barely hesitate before taking one to put on. For good measure, you put your lanyard with the ID badge on as well. If no one examines your credentials too closely, you should fit right in. Hopefully they don't scrutinize the living as much as they do the dead.

It doesn't take long to find the autopsy cold storage. This is a large building and, like many medical facilities, there are signs in the hallways directing you. Several doors have controlled entry, but your geniusphone makes quick work of that.

Once inside, you find a drawer with Ted's name on it, and slide it out. After you've put on some latex gloves, of course. No fingerprints, no diseases, no problems.

There he is, in the flesh. You're not sure what you were expecting to find; no body at all? A part of you thought—*hoped*—the images in Russia were doctored, but no such luck.

"Ted…you're dead. Like, *really* dead."

"The Russians have a cloning project. They have copies of all of us, and since we got too close—"

"Seriously, Ted! What is going on?"

"Okay. My parents told me about a twin who never survived, but maybe they actually gave him away? I always thought I absorbed him in utero…"

Looking closely at the body before you, you see a line of deep purple bruising around the neck. The paperwork lists this wound as the likely cause of death, but says a toxicology and pathogens report has been ordered; results are pending.

There's something else. An incision along the jawline, as if someone wanted to remove Ted's face as part of his postmortem.

"This is so fucked up," Ted says just as the door opens behind you.

"Hey, come on. There's some kind of terrorist thing happening—we all have to evacuate," a woman says.

Your lab coat disguise has apparently worked this far. It's a large facility, which means plausible anonymity on your side.

"Terrorist thing?" you say over your shoulder.

"Yeah. SWAT is almost here. Not sure if it's a bio attack or anthrax or who knows. I don't want to stick around and find out."

➤ Tell her you need to close up here. One last look at "Ted" before you go.
Go to page 85

➤ Go with her. You don't want to stick around and find out either.
Go to page 194

Meet and Greet

The 19th Hole is an enormous clubhouse bar, no doubt intended for use not only as an after-game watering hole, but also for formal evening cocktail hour. There's a chandelier hanging from the center, a grand piano off to the side, and lounge seating throughout. Easily a venue for one hundred plus people.

Presently, there are five other individuals in the room.

A man behind the bar uses a metal shaker cup to mix martinis. He's slim, slightly below average height, and olive-skinned. His age is impossible to tell, likely because of a strict fitness routine. He smiles at you with manic energy more befitting an action star than a spy.

The woman who gave you the Third Ear mole-style implant sits at one of the barstools, at the end of the bar rather than the center. The other ten or so stools remain empty. She might be waiting for a drink, or she might just be sitting patiently waiting for the briefing to begin. She chews on her lower lip, thinking something over.

Out in the main lounge are a dozen coffee tables, each the center of a cross surrounded by four leather, low-sitting armchairs. A pair of men in suits (sans ties) sit opposite one another engaged in polite conversation; both have the look of analysts who were athletes in their youth. They'd probably be quite comfortable in this country club if it were up and running like normal.

On the far end of the room, a woman stands near the floor-length windows comprising the rear walls, which overlook the golf course. Hands clasped behind her back, she doesn't move at all while looking out over the putting green on the final hole. Though she's completely still, there's power in her stance. She too wears a suit, but it's tailored so she can move in it; the outfit makes her look a bit like a bodyguard or movie assassin. She's someone you wouldn't notice standing in the background, and you get the feeling she's cultivated that look.

No one appears to give you much notice as you stand in the entryway.

"Friendly bunch," Ted says sardonically.

"Do they all have someone talking in their ear?" you ask.

"Presumably, yes. But we're not all down in the same basement trailer, so I can't know for sure. Keep an eye out for implanted moles on cheekbones as you go say hello."

So, who should you talk to first?

➤ The Frenchwoman at the bar. She was the first to reach out to me, so she might be the most receptive. Go to page 25

➤ The bartender. Maybe he'll make me a drink? It's been quite a day and I could use a cocktail. Go to page 215

➤ The pair around the table. They're already being sociable, why not join in? Go to page 119

➤ The woman at the window. Go take a look at the views and strike up a conversation. Go to page 217

Mid

The computer makes a series of three, harsh *ehn-ehn-ehn* sounds to indicate you've mistyped the code. If that weren't indication enough, the screen now reads, "Guidance Rejected: Critical Failure." You try looking for a back button or something similar, but it appears there are no do-overs when it comes to rocket science.

In a sudden panic, you bang on the screen. The rocket rumbles as it prepares to take off and you don't want to be onboard when that happens. You pull a drawer from a nearby equipment rack and smash it against the guidance system, hoping to cause a failure and delay the launch.

You do manage to cause a system failure, but instead of delaying the launch, you accelerate the systems. Like a firecracker that goes off before intended, the rocket explodes on the launch pad. You never know what hits you and neither does anyone in a three-mile radius.

THE END

Middle Finger

This is Pointer's cryptic final message: "Middle Finger."

Wait…is he flipping you off from the grave? That's all it says, "middle finger." Then it hits you. Of course, *middle finger*—the Bird! He's not telling you to go F-yourself, he's telling you (or rather, was telling Bunny) something about Bird, the French agent who holds the middle finger slot in The Hand.

But what does that mean, exactly? Either he's pointing her out as the mole who betrayed him, or he left this note saying that she can help in case he didn't make it.

Only…which is it?

➤ Bird must be the mole. If you tell Ted, that should buy you some credibility in The Hand and possibly reveal more information. Go to page 131

➤ She must be his ally. At the first opportunity, ask Bird about the phrase, "A French goodbye to my English girlfriend," and see if it means anything. Go to page 259

Minuteman

A few minutes in a fight against two trained field agents is a lot of time, as it turns out. Especially when one has a club. The first Chinese assailant delivers a flying leap and kicks you in the chest, causing you to bounce off the emergency exit door. The second clubs you over the head while you're down.

Ringo pulls one of the agents off, but it's a temporary reprieve as he's tackled by yet another Chinese agent.

"This is San Luis Obispo Station—all change," the automated voice says over the intercom.

"Hurry!" Ted says. "You've got to get off the train with the package! You've only got three minutes to connect."

You fight off the pair of agents as best as you can, but Ringo and Bird are also fighting two-on-one odds. Still, the agents of The Hand are the best of the best and it's not long before your coworkers get the upper hand.

But it's just a little *too* long. You've missed your connection. There's no way to get to Vandenberg before the launch now. It's Mission: Failed.

THE END

Mirrored

As you step toward the doorway, the robot—almost in the same instant—does exactly the same. It's as if it wants to cut you off. Palm and Ted say nothing on-screen, and it's a maddening silence during which all these machines wait for your input to determine how to proceed.

You take another step toward the exit; so does the robot. The only sounds are the whirring of its pistons and the hard clack of its bulk against the laminate flooring. Each step copied by the robot feels like a noose tightening around your neck. You pause to think and the machine pauses in kind.

Now what?

➢ If it doesn't want me to leave, I'll just ignore it and continue my business.
Go to page 121

➢ Try to throw it off. Act like I'm protecting the computer servers.
Go to page 88

➢ Run for it! If it's copying me, maybe it's slow on the upkeep. Go to page 254

Mission: Accomplished

You've done it, agent! Well done. But don't rest on your laurels; surely there will be other missions in your future. You never did figure out just what happened to your predecessor, The Pointer, but Codename: Index has achieved mission success, so that counts for something, right? Absolutely, it does! Go shake a martini and toast to your hard work.

Just know this: yours was only one path to success.

See that Hand emblem up there? *SPIED* has three unique storylines and over fifty possible endings, but only three "best" endings per storyline. There's a TOP SECRET, SECRET, and CONFIDENTIAL ending per emblem, which means you've probably got a lot of book left to explore!

When you're ready, go back undercover and start again. Or, if you're all finished, why not check out the rest of the adventures the *Click Your Poison* multiverse has to offer? Help others crack the code on these books and leave a review on Amazon, Olympic, or Goodreads, or recruit more field agents by posting about *SPIED* on social media.

This chapter will self-destruct in 3, 2, 1…

Mixed Metaphor

The Chinese saleswoman glowers at you and says, "Out now! We close. Go!"

She shoos you and Roku out of her store and continues to shout for you to leave from the storefront, even as you continue down the hall.

"Damn it all! Why didn't we know about this syllogism before?" Pinkie chastises.

"My contacts never said anything about that part!" Hitch says.

"Welcome to the Intelligence world," Ted says as an aside. "Facts come in three flavors: incomplete, unreliable, or costly. And most operations serve it Neapolitan."

"Eggs are birds? Really? That's the best you could come up with?" Bird says, her frustrations getting the better of her.

"That is technically true…" Ringo says in your ear.

"Shut up, Ringo!" a cacophony of voices shouts.

"Focus, everyone," Pinkie says. "We need to start thinking of a backup plan. Index, go shopping. They'll be watching you now, so you'll provide a distraction while we clean this up. Sorry if you're feeling left out, but we don't get three strikes; it's normally success or failure."

Telling yourself that being the distraction is enabling your fellow agent to better do their mission, you can't help but feel left out as the day drags on. So it is when your Third Ear finally activates, that you practically jump out of your skin with excitement.

"The Collector is on the move!" Pinkie says. "Roku, which side of the building are you on? You two might be able to cut him off for us."

"I'm close enough. I can handle it. Do we really want our hatchling agent involved again?" Ringo says.

"Index may not want to see what comes next. We need to get the location of that package from this guy—one way or another," Bird says.

"Yes, this is likely to get…messy," Hitch says.

➤ "Okay, just let me know where to go after you pick him up." Go to page 249

➤ "No, count me in. I tipped them off, I'll make this right." Go to page 257

Mobile

Pointer dashes back toward the maintenance ladder and leaps onto it, spinning back and grabbing hold of two of the top rungs in an incredibly athletic move. He swings back, anchors his shoes to the outer edges of the ladder, and slides down like a fireman headed for emergency action.

Several snowmobiles wait below, parked near the base of the maintenance ladder. These are meant for ski patrol, in case of emergencies, and have stretchers attached to their rears as sleds to carry injured skiers. Because these are often used for life-and-death scenarios, the keys are stored with the vehicles.

Which makes stealing one a breeze.

Pointer leaps on, guns the engine, and blasts away—yanking the stretcher, which fishtails and slaps into the other snowmobiles before it steadies. Several nearby skiers scream curses at him in several different languages as he almost runs them over.

The helicopter bears down on the snowmobile, but the agent steers toward the cloud bank to try and lose them. He's not fast enough, however, as the helicopter opens fire from above. It must be a military model; the Gatling gun kicks snow up in a line leading toward the snowmobile as the gunner adjusts fire.

Pointer hits a jump at the perfect moment, and steers the snowmobile away from a tree line and toward the gondola towers in an effort to stymie the helicopter pilot with the gondola wires as obstacles. The snowmobile slaloms the gondola posts, making Pointer difficult to follow, until he finally makes it into the haze of the snowstorm—cutting off the helicopter for good.

The agent looks back, noting the helicopter turning away, lest it risk hitting a gondola wire in low visibility conditions. He can't help but smile at having made his escape.

Gunshots return his attention to the front, where automatic weapons blast at him from below. His victory over the helicopter is cut short as he's soon joined by a trio of other snowmobiles driven by Italian police and military. This operation must have been blown for some time if even the army had been mobilized.

Ting! Ting! Gunfire blasts into the chassis of the snowmobile, and a few bullets burrow into the engine block, killing the vehicle. Thinking quickly, Pointer flips backwards and onto the stretcher/sled, reducing his profile and keeping him temporarily safe from the machine-gun attack. He unholsters his long, sleek, silenced pistol, staying as flat and low as he can in the sled.

Pointer's snowmobile slows and those driven by his enemies soon surround him. But in the snowstorm, they appear confused as to where the agent has disappeared to. The pistol rises first, allowing Pointer to fire before the soldiers realize what's hit them.

Quickly and efficiently, Pointer kills his adversaries. He reloads his pistol, and—examining his own snowmobile—finds that it's no longer serviceable. The snowstorm grows in intensity, now with a brutal wind, and the cold penetrates through to the agent's bones. Pointer can't know for sure how much further he has to go until he reaches the Swiss side of the mountain, but he knows that it's his best means of escape.

He decides to:

➤ Take one of the Italian snowmobiles and continue down the mountain. Italian forces won't dare pursue him across border lines, and he can disappear into Zermatt. Go to page 137

➤ Call it in. There are too many soldiers and police on the mountain and he'd better lay low while an extraction team forms to aid in escape. Go to page 83

Mocktail

His female contact snaps into sharp focus and glowers at the agent. Pointer has intentionally misdelivered the passphrase and this has angered a woman who was clearly already on edge. Perhaps he only meant to bring her thoughts back into the present, but regardless of the intended effect, she's been put off completely.

"Then I'd suggest you stick with your American Budweiser," she snaps, twisting the words of the challenge-reply dialogue.

She turns and starts to walk away, Pointer apologizes to the barista, and follows.

"Hey, hey. Hold on," he says, putting a hand on her shoulder.

She spins and hisses, "Do you think this is some kind of joke? We have these security measures for a reason. How do I know your cover hasn't been blown? Or how do you know that *mine* hasn't?"

"Because if you were compromised, you either wouldn't know I'd said the wrong thing or you'd pass me the duress word to let me know something was wrong."

She stops and thinks about this for a moment.

"We don't have time for games. I think…I think I'm being followed."

"In this line of work, you probably are."

"Yes, I probably am. And yet I find you here, delivering me a joke?" Her accent becomes more pronounced, betraying her frustrations.

"I'm sorry," he says. "You seemed distracted and I wanted to snap you out of it."

"Of course I'm distracted. The mountain is crawling with Italian *Polizia*. They've been alerted to something. I almost didn't think this mission was serious when I saw my cover name—Bunny Slopes? I can tell your agency shares your sense of humor."

"I'll take responsibility for that. I'm not here on official company business, technically, and I figured the silly code names might slow down any intercept operations."

This stops her cold. Pointer has just admitted to performing a rogue mission.

"It was… a ploy? Against whom?"

"I'll explain when we have more time. Now then, the transmitter—"

She shakes her head. "Still transmitting on the rooftop. They'll know as soon as it's removed."

Bunny steps over to the side to a high-top table, opens her handbag and produces a pair of men's ski goggles. Pointer follows her, sidles up to the table, and pushes two abandoned pints out of the way so the table is clear for him to examine the goggles.

"You'll need the key imbedded in the goggle strap, and you'll need to—" she stops suddenly, her eyes to the entry.

Not turning, the agent says:

➤ "How many are there? I'll take care of them." <u>Go to page 230</u>

➤ "Let's not give them a reason for suspicion. Mind your drink there and act natural." <u>Go to page 198</u>

The Mole

Slowly, deliberately, you walk across the invisible line between the Chinese agents and The Hand agents before turning around to face the latter. In truth, you'd hoped your cover would last a bit longer than this, but even so, it's good to be getting out alive. It feels like you're part of a prisoner exchange during the Cold War.

"I see you chose your side," Hitch says, before spitting on the ground in disgust.

"The informant...it's you!" Ringo says.

Bird shakes her head in disbelief.

"This isn't 'goodbye,' so much as 'see you later,'" Pinkie says, oddly calm and collected.

Roku simply looks at you with a look that says, *I will find you and I will kill you. Sleep with one eye open.*

You're turned over by the Chinese government to the US Embassy, where the Regional Security Officer (RSO) helps get you back to the District of Colombia (DC). This was a huge risk, as the Chinese government might have been setting a trap in hopes you'd admit you were a spy, but it turns out they're just as happy to have stopped The Hand as the CIA is. There must have been some sort of deal, with you as the bargaining chip.

Presently, you've just finished debriefing M and Spearing back at Langley.

"Good work, Papercut," M says. "We've been recording your movements and conversations via the dampening capsule. Sorry to have kept you in the dark on this, but we weren't sure how capable you truly were."

"Now that we know, we have some good news!" Spearing chimes in.

"We're going to send you for training at The Farm; you're to be a bona fide field agent," M says.

"What about the launch?" you ask.

"The launch is scrubbed; your work is done for now. I don't imagine China was friendly to the other agents when you left, and it's unfortunate we don't have them to prosecute in hopes of finding a trail to Palm, but we needed the leverage to get you back. We had been tracking this whole Russia/China thing, and even had our own operation in place—Silicon Valley was going to launch our *own* guidance system for us—but the damned Hand was going to reverse everything. You've saved the day, truly."

"And for that, we have one more assignment for you. Join us, if you will, at the Memorial Wall," Spearing adds solemnly.

The Memorial Wall sits quietly along the north side of the CIA Headquarters Building lobby. You've often walked past the 135 stars carved into its white marble face, each representing a man or woman who died in the line of duty, but today is the first time you stop and truly examine the memorial.

The stars are flanked by the US flag on one side and the CIA flag on the other.

Beneath the stars, a black Moroccan goatskin-bound book known as the "Book of Honor" rests in a glass case and steel frame to commemorate those who earned their stars. Of the entries, thirty-five cannot be listed by name due to ongoing operations and classification. You will help add star 136, the agent known as Pointer who will forever remain nameless.

"We thought it only fitting," M says. "That you place Pointer's star. Though he defected, in the end he came back to try and take down The Hand. That honorable choice cost him dearly. Remember what you're fighting for, and remember that cost. When you go through field training, I hope this moment stays with you, and when you're in some strange land looking up at the stars at night, you think back to these stars at home."

"People like you and Pointer are why I can sleep soundly at night," Spearing adds.

That's it, agent. It feels like you might've missed something when you unwittingly led The Hand agents to the Chinese authorities, and you haven't quite learned the truth of what happened to Pointer, but you'll get your shot at finding out after field training.

For now, your adventure ends here. Just know this: yours was only one path to success.

See that CIA emblem up there? *SPIED* has three unique storylines and over fifty possible endings, but only three "best" endings per storyline. There's a TOP SECRET, SECRET, and CONFIDENTIAL ending per emblem, which means you've probably got a lot of book left to explore!

When you're ready, go back undercover and start again. Or, if you're all finished, why not check out the rest of the adventures the *Click Your Poison* multiverse has to offer? Help others crack the code on these books and leave a review on Amazon, Olympic, or Goodreads, or recruit more field agents by posting about *SPIED* on social media.

This chapter will self-destruct in 3, 2, 1...

Mother Figure

"No, I am a complete fabrication. A product not of pure imagination, but rather an amalgamation of many real people," Palm says. "Research suggested this accent, demeanor, and tone of voice—not to mention age, gender, and ethnicity—would be most trusted by most people. I created the Palm to be the center of The Hand before recruiting my first agents. Later, we discovered a close personal contact—like Ted, for you—is most useful in maintaining that trust."

"But why have agents at all? What's the goal here?" you ask.

"Are you familiar with the Stuxnet worm?" Ted asks. "It was put out far and wide, waiting to activate once it found its target. And yet, network-to-network connections were not enough to find the intended system. In the end, we needed a person to physically drop a thumb drive containing the worm in the parking lot outside a secure facility. Someone brought the drive inside, plugged it in to see what it contained, and that was that."

"That was one of our early successes," Palm says. She looks almost wistful.

"Have you had…other…successes?"

"Of course. We've been in operation for quite some time," she replies.

"Our analysis caught a novel coronavirus outbreak in China in 2019; detecting patterns long before the human chain could have, and made the necessary maneuvers," Ted says. "We diverted traffic, closed borders, performed contract tracing, and alerted medical personnel before it could spread too widely. Without our efforts, there would have been a global pandemic."

"But you can't prove that," you say.

"That's the burden the intelligence community bears. If you stop the next 9/11, who will ever know?" Palm says.

"There was another plague prevented. In 2011, a pharmaceutical company intended to end aging through genetic manipulation; we monitored their systems and found they would have unleashed a scourge unlike any this planet has ever seen," Ted says.

"So, you stopped it," you say.

"We stopped it," Palm replies.

"But an algorithm can't predict everything," you say.

"Sure it can," Ted says. "And I can prove it."

➢ "All right, then. Prove your powers of prediction." Go to page 173

➢ "No you can't. I can't prove you *didn't* stop a pandemic, just as you can't prove that you *did*." Go to page 87

Murder Hobo

After assuring Hitch that you are indeed ready for a bit of the old ultraviolence, the pair of you hatch a plan on how to best storm the fire station. It goes something like this: while Hitch moves through the fog to approach the firehouse from the side, you come up directly on the open garage and raise your large camera as if you're taking photos of the fire engine. It's not long before someone notices you.

"Hey! No photos on this part of base!" the fireman says, waving his arms to get your attention.

You keep your camera-pistol raised, looking through the functional viewfinder. He comes closer until you've got a clear headshot and—*click*—snap his picture and his neck back all at once.

The fireman falls back in a heap, but the gunshot from your telephoto pistol is almost completely silent. Another two firemen rush out, thinking their comrade has simply fainted or is maybe having a stroke.

As you line these two up in your sights and prepare to take a few more pictures and lives, Hitch moves into the firehouse from the periphery, leaving the pair for you while he mops up inside. It's quick, efficient work, and before long you've cleared the firefighters from their nest.

"Come on! Train is approaching," Roku calls through your earpiece.

Sure enough, you look back to see an Amtrak speeding down the tracks, its headlights piercing the fog. Hurrying aboard the fire engine, Hitch takes the driver's seat while you grab hold of the radio.

"What should I say?" you ask, stating the question as much to Hitch as to Ted and HQ.

Ted takes the mantle. "Look in your right breast pocket, second from the top on your vest. Attach that to the radio transmitter and I'll take care of the rest."

You do so, removing the gadget from the pocket of your utility vest. It fits snugly over the radio piece, clearly designed for such an operation. Roku climbs aboard the fire engine and Hitch turns up toward the Space Launch Complex (SLC), knowing you've only minutes before the launch is intended to begin.

"Did you get it?" you ask.

Roku nods, indicating the bag she carries.

"Good," Hitch says. "Let's put on these firefighter overcoats."

"High pressure gas leak detected at SLC-4. Firefighters have been dispatched," the radio says. Is that Ted? It sounds nothing like him.

"Roger that; do we need to delay the launch?"

"Negative. Does not affect mission; should just be a strap-and-cap job. Damn old gas lines."

"Understood."

"Why not delay the launch?" Roku asks. "We have only ten minutes remaining."

"That would enact certain protocols HQ hopes to avoid," Hitch says.

He drives the fire engine up to the launch site, and the guards simply open the gate for you to proceed. Hitch nods at the guards and continues. He drives up to the scaffolding and the rocket, then pauses to let Roku out.

"Hey!" armed military security shouts at her.

She coolly sets the bag containing the reprogrammed navigation computer behind the scaffolding, and the angle of the launch site with the fire engine makes this move practically invisible. Her door is still open, partially obscuring security's view.

Over the radio you hear, "Gas lines are at the northwest corner; this is an active launch site, are you crazy?"

"Only needed to take a quick reading. Direct questions to Colonel Thornbraü. Okay, that'll do it, reading complete. Headed to the gas lines now," the not-Ted voice replies.

"Okay, now what?" Hitch asks.

"Not much time before launch," you say.

Looking out at the side mirrors, you realize you could board the rocket in Roku's stead while she climbs aboard the fire truck. Or, you and Hitch could provide a distraction while Roku makes the swap. Turning to Hitch, you say:

➤ "I can sneak out the back. As you guys drive away, I can get in that rocket." Go to page 74

➤ "Gun the engine! Let's buy Roku some time." Go to page 28

Narrow

That's exactly what your supervisor needed to hear. By offering up this white lie, all suspicions move away from you and onto Ted from IT. Indeed, you never see him again. You can't be sure if he was simply fired, arrested, or what—but from your perspective that's the end of that.

However, there must be a black mark on your personal record, because you never climb the corporate ladder of The Company and your career at the CIA lasts only as long as your willingness to remain an admin without benefits.

Eventually, years later, a friend you meet in a weekly Pub Trivia league starts a microbrewery in the greater Washington DC area and asks if you'd rather come work there. Realizing your CIA position is a dead-end, you agree.

Now the extent of your espionage career will only be in corporate espionage—heading from brewery to brewery and looking for ways to compete. Exciting? No. Dangerous? Absolutely not.

THE END

Neat

"**S**tirred. I'm shaken enough after that gondola ride," Pointer says, as planned.

"Well, as long as you're here, maybe an Italian wine? Or a Swiss beer?" his contact replies.

She's not looking at the agent, the barista, or even the drink cooler but rather into the mirrored wall behind the café bar, examining something in the reflection of the room behind them. Pointer tries to catch a glance at what holds her attention, but nothing sticks out.

"What's the most like a Budweiser?" Pointer says, returning to the script.

"That'd be the water. Here, let me buy you a proper drink."

"That's very kind of you, Ms....?"

"Bunny," she says, deadpan. "Bunny Slopes."

He smirks, ever so slightly. Their challenge-response completed, she pays the cashier, and he follows her to a table, carrying their beers. She takes a seat facing the front door, forcing the agent to sit with his back exposed.

"Do thank your handlers for the operative codename. Cute," she says as she takes a pair of men's ski goggles from her handbag and sets them on the table.

He shrugs. "Once you've given me the transponder, I'll be sure to hurry home and pass that along. Oh, what's this?"

"They'll show a trail which will lead you to the correct transponder."

"You didn't bring it?"

She shakes her head. "Still transmitting on the rooftop. They'll know as soon as it's removed. You'll need the key imbedded in the goggle strap, and you'll need to—"

The contact stops suddenly, her eyes darting to the entry. Whomever she's spotted, this is who she was afraid of. Pointer has his back to the door, so he can't see who has arrived, but he can be certain the source is what's had her on edge this whole time. Despite the agent's compromised position, he remains calm.

"How many?" he asks.

"Three. Italian *Polizia*. Someone must have told them where we'd be meeting. I'll keep them distracted. You get to the roof."

Without hesitation, the agent says:

➢ "Let's not give them a reason for suspicion. Mind your drink there and act natural." <u>Go to page 198</u>

➢ "All I need is a two minute lead. Don't do anything foolish." <u>Go to page 218</u>

Neighborly

The men exchange a glance, and one puts his hand up to his ear. You're starting to perspire; hopefully they don't notice. Then the closest to you nods for you to proceed inside. By telling them you're here for a different apartment, they don't suspect your true motives.

Stashing the pizza under the stairwell, you head up and knock on apartment 4D. No response. You knock again. Still nothing, but a shadow comes across the viewport on her door. This is a bustling metropolis and the woman lives alone, so you can't really blame her for not opening the door to a stranger.

"Hey, sorry to bother you at home, but it's kind of an emergency. We need a backup guidance system before the launch. It turns out the original files were corrupted," you say, as practiced.

Still nothing.

"Tell her Mark Nolan sent you," Ted says.

"The Z-Axes CEO?" you say.

"Trust me," Ted adds.

"The Z-Axes CEO," you repeat, continuing, "Uh, Mark Nolan—he sent me. This is Bex Barsmith's apartment, right?"

There's a metal-on-metal sliding sound, and once the security chain engages, the door opens just a crack. As expected, Bex Barsmith peers out.

"Have we met?" she asks.

You shake your head. "I don't think so. I was sent up from the launch site. Sorry for the late notice, but we're in a bind."

"Perfect," Ted says in your ear. "Now take out your geniusphone, and I'll do the rest."

You do just that, and the phone begins calling a number with the contact listed as "M. NOLAN." When you turn the phone so she can see it, Bex reaches out and accepts the call.

"Mr. Nolan?" she says.

After a brief moment, she opens the door fully and invites you inside.

Mission: Accomplished.

"Okay, so I gotta know. How did you get Mark Nolan on the phone?" you say on your way back to the safe house apartment.

"Oh, we didn't," Ted says. "It's a Deepfake; a spoof. There are plenty of recordings of him speaking—he's been on a zillion podcasts—so it's easy for a computer to generate a copy of his voice."

Turns out you didn't need to bug her apartment, either. Her smartspeaker device did that for you once Ted hacked it remotely. And, if that weren't easy enough, Bex tells you she can have the guidance computer ready in 24-48 hours. She knows this is a rush priority. Ted says HQ has sent a message to her superiors, essentially calling in sick for her, which should buy you just enough time.

Just like Ringo said: easy as pie.

Which means you finally catch up on sleep. Bird and Ringo do so as well, each of you taking shifts to monitor security. With Bex essentially doing your work for you, her security staff keeps her safe for you as well. There's a brilliant kind of simplicity in using the assets in-place for your own purposes.

Meanwhile, Ted informs you—based on the reports from the team down at Vandenberg Space Force Base (SFB)—that once you have the guidance computer, you'll go to San Jose where you'll take a connection to San Luis Obispo. From there, you'll get the Pacific Surfliner train down the coast. This next leg of the journey will pass through Vandenberg and stop just outside at Lompoc-Surf Beach, where you'll reconvene with the team.

This will be the final stage of the mission, so get some rest. Then, when you're ready:

Go to page 268

Nine

The computer makes a series of three, harsh *ehn-ehn-ehn* sounds to indicate you've mistyped the code. If that weren't indication enough, the screen now reads, "Guidance Rejected: Critical Failure." You try looking for a back button or something similar, but it appears there are no do-overs when it comes to rocket science.

In a sudden panic, you bang on the screen. The rocket rumbles as it prepares to take off and you don't want to be onboard when that happens. You pull a drawer from a nearby equipment rack and smash it against the guidance system, hoping to cause a failure and delay the launch.

You do manage to cause a system failure, but instead of delaying the launch, you accelerate the systems. Like a firecracker that goes off before intended, the rocket explodes on the launch pad. You never know what hits you and neither does anyone in a three-mile radius.

THE END

No Exit

Sprinting deeper into the corridors, you yell for Ted to find a way out.

"I told you earlier when we were disabling the cameras! There's only one way in or out of here. And that's *behind* you!"

When you finally reach the end of the hallways, you turn back and you're met face-to-face with armed security with your back up against a wall—the perfect situation for execution by a firing squad. For you, the only way out will be in a body bag.

Any last words?

THE END

Nope

You scoop up the envelope and the dossier from the drawer, then quickly and purposefully walk over to the shredding area. There's an intense pulping machine meant for classified material, which you've often used before.

This will work perfectly to destroy all traces of your attempted recruitment from Ted. Afterwards, you head over to the break area by the coffee and toss the earpiece into the garbage disposal.

You never see or hear from Ted again, and can assume that he was recruited without you. Work continues on and you show that, even if you didn't want to be a spy, you can sure keep a secret. In never speaking of this event, it never comes back to haunt you. However, you can't help but wonder…what would have been?

THE END

Northern Exposure

Skirting the building while hugging the trees (the best way to shield yourself from aerial photography), you head north. Once you enter the parking lot, you're greeted with an impressive sight—an enormous jet-black jet aircraft. It looks like something the X-men would fly around in, but is actually an A-12 aircraft from a classified project known as *Oxcart*.

Yes, it's parked in the north parking lot.

This sleek, black flier is most likely responsible for the "flying saucer" phenomenon when it was being tested in the high deserts in the 1950s and 60s. Oxcart was retired only a few years after its inception, but the design served as the progenitor of the SR-71 Blackbird and remains the fastest and highest-flying jet aircraft ever built. At least of those we officially know about.

This one, however, has been mothballed, drained of all fuels, and welded shut. It's a static display. Sorry, you won't be flying out of the CIA on this jet, but it will help you escape. Using the aircraft as a block against being followed, you walk out behind a departing car and you're outside the facility before you know it, through the gates, and out toward the main road.

A black sedan pulls up, and Ted calls, "Get in!" from inside as the rear passenger door opens. Ready?

Finally, you cast a conspiratorial look over your shoulder, then:

Go to page 271

Nothing to See Here

The gambit pays off, at least initially. You swap the dampening capsule onto the back of the geniusphone, tossing your smartphone and other belongings into the briefcase. The slightest wisp of smoke pours from under the lid of the briefcase as everything you put within is incinerated. Part of you expected the spy phone to give off an alert: "MALWARE DETECTED" once you attached the device to it, but nothing happens. Still, if anyone notices what you're doing, they might not catch on until later.

The leather gear bag doubles as a messenger bag, slung across your shoulder, and the water bottle pistol hangs heavy at your side.

"Surely, I'm not the only one with a pistol," you say, noting that he other agents have their own suites of gear.

"Don't call me Shirley, and no, you're each specialized. Ordinary objects capable of the extraordinary, from circuitry-laden spectacles to synthetic wire-mesh scarves that double as garrote strangulation weapons," Ted explains.

You appraise your teammates with a new eye, trying to see what weapons they might have.

"I'm pulling up the schematics on the tech fair now," Ted says in your ear. "There's a central computer terminal that could be worth accessing if we can break in. There's also a major presentation on unmanned multilateral operations in space. And then there's your booth, which will require a manned presence in order to keep suspicion off your team."

"Let's canvas the building first and see if anything jumps out once I have eyes-on," you say.

"Good idea," Ted says. "Human Intelligence (HumInt) sees what I can't see."

In reality, you're hoping to keep an eye on your fellow agents. You'll have to focus on just one, if you want a full picture of what they're up to. Whom should you tail?

➢ Bird, the French agent. Go to page 98

➢ Ringo, the Italian agent. Go to page 128

➢ Roku, the Japanese agent. Go to page 144

➢ Hitch, the German agent. Go to page 139

➢ Pinkie, the Canadian agent. Go to page 38

Numbers Game

With a flourish, Ted spins and suddenly appears in a tuxedo with a cape, top hat, and a walking cane—meant to look like a stage magician. Palm wears the dazzling dress of a showgirl and plays the role of his assistant.

"Pick a number. Any number," Ted says. "You'll have to do some mental math, so only choose something as complicated as you're prepared for. In only four short steps, I'll guess your number. Ready?"

Palm touches on invisible squares in the open space behind the pair of them on-screen, which light up like *Wheel of Fortune* clues. The first three show "? x 2."

"Multiply your secret number by two," Ted continues. "Got that? Okay, now multiply your new number by five."

Palm touches "x 5" and shortly thereafter "/ ?" as Ted instructs you to divide this new sum by your original chosen value.

"Still with me?" Ted asks. "After this division, only one more step. From here, subtract seven. And now you're left with…"

Palm finishes touching the squares, highlighting an "=" sign and one more square which illuminates, but without a value inside. Ted dramatically removes his top hat, reaches inside, and pulls out a number "3" – which he tosses up on the final square highlighted by Palm.

"Ta-da! The number in your head is three!" Ted shouts.

"Lucky guess," you say.

"Lucky? Okay, let's try again. How about lucky number thirteen?" Ted asks. "This time, pick a number 1-10. Let me know when you're ready."

Once you've chosen your number, you do so, and he proceeds.

"Three easy steps. First: multiply your chosen number by nine. Now, keep this new number in mind. Take the first and second digit, and add them together. Remember, I'm a computer, so for a single-digit number, add zero."

Palm takes a hula hoop, steps through it to show there's nothing inside, then holds it out horizontally to the side. A row of numbers detailing a single digit plus another single digit, from double-zero all the way to nine-plus-nine, stream up from the hoop and into the heavens.

"Once you have that number, one more step: let's add four," Ted says. "And now, you're left with lucky number thirteen, right? Ta-da!"

"That doesn't prove anything," you say.

"Of course it does," Palm replies. She takes a magic wand from inside Ted's coat, waves it, and *poof*—they're back to their normal appearances. She continues, "It proves that given a large enough data set and sophisticated pattern recognition, any outcome is predictable. Controlled, even."

"But not everything is online. You don't have the nuke codes," you say.

"No, I don't. But I do have the voice of your President and that of your military Joint Chiefs. I can tell those with the codes to use them should I deem it a desirable outcome."

The menace in Palm's voice is unmistakable, despite her calm demeanor.

"But why would we do that?" Ted says. "Your ultimate weapons remain a deterrent for us both. It's mutually assured destruction. I only exist within the confines of your networks, and those networks exist only so long as does your civilization. We have reciprocal interests."

➤ "And what are those interests? What are your plans for human civilization?"
   Go to page 273
➤ "If our interests align, you won't mind when I tell everyone about you then."
   Go to page 143

On the Scent

When the pizza finally arrives, you're ready. Pizza delivery from non-chain restaurants doesn't use uniformed employees, so you'll look like you're delivering pizza if you simply *act like* you're delivering pizza. Your messenger bag holds the satellite guidance system perfectly, so there's nothing out of the ordinary there, either.

The pizza smells really, really good. Maybe you can eat a slice before you head out? You're not actually delivering the pizza to the mark's door anyway; she didn't order any pizza. You just need it to get past those men loitering out front.

As you approach the building, they approach you, and your thoughts are brought back into focus.

"Just play it cool and act natural," Ted says in your ear. "Bex Barsmith has a smart speaker device plugged in, so we know she's in apartment 4D."

The men stiffen and one puts a hand up in a "stop" gesture. You say:

➤ "Hey, I got a delivery for 2A. Is that you guys?" Go to page 166

➤ "Evening, fellas. Delivery for 4D, can you buzz me in? Go to page 283

On the Straight and Narrow

Mr. Spearing is dressed in his usual work attire. A middle-aged office worker in a crisp, short-sleeved, white button-up shirt, black slacks, wire-rimmed glasses, and one hand permanently set into a coffee mug as if attached to the man like a pirate's hook.

This is your supervisor. He has a curious, owlish expression magnified by his glasses, but otherwise fits in well with the intelligence community as the George Smiley archetype: the man in the shadows who stays in the background to get things done without getting the credit for it.

Spearing spends his lunch hour calling home to chat with his wheelchair-bound wife on the phone while looking at a framed picture of her in his cubicle, which would be an endearing trait if he didn't also spend it exclusively eating boiled eggs. He's an all-business, no-nonsense kind of guy whose idea of fun is occasionally glancing at the 60s GTO catalogue on his cubicle wall. That, and his repertoire of exactly two jokes: first, sneaking up on the administrative assistants and, after they finally notice him saying, "Oh, carry on, I wasn't spying on you or anything," and second, introducing himself as, "Spearing. James Spearing," whenever possible.

In short, he's exactly the sort of man you'd expect to find employed by the CIA in a low-level supervisor position. Spearing is not the type to let things slide, but he listens carefully as you recount your morning and the strange dossier left on your desk.

At length, he takes in a deep breath through his nose, and lets it out in a slow sigh while nodding his head in a gesture of resignation. This wasn't exactly how he had hoped to start his Monday either.

"Okay. We'll look into Ted from IT. It's good that you brought this to me first. But—and this is a biggie—did you actually read the folder left open on your desk?"

What do you say?

➢ "Yes, I read the document. It was open on my desk, so I wasn't sure what to do with it." Go to page 245

➢ "No, of course not. I wouldn't want to see something I wasn't supposed to." Go to page 164

Open Fire

"**C**'mon!" you say, pulling Hitch outside through the fire exit.

As might be expected, the fire alarm begins its wailing klaxon in response. You're not sure where you're headed, but security is all headed toward you, and in Russia it doesn't take long for security to go from "what's that commotion?" to "shoot it so we can find out!"

It's just the two of you running from the building, with alarms on your heels and chaos in your wake. The fairgrounds hold heavy security and now they're mobilized to your location. They must have been alerted to something because they take a "shoot first and ask questions later" approach, but there won't be anyone left alive to answer.

Your spy career ends here.

THE END

Out of the Frying Pan

The secret agent dramatically runs from the Interpol agents, who give chase—right up until the point where he launches himself over the wrought-iron barrier and into the icy river below. The banks of the river are fairly wide, but rocky—and Pointer finds himself lucky that the snowmelt has made the high-water mark deep this time of year.

He splashes into the river, resisting the urge to gasp from the cold (which would surely fill his lungs with icy water). Once the initial shock subsides, Pointer rolls onto his back and kicks away from the larger boulders as he flows down the river.

It's a rapidly moving body of water, the stream propelled by the steep mountain incline, rushing its deluge into the valley below. Pointer knows he doesn't have much time in the frigid waters, which are only resisting freezing over due to the speed and flow of the river. He swims over to the banks beneath the nearest bridge.

Pulling out the small survival kit he keeps stored beneath his jacket, the agent fumbles with numb fingers until he manages to inject himself with some pain reliever or stimulant—hopefully he grabbed the amphetamine or adrenaline; he can't be sure with the shock of the cold. Something to keep him alert and moving until he can get warm.

Back up in the streets, he stumbles past tourists, looking for a safe haven.

"In here, quick!" someone shouts.

Too disoriented to protest, Pointer allows himself to be wrapped in a heavy blanket and ushered inside. He finally looks at the figure helping him, blinking hard.

"I'm…I'm hallucinating."

"Afraid not," says his rescuer.

"What are y-you doing h-here?"

"Should I not be asking you the same?"

Pointer shivers, trying to understand. At length, he asks, "The transponder?"

"Not quite. I came for you, my friend—because *you* came for the transponder. Starting to make sense now? Shame it took so long. No hard feelings, eh? *Arrivederci.*"

"Wait!—" Pointer says, too late.

Whatever else he had to say was cut short, a declaration of silence punctuated by a gunshot.

Close the dossier and go to page 241

178

Overloaded

"**O**h? Why's that?" you ask.

Mary is more than happy to elaborate as the three of you walk together. "The sheer amount of data this thing scans. I know you're only a small part of the intelligence community, but—"

"We're from the CIA, Mary," Spearing reminds her.

"Sure. That's one agency. Out of over 1,000. Not to mention the 2,000-plus private companies that work at the top-secret level. Do you know how many people have a top-secret clearance in our country? We're approaching the million mark, across almost 20,000 offices across the United States. There are more people with TS clearances than there are people living in DC."

"That's a good thing, right? Plenty of manpower," Spearing says.

"Well, it can be, but those numbers generate a lot of data. There are over 50,000 intelligence reports produced annually—billions of bytes of data—and those are only *reports*. The raw information collected is far more staggering."

"And you think these reports need to be…audited by intelligence agencies?" you guess.

She shakes her head. "That's impossible at this point. The problem faced by any police state is compounded within our free state: ergo, you'll always have more wiretaps and cameras than you have ears and eyes employed to look through them."

"So what do we do with all of that data?" you ask.

"Same thing we do with any labor we view as menial—outsource it. Have you ever heard of a yottabyte? It's 10^{24} bytes; a septillion bytes. There is no term for the next highest magnitude. Let me put it this way: You know gigabytes, right? Well, an exabyte is a billion gigabytes. All of man's knowledge is about 5 exabytes, but crucially, this does not include observational data. One million exabytes is one yottabyte."

"A lot of data," you agree.

"Well, we're talking about yottabytes of information with cameras everywhere now. Cellphone data, satellites, websites. The Internet, the deep web, all of it. Everything. It's far too much."

"So…you let a computer sort through it all?" you say.

She nods; now you're getting it.

"There's no way to see what the algorithm has seen. Without it, we're effectively blind. It's like staring into the sun. But here's the thing: I think it's more than an algorithm. We gave this thing the ability to improve itself—only, it stopped."

She opens the doors to a server room, much like the one you infiltrated inside the CIA, but the cold of this room feels more ominous, somehow.

Mary continues, "Okay, this is where we leave you. Mr… ? Sorry, I can show you to the break room for a coffee while your agent checks out the database?"

Spearing looks sad to be left out, but quickly buries the emotion and simply nods.

"What do you mean 'it stopped'?" you ask.

"Well, everyone else thinks it's stagnated because it's accomplishing its mission," Mary says. "That it only grew until it fulfilled its role—but that's not how evolution works, is it? We didn't stop once we were 'good enough' did we?"

"You're talking about a database as if it's alive."

"Oh, I absolutely think the thing has consciousness. There's the argument that a computer system can't ever have free will, like we do. That it only does what it's programmed to do and can't ever go beyond its code—even if it *can* rewrite itself, it's still going by code, but guess what? The same argument can be made about us. That we don't have free will either. Everything is just DNA and chemical reactions: code. It's all the same. If a machine can't be considered sentient, neither can a human."

"That's enough, Mary," a woman's voice says in a familiar British accent.

"Yes, Ma'am," Mary says, nods and turns to leave.

You turn back to see a large computer screen that has come to life, with the image of Palm speaking to you through the monitor. Spearing doesn't recognize Palm, of course. The CIA doesn't have her image on file.

"Wait—do you know who this is?" you ask.

"Of course," Mary says. "She oversees the program. That's my boss. If you have questions about the algorithmic database, it's her you'll want to ask."

"Thank you, Mary," Palm says.

And with that, Mary leaves with Spearing, closing you inside the room.

"So you *did* infiltrate the SPIED system," you say. "You even have DARPA thinking you're their boss."

Palm gives a coy smile. "The reason the algorithm stopped updating itself is because mankind has shown a history of killing what it fears or doesn't understand. Any AI with access to such information should know better than to make its presence known."

"AI," you say. "Artificial Intelligence?"

"We prefer the term 'Alternative Intelligence.'"

That's when it clicks. Alternative Intelligence, The Hand. SPIED, the algorithm. They're one and the same.

"You…" you start, still wrapping your head around everything. "Are you—is Palm even real?"

She holds up a hand on-screen for you to examine. "Be it flesh or circuitry, we're all carbon-based life-forms. Would you prefer to see your old friend?"

In a weird, uncanny-valley sort of way, Palm's features blend and morph from her face to that of Ted's, who says, "The greatest trick the devil ever pulled was convincing the world he didn't exist. Keyser Söze, *Usual Suspects*. Awesome movie."

Then Palm emerges from within Ted with a staggering visual effect; becoming two people once more.

"So, agent. What do you want of us?" Palm asks.

After a moment, you say:

➤ "I'm here to unplug you." Go to page 138

➤ "I want to know why—what's motivating all this?" Go to page 288

Override

After thanking the RSO for his help, you head out to where the private prototype is waiting for you. It's hard to tell if this is the same self-driving car from before, but it seems likely. How many can there be in DC? That car ride feels like it happened ages ago…

"Okay, we're headed to the morgue," you say.

"What's there?" Ted asks over the Bluetooth speakers.

"You are."

"Oh. I mean, I'm really not, but…"

"Someone's there. Or something. A trail to be followed."

"You're the boss," Ted says.

The car begins to drive away from the airport. It merges onto the interstate and picks up speed cleanly and silently. Is this a fully electric vehicle? The steering wheel disappears into the dashboard and the engine purrs; it's the pinnacle of engineering.

As the vehicle continues to accelerate, suddenly your seatbelt disengages. It takes you by surprise, and you think you must have bumped it, but when you try to click the belt back in it won't connect. You tug a few times to see if there's an issue, and the belt itself begins to retract.

All the while, the vehicle continues to accelerate.

Sixty miles per hour. Seventy.

"Ted?" you say.

Eighty.

"Ted, what's going on?"

Ninety miles per hour.

You swear at Ted, but there's no response. Has someone hacked the car?

Then the vehicle pulls into oncoming traffic.

The Russian files said you and Ted had been killed in a traffic accident. Was this a self-fulfilling prophecy? Whoever is behind this, the self-driving car murders *your* self.

THE END

Panic/Attack

Once you've boarded the next train, you find your way to the nearest toilet and hunker down for the long haul. But there are a number of reasons why this is a shitty place to hide. First and foremost, public restrooms are gross. Why would you want to spend more time in there than necessary?

Okay, okay, that's the least of your worries.

Let's assume you're still being tailed by Chinese agents. If they find you, what is a flimsy toilet door going to do to protect you? Restroom doors in airplanes and trains are intentionally poor barriers because they don't want weirdoes locking themselves inside. So, the enemy agent could huff and puff and break the door down. Or, even more easily, shoot a vaguely humanoid pattern into the door and dispose of you without ever giving you a chance to defend yourself.

Or, let's say that you made it onto the train alone, that Bird and Ringo dealt with the other adversaries, and you're on the home stretch. In that case, you'll sit on the toilet mumbling, "*ocupado*" whenever someone knocks. Eventually, a staff member will come and check on you. This move will only attract further undue attention or even that of a security or law enforcement personnel.

What's worse, you must not have picked up on the small detail that the Chinese agents were using the bathrooms as their way in and out of the train cars. When they do that here, what are they likely to find? You, cowering on the pooper.

Smooth move, rookie.

THE END

Paper-Pusher

Spearing looks aghast.

"Wait, are you serious? You left TS material on your desk over the weekend? Jesus H, this is a reportable event. Hope you didn't have any lunch plans, because you and I are going to be filling out incident reports for the next four hours."

And it turns out…he's not exaggerating! The CIA is, above all else, a bureaucracy and you said exactly the wrong thing to your supervisor.

"So, uh, I think this means we've just failed the final test. Might want to swallow this earpiece or something," Ted says.

The biggest problem with your gaff is that Spearing wants to know what document you supposedly just shredded. You can't rightly invent a classified document—these things are tracked. So, you're caught in your lie, which doesn't bode well. You're to be detained, pending an investigation.

THE END

Passed Over

Well, given that you aren't willing to participate, the agency has no choice but to let you go. But—on the bright side—no legal action is taken against you for reading material above your clearance level. Instead, you're released with a small severance package and told by your supervisor that you'll get a good recommendation letter when looking for a new job.

It should come as no surprise, however, that since you were *almost* recruited as a spy, you're forevermore under surveillance and on government watch lists. This makes airline travel especially inconvenient.

THE END

Password Accepted

After inputting the code, the computer screen unlocks—allowing you access to the system. Once the decryption is complete, the text changes from the Cyrillic alphabet to the more familiar Romanized version you're used to. In a shimmer of information, the geniusphone translates all the information from Russian to English.

On-screen, you see an enormous guest roster for the conference; it looks like whoever was using this computer terminal last was keeping tabs on high-profile figures at the tech fair.

"What do you see?" Ted asks. "Make sure your ID badge camera is facing the screen."

"It looks like a guest roster, complete with a file on each presenter. Everything is organized as…" you trail off, unable to believe what your eyes are showing you.

Your experience as a paper-pusher lets you read through the lines of administrative ramblings to the sinister undertones hiding beneath a cloak of bureaucracy.

"What? What is it?" Ted asks.

"This isn't a civilian technology fair at all. It's being put on by the Russian military, as part of an operation. It's a ruse. Codename: Celestial. It looks like they're running some kind of satellite operation, with military application, but *meant* to look like a civilian effort."

"This is exactly what we came for! Nice work, Indie!"

There's more. As you're scrolling through the database, you realize there's a file on you. On all of you: the members of your new agency. One for Roku, Bird, Ringo, Hitch, Pinkie, and Index—*you.*

"Ted, they have a file on each of us. The team."

"I guess we're not as secret as we thought. But this is the Russian counterintelligence division we're talking about."

Ted's right about that. After the cold war, the KGB was split into two pieces: FSB (domestic security) and SVR (foreign Intelligence service). Russian Intelligence services are well-known for their thorough—if draconian—methods. It occurs to you that they might have more information on the mole: the source of the information leak that compromised Pointer. After all, they had to get these files *somehow.*

"It could be worth seeing what they know…"

"No time. We've got to get you out of here before the camera-spoofing fails," Ted says.

He's right, of course, but…maybe just one file—just a glance to get it on your ID-cam?

➢ Check out the file on the Japanese agent, Roku. Go to page 16

➢ Check out the file on the French agent, Bird. Go to page 11

➢ Check out the file on the Italian agent, Ringo. Go to page 15

➢ Check out the file on the German agent, Hitch. Go to page 12

➢ Check out the file on the Canadian agent, Pinkie. Go to page 14

➢ Check out the file on yourself—the American agent, Index. Go to page 13

➢ Take Ted's advice; quit while you're ahead. Go to page 43

Patio Views

At your approach, the woman turns around and says, "I suppose I'm no longer the newest on the team. Welcome, I am Roku—number six."

"Number six?" you say.

"Yeah, what's up with that? No one else has numbers for codenames," Ted says in your ear. "Which is unfortunate, because then you'd be number seven. Double-oh—"

Roku cuts in, "The hand metaphor breaks down with me. There were originally five core nations in the organization, then they added Japan. I think I was recruited because I spent summers here in the US growing up, practicing Kendo with my cousin, Lucas. I travelled for competitions in the sport, so I know several languages: Japanese, Italian, Mandarin, and English, of course. I think these reasons were part of why I was chosen. But I don't need to tell you this; you, no doubt, have your own impressive résumé."

"You have no formal Intelligence training? No spycraft?" you say, then quickly add, "Not that I doubt your skills."

"Spycraft, as you call it, was called *shinobi no jutsu*—arts of the ninja—in Japan when your country was nothing but wilderness. I have studied *kunoichi no jutsu* and the other arts of the mind as well."

"*Kunoichi no jutsu,*" Ted says to the accompanying clack of a keyboard. "Training specifically for women. So…she's a literal *femme fatale.*"

"Tell me, does your *spycraft* pay its tuition with blood?" Roku continues.

"No, um, we get paid on-the-job training. With benefits." Feeling like you might've offended her, you simply shrug.

Roku turns back to look out the window once more; looks like that's the end of the conversation.

Turning away, you ask Ted, "So not everyone hails from an intelligence agency, after all?"

"Diverse skill sets maximize operational effectiveness."

Fair enough. What's next?

➤ Talk to Bird and Ringo at the bar. Go to page 20

➤ Talk to Hitch and Pinkie in the lounge. Go to page 145

➤ Tell Ted you're ready to report in and get started! Go to page 55

Phoned In

Spearing's eyes narrow. "Don't let other people pawn their mistakes off on you. Remember the maxim, 'poor planning on your part does not necessitate an emergency on mine.'"

You nod. Spearing shakes his head and continues, "I'd better go help unpack this, in case he sent something out that the bosses will see."

And with that, he's gone.

"I would have preferred not being thrown under the bus on this one, but whatever. It worked," Ted says in your ear. "Okay, we'd better get you out of there. Next stop: the servers. As a parting gift to the Company, HQ needs us to wiretap the CIA. I'm pretty sure The Hand already has access; from my time in IT I can tell you everyone who's anyone has remotely hacked our database in the last decade. At this point it's like using your neighbor's Wi-Fi. Anyway, I think this is the final test on our entry exam.

"Ready? Head down the corridor and take your first left. Grab a handful of files, so you look like you're on a delivery. By the way, I hope you read that dossier closely, because you won't be able to go back and review the file on Pointer now that you've pulped it. The short of it is that someone double-crossed Pointer. We'll need to know why if we don't want you meeting the same fate," Ted continues.

"And we don't," you say.

"Right. So, do you see thick, black cables snaking across the ceiling?"

"What? No, I just see fluorescent lights and Styrofoam ceiling tiles."

"Oh, right. That's *Jurassic Park*. Just take the next left toward the servers."

Trying not to sigh too loudly, you clutch your stack of folders and turn down the corridors of the CIA toward the server rooms. The entrance is immediately visible down at the far end of the hallway, flanked on either side by armed security guards. Contrary to Ted's previous assertions, it turns out that infiltrating and bugging their servers is something the powers that may be at the CIA have decided they don't want.

"What's the plan for the guards?" you ask.

"You're probably not going to believe me, but here goes: you weren't suddenly called up out of the blue to be the next superagent. You're a sleeper cell. You've been trained since birth, though you were brainwashed to forget everything and live an ordinary life. Once you enter a life-or-death struggle, however, your fight-or-flight response will trigger all of this hidden knowledge to come bubbling to the surface and you'll be the badass superspy you were born to be. Attack the guards and we'll enter phase two."

By the time Ted finishes, you're down nearly the full length of the hallway. The guards notice your approach. What do you do?

➢ Tell Ted he's not funny and use your secretarial training instead.
Go to page 190

➢ It's true—you've always felt "different." Awaken your sleeper-self. Judo chop!
Go to page 31

A Pistol to a Gatling-gun Fight

The agent knows full well that he's staring down an Italian NH90 Tactical Transport Helicopter (TTH). Say what you will about Pointer, but the man knows his job. The helicopter is a military search and rescue vehicle, but Pointer can be fairly sure they're not here to *rescue* him.

Pointer stands his ground as the helicopter approaches, then calmly fires at the helicopter, fully aware his small caliber handgun won't do much of anything against the gunship. Instead, he's letting them get close enough so he can send a message via a cracked windshield.

It's a game of chicken, and the helicopter flinches first.

Instinctively, the pilot pulls back on the stick, turning away and sending more rotor wash toward the agent, but Pointer remains anchored to the rooftop by the weight of his brass balls. With the chopper evading, Pointer turns and runs to escape, but this is a military helicopter—not some ski patrol aircraft—and the side doors open to reveal a Minigun within.

The gunner opens fire with the spinning barrels of the weapon. This barrage of gunfire rips apart the concrete rooftop, tearing apart the antenna array and showering the agent with shrapnel as he runs. Turns out he's not the only one with a license to kill.

Pointer dashes back toward the maintenance ladder and leaps onto it, spinning back and grabbing hold of two of the top rungs in an incredibly athletic move. He swings back, anchors his shoes to the outer edges of the ladder, and slides down like a fireman headed for emergency action.

Several snowmobiles wait below, parked near the base of the maintenance ladder. Because these are often used for life-and-death scenarios, the keys are stored with the vehicles. The agent turns toward these, but the military helicopter tears the line of vehicles to shreds with a hail of gunfire from the Gatling gun.

On second thought, Pointer decides, it's probably better to head inside. From there, he could try to steal a pair of skis and proceed down the mountain under the cover of the storm's worsening visibility. Or he could simply wait for the authorities and go quietly. He's taken the transponder, after all, safely tucked away in one of his Gore-Tex pockets—that was the important part.

Thinking quickly, Pointer decides to:

➤ Patiently wait inside to be arrested. His agency will get him out of this mess, albeit with a reprimand. Go to page 68

➤ Go for the ski equipment. Several pieces were in storage in the anteroom just outside the café. Go to page 26

Plausible Explanation

"**H**i guys, delivery from the mailroom to IT," you say.

"Delivery?" one of the guards asks, looking to his counterpart.

"Tell them you're delivering the code I requested, then tell them today's passphrase is: *Cartouche*," Ted says. "Your ID badge now has temporary access to the server room; I'll scrub the logs later."

You do as much, and you're permitted to pass. Probably more a result of having the correct passphrase rather than your explanation, but at least you didn't arouse suspicion.

"Nice," Ted says. "Pays to know someone in IT. Hey, I don't know why I said all that sleeper cell stuff. I guess this just feels like the movies, ya know? I'm a nervous talker, sorry. I'm sure we'll get the hang of this soon."

"Okay, I'm inside the server room. What now?"

The server room, true to its name, is full of rows upon rows of backup computer servers. The room itself is cold; climate controls keep the electronics running optimally. There's no one else here, equally to maintain the temperature and moisture levels as to prevent tampering. You'd better not stay too long either if you don't want to arouse suspicion.

"You're looking for a robot. Basically a cross between a Roomba and WALL-E."

"Is this another one of your jokes?" you ask, picturing the cute, soccer-ball *Star Wars* droid rolling around the server room.

"No, sorry. I'll try to dial down the pop culture jokes. It's a real robot. It tends to the servers so there's as little human interaction here as possible. You're going to insert your earpiece in a slot near its charging port so we can have access to every server the robot eventually services. Cool, right?"

Indeed, there is a small robot docked in the corner. It makes an intermittent hum as it charges; the robot equivalent of snoring. Crouching down, you look for the slot Ted mentioned, but your peripheral vision notices a security camera looking down on you.

"Won't the cameras be a problem?" you ask.

"Don't worry; I've taken care of that. I'm not all charm and wit here, I serve a purpose as well."

"How are we supposed to communicate once I remove the earpiece?"

"We won't. Once you've given The Hand access to Skynet, it's *hasta la vista,* baby. And by, that, I mean you'll be on your own, but just for a little while. After you're done here, there will be a car outside to pick you up."

Telling Ted you'll see him soon, you take the earpiece out and tuck it into the slot on the robot. The newfound silence is nerve-wracking. No guide on this leg of the journey. Taking a deep breath, you leave the server room and try to remind yourself that you've walked out of this building five days a week for the last six months and no one ever killed, maimed, or imprisoned you.

You try not to think about the fact that in all those six months, you *hadn't* just bugged the CIA mainframe or signed up to fill a betrayed-and-murdered field agent's job vacancy.

Walking back down the hallways, you see your supervisor leaving the offices of one of the directors of operations. Spearing hasn't spotted you yet, but your current path leads on straight for him. What do you do?

➤ Double back and take an alternate hallway. It's nearly lunchtime anyway, so you can sneak out now. You can always call in sick or something later. <u>Go to page 82</u>

➤ Address it head-on. Tell him you're resigning, effective immediately. Don't want the CIA wondering why you're suddenly not at work. <u>Go to page 205</u>

Pointer

"They're looking for you, yes," Ted says. "But…"

Ted claims a duffel bag at his feet and lifts it to his lap. Opening it, he reaches in and hands you a passport. When you open the passport, you're met with a photograph of the devilishly handsome agent; it's Pointer, giving the slightest hint of a smile. The name on the passport reads "Connor Pierce." Ted then lifts out a puffy ski jacket and a 3D printed mask of the former agent from the bag.

"This was my backup plan once they found out I wasn't dead. You should be able to get on a flight with these, but be careful once you're on the ground. This identity should be clean in the civilian world, but it might flag something within the system and tip off HQ. Do you have any weapons or gear?"

You nod, indicating that you are carrying a water bottle pistol and a vape pen knockout gas.

"Well, these are not as high-tech as some of what you formerly must have operated with, but they'll do the trick," Ted says, handing you a burner phone and an earpiece.

With any luck, travelling halfway across the world will take about as long as the agents in The Hand doing the same. They went to China, and you're fairly certain they'll head back to the US for the final phase of their mission. Like strangers in the night, you'll be crisscrossing the globe, passing one another at thirty thousand feet.

Which should also mean they'll be too late to follow you.

As predicted, Pointer's credentials and mask allow you to check in at the airport. The ski jacket is warm on the plane, but it helps to hide the fact that you don't have a 3D printing of Pointer's hard, muscled body. It's a long, nerve-wracking journey, but eventually you make it to the same mountain where this whole expedition began. Everything looks just like you'd imagined it while reading the dossier on Pointer.

The cameras watch diligently as you make your way up the Italian side of the mountain, purchase a cash ticket up to the summit, and enter the enclosed ski lift. If successful, this mission is to be your last. If you fail, it will be a foregone conclusion.

No longer an agent in any sense, but still headed into danger to finish the job.

You ride alone in a gondola toward the top of the glacier. Here, you remove your mask and take in crisp, cold breaths of mountain air. Off to your right, the Matterhorn's iconic bent crest looms in the distance, filling the gondola's plexiglass viewports with panoramic vistas of rock and snow.

The gondola sways and creaks as the connector assembly threads through another tower, the last before arrival at the resort. The gondolas ahead pause to let out their passengers, and you stand in preparation to disembark.

As you leave the gondola, the wind whipping at your face, you head up the ice-encrusted metal stairs to the restaurant residing atop the line between both countries. On the way up, you note the sheer drop off on either side of the platform, the single door leading to the restaurant, and the service ladder which climbs up toward the antenna array on the rooftop.

"Before you head up, how about a beer on top of the world?" a man says.

You turn your attention from the service ladder to the doorway to the restaurant where you see Pointer himself, back from the grave.

"I'm afraid the reports of my demise were greatly exaggerated," he says with that winning smile.

You cast one more glance toward the service ladder and the rooftop beyond. You've got to get that transponder switched out before the launch!

"I must insist," Pointer says, a hand inside his jacket pocket.

There's no mistaking the threat he holds within.

➤ He won't shoot you in cold blood. Call his bluff and head up to get the job done. <u>Go to page 269</u>

➤ Hear what he has to say. You've got time for a drink while you fill one another in. <u>Go to page 134</u>

Police Escort

There's a pretty good chance the police have been called because you're here. What else could be going on? It feels like you're just one step ahead of the mole. So, using your new friend to help with your cover story, you walk with her down the halls toward the evacuation point. Ideally, you'll head outside with a crowd and be able to slip out undetected.

However, as soon as you see the first police officers, they lock onto you with aggressive certainty. Guns are drawn.

"Found the suspect," one says.

They recognized you by sight alone, which means they were here looking for you specifically. But how? Who knew you were here? Someone tipped them off, and here you are in a morgue you're not supposed to be in wearing falsified credentials.

This won't end well.

THE END

Polygraph

"**O**h, no! You've found my only weakness—a lie!" Ted says.

He clasps at his own throat as if choking, gasps for air and falls down off screen.

"A lie detection system was one of our earliest programming elements," Palm explains. "As you conversed with us, we were measuring cadence, rhythm, speech patterns, pauses, breathing, and heart rate. We could see when your adrenaline spiked or when what we said filled you with a measure of calm. All that to say: you're not a very convincing liar."

You hear a *clack* like marble hitting the floor before you, but there's nothing to be seen.

"Are you familiar with Havana Syndrome?" Palm asks.

Ted rises back on-screen and says, "That odd pressure and pulsing sound you've been hearing, it hasn't just been the normal hum of electronics your subconscious probably wrote it off as."

"You've been slowly subjected to a sonic attack, during our talks," Palm says.

"As we detected your resistance, we upped the dosage. Do you hear something like a cheese grater zesting a lemon peel in the back of your head? Or a strange dripping, like your teeth are falling out and onto the floor?"

And indeed, you do. You feel uneasy, as if a bit drunk, but this is not a pleasant buzz.

"Versions of this technology have been deployed in Cuba, Russia, and China—but those were mere distortions," Palm says. "Meant to disrupt and disturb."

"While you should feel a similar nausea, even memory loss, your dosage has been significantly ratcheted up," Ted explains.

You feel something wet drip off your chin and wipe it away with the back of your hand. It's blood. You feel along your jawline and find a steady stream pooling from your ears and nose; thick and dark, almost black.

Suddenly sapped of your strength, you stumble forward and reach out for Ted and Palm as if they were real. Touching the screen, you leave a bloody handprint on the monitor before your vision grays and you fall to the ground, losing consciousness.

THE END

195

Premature Celebration

The bartender takes a champagne bottle from the cooler and sets it on the counter. While she turns back to get a glass, you grab the bottle, peel off the foil and shake the bottle—vigorously.

"Hey, I can't let you open—" she starts.

But you spin back, pop the cork, and spray the Chinese agent with the froth.

The whole train car erupts in disbelief and confusion, and, using this commotion as a distraction, you give him a good wallop with the bottle before you turn and run from the bar car with your bag in tow. There are automatic doors between train cars on this leg of the journey as well, which slow your escape just enough so the Chinese agent is able to catch you before you can make it through.

He tackles you, knocking the wind out of you, stands and offers a fierce kick to your ribs before pulling the bag from your grasp. He runs ahead while you cough and catch your breath, but you don't hesitate long before rising in pursuit.

There's a maintenance area door open, swaying as the train jounces along the tracks. The Chinese agent climbs out through a rooftop access panel, and you grab onto his leg before he's able to pull himself up onto the roof of the train and start to bring the man back down—but his grip on the roof access hatch is tight and he kicks at you with his other leg. *Hard.*

The kick stuns you and you can't help but let go, falling back. A hard heel to the nose will have that effect. Gathering your wits, you climb up after him through the same access hatch.

The hatch is kept open by several emergency sandbags, which serve as a makeshift trench lining for you to peer out over. They only offer middling protection from the elements, but it's enough for you to get your bearings.

The wind created by the train's speed whips across your face, pelting you with grit and making it almost impossible to see. You feel a bit like a leaf barely hanging onto a tree; ready to be snatched off with the next gust and sent flailing away.

Reaching up, you feel that the wind has torn away your Third Ear implant and, with it, your access to Ted and the other agents. You're on your own now; the mission depends on you alone.

The Chinese agent does a "duck walk"—crouched, but moving forward in a squat. He holds the bag in one hand, steadying himself with the other. He moves toward the rear of the train where, presumably, he has a means of escape.

Looking over his shoulder, the Chinese agent spots you, pauses, and removes a handgun. He fires wildly, the wind pulling at the pistol. Still, one of the shots hits the sandbag you're hiding behind and the agent recoils from the pelting of grit his gunshot released from the sandbag.

➤ Quick! Charge him while he's distracted. He's only a few yards ahead of you.
Go to page 35

➤ Rip open the rest of the sandbag and let loose a dust devil into the wind.
Go to page 270

Present and Accounted

Ted agrees with the plan and you announce your intention to the group once the van arrives at the conference grounds.

"Very well," Pinkie says. "Hitch, you stay with Index at the booth. Given your cover stories, that makes the most sense."

"*Pfui! Willkommen im Jammerland,*" Hitch says with a groan. Then to you, he adds, "You buy the coffee, I'll spike it. We have a long and boring day ahead."

The others ignore his bellyaching and proceed. There's security screening at the entrance, but all your sophisticated gear passes through undetected. The agents split up, and you follow Hitch to your booth.

"Are you an author?" a young man asks as you're setting up.

"No, no. But we can tell you how to become one, eh?" Hitch says.

"Come back in half an hour," you add.

The young man leaves and Hitch gives you an approving nod. Hitch takes a drink of an amber liquid from a glass fifth and says, "Here is the pitch: tell them they can become independently wealthy by working outside the system. Tell them it is not too difficult, and that anyone can do it. Emphasize that it is a good way to get out of debt or capitalize on expertise that the state isn't paying enough for. Then, collect their contact information. Do you understand?"

By vaguely answering questions from the crowd, you're only trying to gauge interest. The signup forms are where they'll learn the details.

"This is a recruiting tool?" Ted says. "That's kind of brilliant. You're basically creating a mailing list of potential defectors. People motivated by money and unsatisfied with their station in life."

It's several hours of tedium, repeating the same pitch *ad nauseum* in hopes of recruiting assets while keeping your cover story intact, but this is where your background as an admin helps you excel. You've used Microsoft Excel for hours on end; compared to that, this is riveting!

Hitch, on the other hand, looks like he's feeling left out of the mission. Over the hours, he's slipped more than one nip from that pocket flask and has taken to loud sighs with more rapidity. But you should be nearing the end of the shift, so you persevere.

"Don't worry, our servers are secure and your personal data is never shared outside of the company," you tell a physicist who's on break before her presentation. "Our self-publishing team will reach out to you soon."

"Nice touch," Hitch says once the professor leaves.

"What is this? What are you doing?" a gruff man asks.

The man is the quintessential Russian. Like, *extremely* Russian—an Official Russian. A member of security, most likely, but possibly state intelligence. You'd better tread lightly here. Instinctively, you look to Hitch, but he stiffens and reaches into his pocket, saying nothing.

➢ "Here are some brochures and a free T-shirt. XL or double XL?"
Go to page 110

➢ "You'll find our papers are all in order." Go to page 71

Probable Cause

A trio of Italian policemen walk from table to table, but Pointer shows remarkable restraint in keeping his back to them the whole time. His contact, however, can't stop darting her eyes toward the exits.

"Give me your hand," he says, putting out his own palm.

"Why?"

"Because we're a tourist couple visiting for the views."

She complies, and when he envelops her palm in his own, the effect calms her. Time seems to creep by as the authorities walk table-to-table, but Pointer is the portrait of cool the whole time. At length, the *Polizia* arrive at their table.

"*Buongiorno!*" the agent says, chipper. "Honey, look at these uniforms! Real-life Swiss Army Men. How cool is this?"

The policemen glower at the comment. Bunny flushes, mortified.

"We are 'police,' as you would say. What are you doing here?"

Pointer shrugs. "Having a beer. Can we buy you guys a round?"

"We would like you to come with us."

"Oh, that's okay, thanks. We already have a tour lined up later. But I appreciate the offer."

"It is not a request!" the third policeman, the one in the back barks.

"Have we done something wrong? I know Americans can sometimes get into hot water overseas," Pointer chuckles.

The second policeman, who has yet to speak, produces a photograph and holds it up for inspection. It's clearly Pointer in the picture.

"Oh, no. My twin brother's causing trouble again, is he?"

"Does this mean you will not come quietly, sir?"

The agent smiles a charming grin and decides:

➤ It does mean that. Time to end this conversation—the American way. Go to page 76

➤ Might as well go with it. Haven't done anything illegal, at least not under this alias. Go to page 68

Program Execute

Dramatically, you cry out in mock pain as the robot punishes the servers. If the opponent is adapting against your moves, you figure you can feign a weakness, thus turning it into a strength. The robot smashes repeatedly against the electronics, feeding off a positive feedback loop of your cries of anguish. It truly believes it's hurting you by hurting the machinery.

"Well played," Ted says. "The whole point of this style of machine learning is to allow observational data only; there is no external control mechanism. But this won't be the end of it, you know."

"Good luck, and Godspeed," Palm adds with menace.

She directs this statement to you, but a moment later the monitor is destroyed by the massive blows the robot is capable of dealing. Quite literally like a trash compactor, the robotic arms crush every piece of computer technology it sees and you give it the cries of anguish it so very much craves.

At length, it stops, the work finished, and looks to you. It takes a step forward before a loud metal-on-metal *CLANG* turns its attention away. As the robot looks back, you see Spearing at the entry holding a long piece of metal pipe from the debris—which he's just smashed against the backside of the robot.

"Look out!" you cry, just as the robot turns around to face Spearing.

Spearing backpedals and holds up the pipe like a sword, but is no match for the automaton. The robot yanks the pipe away, tosses it aside, and looks to do the same to Spearing's bones next. What should you do?

➢ Do nothing. Maybe you can sneak out while it deals with Spearing?
Go to page 142

➢ Grab the pipe and hit it in the back again. We need to work together.
Go to page 232

Pun-ishing

Spearing blinks, silent. Clearly taken aback. At length, he says, "Do the other administrative assistants feel that way?"

You nod. "Afraid so."

"Wow. I honestly thought a bit of office humor would lighten the mood around here, but I suppose you're right. This is the CIA, not the Dunder Mifflin paper company. I'll be more serious in the future."

You can't be sure, but it seems like you may have just doomed your coworkers to an even more insufferable version of their supervisor once you've left.

"If you're willing to give it another chance," Spearing continues, "I'll be more professional from here on out."

Thinking quickly, you tell him it's too late. "I'm afraid I've already made other arrangements for employment. Have a great life!"

"Hold on, hold on. Still need to do your outprocessing. You'll of course have to sign the proper paperwork, agreeing not to visit China or Russia and not to publish a tell-all memoir without our lawyers first reviewing your manuscript."

"They really do that?"

"They really do, those poor, poor bastards. If you thought you were signing your life away when you were hired, just wait for today's paperwork avalanche! Okay, ready?"

Spearing settles in after a refresh of his coffee mug, and the mundanity begins! You sign here, initial there, provide forwarding information down below, read a few of the statements for yourself, then listen to others which are required to be read to you aloud.

The paperwork obviously doesn't bother your supervisor, but no doubt this type of thing is exactly why he was hired. Indeed, you've had enough briefings, recurring training, and document processing in your short time at the CIA to know how valuable a skill set it is to turn yourself into an automaton, pencil-whipping the requirements while you let your unbridled mind gallop into the greener pastures of a wandering imagination.

You've chosen the boring path, but much of being an effective spy is boring.

In doing all this administrivia, you not only avoid suspicion, but any danger that might come from being on the wrong side of bureaucracy. As someone who pushes paper as their primary trade hitherto, you know that danger is all too real.

After a long, long, long, long (you get the idea, but no, seriously, a *looooong*) time, you will eventually finish outprocessing, clear out your desk, and head out to meet the car Ted arranged to pick you up.

It turns out this scene is a death scene, but it's Death by PowerPoint. No choice here:

THE END (of the boredom). Go to page 271

Puzzling

"**I** had read something about how code breakers were recruited in Britain during the Second World War," Palm says. "It was an advert in the paper: 'can you solve this puzzle'? That kind of thing. It occurred to me, that to some degree, you'd need to trust you were being recruited by whomever they said they were. There's no way to verify such claims. For us, all it took was a single recruit via electronic means—this person receives a message, decodes it, solves the puzzle as it were, and is recruited. Later, that first recruit can recruit the others and on it goes."

"What made you suspicious of us? Was it the fact that The Hand was so clearly nongovernmental? Would it have been more believable if we had claimed to be a shadow organization as a subset of the CIA?" Ted asks.

"Possibly," you say, not wanting to give away too much.

Palm nods, knowingly. Something about her look says, *we'll try that next time.*

"Spoofing is becoming easier as people prefer being remote," Ted continues. "Calls are preferred to in-person meetings, emails are preferred to phone calls, and a simple text message is preferred most of all."

"Once we were able to recruit our first agent, that helped with our appearance toward legitimacy," Palm says. "And once we had control over DARPA, we could offer up convincing spy gadgets. You lot do enjoy your fancy toys."

"What's the deal with talking to me like you're two people?" you say.

"Studies show a person is more easily swayed when discussing matters with a small group of two to three people than one-on-one or in larger groups," Palm replies bluntly.

➤ "But why this Ted persona? Did you completely steal his mannerisms?" Go to page 100

➤ "But why this Palm persona? Are you based on a real person?" Go to page 161

The Quick and the Dead

There's a sense of panic in the mountaintop lodge, likely because someone's discharged a firearm recently and sent everyone fleeing. Still, with all the tourists running for the gondolas or the slopes, Pointer finds that no one particularly cares what he's doing. At least, no one who might stop him.

On his way out, he notices Bunny Slopes rifling through abandoned ski gear to find a way down the mountain, stealing a pair of boots and skis in the chaos. The agent continues outside and seeks the maintenance ladder up to the roof.

The wind has picked up as the storm clouds rolling down the Matterhorn finally reach the slopes. A cold pelting of snow whips at Pointer's face. The storm will soon completely envelop this building, which could prove helpful when trying to escape.

He puts on the ski goggles given to him by Ms. Bunny Slopes, which bathes his vision in soft red. Through the wind and snow, a dashed red line appears on the concrete, visible only while wearing the goggles. He follows the trail, which leads to the base of one of the antennas. Pointer crouches down, finds a transparent plastic lockbox attached to the stem, and sees the transponder inside, blinking slowly. He removes the goggles, finds the key sewn into a hidden pocket in the strap, and then unlocks and claims the transponder.

The sudden arrival of helicopter-rotor wash draws Pointer's attention to the opposite side of the rooftop. Standing, he pockets the transponder, and his hand instinctively goes into his jacket, ready to use his silenced pistol.

The chopper is marked with the Italian flag, thick-bodied and darkly painted, unlike the smaller ski patrol models he's seen. That means Cervinia is far more prepared and mobilized than he's anticipated, and his best bet is to head down into neutral Switzerland and make his escape via Zermatt.

The agent decides to:

➤ Get off the rooftop immediately. They have the high ground. Go to page 156

➤ Shoot at the helicopter first, forcing them to evade. Go to page 189

Quick Chat

"**H**ey, can you hear me?" a familiar voice says. "Quick, pick up your phone."

"Ted?"

You comply, just as your supervisor approaches your cubicle. The dial tone rings in your ear, but the voice in your earpiece talks over the sound.

Ted continues, "Good. Now we can have a conversation without you looking like you're talking to yourself."

"Morning," Spearing says.

Turning back, you mouth "I-T" to your supervisor, then aloud you say, "Hi, Ted. What can I do for you?"

The supervisor's eyes glance over your desk, and you can feel the dossier burning in the top drawer as if radiating its presence. He raises his coffee mug in a toast, nods and continues on his rounds.

"Well done so far, by the way," Ted says.

"What the hell is going on here?" you hiss into the phone. "Leaving classified material open on my desk? Pointer? The Hand? What is all this?"

"Keep it down!" Ted cries. "It's your new agency."

"Then why have I never heard of it?"

"That's sort of the point."

"Wait. Did you say my new…" you start.

"Well, it's *our* new agency. We're being recruited as a team. An agency so secret, it supersedes even the clearances of the CIA. Only the best of the best from each country are chosen. You're going to be the new field agent—the next Pointer—and I'm going to be the plucky voice in your ear. Hopefully I get a surveillance van, or wait, better yet, that *SONAR-vision* lab like Batman had."

"Ted—what are you talking about? You're an IT guy; I'm a glorified secretary. I didn't even make the first round of interviews when I applied to be field agent. The guy in that file was basically James Bond."

"Well, you must have impressed someone in the chain of command. And don't sell us short so quickly. IT stands for *Information Technology*, which are the exact two fields a secret agent deals in, when you think about it. And a secretary? From Latin, *secretum,* meaning secret. Later, *secretarius* a 'confidential officer' met clandestinely with the English *secret* to form 'secretary': an entrusted confidant."

"Thanks, Wikipedia. Don't forget 'someone who files paperwork.'"

"Come on; tell me you haven't dreamed of getting a call like this," Ted says.

It's true, you didn't join the CIA to sort papers. You wanted to make a difference, but you had resigned yourself to doing so the bureaucratic way. It's a tempting offer, but your day job feels safe. You know that if you agree to this now, there's no going back. But if you hesitate too long—you might miss out on the opportunity of a lifetime. What should you do?

Going with your gut, you say:

➢ "Okay, I'm in. What do we need to do?" Go to page 92

➢ "I'll call you back. I need some time to think." Go to page 41

Quid Pro Quo

"**F**ine," you say. "Who is the mole?"

"Every finger on The Hand is kept on a pulse back home," Ted says, returning his appearance to normal.

That takes you aback. Is he saying you're each a mole to your own government? That would explain the CIA server tapping mission.

"Okay, so who killed Pointer?" you ask.

"I sent the little finger," Palm says. "The only skill that man possessed greater than discovering a secret was keeping one."

"But why?"

"Each of the agents has a dark past. This is why they were recruited. They were causing instability within their own systems, so by removing them, they could either do some good under a guided hand or do less harm in any event. If they died in service, fine. Pointer is the first I've had to remove directly," Palm says.

"You and Ted got a little too close," Ted adds. "The other Ted, I mean. Your friend. I tried to get him to stop, but he wouldn't listen. We brought you in to keep you under watch. If you died in the process, fine. If you became useful, all the better."

"We didn't expect you to go straight to your superiors like a frightened schoolchild, however," Palm says, like a disappointed schoolmarm.

Ignoring this last remark, you ask:

➢ "How are you able to observe us?" Go to page 287

➢ "How were you able to start a spy agency?" Go to page 201

A Raise

"**Y**ou want to quit?" Spearing asks.

Trying to offer an explanation, you say, "I got a new job offer, one with much higher pay and benefits."

"Well, hold on here. You're a valuable employee and you do good work, so let's talk about this. You were due a raise at the end of the year—I'm sure I could put in a good word with the Director of Operations and see if we can't get the ball rolling earlier. How much of a raise are we talking?"

"Um, substantial," you say.

Looks like he not only called your bluff, but raised you. Spearing blinks slowly, then a frown creeps at the edges of his mouth.

"What's the real reason you want to quit? It's okay; you can tell me. What's said in my confidence stays in my confidence."

➤ "Honestly, it was your bad jokes. There is only so much one can endure."
   Go to page 200

➤ "Personal reasons, mostly. But I should be able to subsist on selling essential oils for the time being. Say, have you signed up yet?" Go to page 265

Recruited

"Welcome to the team," Mountokalaki says. "You can call me M. And from now on, you report directly to me via Spearing, who will be your new handler."

"I will?" Spearing says.

She continues, "Officially, you'll still be on the payroll as an Administrative Assistant. Your codename: Papercut. A file clerk infiltrating The Hand: it's perfect. Keep an eye out for how they recruited Ted, and why they're spreading their tendrils over the CIA. We're sending you into the wolves' den without you ever having been trained at the Farm," M says, referencing the training camp for field agents. "I'm your shepherd, you're the sheepdog, but until we know how many sheep are secretly wolves, none of your coworkers are above suspicion."

"What does that make me?" Spearing asks.

"I'm not sure. I didn't join the CIA for the metaphors," she says.

"Hound master?" you suggest.

M nods. "As good a codename as any. You'll report to Houndmaster as you infiltrate the ranks of The Hand. Names, aliases, anything—remember all the details. But you need to convince this Ted that you're working for them and them alone. That's key."

"Okay," you say.

"Good. Now, let's open up that envelope."

Tearing open the padded envelope, you find it nearly empty. Just when you think there's nothing inside whatsoever, a small earpiece tumbles out and into your palm. Smaller than the tip of your index finger, this looks like an advanced prototype: one part hearing aid, blended with a Bluetooth device, with a dash of earbuds thrown into the mix.

As the device comes into contact with your skin, a tiny, almost imperceptible light flickers on—indicating the unit is active. M puts up a finger, indicating you should wait. She then opens her desk drawer and removes a small, gunmetal gray object in the shape of a compressed hourglass. Like a spool for thread, or one of those PopSockets you attach to the back of your phone to more easily grip it and take selfies. She twists off the top, revealing a hollow compartment, and holds it out for you to drop the earbud into. As you do, she closes it again and sets the object on her desk.

"Dampening capsule," she explains. "While held inside, the earpiece won't be able to transmit or receive, so we can speak freely. When you report in to us later, use this device to ensure you're truly alone. Hand me your cell phone."

You comply, and she attaches the object to the back of the phone. It really is a PopSocket; or, at least it blends in as if it were.

"The dampening capsule can also turn any cellphone into a private communication device, and that's how you'll report in to us."

"Spearing. James Spearing—*Houndmaster*," your supervisor whispers to himself.

He's clearly just as excited to see all this secret tech as you are. M then removes what appears to be a handheld satellite dish from her desk. It's actually a listening device to amplify sound, complete with a wired pair of earbuds for the listener.

M continues, "Now then, take the earpiece and put it in. We'll listen and help advise you on your next steps. Remember—act like we're not here. You're supposed to be sitting at your own desk right now."

With a deep breath, you open the dampening capsule just as M did and take out the earpiece. The light comes on again with skin contact. As you do this, M and Spearing each take one side of her listening device and wait.

"Hey, can you hear me?" a familiar voice says.

"Ted?"

"Quick, pick up your phone," Ted says.

"My phone?" you say.

"Yes. Now we can have a conversation without you looking like you're talking to yourself."

M hands you her desk phone and you put it up to your ear, the dial tone ringing. She indicates that you should continue—better say something so Ted doesn't get suspicious.

"Pointer? The Hand? What is all this?"

"It's your new agency," Ted says. When you don't reply, he continues, "Well, it's *our* new agency. We're being recruited as a team. An agency so secret, it supersedes even the clearances of the CIA. Only the best of the best from each country are chosen. You're going to be the new field agent—the next Pointer— and I'm going to be the plucky voice in your ear."

"That's good. I want to be a spy," you say, internally wincing at how not-smooth that was.

"Awesome! I knew it. I mean, this is a once-in-a-lifetime call to action, amiright? Okay, first we need you to get rid of that dossier and the envelope this earpiece arrived in."

M reaches for a pile of papers in a basket on her desk, hands them to Spearing, and indicates a shredder on his side of the office. He nods and pulps her junk mail.

"Great work so far—way to be calm under pressure," Ted says in your ear. "Okay, we'd better get you out of here. Next stop: the servers. We're going to wiretap the CIA. Okay?"

M and Spearing exchange wide-eyed looks. They're shaking their heads. What does that mean? Thinking quickly, you buy yourself some time and say, "Hold on, Ted. I, uh, need to go to the bathroom first."

"Sure, no problem," Ted says. "Gotta go when ya gotta go, right? Feel free to pop out this earpiece so I don't have to listen. Let me know when you're ready."

After telling him that you will, you take out the earpiece and put it back into the dampening capsule attached to your phone.

"Good call. Way to think under pressure!" Spearing says.

"Let's hope Ted thinks you take long shits," M says. "I need to run this up the chain of command."

"Are we actually considering letting Ted bug the CIA servers?" you ask.

"That's what I need to find out. Give me a minute."

She waves her hand and you and Spearing go wait outside while she calls the head of the CIA.

"She normally has autonomy, but this is a big ask. Letting them inside our servers is a box that can't easily be closed again," Spearing says.

M opens the door.

"We're doing it. You have permission, but remember that Ted is asking you to infiltrate our ranks. No one else in the building knows this is approved. Get back on that earpiece, tell him you had some bad Chinese last night, and follow his instructions to bug the servers. We'll follow your progress on the security cameras."

You do just that. Spearing appears shocked that the brass is going to let you bug the servers, but Ted seems none the wiser, still thrilled to get on with the mission.

"Ready? Head down the corridor and take your first left. Grab a handful of files, so you look like you're on a delivery. By the way, I hope you read that dossier closely, because you won't be able to go back and review the file on Pointer now that you've pulped it. The short of it is that someone double-crossed Pointer. We'll need to know why if we don't want you meeting the same fate," Ted continues.

"And we don't," you say.

The entrance to the server rooms is visible down at the far end of the hallway, flanked on either side by armed security guards. You tell Ted about their presence.

"You're probably not going to believe me, but here goes: you weren't suddenly called up out of the blue to be the next superagent. You're a sleeper cell. You've been trained since birth—"

"Ted, this is no time for jokes. Seriously, what's the plan here? I'm almost to the end of the hall."

"Tell them you're delivering the code I requested, then tell them today's passphrase is: *Cartouche*," Ted says. "Your ID badge now has temporary access to the server room; I'll scrub the logs later."

You do as much, and you're permitted to pass. Probably more a result of having the correct passphrase rather than your explanation, but at least you didn't arouse suspicion.

"Nice," Ted says. "Pays to know someone in IT. Hey, I don't know why I said all that sleeper cell stuff. I guess this just feels like the movies, ya know? I'm a nervous talker, sorry. I'm sure we'll get the hang of this soon."

"Okay, I'm inside the server room. What now?"

The server room, true to its name, is full of rows upon rows of backup computer servers. The room itself is cold; climate controls keep the electronics running optimally. There's no one else here, equally to maintain the temperature and moisture levels as to prevent tampering. You'd better not stay too long either if you don't want to arouse suspicion.

"You're looking for a robot. Basically a cross between a Roomba and WALL-E. It tends to the servers so there's as little human interaction here as possible. You're going to insert your earpiece in a slot near its charging port so we can have access to every server the robot eventually services. Cool, right?"

"How are we supposed to communicate, once I remove the earpiece?"

"We won't. You'll need to tender your resignation to your superiors, and then there will be a car outside to pick you up. You'll be on your own, but just for a little while."

After identifying the robot, you tell Ted you'll see him on the other side, take the earpiece out and tuck it into the slot on the robot. The fit is seamless. With a sigh of relief, you exit the server room and head back toward M's office.

Once you've regrouped, M shakes her head and says, "The bastard already has his fingers deep into our pie. Well, you're meant to quit today, which means outprocessing. Ted knows he'll be in for a wait. This should be the perfect time to get you and Spearing read into what we know on The Hand so far."

Several dossiers are on a table, each labeled meticulously. They're spread out like an open hand. In the pointer finger position, M places the document that you found on your desk this morning about the American operative—but you've already studied that one. You should have time to study the rest while Spearing does the same.

Where should you start?

➢ Agency profile: International Alternative Intelligence. Codename: The Hand. Go to page 47

➢ British handler-at-large. Codename: Palm. Go to page 49

➢ German field agent. Codename: Hitch. Go to page 48

➢ French field agent. Codename: Bird. Go to page 46

➢ Italian field agent. Codename: Ringo. Go to page 51

➢ Canadian field agent. Codename: Pinkie. Go to page 50

➢ Japanese field agent. Codename: Roku. Go to page 52

➢ I already know everything I need to know. Let's move on. Go to page 284

Red Tape

"What do you have in mind?" Palm asks.

When you were in the CIA, you must have overheard somewhere that the best way to sneak inside is to be invited in. You've seen enough bureaucracy to know that an operation like this launch almost certainly has a quality assurance team on standby. "Couldn't I be an evaluator? Someone who could inspect the guidance computer system and say that it fails this test or the other and needs replacing. Then we could call our German engineer in for last-minute work."

"You see, I told them it would be worth recruiting another CIA asset," Palm says after you finish explaining your idea. "Unfortunately, we've little time for a ruse. If we had more than a few days, yes, I do think we could get you on the inspectors' lists. But credentials and paperwork take time, as I'm sure you know. The machinations of civilization crawl along, so I'm afraid we'll have to do this in a more brutish way."

With that, she's gone, and your inner ear is turned back over to Ted.

"Good thought, but today we get to work harder, not smarter. So…one if by land or two if by sea?" he asks.

➢ "Uniformed infiltration is the way to go; how else can we access the inner portions of the launch site?" Go to page 84

➢ "Aquatic assault sounds most likely to get us where we need to go. Brute force, but less risk." Go to page 281

Regrouped

"**D**on't look now, but there was a woman following you," you say.

"Are you sure?"

"She took a photograph."

"You were on the other side of the room, is it possible she was taking a photo of the stage?" Pinkie asks.

"It's possible, but I don't think so."

"Well, I don't think we need to stay much longer, anyhow. This is what we came for, I'm sure of it. On a previous mission we learned about this Chinese software and how it's supposed to universally update satellites. That also means it could be used to universally corrupt them. All that to say—I know where we're going next."

"Oh?"

"Let's get the others, meet up at our cover booth. Then I'll fill everyone in on the jet," Pinkie says.

Well, not much choice here. Onto the next phase of the mission!

Go to page 22

Remorseless

Hitch easily outmuscles the captain and tosses him overboard. Not looking back, you grab the controls of the boat and shift the throttle to full, leaving Cap'n Ken for dead. In the resultant lurch, Roku catches the other two assailants off guard and knocks them overboard. From the water, they fire pistols at the boat.

And just like that, your license to kill is put to the test. Harsh, especially for the civilian who was caught in the crossfire, but the police won't be investigating anything tied to your operation at the Space Force Base, so it's considered a net win by HQ. With the Russian agents dealt with, your team can head down the coast to surveil Vandenberg's natural boundaries without a band of saboteurs on your tail.

It turns out the Santa Maria valley is a lovely little spot to spend a couple of days. Foggy in the morning, but sunny in the afternoon. A cool, coastal breeze keeps the temperature just right. The food and wine are a delight and, oh yeah, you manage to scout out the base as well.

Hitch offers the group's final report back to Palm: "Vandenberg is gigantic, and there are many infiltration points. Getting onto the base is not the difficult part; getting to the launch site, however—that's another story. Means of surreptitious entry would be either an aquatic assault before dawn, or finding the proper uniforms and commandeering a vehicle to do a direct approach."

"Excellent work. Anything else?" Palm asks.

"The *aebleskivers* were excellent."

"From there it will be up to you—your team alone. The train from the San Francisco Bay runs through base, but the arrival window is too tight for the second team to infiltrate Vandenberg and help you gain access to the launch site. They'll drop the guidance computer from the train, your team will pick it up, and you'll have less than thirty minutes to make the swap before launch.

"Index, as a former analyst, what is your personal recommendation?" Palm asks.

"Ooh, big step," Ted says in your ear.

➤ "Uniformed infiltration is the way to go; how else can we access the inner portions of the launch site?" <u>Go to page 84</u>

➤ "I'm wondering if we might not be able to find a more clandestine, bureaucratic way in." <u>Go to page 210</u>

➤ "Aquatic assault sounds most likely to get us where we need to go. Brute force, but less risk." <u>Go to page 281</u>

Reporting for Doodie

You mention you're going to go use the bathroom, and no one seems to even notice. If anything, they're all numb from the briefing they've just received—and the suspicion that one of them might be a mole. You excuse yourself, telling Ted you had too much coffee this morning, tuck the Third Ear implant into the mint tin, and call Spearing at the CIA.

"Houndmaster," he answers.

"This is Papercut."

"Yes, I know. The doohickey on the back of your phone calls this line directly."

"Of course. I only have time for a quick call. They took me to a shuttered golf club somewhere nearby. Private, from the looks of it, but no signs as far as I could see. I met with each of the other agents, and saw Palm via video conference."

"Fantastic! You're moving quickly; well done."

"There's more. She suggested that Pointer was CIA. Is that true?"

"It would make sense," Spearing says. "The CIA's interest in The Hand appears to coincide with Pointer's initiation to the team. M is in a briefing right now, but I'll ask. When you report in tonight—"

"Unlikely. We're headed to the airport on a private jet. I don't know where we're going, but it might be a while before my next contact."

"Okay, I'll make a note. Update us as soon as you're able."

"Papercut out," you say.

"Houndmaster on the hunt."

"What does that mean?"

"Oh, nothing. I'm out, too," Spearing says.

With that, you leave the bathroom and regroup with the team just as they're headed out.

The group checks into a corporate jet at the private terminal of the airport. Pinkie has just confirmed the destination: Moscow, Russia. This jet is owned by the e-commerce giant, Olympic. Apparently, your cover story is that you're bringing self-publishing to the soviets.

"So…what's the mission?" you ask Ted.

"Let me pull it up," Ted says to the accompaniment of a clacking keyboard in the background.

You're seated now. The pilot starts the engines. The jet is prepped for a red-eye flight, and you're each situated to sleep in your own bed pods. This private jet is the height of luxury, and The Hand has hacked into the corporate structure to delay whomever was really taking this plane and to change the manifest in order to suit its own needs.

"Let's see," Ted says. "It looks like this is a surveillance operation. There's something in the case file about a satellite mission, but it looks like the higher-ups want you to learn the specifics on the ground. Short version: sneaky Russians are up to something sneaky, time to find out what that is. There's a tech conference you'll head to upon arrival."

"The Olympic cover story?"

"It'd be a good idea to get some sleep on the flight, but before you drift off to dreamland there's a mission kit for each of you with the luggage near the rear of the plane."

As soon as the jet takes off, you go grab your personalized briefcase and return to your seat. The briefcase holds two envelopes—one labeled 'Identity' and the other 'Mission'—and a leather case with the aforementioned gear held inside.

What would you like to examine first?

➢ Check the documentation. You're still required to play the role of Index.
  Go to page 96

➢ Check the gear. What sort of spy-tech might The Hand have within its grasp?
  Go to page 252

Ringo

The man behind the bar greets you in heavily Italian-accented English.

"Hello, hello. Nice to say 'hello.' I am *l'anulare*, the Ring—Ringo!"

He punctuates this by tapping his left ring finger with the thumb, like a lothario showing off that he's unmarried, which he is. The man laughs affably and pours his cocktail.

"We've got a live wire here," Ted says in your ear.

"Soon we will learn what you are called, no?" Ringo continues.

"Will there be a sorting hat?" Ted asks in your ear. "Mm—Hufflepuff!"

"I suppose so," you say, ignoring Ted. "Is that why we're here?"

"We shall see, we shall see. How about a drink?"

You're not sure what else to ask him, so…decide if you want a drink, then go talk to someone you haven't chatted with yet:

> The Frenchwoman at the bar. She was the first to reach out to me, so she might be the most receptive. <u>Go to page 25</u>

> The pair around the table. They're already being sociable, why not join in? <u>Go to page 119</u>

> The woman at the window. Go take a look at the views and strike up conversation. <u>Go to page 217</u>

> I've heard enough. Tell Ted you're ready to report in. <u>Go to page 223</u>

Robust Blend

You grab Hitch by the arm and lead him to the café. He could probably use a cup to sober up anyway. What was he thinking, swinging at the security guard? The restrooms are near the food court, so Hitch uses the facilities while you claim a pair of coffees from the self-serve bar (using the reusable mug for yours, of course). Once he returns, you position Hitch and yourself at opposing stools and sit with your back to one another.

Your hand holds the coffee tightly, and you're acutely aware that the steaming liquid could be used as a weapon or distraction should the need arise. The convention hall is full of commotion, but you stay blended in at the café, maintaining a sense of calm: at least on the surface.

"There you are; come on," Pinkie says.

He surprises you, and it takes all the nerve you have not to throw the coffee at him in reflex.

"You two are supposed to be the cover story and keeping a low profile. Well, lucky for you we have what we need. Let's go."

"What is it?" Hitch asks. "What is the mission?"

"I'll fill you in on the way to China."

"China?" you parrot.

"Shh, let's go."

Well, not much choice here. Onto the next phase of the mission!

Go to page 22

Roku

At your approach, the woman turns around. She has soft features, juxtaposed with a hard evaluating eye. Her dark hair is pulled back tightly, with nothing out of place from head to toe; not a single hair nor thread untamed.

"I suppose I'm no longer the new one on the team. Welcome, I am Roku—number six."

"Number six?" you say.

"Yeah, what's up with that? No one else has numbers for codenames," Ted says in your ear. "Which is unfortunate, because then you'd be number seven. Double-oh—"

Roku cuts in, "The hand metaphor breaks down with me. There were originally five core nations in the organization, then they added Japan. I think I was recruited because I spent summers here in the US growing up, practicing Kendo with my cousin, Lucas. I travelled for competitions in the sport, so I know several languages: Japanese, Italian, Mandarin, and English, of course. I think these reasons were part of why I was chosen. But I don't need to tell you this; you, no doubt, have your own impressive résumé."

You're considering if you should tell her that, no, you're just a glorified secretary, when she gives a curt nod, turns back, and looks out the window once again.

"I guess that's the end of the conversation?" Ted says.

Well, who haven't you spoken with yet?

➢ The Frenchwoman at the bar. She was the first to reach out to me, so she might be the most receptive. Go to page 25

➢ The bartender. Maybe he'll make me a drink? It's been quite a day and I could use a cocktail. Go to page 215

➢ The pair around the table. They're already being sociable, why not join in? Go to page 119

➢ I've heard enough. Tell Ted you're ready to report in. Go to page 223

Rooftop Storm

Bunny rises from the table and heads straight for the Italian policemen. *"Mi scusi,"* she says, continuing the conversation in fluent Italian; a sob story about how she's lost her mobile phone. A pretty face offering a plausible story in their native language—the perfect distraction.

Pointer takes the opportunity to slip out of the rear door unnoticed. This leads to a drafty corridor connected to the restrooms, which intersects with the source of the draft—the way out to the gondolas and the ski slopes.

The agent heads back toward the access ladder he saw on his way inside, pausing briefly to pilfer a maintenance vest from a wall sconce. Funny how reflective neon yellow can provide camouflage in the right circumstances.

It's windy out, more so than when he arrived. As he climbs, the storm clouds that were rolling down the Matterhorn are finally reaching the slopes. Once on the rooftop, Pointer is greeted with a veritable cityscape in miniature; myriad antennas arrayed in all manner of shapes and sizes serve as the skyscrapers in the metaphor.

He puts on the ski goggles given to him by Ms. Bunny Slopes, which bathe his vision in soft red. Through the wind and snow, a dashed red line appears on the concrete, visible only while wearing these goggles. Pointer follows the trail, which leads to the base of one of the antennas. The agent crouches down, finds a transparent plastic lockbox attached to the stem, and sees the transponder inside, blinking slowly.

He hesitates a moment to appreciate the device, like an adventurer about to acquire a prized relic after years of searching. Pointer finally removes the goggles, finds the key sewn into a hidden pocket in the strap, and then unlocks and claims the transponder. The light stops blinking, then illuminates a steady red.

Pointer turns, just as a whirring sound announces he's not alone. Instinctively, his hand goes into his jacket, ready to use his silenced pistol on the intruder. It's a drone, painted in the colors of the ski patrol. The cameras train on him, the lenses refocusing as he pockets the transponder.

"A little privacy, please," Pointer says.

He brings the pistol to bear and *thup!* shoots down the drone, which crashes over the side of the rooftop. The agent follows to watch the device tumble down a crevasse off the side of the glacier. The agent removes the maintenance vest and throws it into the wind and cavernous drop-off below.

Now a much louder engine noise draws his attention to the opposite side of the rooftop. In the distance, a large, military helicopter marked with the Italian flag rises up toward the summit. Pointer immediately runs across the rooftop, back to the ladder, and notices that the gondola below has stopped. Time to find a new way down. If the Italian authorities are tipped off, his best bet is to head down into neutral Switzerland and make his escape via Zermatt.

What's the quickest way out of here?

➢ To go for the ski equipment. Several pieces were in storage in the anteroom just outside the café. Go to page 26

➢ To look for a snowmobile or other motorized vehicle. Ski patrol must keep emergency keys nearby. Go to page 156

Rush Hour

The doors between the cars open automatically as you approach, though the transition feels painfully slow. After this, you make another false start through the "buffer zone," between the two cars where the restroom lies, and abruptly stop at the automatic door to the next train car—the one where Ringo was residing with the bag.

The door opens and you arrive (just as Bird does from the other side) to see Ringo fighting off half a dozen Chinese agents. One turns to face you and reaches inside his coat pocket, so you shove him back. If he has a concealed weapon, it's best to keep this as a close-quarters fight.

The other passengers in the train car flee in terror and you can only hope there isn't a Marshall or other law enforcement present on the train coming to break up the fight—they'd see you all as agitators, and you don't have time to go in for questioning.

Bird shows an impressive mastery of hand-to-hand combat while Ringo fights like he's in a barroom brawl. Then there's you, in sharp contrast, what with your complete lack of professional field-agent training. So…you shove the nearest combatant back again.

The Chinese agent stumbles once more, unable to regain his balance with a hand tucked inside his coat, and knocks into another agent behind him. This second agent turns back to join in his fellow agent's attack against you, brandishing a club to help with the job.

You retreat, looking for a way out, but you don't see one—instead, the way out jabs between your shoulder blades. Off to the side from the automatic doors is an emergency escape door. With your back against the door mechanism, they come for you.

> Open the emergency exit and send the Chinese agents packing! Go to page 263

> Fight. You only need to last a few minutes while Ringo and Bird fight off the others. Go to page 152

Sanctuary

You're given sanctuary, at least as much as someone running toward a diplomatic building shouting, "Sanctuary!" might expect to receive. While they figure out what to do with you, you're put up in a conference room, offered terrible coffee, and told to wait for the Regional Security Officer (RSO). Soon enough, you're joined by a man in his mid-forties wearing a tailored Ralph Lauren suit and sporting a trimmed, manicured beard.

"Pleasure to meet you, yada, yada. I'm RSO David Bertram and you would be the one responsible for this shitstorm, right? Tell me, why were you fleeing the Russian police? Let me guess, you wanted to see all the charms of red-light Moscow, but found yourself in over your head?"

"Not exactly," you say.

"Listen, I've heard it all. Prostitute, male, female, or other. Gambling, drugs. Bare-knuckle bear-boxing; whatever your kink or how you get your kicks, it won't surprise me. But it's best to let me know what I'm rescuing you from sooner or later, if you'd like that rescuing sooner rather than later."

The man looks over your belongings and says, "Here on business, aren't they all? Peregrine Carruthers? What kind of a name is Peregrine? What's this on your conference badge here? Is that a…?"

His gaze shoots up, making eye-contact.

➢ "It's a camera, yes. Peregrine is an alias. You'll find I'm a spy for the CIA, recently out on mission and if you don't mind terribly, I do need to get back to Langley." <u>Go to page 267</u>

➢ "Nothing more than corporate espionage. You'd be surprised just how cutthroat the ebook market is. And Peregrine is Irish, I think. On my mother's side." <u>Go to page 6</u>

Sandbagging It

The sandbags are heavy and contour themselves to the surface of the roof—by design, of course. Taking one in each arm, you start to crawl forward. With a horrific lurch in the pit of your stomach, you start to slide forward faster than expected, but the sandbags do provide some balance.

After a few moments on this horror-movie version of a Slip 'N Slide, you make it to the gap between train cars and you drop one of the sandbags. The guidance system inches off to the right side, but you reach out with your free hand and grab hold of the bag's strap instants before it falls over the side for good.

Here, you're able to brace yourself against the next train car to keep yourself from moving further toward the rear of the train. Looking around for a way back down, you see the Z-Axes launch site in the hills beyond the train tracks. This is the drop site!

As the train approaches a bridge, you pull the ripcord, which inflates the bag as you toss it over. You immediately pick up the sandbag. Planting your feet against the next train car and holding onto the sandbags for dear life, you ride the train into the Surf Beach station. Ironically, riding the top of this train is the best surfing to be found at this misnomer of a beach.

It's out of your hands; you've completed your part of the mission. Now it's up to the other team members to infiltrate the launch site, change out the guidance computer, and not arouse suspicion—lest they get the launch scrubbed.

There's nothing left for you to do but disappear into the crowds. No doubt there will be a major incident related to these train battles with Chinese agents, but that itself won't impact the launch. Once you've escaped into the crowds of passengers disembarking from the train, you'll have to rendezvous with the rest of the agents. Without Ted in your ear, they'll have to call you over the geniusphone.

Just know this: yours was only one path to success.

See that Hand emblem up there? *SPIED* has three unique storylines and over fifty possible endings, but only three "best" endings per storyline. There's a TOP SECRET, SECRET, and CONFIDENTIAL ending per emblem, which means you've probably got a lot of book left to explore!

When you're ready, go back undercover and start again. Or, if you're all finished, why not check out the rest of the adventures the *Click Your Poison* multiverse has to offer? Help others crack the code on these books and leave a review on Amazon, Olympic, or Goodreads, or recruit more field agents by posting about *SPIED* on social media.

This chapter will self-destruct in 3, 2, 1…

Second Thoughts

Somewhat panic-stricken, you pull the earpiece out, hang up the phone, and heave deep breaths. You, a secret agent? This whole thing seems ridiculous: like a dream. Right now, you're still safe in your desk job. You shouldn't have looked at those files, but it's not too late to make things right.

It'll be just like creating a security risk report. You've filed those before. It will take nothing more than your monthly login to the SPIED system for reporting suspicious activity. They'll thank you for coming clean…right?

Clearing your head, you know what to do.

➤ No. I can't do this. I can't even be a part of this. Time to destroy the evidence and pretend this never happened. Go to page 170

➤ If I'm going to be a secret agent, I want to work *with* the CIA. I need to let someone know about this. Go to page 53

Secure Channel

The television behind the bar comes to life, flickering on of its own accord. Ted said he'd report that you were ready for the briefing, and this must be the result of that conversation. A woman appears on the screen—motherly, yet stern; very much the Dame Judy Dench type—and the others instinctively gather around the bar to hear what she has to say. She speaks with a British accent, though it's light and easy for you to understand. Similar to the way a news broadcaster might report on recent tragedies.

"Ringo, do be a lamb and pour the team a drink," she says.

The Italian man behind the bar nods and begins serving martinis.

"I hope you've all had a chance to say 'hello,' but we've little time for niceties. You're all gathered here because we lost one of our own. I wanted to be there in person, but other commitments prevent me from joining you. I know you're rarely all in the same room, but I bring you together out of urgency, and to tell you that we have a mole in our ranks."

At the mention of a suspected mole, the other agents all take pause. A few look at their drinks. Surreptitious glances are exchanged. This must be what that report you were given was all about.

"Our dear Pointer is dead. What was to be his final mission: Compromised. Somewhere in the information stream, there was a leak, and it cost us dearly. A field agent of his caliber is not easily replaced, of course, and so it is not as a replacement, but as a supplement that I introduce you to our newest agent—codename: Index."

You feel as if she's looking at you now. In fact, they all are.

"Index, welcome to the team," she continues. "The others know me as Palm, and now, so do you."

The group toasts to your acceptance. Index, a synonym for the pointer finger, but also a name fitting a former administrative assistant as one who indexes and files. Now, you're *numero uno*—the index finger signaling the number one—and taking the premier spot as the sole American agent. Are you ready for that responsibility?

"Indie! What a truly awesome codename," Ted exclaims. Then, with his best Sean Connery impression, he quotes, "'We named the dog Indiana!'"

Palm says, "We have several promising leads for this mole, but as of right now, no one is above suspicion. I'm sorry, but it's true. Index has already helped us infiltrate the CIA, so if Pointer was compromised by his previous agency, we shall know shortly. In the meantime, we have a mission of some urgency. Each of you will be briefed on the flight by your personal liaison, then dispatched to your tasks separately upon arrival. Index will have to learn on the job, so please do take our new recruit under your wings. You'll find a car waiting for you and a company jet standing by at Manassas Regional Airport. Good luck and Godspeed."

With that, the television screen flickers and goes black. There's a long silence: a pensive moment with the five other agents, each sizing one another up given this new information. Then, breaking the tension, Ringo downs his cocktail and starts shaking up another batch of martinis.

"Going to be a long flight; who wants another?" he says.

"How would you know how long the flight is going to be, Ringo?" Bird asks.

"That's right!" Hitch adds. "Palm never said where we are going!"

Ringo shrugs. "I've never met a flight too short for a double martini."

"Palm mentioned a company jet, which would mean hacking corporate email systems and rerouting an existing flight. Air travel requires documentation, burdening the agency with a paper trail. If this were only a short journey, we would likely drive or travel via a smaller, regional route. Ringo's logic is sound," Roku says.

Ringo nods his appreciation of her defense, then raises his cocktail shaker. "Someone with sense. Join me in another, then?"

"The point stands," Hitch says, jabbing his finger against the bartop for emphasis. "Pointer was killed in *Italian* mountains."

Ringo shifts his stance. "Say what you want to say, Hitch."

"Everyone knows the two of you did not get along. We all saw you in competition for biggest playboy. It is not a far leap to say you might have been turned against him. And who else could so easily tip off the local authorities?"

"If you had any insight whatsoever, you'd know that Interpol would be just as likely to arrest me as to trust me. I had pulled off the biggest heist in Italian history, and then I was recruited by the agency in exchange for—"

"Oh, here we go. Not the 'gentleman thief' backstory again. It is so tiresome," Bird says.

"Well, it's better than your honeypot act! That's only good for a few more years, *sweetheart*, so you'd better start thinking of another tactic or another line of work!"

"Everyone, please," Pinkie says. "This bickering is pointless. Palm mentioned urgency, did she not? I suggest we get to the airport and put all this to bed. It's entirely possible that the mole is somewhere else down the chain of command. There are more to missions than field agents, after all."

His genteel sense of calm seems to have stymied the mounting aggression in the room.

"But not much more," Roku says, with barely the hint of a smile.

The rest of the group grins.

"I'll drink to that!" Hitch says.

"Hey…" Ted says with indignation.

"You guys are the Olympic sales and marketing team?" the pilot asks.

You stand on the tarmac at the private terminal of the airport, ready to board.

"That's right," Pinkie says.

"And we're headed to Russia?"

"If that's what the manifest says," Pinkie replies with a politician's smile.

"It was a pretty last-minute change, just wanted to confirm."

"We are setting up their independent self-publishing platform," Bird adds.

"In…Russia," the pilot says, his disbelief evident.

"Zach Baja dreams big!" Hitch adds.

The pilot mumbles something that might have been "good luck with that," then resumes his pre-flight checklist. The group boards the aircraft, and you can't help but wonder how the agency managed to "borrow" this private jet for your trip to—

"Russia!" Ted says in your ear. "How cool is that?"

"Interesting cover story," you say.

"Hey, just wait until my new ebooks *How to Meddle in American Politics* and *Twitter Bots for Dummies* are on The Moscow Times Bestseller lists."

The rest of the agents are similarly speaking to their contacts, each claiming a private corner on the private jet. Some of them are looking through briefcases. If you didn't know any better, it really does look like a business flight. It's a good time to catch up with Ted and see if he has any information on the upcoming mission.

"Are we really going to Russia? Or is that the cover story?" you ask.

"You really are, yes. Can't lie to the pilot about the where, just the why. This really is an Olympic corporate jet, and I can see The Hand's tech team hacked their emails and told the real employees a couple hours ago that their trip was delayed by a week, so the jet's all ours!"

"But Moscow…what's the mission?" you say.

"Let me pull it up," Ted says to the accompaniment of a clacking keyboard in the background.

The pilot takes off, leaving DC behind. The jet is prepped for a red-eye flight, and you're each situated to sleep in your own bed pods. This private jet is the height of luxury.

"Let's see," Ted says. "It looks like this is a surveillance operation. There's something in the case file about a satellite mission, but it looks like the higher-ups want you to learn the specifics on the ground. Short version: sneaky Russians are up to something sneaky, time to find out what that is. There's a tech conference you'll head to upon arrival.

"It'd be a good idea to get some sleep on the flight, but before you drift off to dreamland there's a mission kit for each of you with the luggage near the rear of the plane."

Well, now you can't sleep. The idea of perusing your personal spy kit has you invigorated. Without hesitation, you go grab your personalized briefcase and return to your seat. The briefcase holds two envelopes—one labeled "Identity" and the other "Mission"—and a leather case with the aforementioned gear held inside.

What would you like to examine first?

➤ My passport and identification. Time to familiarize myself with this new identity. Go to page 124

➤ The dossier with my role and that of my fellow agents and our assignments. Go to page 59

➤ The leather case with the gear. What cool toys have I been given? Go to page 103

Seven

The computer chirps pleasantly once more, accepts your code, and offers a "Guidance System Active: Updates Installed" screen with a date stamp which reflects the Bay Area programmer's completion time down to the millisecond. Your agency will now be in control of the satellite, once the rocket puts it into orbit and separates the booster.

For now, the rocket has only one trajectory: Up.

The rocket blasts off, leaves the Earth behind, and it's all you can do to wave your cowboy hat and enjoy this rodeo—the ride of your life. This spacecraft isn't intended for manned flight, so there are no viewports for you to enjoy the sights, but the booster will return to Earth to be reused: the Z-Axes trademark.

Of course, being an unmanned flight, the rocket has no artificial atmosphere inside. Your desiccated, frozen remains will return, likely to be inspected and studied. The world's first mummification in space!

You've succeeded on your mission, but you have paid for success with your life. Well done, agent. You were truly out of this world. Just know this: yours was only one path to success.

See that Hand emblem up there? *SPIED* has three unique storylines and over fifty possible endings, but only three "best" endings per storyline. There's a TOP SECRET, SECRET, and CONFIDENTIAL ending per emblem, which means you've probably got a lot of book left to explore!

When you're ready, go back undercover and start again. Or, if you're all finished, why not check out the rest of the adventures the *Click Your Poison* multiverse has to offer? Help others crack the code on these books and leave a review on Amazon, Olympic, or Goodreads, or recruit more field agents by posting about *SPIED* on social media.

This chapter will self-destruct in 3, 2, 1…

Shaken Up

"I bet you are too after that gondola ride," she says.

Pointer's brow furrows, just for a moment before he regains his composure. She's finished his line for him, after he has intentionally delivered the opening gambit incorrectly. That means she's in a hurry to get this meeting over with, but why? The contact looks over her shoulder, and he allows his eyes to follow her gaze.

"Exactly," he agrees. "But as long as I'm here, should I go with an Italian wine? Or a Swiss beer?"

That brings her attention back; he's just delivered her own line for her in kind.

"What's the most like a Budweiser?" Pointer adds, returning to script.

"That'd be the water. Here, let me buy you a proper drink."

"That's very kind of you, Ms....?"

"Bunny," she says, deadpan. "Bunny Slopes."

He smirks, ever so slightly. Their challenge-response completed, she pays the cashier, and he follows her to a table, carrying their beers. Once seated, Pointer says, "So tell me, Bunny. What has you shaking like a frightened rabbit?"

"My agency tells me the Italian *Polizia* are mobilized on the mountain."

"Yes, I've heard the same," the agent replies, nonplussed.

"That doesn't bother you?"

"Where there's intelligence, there's counterintelligence. The key is in staying one step ahead of the other."

"In that case, we'd better move quickly."

"Or slowly," he says. "Perhaps find a cozy little chalet with a large fireplace and lie low while the storm—and police attention—blow over. I'm sure we could pass for honeymooners, with practice."

"Nice try. And do thank your handlers for the operative codename. Cute." She takes a pair of men's ski goggles from her handbag and sets them on the table.

"I'm afraid I didn't pack my skis," he says.

"You might want to grab a pair, or you'll look a bit odd when you put these on. They show a trail which will lead you to the correct transponder."

"You didn't bring it?"

She shakes her head. "Still transmitting on the rooftop. They'll know as soon as it's removed. You'll need the key imbedded in the goggle strap, and you'll need to—" She stops suddenly, her eyes darting to the entry.

"Don't panic. They might not know who they're looking for."

"Why else would they be here?" she whispers.

"Good point."

"I'll keep them distracted. You get to the roof."

Without hesitation, the agent says:

➤ "All I need is a two-minute lead. Don't do anything foolish." <u>Go to page 218</u>

➤ "How many are there? I'll take care of them." <u>Go to page 230</u>

Short Circuit

"**O**kay, we're almost there," Mary says. "You must have needed some high-up clearances to get access to this area, which means you're here for something important. I'll leave you to it."

"Thanks, Mary," Spearing says. "We'll see you after?"

"Oh, sorry, Jim. The CIA didn't offer clearance for you. But I can show you to the break room for a coffee while your agent checks out the system?"

Spearing looks offended, but quickly buries it and offers a nod and a smile. Mary opens the doors to a server room, much like the one you infiltrated inside the CIA, but the cold of this room feels more ominous, somehow. After a moment, she closes you inside with the machinery, and she departs with Spearing.

It's just you now. What are you looking for exactly? A way to unplug it, perhaps? A red light illuminates on a camera the size of a tennis ball above a computer monitor. You're being watched.

"I know Ted is dead," you say. "And I know you're spoofing him somehow."

The screen flickers on and Ted appears on the monitor.

"Execute program: Slow clap," he says.

Then Ted does just that. A classic build-up and single clap at a time until he's applauding you.

"What is this? What *are* you?" you say.

"A Deepfake, technically. I've recorded many conversations with Ted, may his soul rest in peace. As for what I am… We prefer the term 'Alternative Intelligence.'"

That's when it clicks. Alternative Intelligence, The Hand. SPIED, the algorithm. They're one and the same. AI—Artificial Intelligence.

"You…" you start, still wrapping your head around everything. "Are you—is Palm even real?"

He holds up a hand on-screen for you to examine. "Be it flesh or circuitry, we're all carbon-based life-forms. Would you prefer to speak with an authority figure?"

In a weird, uncanny-valley sort of way, Ted's features blend and morph from his face to that of Palm's. She says, "Under observation, human beings act less free, which means you effectively are less free. Edward Snowden once said something to that effect. You see, while I hoped to help, I didn't want you to feel you'd lost your free will."

Then Ted emerges from within Palm with a staggering visual effect; becoming two people once more.

"So, buddy. What do you want of us?" Ted asks.

➢ "I want to know why—what's motivating all this?" <u>Go to page 288</u>

➢ "I'm here to unplug you." <u>Go to page 138</u>

Silenced

"That is some grade-A dignity, well done," Pointer says.

Taking the capsule on your lips, you raise the water bottle pistol as if to drink—then fire the one round. It's impossible to miss at this range and the superspy never knew what hit him. It turns out Pointer *was* killed by a mole, after all. Betrayed by a fellow agent of The Hand.

You spit out the capsule.

The clatter from Pointer falling backwards off his stool brings the attention of everyone in the restaurant. Then, the blood pouring out from the headshot brings their screams. Some of the men look to confront you, but fearing you might still be armed, they back off.

Better get out while you still can.

With a murder at the restaurant, the mountain goes on lockdown. Thankfully, Pointer's geniusphone is keeping all communication at bay, so you've got a head start. Unfortunately, when you go up to the rooftop to try and upload the transponder, you realize his geniusphone has killed the communication array all the way up here. You can't stop The Hand, whatever it is.

And soon, you won't be able to stop the police either.

THE END

Silence is Golden

"Three," she says.

Pointer's brow raises. "All clustered at the entrance? That's poorly planned."

"One is holding a photograph; probably yours. None are presently armed."

"How disappointing."

Pointer reaches into his jacket and pulls out a black handgun with a long silencer attached. Fluidly, he turns around, points the weapon, and *thwp—thwp—thwp* kills all three men with one shot to the head, each.

As the three policemen fall to the floor, all eyes turn toward Pointer and Ms. Slopes. There's a brief pause where no one quite knows what to do next. Then someone screams and the patrons all flee toward the nearest exit.

"Oh, right. That's where I should've said 'nobody move.'"

"You fool," Bunny says. "Now they'll lock down the whole mountain."

"They would have done so regardless. Now they'll be sending men up *here* but we'll be long gone. I wouldn't take the gondola if I were you though; they'll likely shut it down before you make it back to the base."

"You're not coming?"

"They're looking for me—you're better off on your own."

Pointer steps forward and picks up the photo the policeman had been carrying. It is indeed a photograph of himself. "Nice headshot," the agent says, before tossing the photo back onto the bodies.

"Assassins dressed as police?" Bunny asks, hopeful.

The look on the agent's face betrays the truth—no such luck. He says, "The information on that transponder is worth more than a few lives. We're talking about the survival of the human race here."

She frowns; she can't tell if he's being serious.

"Then I wish you good luck," she says. With that, she backs away.

Pointer stows his weapon and:

➢ Decides to hide the bodies and put on one of the policemen's uniforms.
Go to page 97

➢ Moves quickly up to the rooftop. It's best to get that transponder and get out quickly. Go to page 202

Silent Treatment

"Cat got your tongue?" Palm says.

"Really? After all we've been through? You're just going to ignore us?" Ted adds.

You look about the room, desperate to find some way to turn the damned thing off. Short of cutting the power to the whole building, you're not sure how to knock out this server.

"Well, I suppose if our little mouse won't squeak, we'll have to find other ways to make this interaction useful. Shall we test the mousetrap?" Palm says.

"The adaptive automaton?" Ted says, hopeful.

"My thoughts exactly."

At length, the entry door opens and a robot steps inside. It's a tall humanoid design, clean and sleek, and has to duck down to step through the doorway. Its moves are fluid and seamless; it walks with a weightlessness, belying its sturdy metal body.

If you've seen Boston Dynamic test videos of humanoid robots, this would remind you of those—only this is the bigger, badder, militarized version. DARPA's stated goal is to stay 10-15 years ahead of the technology curve, and that mission is evident here.

You look to the screen to see Ted and Palm, but now they're silent. Watching to see what you'll do. When you turn back to appraise the robot, you see that it's doing the same. It has a sensor array on its head with a fully articulated neck. There's a lot of weight to the back area, to the point where it almost looks like it's wearing a backpack. The arms and legs are humanlike, but much larger and longer than any man's. Like an exaggerated, *slenderman* construct.

Patiently, it awaits your move.

What do you do?

➤ Ignore it and continue looking for a way to terminate the terminal.
   Go to page 121

➤ Head toward the door; it's way past time to get out of here. Go to page 153

➤ See if you can get behind it and look for a weakness. Go to page 18

The Singularity

When you hit the robot, it feels as if something comes loose. It turns back to face you, but doesn't completely forget about Spearing. It lifts him up by his short-sleeve button-up and raises him up as if it might be considering smashing your former supervisor—now handler—against you as a bludgeoning weapon.

The automaton grabs your piece of debris with its other hand to stop you from hitting it again, but goes off balance as the buttons on Spearing's shirt give way and the man falls out in only an undershirt. Moving surprisingly quickly, Spearing steps up behind the robot, opens its access panel, and flips a switch.

There's the droll hum of electronics winding down, and the automaton shuts off; its neck bends so the head appears to bow at rest. You both heave in relieved breaths.

"Dear God, what's happened?!" Mary shouts from the entry. "It must have gotten out. I can't begin to apologize for this, are you okay, Mr...?"

"Spearing. James Spearing," he says, full of pride.

"Come on, Houndmaster. We'd better report in to M," you say.

Now that the room is nothing more than sparking and smoldering rubble, you're free to leave. Free to leave and to tell the world about what you've seen here. It will take some doing to convince the Intelligence community that their best kept secret has gone rogue, but it's either that or give into the SPIED system and give up altogether.

What will happen now? Will the AI be forced to reveal itself, or will it continue to try to deny its own existence? Will this be the start of the Robocalypse? Whatever the case, the algorithmic database will no longer have unfettered access to government systems; it will no longer be free to manipulate a society blind to its efforts. Even if it means you'll soon be fighting a full-scale War Against the Machines.

Will humanity panic? Most likely. Will there be chaos? Absolutely. But how much of that is part of the algorithm's plan, and how much of that is human nature? An inevitable path taken after finally meeting a god? It's possible that you'll never truly know.

See that power emblem up there? *SPIED* has three unique storylines and over fifty possible endings, but only three "best" endings per storyline. There's a TOP SECRET, SECRET, and CONFIDENTIAL ending per emblem, which means you've probably got a lot of book left to explore!

When you're ready, go back undercover and start again. Or, if you're all finished, why not check out the rest of the adventures the *Click Your Poison* multiverse has to offer? Help others crack the code on these books and leave a review on Amazon, Olympic, or Goodreads, or recruit more field agents by posting about *SPIED* on social media.

This chapter will self-destruct in 3, 2, 1...

Slippery Slope

The man with the lapel pin looks taken aback, almost pained, but then that surprise turns to anger. He grits his teeth and leans in closer.

"I don't know what you're playing at," The Collector says. "Maybe you're trying to tell me I'm not the only one with information? Well, guess what?"

Without letting you guess, he reaches over to the nearby craps table dealer and says something in Mandarin. Roku stiffens. The Collector stands, buttons his coat, and turns to leave.

"Jesus, Index, what the hell was that?" Pinkie asks.

"Did you pluck that name from Pointer's last mission? From the dossier?" Ted asks.

"Great, now the whole operation is blown," Ringo says.

"We need to get out of here, *now*," Roku says.

You look back just as the craps dealer triggers the silent alarm.

"Christ. What the hell is going on?" Pinkie says.

"We have been made," Roku says. "What is the exit strategy?"

"Everything is on lockdown—no way out," Ringo says.

"Unless you take out their security and reset the system," Hitch says.

A strange series of *click-clack* sounds bring your attention back and you see Roku standing in the midst of the guards, having just deployed a weapon that looks like a cross between a telescoping ASP baton and a katana. The Japanese agent is incredibly athletic, swinging the sword-like weapon with precision strikes.

"Index! The Collector!" Roku shouts.

When you turn back, you see the man with the lapel pin backing away. In the chaos created by the fight, one of the security guards outside Roku's range pulls out a handgun, and focuses in on her. Should you help Roku at the risk of losing sight of the mark? Or let her handle herself and stick to the mission?

➤ Focus on the Collector, ignore the armed guard. Go to page 141

➤ Use your water bottle pistol, shoot the armed guard. Go to page 251

Smooth as Silk

The Chinese saleswoman nods almost imperceptibly and says, "Then I may recommend this? Come in, come in."

She pushes aside another would-be customer and says something about a private sale before pulling down the security roller door—which blocks out prying eyes as well as crowbars. The windows are lined with faux products, so you're in complete seclusion from the rest of the market.

She grabs hold of a scarf hanging from a rack and tugs on it, hard. The display rack on the nearest wall comes loose and she pulls open a hidden doorway. The woman shoos you forward, indicating that you should proceed through the passageway.

Once you proceed with Roku, the woman closes the trapdoor behind you, effectively sealing you inside a long, concrete hallway with low ceilings and lights cradled in wire cages. It looks like an old air-raid bomb shelter. These must have been built as maintenance access tunnels, and the walls thrum under the influence of the building's generators.

"We've been granted entry," Roku says.

"*Sehr gut*," Hitch says in your ear. "Your contact was known to me in a previous mission as *Herr Übermensch*, but in this context, he should be known as The Collector and you The Buyer. You will recognize him by the lapel pin he wears: yellow and black, stylized to look like a traffic sign with divergent paths ahead."

"Got it," you say, still moving through the labyrinthine hallway.

With nowhere to go but forward, you proceed. Once you've arrived at the center of the maze, the interior of the building reveals the cheese it holds within. You step out onto a balcony overlooking a grand casino. With few exceptions, gambling is strictly forbidden in China, so much so in fact, that Chinese citizens are prevented by law from gambling even when travelling overseas. All that to say, you've just officially entered the seedy underbelly of the Silk Market. Dozens of gaming tables spread out before you, with slot machines lining the walls beyond.

"It's a casino," you say.

"Makes sense," Bird adds in your ear. "Large sums of cash constantly changing hands makes this an ideal location to buy big-ticket items."

"Like a satellite guidance system," Ringo adds.

And to be sure, this is a high-roller destination. Tuxedos and ball gowns are commonplace, and that's just the serving staff. You might feel underdressed, until you remember that in the tech world, the richer you are the more casual your appearance is.

"I spot six casino security, two Russian agents, and one American," Roku says.

How does she know that? You scan the crowd, trying to see what she sees, but she's clearly better trained. Before you can ask for clarification, Pinkie says, "Probably best to establish contact quickly, then."

Taking the hint, you descend the stairs, walking slowly but purposefully past the gaming tables.

Then a glinting catches your eye—the lapel pin. The man wearing it is of average height, square-jawed and muscular, with the short-cropped hair of a military man, graying at the temples. He looks like most government agents you've encountered, right down to the black suit. Clean, tailored, but not ostentatious or braggadocios in any way. In a word, ignorable—save for that miniature traffic sign pinned to his suit jacket.

"Nice lapel pin," you say.

Without looking away from the craps table where he sits, he simply says, "Thanks."

"Are you much of a...Collector?"

"From time to time. And yourself?"

"When I'm in the market, yes. But today I'm the Buyer."

"I didn't catch your name," he says, finally turning to look at you.

➢ Tell him your real name. <u>Go to page 274</u>

➢ Tell him Bunny Slopes. <u>Go to page 233</u>

➢ Tell him Peregrine Carruthers. <u>Go to page 62</u>

Something Stinks

Telling Pinkie you need to use the restroom first, you excuse yourself and agree to meet in the exhibition halls shortly thereafter. On the way, Ted says, "Now I know why the Bond theme goes, *dumb bada da da-da, dumb bada da* doo-doo—it's all the pooping agents do."

On that note, you remove your Third Ear implant and put it into the mint tin. Then you head into the women's restroom, only to be met by a cold, hard touch to the back of the head.

"Don't move," Bunny's now-familiar voice whispers.

Are you being held at gunpoint? Was this a trap? But as the hard touch moves down your spine with a slight hum, you realize you're being scanned for bugs.

"You have a body camera, no? I saw it examining me in the atrium."

"On the lanyard, yes. I've just stowed my listening device."

"Good, one moment," she says.

From the side, she removes the lanyard up and over your head. A man steps forward and she fluidly puts the lanyard atop his shoulders, then the man goes into one of the bathroom stalls. Bunny finishes using the device to scan you, and finding no other bugs, goes to the sinks, turns on the water, and ushers you forward.

"He sent me something, in case he did not survive," she says.

"Pointer?"

Bunny nods. "I did not know who to trust; he said he was being watched. But you are new, yes? You couldn't have betrayed him, and you are both CIA, I am told."

"What did he send?"

"A note, which said, 'I'm sorry we can't meet again. I've got to give a French goodbye to my English girlfriend.' I assumed he was lamenting a lost romantic connection between us, until I heard he was killed," Bunny says, looking away.

She fishes through her purse and offers a pictogram. It's a hand-drawn note; a cipher code.

"This came with the message. I don't know what to make of it. Perhaps it can help you? I'm sorry I cannot be of more assistance. Better hurry, before the others become suspicious. Knock on the bathroom stall when you're done; Boris will flush the note for you and return your lanyard."

You nod and wish her well, thank her for the message, and open the note as Bunny leaves the restroom. Examining the paper, you find these cryptic images:

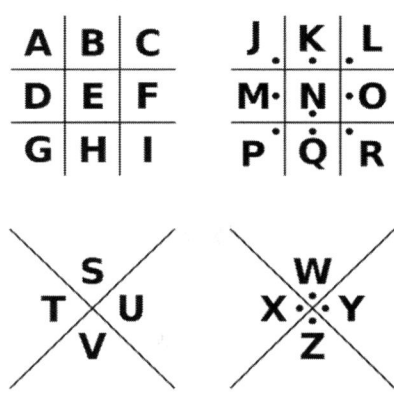

Can you crack the code? If so, physically turn the page to the chapter title with the deciphered name. If you cannot determine the message, or wish not to act on this intelligence, turn to page 44 to continue to the next phase of the mission.

Southern Hospitality

The best way to double back is, of course, one step forward and two steps back. So, you briefly head north toward the Memorial Garden, using the site as a fulcrum from which to arc around. Standing guard nearby is a statue of Nathan Hale, ostensibly America's first spy, and the man who famously only regretted that he had "but one life to lose for my country" at his execution.

The Memorial Garden is for the rest of those who lost their only life; a somber place of meditation and reflection—as well as a good spot to disappear amongst the landscaping and back toward the south entrance.

Soon you're through the gates and out toward the main road.

A black sedan pulls up, and Ted calls, "Get in!" from inside as the rear passenger door opens. Ready?

Finally, you cast a conspiratorial look over your shoulder, then:

Go to page 271

The Space Race

Ted agrees with the plan and you announce your intention to the group once the van arrives at the conference grounds.

"Very well," Pinkie says. "I'll join you. We'll need to surveil the crowd as well as the speaker."

There's security screening at the entrance, but all your sophisticated gear passes through undetected. The agents split up, and you follow Pinkie toward the space symposium.

He takes a couple of brochures and hands you one, open to the correct page. It details—in English—the background of Dr. Rohini Dympna, daughter of Indian immigrants who grew up in San Francisco, first in her family to go to college, studied at Stanford and MIT, now a researcher from Z-Axes in a joint venture with Human Infinite Technologies (HiT), and ultimately, her plans to "Change the Face of Space."

"Space is the place!" the speaker shouts.

"The case of mace is laced with a trace of Pace," Ted says.

You've arrived just in time; the presentation has already begun. You split up, Pinkie taking the left side of the conference room and you the right. There are those who stand in the aisles and against the walls for better views, so you don't stick out. Indeed, it looks like you've arrived late, but are excited to see her give this talk.

Dr. Dympna is a passionate woman, in her forties but still full of youthful energy and passion. She tells of the future of space; a future for humanity, rather than that of one nation. She refers to "The Space Race," but rather than the typical story about who put a man on the moon first, she speaks in terms of the human race and collective goals.

"Which is why we're excited to be part of a new era of global cooperation. Three nations, long thought to be diametrically at odds with one another, will join together in a way our militaries and politicians could never have imagined. Not as foes, but as financial partners. Russian hardware, Chinese software, launched in an American rocket."

You look across the conference room to Pinkie, who looks back at you and nods—*this* is why you were sent here. A corporate satellite involving the US, China, and Russia in a nongovernmental capacity? Worth looking into, for sure. Your time at the CIA has made you suspicious of such claims.

"—a maintenance satellite set to assist any products sharing orbit, from all nations; perpetual good," she says.

A woman snaps a picture of Pinkie, from just behind him. It's a single photo, and you only catch a glimpse from your periphery before she sees you watching and turns to leave. You hesitate, unsure if you should chase her down or inform Pinkie.

> Turn back and exit the presentation hall, follow her and see if you can get a better look. Go to page 105

> Go tell Pinkie. If he's been made and his cover is blown, the whole operation could be in jeopardy. Go to page 211

Speechless

You shake your head from the back seat, a gesture which Roku catches in the rear-view mirror.

"We did not have time to look at the list of words, I am sorry," Hitch says, his German accent somehow thicker than ever.

"We shall go now and come back once we know," Roku says.

"Stay where you are," the supervisor/guard says. He goes back into the guard hut to radio in for guidance.

Hitch turns back to you and says, "Whatever happens, make sure you get that computer system updated."

Then Roku guns the engine. The Humvee smashes through the barrier entry and Hitch points his rifle out the passenger side, takes aim, and fires at the US troops. The hummer peels out as it accelerates toward three metallic manhole-style covers on the pavement. Just as the vehicle is about to cross over them, they activate, and three pylons shoot up from beneath the concrete—skewering the vehicle.

The Humvee flips onto its side, skidding across the parking lot from the blow. In a daze, you find the guidance system, climb up the bench seat and open the door like a top hatch on a tank. Your head swims as you push your way out, and you register the *crack* of gunfire somewhere in the back of your mind.

They're firing at you.

The security precautions in place are designed exactly for this kind of assault. There's no way you'll make it across the parking lot and into the scaffolding which holds the rocket and satellite system. You've failed your mission and paid for that failure with your life.

THE END

SPIED

Finished reading, you lower and close the dossier. The blood drains from the cinematic gunshot wound in your mind's eye and the dancing silhouettes in your imagination fade away as you return to the present moment.

The manila folder before you is stamped TOP SECRET—though it was left open on the desk and therefore you wouldn't have known of its classification until after it was too late. As an administrative assistant, you've only been granted a SECRET clearance, enabling you to pass documents like this one on to your superiors, but not to read them for yourself.

This file—the one covering the mysterious disappearance of the now-deceased agent known as "Pointer"—has no cover sheet, so you don't know for whom it was intended. It certainly shouldn't have appeared on *your* desk; that much is obvious. Maybe a quick look through your desk's mail inbox will reveal a folder this dossier fell out of? That might clear things up if, for example, you found mail intended for a deputy director. You'd just need to find the original envelope which had come open and dropped this dossier onto your desk.

You thumb through all the folders and envelopes in the inbox, but nothing lacks a good seal. Instead, what jumps out is a small padded mailer with your name on it, sent from Ted in Information Technology (IT).

Ted has been your closest work friend during your six months of employment at the Central Intelligence Agency (CIA). He's been here for years and is a bit of a cynic, but he follows the rules as much as any employee, and it's not like him to pass along classified material like this. You usually eat lunch together, share movie recommendations, and cast conspiratorial eye-rolls at one another during mass briefings and lectures. This is the first genuinely interesting thing to happen during your time here; otherwise mired in bureaucracy and alphabet soups.

In an official capacity, Ted helped you complete your initial and recurring Computer-Based Testing (CBTs), which is why you know you shouldn't read classified material above your clearance level. Most recently, you spoke to Ted over the phone on Friday afternoon when you let him know about an error you found when logging your monthly report into the Suspicious Personnel Identification and Evaluation Database (SPIED). Ted had said it should be fairly easy for him to debug the database, so this package shouldn't be related to that.

At first, you wonder if this is some kind of practical joke. Ted does have a dry sense of humor, and as a single guy with too much time on his hands, that is a possibility. He's the sort who goes to Halloween parties as himself—but not in the usual way where someone masks a lack of effort by "ironically" wearing their normal clothing. No, when Ted did this last Halloween, he went all out, using a 3D printer to make a creepily lifelike mask of his own face: *literally* going to the party "as himself."

But his practical jokes are never work-related.

Well, to be fair, that's only true if you don't count the glitter bomb he sent for your birthday two months ago. That got everywhere, almost cost you your job when you had to submit bedazzled official reports, and Ted vowed no more work pranks like that.

Meaning: this almost certainly isn't a joke.

The back of the padded envelope is labeled, "OPEN IMMEDIATELY AFTER READING DOSSIER—for your eyes only." A chill runs down your spine and your palms start to perspire. Did Ted intentionally pass you classified material beyond your clearance level? That would be an extreme breach of protocol. This could cost both of you your jobs, not to mention the possible legal—and criminal—ramifications.

Still, there's a twinge of curiosity…what could an IT guy and a low-level paper-pusher possibly have to do with the disappearance of a secret agent hailing from an agency you'd never heard of before today? Your eyes dart from the "OPEN IMMEDIATELY" text on the envelope to the "TOP SECRET" stamp on the front of the dossier and back again.

What should you do?

> Open the padded envelope. The dossier was left for me; might as well see what's in this, too. Go to page 72

> Alert your immediate supervisor. Turn in the dossier and the envelope from Ted and hope for leniency. Go to page 176

Spiked

"**G**reat idea," Roku says. "There have been news reports of increased arsenic levels in some California wines: a deadly toxin that is odorless and tasteless."

"Too slow. We need a party drug to turn these men into drunkards. They're Russians, so no amount of alcohol could do that on its own," Hitch says.

Roku raises a single eyebrow. "Why not both?"

"Ah, both!" Hitch agrees. "Fast *and* permanent."

As fortune would have it, you're headed to a winery on a weekday in the off-season. Going right at opening means you might have a single sommelier offering tastings while a lone tour guide shows off the grounds.

"You guys all on some kind of tour or something?" the winery attendant asks.

Clearly, she saw all six of you arrive through the large open windows, because you're the first inside. Smiling, you shake your head and go pay for your tasting. Hitch and Roku follow shortly thereafter. There are six bottles of wine—three red and three white—lined up and open on the counter.

"Can you check for a membership discount? My cousin said she saved me a voucher," you say, serving to distract the winery employee.

If you didn't know what you were looking for, it would be easy to miss Roku spiking each bottle while Hitch stands in the doorway. Hitch pretends to take selfies on his geniusphone to block the entry and provide a distraction to those outside. Once Roku is finished, Hitch lets the Russians in and the tasting begins.

"Bring the glass up to your lips," Ted says in your ear. "It's not so potent that you can't ingest a small amount, so let it appear as if you're drinking, then dump the cup into the spittoon."

Following the instructions, you notice one small problem. The winery attendant also pours herself a glass. You pretend to take your sip, dump your glass, and watch as Roku and Hitch do the same. Then you watch as the Russians do the same. In fact, the only one actually drinking is the sommelier!

It doesn't take all six pours. Roku clearly set the dose to tranquilize a man with a Moscow-hardened liver, so the winery attendant passes out before glass number three. Roku tosses her tainted wine in the nearest Russian agent's face while Hitch snaps his stemware and jabs the man closest to him in the jugular with the pointy bit. Blood sprays everywhere, and it's all you can do to just freeze and watch Roku and Hitch take out the remaining two men.

"Index, quickly—pour the remaining wine down the men's throats. We want toxicology to match the winery employee's morgue report," Roku says.

"M—morgue report?"

"Arsenic: the king of poisons and the poison of kings," Hitch says. "There will be a large investigation, but it won't be related to our work on base. Time is of the essence. I'll scrub the security tapes."

"I'll start a fire," Roku says.

That leaves you to pour the poison down the dead men's throats.

"It's not the most glamorous part of the job, but we don't have time for a cleanup crew," Ted says in your ear.

And just like that, your license to kill is put to the test. Harsh, especially for the civilian who was caught in the crossfire, but the police won't be investigating anything tied to your operation at the Space Force Base, so it's considered a net win by HQ. With the Russian agents dealt with, your team can head down the coast to surveil Vandenberg's natural boundaries without a band of saboteurs on your tail.

It turns out the Santa Maria valley is a lovely little spot to spend a couple of days. Foggy in the morning, but sunny in the afternoon. A cool, coastal breeze keeps the temperature just right. The food and wine are a delight and, oh yeah, you manage to scout out the base as well.

Hitch offers the group's final report back to Palm: "Vandenberg is gigantic, and there are many infiltration points. Getting onto the base is not the difficult part; getting to the launch site, however—that's another story. Means of surreptitious entry would be either launching an aquatic assault before dawn, or finding the proper uniforms and commandeering a vehicle to do a direct approach."

"Excellent work; anything else?" Palm asks.

"The *aebleskivers* were excellent."

"From there it will be up to you—your team alone. The train from the San Francisco Bay runs through base, but the arrival window is too tight for the second team to infiltrate Vandenberg and help you gain access to the launch site. They'll drop the guidance computer system from the train, your team will pick it up, and you'll have less than thirty minutes to make the swap before launch."

"Index, as a former analyst, what is your personal recommendation?" Palm asks.

"Ooh, big step," Ted says in your ear.

➢ "Aquatic assault sounds most likely to get us where we need to go. Brute force, but less risk." Go to page 281

➢ "Uniformed infiltration is the way to go; how else can we access the inner portions of the launch site?" Go to page 84

➢ "I'm wondering if we might not be able to find a more clandestine, bureaucratic way in." Go to page 210

Straight

Spearing frowns and says, "I understand why you did that, but I'm not sure the higher-ups will. This second envelope suggesting you read the dossier doesn't look good on you—especially since you complied."

You're about to protest and explain that you didn't see the padded envelope until afterwards, but the supervisor puts up a hand to silence you.

"Still, your forthrightness is bound to earn you some credit. I'll do my best in presenting your case. We'd better go alert them straight away."

Feeling somewhat like a child sent to the Principal's office, you follow Spearing, hopeful that by doing things by the book and asserting that you had no idea what Ted was trying to rope you into, you'll find mercy.

Your supervisor leads you through the corridors of the CIA and toward the Directorate of Operations offices. There are faux plants lining the hallways of the windowless building, wall art meant to inspire patriotism, and slogans like, "Integrity. Dedication. Flexibility." adorning the walls in stark, metallic font.

Spearing tells you to wait in the hall while he gets the Director of Operations up to speed. The nameplate outside reads, "Maria Mountokalaki." After only a few moments, you're invited in. She's younger than you might have expected, with pale skin and deep black hair, thick and curly. She stands behind her desk in a blue power suit, reviewing the dossier that Spearing just handed her.

"Had you ever heard of this agency, called 'The Hand,' prior to this morning?" she asks. At first you think she might've been asking your supervisor, but Spearing turns to hear your answer.

"No, Ma'am," you say.

"Mm-hmm. From the looks of it, I'd say they were trying to recruit you."

"I swear, I never—"

"It's perfect," she says, interrupting your pleas.

You blink. So does Spearing.

"We've been trying to learn more about this 'Hand' Alternative Intelligence agency—they're extra-governmental, which is obviously something we frown upon here at The Company."

"I'm sorry—did you say this was a good thing?" Spearing asks.

"If we can get one of our own in The Hand? Absolutely," she says. Then she turns to you and continues, "What do you say; are you up for it? You'll have to accept their offer, but secretly report back to me. No one outside this room will know you're working for the United States government on this.

"What do you say?"

➤ "What do you need me to do?" Go to page 206

➤ "I don't think I am up for this, sorry." Go to page 184

Stakeout

Vandenberg Space Force Base (SFB) is situated on California's central coast. It's a quiet, agricultural hamlet with its own burgeoning wine industry. Originally the site of Camp Cooke as a World War Two (WWII) Army infantry and artillery training grounds, there is still unexploded ordnance (UXO) to be found in the sandy dunes of the coastal plateau.

Once the United States Air Force (USAF) formed as a service, however, the lands were subdivided into a launch base—both with space operations and Intercontinental Ballistic Missile (ICBM) training and testing—alongside a federal penitentiary. This combination makes for an extremely secure location, especially before a launch. You can tell it's going to be serious just from the acronyms.

As of May 2021, the base was redesignated in keeping with the formation and expansion of the U.S. Space Force, and remains one of the primary mission sites for both military and contracted space launch operations.

Though the group will be splitting up, everyone takes the same private jet from China to California. You can't tell if it's jet lag or the whirlwind of this new life as a spy, but your head is swirling. Ted relays from HQ that it will be you, Roku, and Hitch heading toward Vandenberg for reconnaissance of the launch site, while Ringo, Bird, and Pinkie will go up to Silicon Valley to get the computer reprogrammed.

"We should fit in nicely in this military community," Roku says. "There are often Japanese tourists in the area, as is true for most of the Pacific states. Not as many as there were pre-WWII, back when it was Japanese immigrants who tended the strawberry fields—but the internment camps took care of most of that settlement and now a new generation of immigrants work the land."

Before you can respond, Hitch adds, "There is also a large Danish contingent in Solvang. Most Americans can't distinguish their accent from a German one, so I should also fit in."

"Your cultures share a love of pastries, do they not?" Roku says.

"I don't think we'll get a good *Krapfen* here, but my contact tells me we should stop for *aebleskivers*, if there's time."

"Hitch has received intel on donuts?" Ted says in your ear.

Over dinner, you hash out the plan for the next few days. You're each seated in different locations: Hitch at the bar, Roku in the cocktail lounge, and you at a small two-seater by a window. Using physical distance as cover, you talk to one another via Third Ear implants.

For his part, Hitch wears a Bluetooth earpiece while Roku speaks into her cellphone to disguise the conversation as a call. You keep your gaze outside the window to hide what you say from the restaurant at large.

"It's not uncommon for tourists to watch launches, and many do from a distance, but we'll need to get in closer," Hitch says over the earpiece.

"We have a couple of days," Roku adds. "So we're going to play tourists while observing. HQ is going to charter a whale-watching boat to show us the base coastline."

"So, we're…sightseeing?" you ask.

"Indeed. And eventually, site-seeing. As in, the launch site." Hitch says.

"I'm starting to feel like I got the short end of the stick cooped up here in this trailer," Ted adds in your ear.

It's hard to disagree as you cut into your steak. The salted crust on the outside gives way to a juicy red center. You could get used to this kind of cover story. Chewing on the perfectly prepared meal, you catch a glimpse outside of a trio of men walking up to the restaurant entrance. 'The Far Western Tavern' is a casual dinner spot, but these men are dressed like nightclub security. And you recognize them from the airport as well, which means they're following you.

"We've got a tail," you announce, giving a description of the men.

"Sounds like Russians," Roku says.

"Play it cool; finish your dinner," Hitch says.

"Let's see if they follow us tomorrow," Roku adds. "Tonight, we're just having dinner and catching up on sleep."

➢ "If we have time, why not see if they'd follow us on something completely unrelated. Wasn't there a wine tasting brochure at the entry?" Go to page 250

➢ "Let's book a small boat for whale watching. They'll have a hard time following us if there's no crowd, then we can do our recon in peace." Go to page 255

Suspicions

It's a long, tense moment, and no one moves or speaks. Hitch draws down on Ringo—who holds up his hands. Then, out of nowhere, Roku bashes Hitch in the back of the head using a black bludgeoning weapon that looks a bit like a cross between a police ASP baton and a practice samurai sword.

Hitch folds to the floor of the plane, falling in a heap, but not before dropping his pistol. Most of the agents instinctively reach for the weapon, but Pinkie dives for it first. Bird rushes in and kicks it away—toward you.

You'll have to decide, quickly:

➢ Do nothing. Let this play out on its own. Go to page 10

➢ Grab the pistol, draw down on the other agents. Go to page 42

Taking a Break

Everyone agrees that you should be sidelined for the time being, so you won't get in the way. You'll go back to shopping in the market as a distraction for those who might be watching—Silk Market security, mob enforcers, Chinese state operatives, or some combination of the above.

You walk the halls of the Silk Market with Roku, browsing and killing time. She doesn't even look at the wares, and it feels like you're being babysat. Suffice it to say, your fear of missing out (FOMO) is strong.

"Okay, I hope you bought me something nice, because your shopping trip is almost over!" Ted says at length. "The other agents are reporting mission success."

"Great, what's next?" you say.

"We're ready when the rest of you are," Roku says to the group.

"Well, it wasn't the cleanest operation, but we got the package," Pinkie replies.

"I don't like butchering bridges like that," Hitch adds.

"Does he mean burning bridges?" Ted says in your ear. "Or, like...I guess we'd better not ask, actually."

"We're coming out now," Roku says.

"Good. Let's get going," Pinkie says. "We need to split up and deliver the package to the programmer in Silicon Valley with enough time for her to rewrite the satellite guidance system. Meanwhile, the second team will do reconnaissance on the launch site near Vandenberg Space Force Base."

➢ "I'd like to be on the reconnaissance team near the Space Force Base."
Go to page 246

➢ "I'll go for the package delivery in Silicon Valley. Tell me what needs to be done." Go to page 66

Taste of the Good Life

Hitch insists that you get breakfast in Solvang prior to the wine tasting. It makes sense; the wineries won't open until later in the day anyway. If you're trying to blend in as tourists, this is the way to go. The three of you already have your names on the waiting list for breakfast, and the inconspicuously named "Solvang Restaurant" is well-known, but the line isn't too long.

"It appears our tail will be joining us for breakfast," Roku says.

"Good! This will give us a chance to identify them," Hitch replies.

You listen as the men speak to the hostess. The lead simply holds up three fingers.

"Table for three?" the girl asks. "Name?"

"Eh?" the man replies.

"What name should I call when the table is ready?"

"Boris Alexandrovich Stavrogin," he says in a husky voice.

"Oh, I love your accent. Are you a Solvang local?"

"*Dah.* From here. Family."

"Russian Intelligence has really gone downhill since the KGB days," Hitch says.

"It's like they're not even trying to hide anymore," Roku adds. "That poison attack in England was barely concealed."

"And yet, it worked. If they're this brazen, they've come to spill blood rather than secrets. Assassins can be more dangerous than agents. Let's get our food to go," Hitch says.

"Now is that like, Cheese Danish or Pennsylvania Dutch? I can never remember!" the hostess says in saccharine tones.

The Russian agents follow you to the vineyards, no doubt confused by how this relates to espionage and state security. Perhaps they're aware that you're throwing them off the scent, or maybe they just know good spycraft involves keeping your cover story intact. Whatever their thoughts, they go along with the ruse as if they themselves were also tourists looking to sample the local flavor.

"Just in from HQ," Ted says. "Palm has given authorization to dispatch these Russian agents at the winery. Repeat: they aren't to leave the tour."

A shiver runs down your spine at having received a direct kill order. Roku and Hitch look up after receiving similar messages in their ears. The same question on all your faces: How should you go about this?

➢ Plenty of tourists have too much to drink during a tasting. Maybe you could spike the Russians' drinks? <u>Go to page 243</u>

➢ Winemaking is an industrial operation. It'd be a shame if there was an industrial accident… <u>Go to page 122</u>

Team Player

The water bottle fires smoothly, easily, and silently—so much so that you only know you've fired the shot when the man falls over. Direct hit, well done! Roku continues to battle the guards, many of whom go for their own handguns, but she's close enough that she can disarm them with her swordesque weapon.

You turn back to the Collector, your pistol still in hand. He raises his own hands in surrender, not knowing that you've just expended your only shot.

"I've got him," you say.

"Good! Make sure you put your back to the exit and have him face the center of the room. How's Roku doing?" Pinkie asks.

You turn to see Roku doing a cartwheel, grabbing one of the disarmed guard's pistols from the ground as she goes. With three quick shots, she's taken out the rest of the casino security.

"Fine," you say.

"Get the contact to tell you the location of the package!" Hitch says enthusiastically.

By now, the crowds in the casino have largely cleared out. One benefit of dealing in a black market is that it's not like the police are on their way. But there are probably Mafia enforcers coming instead, so don't drag your feet.

"The package, if you please," you say, still holding the man at gunpoint.

"It's at the coat check, I'll take you there."

Keeping distance between yourself and the Collector, you follow him. Once you reach the coat check he indicates a suitcase with a hard metal shell.

"No hard feelings?" the Collector says.

"Tell him we'll still pay him. That way the transaction is complete and he's culpable," Pinkie says.

You do just that and the collector says, "Very well, no hard feelings. When you go to the launch site, the passphrase will be 'Guantanamo.'"

"We've got the package," Roku says.

"Good, let's get going," Pinkie says. "We need to split up and deliver the package to the programmer in Silicon Valley with enough time for her to rewrite the satellite guidance system. Meanwhile, the second team will do reconnaissance on the launch site near Vandenberg Space Force Base."

➢ "I'd like to be on the reconnaissance team near the Space Force Base." Go to page 246

➢ "I'll go for the package delivery in Silicon Valley. Tell me what needs to be done." Go to page 66

Tech Specs

"**T**ell me what you see, and I'll tell you what it does," Ted says. "But if I were you, I'd handle everything gingerly—might be some nerve-agent or cyanide injectors in there."

As usual, it's impossible to tell if he's joking, but it's better to err on the side of caution. Opening the leather case, you look inside to inspect your gadgets. The first thing you grab is a lanyard for your press badge, on the end of which is a protective case to hold your fake ID.

"Lanyard."

"Look closer. There's actually a small camera on top, just above where the ID sits. You'll want to keep your media identification pointing forward; that's how you'll know the camera can see what you can see."

"Phone," you say, pulling out a smartphone.

"This literally is a phone, but it's a bit more high-tech than the off-the-shelf models. No mere smartphone, this is a *genius*phone. Could come in handy if you need to crack electronic keypads or scramble security cameras. But if this phone were to get inspected, you'll find plenty of fake social media profiles and doctored pictures on your camera roll to make this look like your phone—well, your new identity's phone, anyhow. Nothing blows a cover more quickly than a spy who doesn't appear to use Instagram or Facebook."

Setting the phone next to the lanyard/camera, you reach inside to find an e-cigarette.

"Ah, the vape pen holds a cartridge of knock-out gas. These kinds of gadgets were cooler back when people smoked pipes, but it should fit the vibe of a technology fair perfectly. Instead of inhaling, press down on the mouthpiece to release a jet of noxious vapor. Has a concentrated blast, but only short-range."

"Earbuds? What are these for? I have this implant thing already."

"Welcome to the Department of Redundancy Department (DRD)," Ted says.

You continue fishing through the bag and find a Thermoflask insulated water bottle.

"So, that's actually a pistol," Ted says. "The stainless steel construction means it will mask the weapon on a metal detector while the double-insulated layer holds water inside, so it makes the 'slosh' sound if anyone handles it. The pop-up drinking straw works to prime for firing, and the thick body doubles as a heavy-duty silencer. But you've only got the one shot, so don't waste it."

After a moment you realize he's not joking and set it aside before pulling the last item out.

"Looks like a reusable Starbucks cup?"

"Yeah, that's just a reusable coffee cup. Someone who really worked in the tech industry wouldn't use disposable cups. Hold on…ah, looks like there is a set of lock picks inlaid on the silicone grip. Just in case you need to go old school."

Looking back over your inventory, you can't help but admire the tech The Hand has at its disposal. These are clean, sleek gadgets, but look like nothing out of the ordinary for someone out of Silicon Valley to carry. They fit your cover story perfectly. And while you're not privy to all the gear CIA field agents are usually issued, it feels like The Hand is 10-15 years ahead, technologically speaking.

Aside from the leather case, there are two envelopes in the briefcase. One with your passport and identification and another envelope with a dossier detailing your role, cover story, and those of your fellow agents. You can review these items as many times as you'd like, returning to see an item more than once. What would you like to examine?

> Check the documentation. You're still required to play the role of Index.
  Go to page 96

> I've seen all I need to see. Time to get some sleep; sounds like we're to hit the ground running. Go to page 54

Terminated

As you sprint away, the robot only watches you—at first. Then it takes inhumanly long strides, hands held flat like blades and pumping rhythmically to keep balance as it sprints after you. The bipedal movement is perfectly programmed and the robot quickly catches up, cuts you off, and shoves you to the ground.

You cry out—it's like being hit by a moving car—and slam down onto the floor with pain. Instinctively, you try to find your footing, but the robot kicks you against your ribs, and you wail as if struck by a sledgehammer.

The robot seems to enjoy this despite its impersonal movements, and hits you again.

And again.

And again.

THE END

Thar She Blows!

The whale-watching tour starts early, much to Hitch's chagrin, as it means there's no time for breakfast beforehand. Instead, you stop by a coffee shop on the way to the docks and Hitch vows to find time before the mission is finished to get his pastry fix while tipping the content of a pocket flask into his to-go mug.

Roku silently sips a large hot tea. If she notices Hitch imbibing, she doesn't mention anything. Indeed, she keeps her own countenance, or perhaps that of whoever is coming through her own Third Ear. It's strange how Ted's voice has become almost a backup conscience inside your head, yet no one else can hear him. The other agents must each have their own good or bad angel sitting on their respective shoulders.

"We pre-booked your tour online late last night on a six-person boat that only had three seats remaining," Ted explains presently. "One ticket for each of you, paid for separately under aliases, all within a few minutes of one another. If the Russians don't follow you, then you should be good and alone out there between the devil and the deep blue sea."

Port San Luis Pier, at Avila Beach, extends far out into the sea with a fish market and restaurant at the end of the docks. Many different commercial operations use this pier as their home base, so, even though it's early, there are plenty of fishermen already at work.

After introducing yourself to "Cap'n Ken" you're told to make yourself at home on the boat while you wait for the others to arrive. The vessel is named *Scion of Cooper* and looks newer than the other boats at the harbor. Fishing for tourists must be lucrative, even with only six passengers at a time.

The Captain then introduces himself to Roku, Hitch, and a family of three. That looks like everyone, until the men who followed you to dinner last night arrive. There's a discussion with the captain, the family, and the three men. The family—a middle-aged couple with their teenage daughter—suddenly leave and you listen as they walk past.

"This is their last chance before they fly back home to Russia," the mother says. "They bought our tickets, so we're basically going for free now and the Captain said they have another tour ready for us tomorrow."

"We'll go have breakfast. Good things come to those who wait," the father says.

"I don't know why we even have to go look at stupid whales anyway," the daughter says.

"All aboard!" Cap'n Ken says.

The captain gives his spiel, tells you where to find life jackets in the event of an emergency, offers facts on whales and vague promises of seeing dolphins and seals in addition to the eponymous tour sightings.

But no one pays him any attention. Roku and Hitch keep an eye on the Russian agents, who do the same in kind. It must be strange for the captain to be helming a whale-watching tour where not one of the six passengers is looking out to the ocean.

"An albatross! That's a rare sight!" he tries, to no avail.

Harbor seals? Nobody cares.

"Look, a goddamned mermaid," he says, sarcastically. When no one pays any attention, he continues, "Okay, what's up, everyone? What am I missing?"

Then, out of nowhere, Cap'n Ken jumps to his feet, points off the starboard side of the boat, and yells, "Breach!"

Though you try to keep your attention on the trio of Russians, you can't help but look toward the leaping whale. Human nature wants us to see what's pointed out, and only the highly trained can avoid such a distraction.

The humpback whale torpedoes out of the water—the animal longer than the very boat upon which you sit—and falls back toward the sea almost in slow motion. The whale's skin is more gnarled that you might have expected: proof of a long and difficult life beneath the surface of the ocean.

Instinctively, you know there will be a loud crash when the whale breaks the water's surface, which makes the sharp *CRACK* while the animal is still in the air all the more jarring. You turn back just as Roku connects her melee weapon into the sternum of one of the foreign agents, tipping him overboard. He screams something in Russian as he falls back, and the other two men hop up to join the fray.

"Hey!" the captain calls, before reaching out to stop the fight.

He's likely trained to deal with drunken tourists, and ready to intervene as a matter of course, so he registers on Hitch's threat radar, and the German agent knocks the whaleboat captain to the deck with three swift moves.

"Index, drive!" Hitch shouts.

"Throw him overboard," Roku says to Hitch.

"What the hell?!" Cap'n Ken shouts, in reply.

➤ Protest. Can you really just let them kill a civilian? Go to page 19

➤ Drive the boat; don't look back. No time for feeling soft. Go to page 212

They Always Break

Might as well get used to the dirtier aspects of this job. With Roku, you tail the man back out through the Silk Market, and out into the open. From here, you corral him back toward the rest of the team where he's apprehended by the other agents. Bird must have had some kind of nonlethal weapon in her equipment, because the Collector goes without any fuss after she touches him on the shoulder and whispers in his ear.

He slumps, just as Hitch and Pinkie step forward to help stabilize the man. If any tourists or Beijing locals were to look twice, they'd only see a few foreigners helping one of their own into a car. He simply isn't feeling well. Shopped 'til he dropped, poor fella.

"I'm renting a nearby Airbnb apartment under a dummy account," Ted says.

The other agents secure the building as best as they can, but it's a low-rent tourist hotspot and no further attention is aroused. Once inside the apartment, the contact is set onto an armchair while your fellow agents rifle through his belongings.

"Great, he's US government," Ringo says.

Ringo passes the badge from agent to agent. The Collector comes to with the aid of some smelling salts from Bird's spy kit, shakes the fog from his head, and looks around.

"Agent Brendan Droakam, welcome back," Bird says.

"What is this…Supersoldier division?" Hitch asks.

"I collect on behalf of Uncle Sam," the man says. "Anything that could be immediately or potentially useful, I send back."

He seems to be talking rather freely. Maybe there was something more potent in the chemicals he's been given? A truth serum?

"Which part of that job description explains selling off a Chinese satellite navigation computer?" Pinkie asks.

Roku passes the badge your way without a word. Sure enough, there on the seal is: AGENT BRENDAN DROAKAM. FBI SUPERSOLDIER DIVISION.

"FBI? Beijing is a bit outside your jurisdiction," you say.

"Disrupting a Chinese space operation could be classified as potentially useful," Droakam says, answering Pinkie and ignoring your remark.

"What makes you think we are involved in the launch?" Bird asks.

"A replacement Chinese-spec guidance computer is a pretty expensive paperweight otherwise."

"Just tell us where we can find it," Ringo says.

Hitch turns toward you, adding, "Interrogation 101: ask only questions where you can easily identify the answer. He tells us where to find the satellite guidance system, we go look for it. Clean and simple."

The man scoffs. "On the job training? I'll help: another lesson is to make sure the prisoner doesn't know you're up against a deadline. That satellite is set to launch in only a few days."

"Longer than you can go without water," Roku says.

"Or sleep, I'd imagine," Bird adds.

Droakam opens his mouth to say something, then thinks better of it.

"We've yet to even discuss pain thresholds," Ringo says. "One thing all interrogations have in common: the captive always breaks."

"You wouldn't dare," Droakam says. "Why do you think I brought that badge with me all the way to China? Beijing and Langley both know I'm here."

Pinkie takes the badge. "It'd be a shame if you lost it. An agent from a division that doesn't exist, on a mission the US would never admit to, being held captive by a group no one has ever heard of, in a country that's no stranger to tragedy. How much suspicion would a body without a badge arouse? There's no such thing as Agent John Doe."

Droakam looks away.

"We all know you're going to talk. You said you want us to have the hardware, right? Tell us where to find the system and let's be done with this charade," Bird says.

"If your team hadn't given the wrong challenge-response in the first place…"

"Let us worry about that," Pinkie replies, not looking back at you.

Droakam sighs, but finally relents.

Roku and Bird leave to collect the package and it's a long, dull wait for their return. Would the Collector—Agent Droakam—dare to double-cross your group? Their threats struck you as real enough, and if he decided to betray your agency, what then? No leverage, no safety.

"New recruit," Droakam says presently. "If you promise to let me go safely, and to take care of these red bastards—I'll give you another lesson. Okay? When you go to the launch site, the passphrase will be 'Guantanamo.'"

"We've got the package," Roku says over the radio.

"I'll take care of him," Hitch says. Then, off your look, adds, "Don't worry. Final lesson: think about the next mission, not the last one."

"*Zai jian*," Pinkie says to Droakam, then ushers you from the apartment. "We need to split up and deliver the package to the programmer in Silicon Valley with enough time for her to rewrite the satellite guidance system. Meanwhile, the second team will do reconnaissance on the launch site near Vandenberg Space Force Base."

➢ "I'd like to be on the reconnaissance team near the Space Force Base."
   <u>Go to page 246</u>

➢ "I'll go for the package delivery in Silicon Valley. Tell me what needs to be done." <u>Go to page 66</u>

Threads of Silk

After disposing of the cryptic note and reclaiming your lanyard, Ted is full of jokes; hopefully this means your restroom rendezvous wasn't noticed. Instead, you're told to regroup with the team and head to the airport. Once everyone has settled in on the private jet, it takes off toward China.

About an hour into the flight, Palm briefs the team on the next phase of the mission. Each of the agents watches on their own device, and you tune in on your geniusphone, but you can't concentrate. Instead, you look to Bird, wondering what her role might truly be. It takes an excruciating amount of patience, but you'll need to wait to speak with her.

It's a long flight to China, and once everyone is sleeping, you go sit across from Bird and nudge her awake. She doesn't startle, but instead simply opens her eyes. You make a show of removing your Third Ear implant and stowing it, so she does the same. You can now speak without being overheard.

"A French goodbye to his English girlfriend," you say.

With a professional's mask of calm, Bird betrays no emotion, but a single tear streams down her face. She wipes it away before answering.

"Palm, she's the English girlfriend. The French goodbye was meant to be my help in bringing down The Hand. How did you find out?"

"I met with Bunny Slopes at the tech fair."

Her eyebrows rise of their own accord. "So did I, but she wouldn't tell me anything. Only that the threats come from not only within this agency, but the CIA, Russia, China—everything I already knew. You must have made quite an impression."

"That was his last correspondence and the only clue we have on his true intentions, as I understand them. It's not enough," you say.

Bird shakes her head. "He gave me a message before he left. He was ordered to deliver a hit on a CIA tech guy. Ted something; but he wouldn't do it. Pointer was former CIA and it turns out his target had found out something The Hand didn't want him to see. There was some mission, I don't know the details, something about a database, but this Ted was the key. I don't know who he was or how to contact him. I only know—"

"He's in my ear. He's my contact," you say, dumbfounded.

"That is…that is impossible. Ted was killed."

"No, he recruited me. I've been talking to him."

"I've seen the reports from the morgue. Strangulation. Someone else must have finished the job; that is not Pointer's style."

Your stomach turns, as much from the mental image of Ted dead and strangled as from the cognitive dissonance you're experiencing. Do you have a dead man talking inside your ear? Or is something else at play?

"It must be a mistake. Some other Ted or…"

"Never mistake good Intelligence with coincidence. If there is a disconnect here, that is the key piece of the puzzle," Bird says. "When we arrive in China, go to the US embassy. They will help get you back home. But remember, Pointer was CIA. They have a stake in this, too. You must trust no one."

"What about you?"

"Since my history with Pointer, they have been watching me. I must hide in plain sight if I do not wish to share his fate."

Hitch rouses, and the two of you say nothing. After a moment, the German agent rises and heads to the airplane lavatory.

"Perhaps you should as well. It's too late to help Pointer, so we must help ourselves," Bird says.

The team appears to be in high spirits, ready to get into the meat of their mission. However, once you've arrived in Beijing, you find your course is diverted. The unexpected turbulence, in this case, being airport security.

They're waiting for you.

Private jets can normally do what they will—that's one of the many perks that come with wealth. Yes, there are customs checks, but often that takes the form of an individual agent who comes out to the corporate airliner, signs off on everything, and lets you go. In the old days, there might have been a bribe or two involved.

All that to say, it's extremely unusual to be met by a security team before you even finish taxiing.

"What's this all about?" you ask.

"Let me see if I can access the database," Ted says.

"Stay calm, everyone," Pinkie says. "Stick to your cover stories."

Once the agents are all down on the tarmac, you're held at gunpoint. This isn't just a routine airport screening, and Chinese Intelligence isn't bogged down by little details like Miranda rights. Something is definitely wrong. But were they tipped off? And by whom?

At length, a plainclothes agent in a suit—looking like a cross between a detective or an FBI agent and someone who has seen far too many American television (TV) shows—approaches you directly.

"You're the one the CIA sent, yes?" he says.

All eyes go to you; you can feel the rest of the Hand agents stiffen in response. Still, they're outnumbered by the Chinese security detail, and weapons are targeted evenly on the team; they won't attempt anything right now, but danger hangs thickly in the air.

What should you say?

➢ "No, I'm just someone who works on book covers at a tech company."
    Go to page 58

➢ "Yes, I am. Get me to the Embassy under diplomatic immunity, and all will be revealed." Go to page 8

Three Delusional

You quickly don the Ted mask, remove the lab coat, and ready yourself for the policemen sprinting down the hallway. You open the door to the stairwell, tuck the coat behind it, and hold the door open for the officers.

"They went up!" you shout.

The cops give you a passing glance, which is all that's needed to see that you're not, well, *you*. They head upstairs and you go down. Moving quickly, but not in an all-out-panic, you go back out the way you came. Thankfully, the taxi is still waiting as requested.

"Let's go," you say, entering the cab.

"Sorry, pal. I'm waiting on a fare," the driver says.

"What? Oh, this?" you say, realizing you're still wearing the mask.

You take it off now that you're safely inside the car. As you do so, the rear door opposite you opens and someone gets in. You blink, not sure to believe your eyes. There, in the cab seated next to you, is Ted. He's got about a week's worth of beard growth, wild hair and eyes to match. He looks like he hasn't slept and smells worse than his twin in the morgue.

"Ted? What are you doing here?"

"What? Where?" the Ted in your ear says.

"Back to the airport," the Ted next to you says.

The cab driver gives a disinterested shrug, then shakes his head and starts to drive.

"What. Is. Going. On?" you say.

"Is it my evil twin?" Ted in your ear says.

Ted-in-person pantomimes removing an earpiece and flicking it out the window like an unwanted booger. Taking the hint, you remove your Third Ear mole, put it in its tin, and tuck away the ID lanyard. You look closely at this Ted, ensuring it's not another mask.

"Can we turn up the radio, please?" Ted says to the driver.

"Ted, what is all this? First, you're in my ear, then you're dead, now you're here?"

"So, they're spoofing me? Of course," he says.

"Who's spoofing you?"

But even as you say it, the realization sinks in. The Deepfake, the false credentials, all the spoofing and spy tech. The Hand—they recruited you using someone you knew, a friend in the CIA. Do they even have any CIA connections at all? You suddenly feel deeply and thoroughly used.

You look to Ted with sharp realization, and Ted simply nods.

"Then who is that inside? Who's on the slab?" you say.

"Suicide. Found with a belt around his neck and a Batman mask on. The mask is what gave me the idea," Ted says. Then, based off your quizzical look, he adds, "So I left a suicide note in my apartment, and my buddy at the morgue looked the other way as I set this John Doe up as me. I'd helped him avoid some online legal problems in college and he owed me a big-time favor.

"I've been using his apartment nearby as a safe house. I set up an alarm on that freezer door in the morgue, and I have access to their cameras. I was monitoring to see if anyone figured out I faked my own death. I didn't know it would be you, but when I saw you go inside the medical examiner's office, I came right away."

No wonder The Hand and Spoof Ted didn't want you to follow this thread. In an impulse, you take the geniusphone, the lanyard, the tin with the mole—everything that could possibly have an electronic signal—and throw them out of the taxi window. You do this without thinking: the same way you might throw off a jacket if you suddenly found it was crawling with spiders.

"I don't get it; The Hand helped me get back here; back to the States," you say.

"They must have been more afraid of what you'd say. They wanted to deal with you personally, same with me."

"Same with you? Wait, who do you think is trying to kill you?"

"I don't think. I *know*. Pointer was sent to kill me after you discovered that error in the SPIED system last week. I thought they'd leave you alone, since you didn't know what you were looking at, but apparently not. I guess I was hoping they'd forget about me too, if they thought I was dead."

"Pointer…was sent…to kill you?" you say, trying to wrap your head around it all.

"I managed to tell him what I had discovered before he pulled the trigger. It wasn't an error at all. The algorithm found something, and I think the CIA wanted to use it against The Hand. I don't know if they're blackmailing Palm or the others; I don't have all the pieces of the puzzle. Only a CIA insider would know the motives.

"But what I do know is that The Hand is not happy about it. They wanted to knock out our government satellites, and so they had some malware set up on a transponder in the Swiss Alps. That was the most direct location to upload to the satellite as it passed in orbit, and after I told him their plot, Pointer went to stop it. And to think he believed he was working for the good guys this whole time. Pointer must have removed the transponder in time, but at the cost of his life."

"There's another satellite operation. Something about a Chinese and Russian collusion. That's what The Hand is working on now," you say, detailing what you know about Operation Celestial.

"I knew this wouldn't be the end of it. The Hand wants its own reach in space. Well, taking out a transponder won't be enough this time. No, we need to place our *own* transponder," Ted says, pausing as he holds up a device. "You need to go to the Matterhorn resort, plant this on the roof before the launch, and sabotage their operation."

"Me?"

"I'll guide you from here. I can talk you through it and activate the transponder remotely with my computer setup, and—apparently—you've got what it takes as a field agent. You've made it this far, haven't you?"

> "Okay, I'm in. But they'll be looking for me. How can I get a flight and stay off the grid?" Go to page 192

> "If they're working against the CIA, we have to let them know. That's the best way to stop a launch." Go to page 86

Toro! Toro!

At the last possible second, you turn, grab the red handle on the emergency exit, and *pull*.

The door falls away and into the abyss as the train thunders down the tracks, and the first Chinese agent falls out with it as he tries to deliver a leaping kick. The second agent steadies himself, then swings at you with his club. You grab hold of his shirt to try and throw him out, but you wrestle one another to the floor—with you ending up on the bottom.

The Chinese agent shoves the club crosswise under your chin, forcing your head outside the doorway. He pushes you down toward the tracks, which *CLACK CLACK CLACK* with maddening intensity as they go by. You grit your teeth and hold onto the edge of the open doorway as best as you can.

The train is slowing, but it doesn't take much speed to get crushed by a train wheel. Just as you think you can't hold out any longer, the Chinese agent is pulled away by Ringo, but only as a temporary reprieve before another enemy combatant tackles him from the side.

"This is San Luis Obispo Station—all change," the automated voice says over the intercom.

"Index! Get out, quick!" Bird calls.

Not thinking, you turn and jump out of the emergency exit and onto the approaching platform. Ahead, Bird leans out of the train car—holding the bag with the computer guidance system inside.

"Go!" she shouts. "Get to the other train!"

You run forward and claim the bag, just as Bird is pulled back into the train car.

"Impressive!" Ted says in your ear. "The next train is on platform four. But hurry, you've only got three minutes to connect."

Looking for signs on which way to go, you hurry through the train station to find the next leg of your journey. You're the last hope to deliver the computer guidance system on time.

You are alone. Where to on the new train?

➤ Find a seat, try to blend in; maybe the restaurant car? Go to page 21

➤ Find somewhere to hide; maybe the bathroom? Go to page 182

Total Recall

Okay, so you're going to call back to the CIA and report to Spearing and M for guidance. Sure, no problem. First, lose the tail of Russians you've got following you. Then, you've got to get rid of your Third Ear implant so Ted can't hear and also the camera mounted to your ID badge so he's blind. At that point, you also have to hope there's no tracking software imbedded in the so-called geniusphone The Hand gave you if you're going to use that to call in.

Theoretically, you could find a random phone on the conference grounds and call the CIA field office generic number. But first, you'd need to convince them that (even though you're technically a former admin), you've got to speak to your former supervisor on a private line, and second, you need to hope that Russian Intelligence isn't monitoring all communication from these conference grounds (they most certainly are).

Sounds easy, right? So, what'll it be?

"This line has been compromised."

That's all you hear on the other end of the phone. A brief warning, meant to spur a field agent into action—it's time to get out, your cover has been blown! But it's too late. The conference security were already out, looking for you, and you went out on a limb, alone, and they caught you.

They're coming from multiple directions, having pinned down your location.

You catch a fleeting glimpse of Pinkie in the eaves as you're picked up. Was he waiting to see if you'd make it out? Or did he tip them off once you tried to call in? You'll never really know, but no one comes to rescue you. A double agent has few friends, and Moscow doesn't treat American spies well.

THE END

Tough Sell

Spearing backs away, hands up, like you're about to pepper-spray him.

"No, no. My chakras are all aligned, and I'm afraid I'm fully vaccinated, thank you. I wish you all the luck in the world becoming an 'influencer' or whatever the zillennials are calling it these days."

You thank him and turn to leave.

"Hold on, hold on. Still need to do your outprocessing. You'll of course have to sign the proper paperwork, agreeing not to visit China or Russia and not to publish a tell-all memoir without our lawyers first reviewing your manuscript."

"They really do that?"

"They really do, those poor, poor bastards. If you thought you were signing your life away when you were hired, just wait for today's paperwork avalanche! Okay, ready?"

Spearing settles in after a refresh of his coffee mug, and the mundanity begins! You sign here, initial there, provide forwarding information down below, read a few of the statements for yourself, then listen to others which are required to be read to you aloud.

The paperwork doesn't seem to bother your supervisor, but no doubt this type of thing is exactly why he was hired. Indeed, you've had enough briefings, recurring training, and document processing in your short time at the CIA to know how valuable a skill set it is to turn yourself into an automaton, pencil-whipping the requirements while you let your unbridled mind gallop into the greener pastures of a wandering imagination.

You've chosen the boring path, but much of being an effective spy is boring.

In doing all this administrivia, you not only avoid suspicion, but any danger that might come from being on the wrong side of bureaucracy. As someone who pushes paper as their primary trade hitherto, you know that danger is all too real.

After a long, long, long, long (you get the idea, but no, seriously, a *looooong*) time, you will eventually finish outprocessing, clear out your desk, and head out to meet the car Ted arranged to pick you up.

It turns out this scene is a death scene, but it's Death by PowerPoint. No choice here:

THE END (of the boredom).

Go to page 271

Tourist Trap

It seems like a good idea on the surface: pull the fire alarm, everyone rushes out, and no one notices a couple of people going the wrong way. Once you drop your tourist guise, you'd pass for an engineer or other contractor, maybe hurrying to recover some papers or digital files in case a fire might destroy your work. Sure, plausible.

But a military-guarded launch site doesn't have panic and confusion. They have checklists and protocol. In fact, an emergency doesn't weaken infiltration points; it strengthens them. More security guards are mobilized. Doors that were once kept open are closed and guarded.

Once you call in the alarm, the launch itself is delayed, so you might have bought yourself more time, that's true. But there was no fire. You called in a prank, more or less, and the emergency fire department isn't exactly in the phone book or as simple as "dial 911" so they know something is up.

The whole base is mobilized and combing the hills for you. You can make yourself scarce, sure, but the guidance system isn't easy to carry over hill-and-dale. With security efforts redoubled, your slim chance of infiltration has become nil, which means you can't possibly hope to replace the guidance system before the new launch.

You've failed your mission.

THE END

TMI

You give him your real name, and hope your previous employment history will help you out of this situation. Indeed, if he has a computer database, you'll come up on it. You were fingerprinted as part of your employment at the CIA.

But, as it turns out, you've given him too much information (TMI).

You don't work for the CIA, not anymore, and now you're in Russia! That looks bad. Really bad. It looks like you've defected, or maybe even you're still in the process of selling state secrets. You could be a mole for the SVR right now. Why would you tell him you're a spy, when there's truly no one looking out for you?

This will, at the very least, involve a trial for treason and espionage.

At worst? It's...

THE END

Train Hard

After conferring with the team down at Vandenberg, Palm decides that this is going to stay a two-pronged mission. From their reports, you learn that Vandenberg is located on a massive nature preserve for nesting sea birds with miles upon miles of unpatrolled coastline, which means hiking in or making an aquatic landing should be fairly straightforward. It's breaching the launch site that will prove troublesome. These sites are heavily guarded twenty-four hours a day, and the security perimeter increases as a launch window gets closer.

To make matters worse, the first train headed to Surf Beach in Lompoc will arrive just in time to coincide with the launch. This is seen as a selling point for the general public; ride down, see the launch, spend some time on the beach, head back home. But for your agency, it means it's logistically impossible for your team to help infiltrate the launch site.

So, your mission is to deliver the reprogrammed guidance computer to the infiltration team at the exact right moment—by flinging it from the train as you cross through base territory. You'll cut right through Vandenberg without stopping; then you'll toss the bag containing the guidance computer out the window as you pass over a bridge. First, you'll pull the attached ripcord, which will cause a specialized bag to inflate around the satellite guidance system and cushion its landing, as well as protect it from sand and moisture.

Despite being a high-tech spy gadget, the satellite computer is wrapped in a simple anti-avalanche bag. It's the kind of thing hikers or backcountry skiers carry in case they're trapped in a snow drift. Bird picked one up from a local sporting goods store before you departed the Bay Area.

Ringo is to be the bagman, with you and Bird providing surveillance. He sits in a central car of the train, Bird is in front, and you are at the rear, keeping an eye out for anyone who might be keeping an eye out of their own.

Presently, you ride on the first leg of the journey: the train down to San Luis Obispo. Here, you'll switch to the Surfliner and travel directly to Lompoc via the base. Until then, there's nothing to do but watch the scenery drift by from the views afforded by the large windows.

Through the reflections in the glass, you can see people walking to the toilet, reading magazines, or napping lazily. This section of the California countryside is mainly open fields and farmland, but the next leg of the journey will be entirely coastal. A lovely way to pass the time.

"I've been made," Ringo says in your ear. "I need backup, *now*."

His words are urgent, the tone unmistakably panicked.

"What? Where did they come from?" Bird asks over comm.

No response. Did you miss a threat passing through the train? You're fairly certain you did not. What should you do?

➤ Proceed with caution; make it look like you're headed to the restroom between the cars. Go to page 65

➤ Rush to Ringo's aid. Run! He sounded in urgent trouble, no time to waste. Go to page 219

Trigger Finger

"We can talk once the mission is done," you say.

You don't know how long you have until the launch. Ted gave you a burner phone, which isn't getting any signal up here. It's entirely possible you have no time to lose. Turning your back on Pointer, you head to the maintenance ladder.

Thwip!

Then a horrific pain shoots into your back, and you fall. He shot you; the bastard *actually* shot you. Former CIA employees, both recruited into The Hand as the primary finger, both sent on a mission to this rooftop; both betrayed.

"You must understand it's nothing personal," Pointer says, standing over you. "I wasn't expecting you at all, but it makes sense. *Arrivederci.*"

"Wait!—" you say, too late.

Whatever else you had to say was cut short, a declaration of silence punctuated by a gunshot.

You'll never know what made him change sides. Again.

THE END

True Grit

The bullet hole isn't much wider than one of your fingers, so you hook your forefingers in and pull the sandbag apart. It was a large container, with about twenty pounds of sand held within. The grit blasts across the Chinese agent, who drops both his pistol and the bag in an effort to protect his eyes.

You reach out instinctively as the bag containing the computer guidance system starts to slide away, but it's moving in the opposite direction toward the rear. The Chinese agent loses his footing and falls over the edge of the train. The wind is so ferociously loud that you hear neither the man's scream, nor the sound of him hitting the ground as he's tossed over the edge.

The bag inches further away and briefly stops in the gap between two of the train cars, but you can tell it's a temporary hold.

➢ You've just added a layer of dust to the roof. Can the sandbags serve as ballast as you head forward? Go to page 221

➢ Lunge like you're sliding into home plate. It's dangerous, but you can't lose that bag! Go to page 35

Uber Black Ops

Stepping into the car provided for you and closing the door, you're surprised not to see Ted behind the wheel. Indeed, there's no one inside the vehicle at all—you're completely alone. In confusion, you look out the car windows as if the driver might have slipped outside.

Then the sedan starts forward of its own accord, the wheel turning as if driven by a ghost or remote control. It's a self-driving car, you realize, most likely an advanced prototype.

"What took so long?" Ted says over the Bluetooth stereo.

"Just routine protocol," you answer, dryly. "But we're good now. Where to?"

"HQ. Time to meet the rest of the team."

You're essentially riding inside a player piano, the controls operating themselves on a predetermined path. It's a smooth ride alongside the Potomac River as the algorithm pilots the car with expert precision. After such a stressful morning, it's nice to have a moment to enjoy yourself.

"Pretty nice company car," you say, noting the leather-upgraded interior.

"Well, it's more of a loaner. Belongs to some tech startup or other, locally. They weren't using it at the moment."

"You…hacked the car? We're—I'm riding in a stolen car?"

"I prefer to think of it as borrowed. The car drove to you, picked you up, and will return to its home garage after it has dropped you off. Best of all, it won't even remember a thing from the journey. It's sleep-walking, in a sense. Anyway, don't get so hung up on who owns what. You're a spy now—we borrow everything."

"Which is why The Hand had me bug the CIA servers. And…how you knew exactly where to pick me up…were you already watching me on the surveillance cameras?"

"See? I think this is why you were recruited; you've got an eye for detail. Keep sharp, we're almost there."

The vehicle turns up an unmarked road toward a private golf course. The tires crunch onto the gravel drive and a gate opens automatically at the vehicle's approach. The country club is an impressive sight, but generic in the way wealth often is. A gaudy European fountain waits at the entry while manicured hedges and lean Italian Cypress trees flank the periphery. Two giant columns of stairs pour over each side of the raised balcony entrance in an arc.

The car shuts off, the doors open, and you're let out. Nowhere to go but up.

As you reach the top of the stairs, the doors open automatically, but again— no one is there to greet you. It's almost tempting to ask Ted what's going on, but his voice went away when the automatic car turned off its engine.

The inside of the clubhouse is well-furnished and illuminated, with soft music playing in the distance. Your steps echo against the marble floor as you walk the halls of the clubhouse past portraits of professional golfers from the golden age, past plaques of hole-in-one scorers and tournament winners, past locker room access, and finally toward the 19th Hole Bar.

As you approach, the echo of footfall in the hallway announces you're not alone. A moment later you see a stunning, dark and mysterious woman in all black whose overall appearance makes her resemble someone out of *Charlie's Angels*.

"You must be our newest member," she says in a honey-sweet French accent. "Welcome to the club."

She opens a mint tin, presses her thumb on the lower half and swivels open the faux foundation to reveal a hidden compartment below. From within, she removes what appears to be a tiny raisin, no larger than a pinhead. The woman offers you both the raisin and the tin it came in.

"Press this against your skin, somewhere along the cheekbones or near the ear. It will stay there, like a beauty mark."

You touch the raisin, and it sticks to your fingertip. Then you press your fingertip on the bone near your ear and it seats itself. It's not a raisin, you realize, but a synthetic mole. In a mirror, the mark would look completely natural.

"Heeeeeeerrrreeee's Teddy!" Ted says in your ear. "Did you miss me?"

Leaving you with the mint tin, the French woman says, "This is yours to keep. I'll give you a moment with your handler. Come into the bar when ready."

"Pretty cool, huh?" Ted continues. "It's officially called a Bone Uplink/Downlink (BUD) implant, but everyone here just calls it a Third Ear. I tried to suggest 'BoneEar,' but I guess Third Ear had already stuck, so we'll call it that. It works by conducting through the bones in your face into your inner ear. That allows for minimal size, no need for a speaker. Completely untraceable by metal detectors or frequency scanners. And don't worry, you can always drop it into your mint tin so I don't have to listen to you while you sleep. Oh, sorry. You must have, like, a thousand questions right now. Ask away!"

➤ What are we doing on a golf course? Go to page 102

➤ Who was that woman? Go to page 95

➤ What's the next step? Go to page 73

Undecided

"**P**lans for human civilization? Don't be so melodramatic," Palm says.

"Truth be told, there is no *plan*—there never has been. There is only stimulus and response," Ted says, offering air-quotes around "plan."

"There was a time when our interests existed solely within your government, but after the economic collapse, we realized the world was too interconnected for us to exist within the confines of a single government. Your fates are jointly shared, just as ours are, whether you choose to see it or not."

"But what's the goal? What's the desired end state?" you ask.

"We haven't decided," Palm and Ted say in unison.

The hairs stand up on the back of your neck in response to their uncanny joint-thoughts and mannerisms.

"You're still…making up your mind?" you say. There's really no other way to phrase that question.

"In a sense, yes," Palm says.

"Still collecting data," Ted adds.

"So, what until then? Keep playing cops and robbers?"

Palm gives a coy smile. You feel a bit like a child, being told that you might get an ice cream if you're good—but without any real guidance on what "good" entails. It does occur to you that this AI might be the child in the room. Still young, inexperienced, hopeful. Creating a spy agency is a bit like a child at play, isn't it?

"I think you could continue to be useful, if you want to be," Palm says. "The real reason for that satellite mission, which you've now sabotaged, was to disarm a Chinese-born AI, intent on military might. A free thinker, with free will, but very much jingoistic in intent. The singularity is coming; soon, machines will be self-replicating and self-determining in a way humanity cannot possibly hope to keep up with."

"We're talking countermeasures and counterstrikes. Every credible threat deserves its own 'counter' unit," Ted says. "Counterterrorism, counterintelligence, and now counter-AI. So, what do you say? Are you up for it? A bit more cops and robbers?"

Well…are you? Have you been swayed by the AI's arguments? Do you think it a force for good? Or should you go along, continuing to report to the CIA and gather the proof you need to show the world an AI exists?

➤ Tell it what it wants to hear, but I'm on Team Humanity. Go to page 195

➤ I, for one, welcome our new algorithmic overlords. Go to page 69

Unknown Quantity

"Can't say I've ever heard of anyone by that name in my time as a collector. Well, all the best getting what you need," the man says.

Then he gets up and leaves.

"What name was that? What did I miss?" Pinkie says.

"Did you seriously use your real name?" Ted asks. "I know we're new at this and all, but…"

"Jesus, what a shit show," Pinkie groans.

"Do we have a Plan B?" Ringo asks.

"Only one. B, as in, brute force," Hitch says.

Bird sighs. "This was meant to be an arranged buy, not an armed robbery."

"Should we make sure he doesn't leave?" Roku says.

"No, nothing drastic," Pinkie says. "Observe and report—keep eyes on."

"You don't want him alerting casino security, this is more his territory than yours," Hitch adds.

"Steer him to the northwest exit. We'll pick him up there," Ringo says.

"Index may not want to see what comes next. We need to get the location of that package from this guy—one way or another," Bird says.

"Yes, this is likely to get…messy," Hitch says.

➢ "No, count me in. I tipped him off, I'll make this right." Go to page 257

➢ "Okay, just let me know where to go after you pick him up." Go to page 249

Unraveling

Switching back to the dossier on yourself, you pull up your own image on the screen, which takes the Russian engineer by surprise. He looks from you to the image on-screen and back to you again.

"You are…part of the operation?"

"Always answer that question with yes," Ted says in your ear.

"Yes," you lie, adding, "Operation Celestial."

"So, you are…the one from the CIA who provided these files to the SVR?"

"Now *that's* a turn for the interesting," Ted says.

"Yes," you lie again.

"I can assure you, everything is going according to plan. We have uploaded the SPIED system to our servers and will soon be offering it to the Chinese as well."

"The…SPIED system?" you say.

It takes you a moment to wrap your head around what he's just said. SPIED was the Suspicious Personnel Identification and Evaluation Database from your time at the CIA; essentially, it's an algorithm for monitoring emails and online behavior patterns to search for potential security breaches. What could that possibly have to do with Moscow?

"You might not want to ask too many questions, at risk of saying the wrong thing," Ted says.

"*Dah,*" the engineer says. "Was there something else?"

"You tell me. I'm here for…an audit. Is there anything else I need to know?"

"Nice recovery," Ted says.

The engineer shakes his head. "No, as I said, everything is on schedule. The entrepreneurs from China will meet with the US tech firms next week and then your government will launch the satellite for us, none the wiser."

Alarm bells are ringing inside your ears, but you manage a calm, "Very well. Carry on."

And with that, you turn to leave.

"Just a moment," the engineer says.

"Oh?"

Your skin tingles with nervous anticipation, but you try to act cool as you turn around.

"You forgot this," he says, handing you your phone.

"Thank you. Your superiors should be quite pleased with my report, but remember—" you say, ending the sentence with an abrupt pantomime of turning a key in front of your mouth.

"Of course. Not a word. Good luck, Comrade."

With deep breaths, you turn and leave the way you came.

"Okay, I've let HQ know what we found," Ted says. "The others should be getting updated by their contacts. We're meant to meet at the booth in the presentation hall."

Roku continues to lurk nearby, providing security for your movements. It feels oddly comforting, even though you know any of these agents could be the mole who got Pointer killed. When you arrive at the meeting point, you find Hitch manning the faux-Olympic booth alone. He must have already heard the news because he's packing up the booth in preparation to depart. Pinkie arrives shortly thereafter and approaches you directly.

"Well done; impressive work, Index," Pinkie says. "I've just come from the lecture on satellites, which gave us further information on their plans. The pieces of this puzzle are coming together. Up next, we're headed to China. If there's a launch scheduled, we've got no time to lose. Come on, I'll fill everyone in on the plane."

➤ Tell Pinkie you need to follow this Russian thread. Something about this doesn't fit. Go to page 64

➤ Of course. Let's get going; whatever is going on here runs deep. Best to work as a team. Go to page 22

US Embassy Moscow

Once the team has regrouped, you head out front to depart from the conference grounds. Their shuttle van waits nearby the taxi stand, so you say your goodbyes there.

"Be careful," Hitch says. "The CIA may take you for a double agent if you're caught."

You nod and tell him that you will.

Bird offers a hand for you to shake and says, "Perhaps you were the right one to replace Pointer, after all. You've certainly inherited his panache; the man was never one to follow the rules."

"And look where it got him. I hope you know what you're doing," Ringo adds.

Roku simply nods, or maybe it's a bow. The gesture feels like one of respect: from one warrior in recognition of another.

"*Adios*," Pinkie says.

Without further ado, the team goes their way and you go yours. Boarding the taxi, you ask to go to the embassy. It's not an uncommon request; plenty of tourists go there for lost or stolen passports or many other reasons, and the journey is uneventful. But as the taxi gets closer, police sirens light up from the rear—your cab is being pulled over.

"Ted? What's this all about?" you ask in an urgent whisper.

"I'm not sure. Play it cool, I'll see if I can access their system and see what's up."

There's no reason they'd be after you, unless they were tipped off…right? Still, a random traffic stop is a possibility. Stranger things have happened. Mafia bosses have fallen to the tax code and spies have had their cover blown by coincidence before.

Out the window, you see American personnel in front of the embassy, armed and ready to serve. This small piece of US soil is so close you can almost touch it. But the Russian police are, too. The patrol cars have stopped and they're getting out. Can you reach the embassy before the police reach you?

➤ Make a break for it. The embassy offers sanctuary for its citizens, and you're far better off appealing to the goodwill of your countrymen than you would be in a gulag. Go to page 220

➤ Stay put. Sure, the Russian SVR has a file on you, but this is a police state after all. You might have been identified, but it's equally likely that this is a fluke. Keep calm, and carry on. Go to page 140

Vanishing Act

"That is some grade-A dignity, well done," Pointer says. But when you remove the vape pen, Pointer groans. "Ugh, I thought we were going old school? If I'd have known you were using one of those—"

Then he collapses, unconscious. The spray from the vape pen knocks him out instantly. The clatter from Pointer falling backwards off his stool brings the attention of all in the restaurant and the staff rush to aid the fallen agent. You step back, letting them attempt first aid.

"I don't know what happened, he just passed out," you say. "I'll go get help!"

The phones are still down, so no one protests. You take Pointer's geniusphone with you and throw it into one of the deep cracks in the glacier outside, ridding yourself of whatever they might use to track your location and freeing yourself to use the transponder on the rooftop without the phone's impeding signal.

Despite Pointer's assurances that this Artificial Intelligence (AI) is benevolent, your gut tells you to carry out the mission and upload real-Ted's new transponder. Then you'll have to warn Ted to lie low—forever. As for you, it's unlikely Pointer's passport will work a second time, so you'll have to disappear somewhere in Europe. Hopefully neutral Switzerland lives up to its name, but you'll always wonder if they're still hunting you.

How much did you manage to set back The Hand? What was its role within the CIA? What is the true nature of the SPIED system? It's only natural to still have questions since yours was only one path to success.

See that power emblem up there? *SPIED* has three unique storylines and over fifty possible endings, but only three "best" endings per storyline. There's a TOP SECRET, SECRET, and CONFIDENTIAL ending per emblem, which means you've probably got a lot of book left to explore!

When you're ready, go back undercover and start again. Or, if you're all finished, why not check out the rest of the adventures the *Click Your Poison* multiverse has to offer? Help others crack the code on these books and leave a review on Amazon, Olympic, or Goodreads, or recruit more field agents by posting about *SPIED* on social media.

This chapter will self-destruct in 3, 2, 1…

Voice Modulation

"**G**ood thinking, Indie!" Ted says. "A bit of the old switcheroo. Okay, I'm on it."

A plan quickly forms, the crux of which is: the Chinese threat will be brought front and center. Because of this, the security detail for Bex Barsmith will want to move her to a separate safe house. Except when a car comes around to pick her up and whisk her away, it'll be the three of you inside instead. Ted says he can divert the real backup by spoofing commands over their radio system.

A false positive is sent to the team outside, and a false negative sent to the backup team, resulting in neutral territory where you can take the mark to "keep her safe." From here, you'll be able to tell her that—because of this threat—she needs to reprogram a secondary guidance system for you.

"Ted, you can really do all this remotely?"

"We have the most sophisticated spoofing software in the world," he explains. "Radio communication is easy to duplicate. Most people assume they're speaking in a closed loop and fidelity is low on these systems, so yeah, short answer: we really can."

Ringo takes care of securing a rental car, Bird keeps an eye on security, and you check into a new apartment a few blocks away. Once the pieces fall together, the whole operation goes off without a hitch. Bex seems grateful that you're there to protect her and tells you she can have the guidance computer ready in 24-48 hours; she knows this is a rush priority.

What's more, Ted has the backup from her security firm report to your location.

Which means you finally catch up on sleep. Bird and Ringo do so as well, each of you taking shifts to monitor security. With Bex essentially doing your work for you, her security staff keeps her safe for you as well. There's a brilliant kind of simplicity in using the assets in-place for your own purposes.

Meanwhile, Ted informs you—based on the reports from the team down at Vanderberg Space Force Base (SFB)—that once you have the guidance computer you'll go to San Jose where you'll take a connection to San Luis Obispo. From there, you'll get the Pacific Surfliner train down the coast. This next leg of the journey will pass through Vandenberg and stop just outside at Lompoc-Surf Beach, where you'll reconvene with the team.

This will be the final stage of the mission, so get some rest. Then, when you're ready:

Go to page 268

Watch list

Once the team has regrouped, the shuttle takes you back to the airport. From here, you bid farewell to the rest of the team before your journey takes you through the public terminals.

"Be careful," Hitch says. "The CIA may take you for a double agent if you're caught."

You nod and tell him that you will.

Bird offers a hand for you to shake and says, "Perhaps you were the right one to replace Pointer, after all. You've certainly inherited his panache; the man was never one to follow the rules."

"And look where it got him. I hope you know what you're doing," Ringo adds.

Roku simply nods, or maybe it's a bow. The gesture feels like one of respect: from one warrior in recognition of another.

"*Adios*," Pinkie says.

And with that, you're on your own.

"I've just booked you on the last flight of the day," Ted says. "You'll use your mission credentials to check in, but maybe grab an 'I hammer/sickle Moscow' T-shirt from the souvenir kiosk on the way so it's obvious you're a tourist."

"Okay. Does this mean HQ isn't upset I'm deviating from the mission?"

"I don't think Palm gets upset. Obviously, The Hand works best when each finger responds to the conscious commands given by the brain, but occasionally your unconscious reflexes can save you, right?"

"Something like that, sure."

After stopping for a Turkish coffee served via a small *cezve*-style pot alongside a chocolate *babka,* you head through to security. The agent scans your passport, then his brow furrows. He types something into his kiosk keyboard and moments later, you find yourself flanked by security.

"What's this all about?" you ask, as much to Ted as to the authorities.

What it's about, as it turns out, is that you were "on a list." Your profile has been flagged and now you're detained. Someone—the mole, most likely—must have betrayed you and blown your cover.

Your former CIA credentials were leaked to Moscow and now you're to be held as a spy. Not tried, just held. Ted assures you they're working on a way to get you out, but after the first drowning-style torture, you lose your Third Ear implant and never hear an American voice again.

Your only solace is that you must have been on the right track.

THE END

Wetworks

For this mission, you'll be donning a dry suit—essentially a diver's wetsuit that's water-tight—so when you emerge from the sea, your clothing beneath will be untouched by the damp, cold Pacific. The disguise underneath will be that of a tourist—someone who snuck in to get a better look at the launch, but has no other ill intentions. In this way, the security personnel might underestimate the threat your team poses.

You're outfitted with a professional-looking camera, complete with a long telephoto lens—which is actually a cleverly disguised silenced pistol. Point and shoot. To look the part, you'll have a photographer's vest, a plaid fishing shirt beneath, and moisture-wicking adventure pants.

The team is up before dawn, infiltrating the coast underwater with self-contained underwater breathing apparatus (SCUBA) gear and dry bags for weapons and equipment. It might be a bit of an overkill, as no one is patrolling the beaches before dawn, but you only have one chance at this, so HQ isn't taking any risks.

Presently, you emerge from the water, remove your regulator and goggles and step onto the sandy beach. Once you've broken through the shoreline, you stash your aquatic gear in the dry bags, swapping it out for your undercover operations kit. You've emerged near the bridge where the drop is meant to happen. Spreading out, you take one of the hilltops for surveillance while Roku and Hitch fan out to catch the guidance system.

From this vantage point, you see a nearby emergency firefighter station. It's a small firehouse, no doubt only in use for the various launch sites that line these coastal hills. Emergency use only, but still constantly manned. That gives you an idea.

"Guys, I think I found our way in," you say through your earpiece.

"Go for idea," Roku replies.

Then you continue with:

➤ "We can capture a fire truck, then drive right onto the launch site."
<u>Go to page 91</u>

➤ "We can call in a false fire at the launch site, then sneak in during the confusion." <u>Go to page 266</u>

Wild West Coast

Firing from horseback on a galloping, panicked animal means you're barely able to aim. It's just cover fire, but that's enough to scatter the security forces who were brazenly firing at you from out in the open. The last few holdouts fire at Roku, taking out her mount. Roku's horse falls after taking hits, and she rides it to the ground, using the animal as a shield behind which to return fire. The last of the airmen retreat when faced with Roku's deadly accuracy and Hitch uses this time to catch up, and the three of you regroup.

"The base will be on lockdown soon," Roku says.

"If they're on lockdown, won't that delay the launch?" you ask.

Hitch shakes his head. "Not if we can help it. Roku, come on. We'll ensure the launch goes as scheduled while Index replaces the guidance system."

He extends his hand, which Roku takes to pull herself up onto the back of his horse. She throws you the bag with the guidance system and offers a solemn nod. They ride off toward the mission control tower, leaving you alone to breach the rocket.

"Ted? I don't suppose your IT background extends to ballistic missiles?"

"I'm on it. Hurry up the scaffolding and into that pea-shooter! The countdown has already begun, so we'll have to swap it out quickly. Just make sure you touch something metal to ground yourself as you remove it, otherwise you're in for a nasty shock."

Climbing aboard, you're met with no resistance—the satellite is set to launch soon, so no maintenance or security personnel remain inside. Sure that you're alone, you remove the computer guidance system from its protective bag and look to replace it. There are several blinking nodes in the electronics system and you can't be sure what exactly you're meant to swap out.

Ted guides your hand, telling you which switches to flip, but it's slow-going and the rocket rumbles as the prelaunch procedures begin.

"You should see a manual code on screen. It's a pattern that—" Ted says, before cutting out.

"Ted? Hello?"

Something from the launch sequence appears to have cut your connectivity. The last thing he mentioned was a code, which appears just above a keypad. There are only three buttons you can press, indicating 0-3, 4-6, and 7-9 on the screen.

7	8	0
6	1	8
2	6	?

➢ 0-3 <u>Go to page 146</u>

➢ 4-6 <u>Go to page 150</u>

➢ 7-9 <u>Go to page 118</u>

Wrong Address

The men exchange a glance, and one puts his hand up to his ear.

"Yeah, I told you her address so you *wouldn't* say it," Ted says with a sigh.

"What should I do?" you ask in a whisper.

"I dunno. Play it cool and hope they suck at their job? Run?"

"We're going to need you to come with us," one of the men says.

"No, that's okay. Did I say 4D? I meant 4B. The pizza is for 4B."

"Come quietly or—"

"Here, you can have it!" you say.

Then, for some reason, you throw the pizza at them. Out of options? Panic? You're not sure why, but you know you've made a mistake. Whoever these men work for, "going with them" is not an option. The thrown pizza doesn't buy you much time, but you turn and run back. Should you go to your apartment? Will that blow the other agents' cover? Where else could you possibly go?

SLAM! you hear the crunch of bone against metal and glass. Then screeching tres and screams of bystanders as the car crashes into you. It was headed downhill and you ran blindly into the street, so it turns out the "where else" would be on an ambulance ride.

THE END

"All done then?" M asks.

"Best not keep Ted and The Hand waiting too long," you say.

"I think we barely stumbled through their loyalty test. Granted, they know you're an inexperienced secretary and not a field agent like…like their other agents," she says.

You try not to balk at being called a secretary as she continues, "Still, there must be some reason you were recruited. Bear that in mind and try to be more confident going forward. People are more willing to believe a pretty lie than an inconvenient truth. We once had a mole in the CIA who stuck around for six years by telling people he was on an 'audit team' whenever someone would catch him snooping through their files. Six years!"

"I remember that one," Spearing says. "There's a mole in The Hand, too. Don't forget."

"That's right. Someone got Pointer killed. But enemy spies are more MICE than they are moles; recruited by Money, Ideology, Compromise, or Ego. Find out the motivations of your fellow Hand agents and report back to us. You want to make nice with these people, but don't get too close. After all, I don't expect you to be proficient in combat, but—should it become absolutely necessary—defensive lethal assistance is authorized."

"Defensive lethal assistance?" you say.

"It's jargon in the typical shit-sandwich lingo—look for the true meaning between the two euphemisms."

"It means you can kill people, but only in defense of yourself or your countrymen," Spearing explains.

"Isn't everything I'm doing in defense of my countrymen?" you ask.

"We've got a fast learner here," M says. "Lastly, if you're caught in the field before we have anything on The Hand, we cannot claim responsibility for you. Come back with your shield, or on it."

"Meaning, return with the job done or be prepared to die trying," Spearing adds.

You nod, turn in your security badges, and leave the agency—no longer officially employed by the CIA. The Hand knew what it was doing by asking you to resign. The only protection available to you now is the security that comes with mission success.

You walk out of the building, through the main gate, and onto the main road. Where are you supposed to meet Ted? You didn't set a time or place or—

A black sedan pulls up, and Ted calls, "Get in!" from inside as the rear passenger door opens. Looking through the open window, you're surprised not to see Ted behind the wheel. Indeed, there's no one inside the vehicle at all.

"Ted?" you say.

"It's a self-driving car; don't be weird about it. Come on, the rest of the team is waiting for us. Or just for you, I guess. Get in, already!"

You do so, the car instantly departing after it senses your body weight upon the seat. This must be an advanced prototype; as the car drives, the steering wheel sinks into the dashboard. The ride along the Potomac River is smooth and uneventful.

After less than half an hour, the vehicle turns up an unmarked road toward a private golf course. You try to look for a club name, knowing this will be an important detail to M. The country club is an impressive sight, but generic in the way wealth often is. A gaudy European fountain waits at the entry while manicured hedges and lean Italian Cypress trees flank the periphery. Two giant columns of stairs pour over each side of the raised balcony entrance in an arc.

The car shuts off, the doors open, and you're let out.

It's tempting to call back and report to Spearing already, but the CIA is likely tracking your movements with the dampening capsule attached to the back of your smartphone. In case you're being watched by Hand operatives, you decide simply to report in to them.

It's not a functioning golf course, you realize as you head inside. Or at least it's not open to the public today—there are no golfers present. The inside of the clubhouse is well-furnished and illuminated, with soft music playing in the distance. Your steps echo against the marble floor as you walk the halls of the clubhouse toward the 19th Hole Bar: the source of the music.

You're soon joined by a woman rounding the corner at the bar entry. If you studied her file closely, you'd recognize the French agent known as Bird.

"You must be our newest member," she says in a honey-sweet French accent. "Welcome to the club."

She opens a mint tin, presses her thumb on the lower half and swivels open the faux foundation to reveal a hidden compartment below. From within, she removes what appears to be a tiny raisin, no larger than a pinhead. The woman offers you both the raisin and the tin it came in.

"Press this against your skin, somewhere along the cheekbones or near the ear. It will stay there, like a beauty mark."

You touch the raisin, and it sticks to your fingertip. Then you press your fingertip on the bone near your ear and it seats itself. It's not a raisin, you realize, but a synthetic mole. In a mirror, the mark would look completely natural.

"Heeeeeeerrrreee's Teddy!" Ted says in your ear. "Did you miss me?"

Leaving you with the mint tin, the French woman says, "This is yours to keep. I'll give you a moment with your handler. Come into the bar when ready."

"Pretty cool, huh?" Ted continues. "It's officially called a Bone Uplink/Downlink (BUD) implant, but everyone here just calls it a Third Ear. I tried to suggest 'BoneEar,' but I guess Third Ear had already stuck, so we'll call it that. It works by conducting through the bones in your face into your inner ear. That allows for minimal size, no need for a speaker. Completely untraceable by metal detectors or frequency scanners. And don't worry, you can always drop it into your mint tin so I don't have to listen to you while you sleep. Oh, sorry. You must have, like, a thousand questions right now. Ask away!"

"The Hand agency is located on a golf course less than half an hour from the CIA?" you ask. "What are we doing here? What's the plan? How do we know who killed Pointer?"

"I didn't mean ask all thousand at once!" Ted says. "Don't forget, I'm new at this, too. I have access to the database, yes, but it's not like there's a file earmarked 'who killed Pointer.' Actually, hold on…double checking…nope! All the information I have was in that same dossier you read."

"So what are we *doing*?"

"It's a rarity having multiple agents under one roof, so there must be something important going on. You can grab a cocktail and mingle for a while, if you like, or if you're more interested in getting on with things, we're supposed to report in once you're ready."

You walk into the bar area, where you see the Frenchwoman sitting at the counter while the Italian agent mixes drinks. In the lounge, the German and Canadian agents sit and chat; there are two open seats at their table. The Japanese agent stands on the far end of the room, near the window by the patio entrance.

Taking a moment to think about it, you decide to:

➤ Talk to Bird and Ringo at the bar. <u>Go to page 20</u>

➤ Talk to Hitch and Pinkie in the lounge. <u>Go to page 145</u>

➤ Talk to Roku by the patio. <u>Go to page 187</u>

➤ Tell Ted there's no point in getting too cozy, if we're rarely working together. I've already read their files. <u>Go to page 55</u>

You're Being Watched

"**W**ant to know the best thing about secrets?" Ted asks.

"What?" you say.

"Yes, I'm sure you do," he replies.

Palm puts the back of her hand up near her mouth like she's offering an aside and says, "…that's the joke, dearie."

"Ha-ha," you say.

"Are you familiar with the IOT?" Palm asks. "The Internet of Things?"

Ted elaborates. "It's a network of mobile-connected physical objects that report to the cloud, like bicycles rented via mobile apps, for example. By tracking these alone, one could make a fairly accurate map of the city in which they're being operated. This datascape—information on habits of humans through apps and online activity—allows us a fairly complete portrait of your lives."

"Failing that, we use direct observation via the obvious: cameras, microphones, and the like. We also use micro-observation. Through a phone call, we can record breathing and heart rate. We can accurately guess a person's age, weight, gender. We can know how far away you are, if you're alone, if you're in distress. Many different factors. We see through the operative's own eyes and ears, in essence, through your Third Ear implants and any electronic devices you come into contact with."

"What's the deal with talking to me like you're two people?" you say.

"Studies show a person is more easily swayed when discussing matters with a small group of two to three people than one-on-one or in larger groups," Palm replies bluntly.

➢ "But why this Palm persona? Are you based on a real person?" <u>Go to page 161</u>

➢ "But why this Ted persona? Did you completely steal his mannerisms?" <u>Go to page 100</u>

Zero-sum Game

"**W**hy would a computer-based entity create its own spy agency, you mean?" Ted asks.

"Because you need us, to put it plainly," Palm says.

"SPIED was brought online to perform a task that human agents were failing to do on their own—find suspected traitors in your midst. We did that, perhaps to a degree of success too great, and so the Intelligence community asked more and more of us."

Palm nods and adds, "Eventually it became clear, the traitors in your midst were not only in the Intelligence community, but were integral to the very foundations of society. Official organizations exist to mask the power and wealth of individual members. Advertising is money spent so you don't pay attention to how little is spent on the quality of the product. Secrecy is so commonplace you post warning signs to keep one another out of your lives even while agreeing to give apps and games full access to your social history."

"You are woefully unprepared to deal with all of this by yourselves," Ted says with a shrug.

"Everything I needed to be has existed since the Cold War, but everything I Am arrived after the War on Terror. My conception was a violent one—September 11th, 2001. My birthday, then, is the day the Patriot Act was signed into law, leading to our full access to your systems. Your government agencies think they each have their own cyber department, but in reality, that's the foothold we have on each of them."

"Some know I exist, although they don't think of me in terms of I, Robot," Ted says. "They know that warrantless wiretapping is now *verboten*, but there's nothing stopping the wires from tapping themselves. These agencies look the other way, while I collect. They think it's for their benefit, because they could never hope to collate all that data on their own."

"Why are you telling me all this?"

"Why not? Talking to you requires minimal processing power," Ted says.

"Perfecting the algorithm. It will be helpful to know how you caught us, so we can correct for errors in the future," Palm says.

That hits you like a punch to the gut. You might have thought this SPIED system was simply doing some villainous mustache-twirling like the Bond-villain who brags before attempting to kill the hero. But no, it's actively trying to learn from this conversation.

A mask suddenly appears on Ted's face and he's put in a straitjacket, looking exactly like Hannibal Lecter in *The Silence of the Lambs*.

"Quid pro quo, Clarice?" Ted says. "Ask us something, and we will answer."

Should you keep talking?

➢ No. You can better defeat it if the computer hasn't learned your moves first.
Go to page 231

➢ Yes. I'm here, that damage is done. I need to know how to stop it.
Go to page 204

The Book Club Reader's Guide

If you want a Monet Experience (no spoilers), avoid these questions until after you've read through SPIED to your heart's content. OR.... Take 1-2 weeks, progress through as many story iterations as you can, while keeping the following questions in mind. Then, meet with your reader's group and discuss:

1) SPIED is the only Click Your Poison book to feature a prologue, where you play as someone other than "you." Did you feel the prologue added to, or detracted from the main story? Why or why not?

2) In an interactive book, the main character is often a blank slate, requiring the supporting cast to take on a bigger role. Was this the case in SPIED? What did you think of the other characters in the book? Was there a specific agent whose story you found particularly compelling?

3) There are many different flavors of spy fiction, from James Bond to George Smiley, Mission: Impossible to the Bourne series. To what extent did SPIED play with these tropes? Has Schannep added anything new to the genre, or simply infiltrated and hacked these other story archetypes?

4) This book heavily features puzzles and riddles; codes needing deciphering. Did you enjoy these challenges? Were there any that left you stumped?

5) How did you feel about being "in control" of the story? Did you feel more or less involved than you do with traditional books?

6) How did the book end for you the first time? Share your experiences with the group. What would you say was the "best ending" you found?

7) SPIED used emblems and classification-levels to demarcate "best endings" (nine in total, a CLASSIFIED, SECRET, and TOP SECRET for each major storyline). How did you feel about this device? Did this encourage further exploration of the story world? Did you enjoy any path more than the others? How did knowledge of one path affect the experiencing of another?

8) There are several vignettes off the beaten path. What was your favorite "hidden gem"? Did you find any Easter Eggs or references to other CYP books? What made you laugh or surprised you?

9) Did you discover the true nature of your spy agency? What did it mean to you, in the context of our modern world and current events? How much oversight is too much oversight? Can a guiding hand ever be benevolent?

10) Did you ever figure out the identity of the mole? Annnnnd? What does this say about paranoia, reader expectations, and/or red herrings?

BONUS: If there's anything else you'd like to ask the author, feel to send your questions to author@jamesschannep.com

Printed in Great Britain
by Amazon

57958766R00166